THE DEMONS ARE GROWING BOLDER...

The assassin muttered something under her breath, and suddenly Frej's spell on her broke. The woman wasn't just a human; she was a Witch. She reached into her pocket and pulled out a second vial etched with runes.

"Don't move, or I'll blow this whole room to pieces." She waved the bottle for emphasis.

One of the police officers took a tentative step forward. "Easy now, we just want to talk."

She wasn't interested. She threw the bottle to the ground. Luckily, Frej trapped it in an orb of air before it shattered.

The woman lunged for the door, but the officers tackled her to the ground. "You're under arrest—" began one of the officers.

Inside Frej's orb of air, the bottle began to crackle and fizz as the spell seeped from the loosened stopper. He swore and reinforced the magic surrounding it as the explosion erupted, but the enchanted bomb was strong and tore through the shield.

"Frej!" Erin screamed.

❖

BOOKS BY
KATHRYN BLANCHE

Laila of Midgard series

Caught by Demons
Summoned by Demons
Infiltrated by Demons
Hunted by Demons

Hunted by the Holidays
(A Laila of Midgard Novelette)

HUNTED BY DEMONS

LAILA OF MIDGARD
❖ BOOK 4 ❖

KATHRYN BLANCHE

DEDICATION

To Jason. Your compassion and understanding mean more to me than you will ever know. May you rest in peace.

HUNTED
BY
DEMONS

PROLOGUE

Marius watched his faint reflection in the dingy window. The face that stared back looked ghostly and haunted with dark circles under his eyes hinting at many sleepless nights. Crumpled in his hand was yet another death threat from Izel, whose patience was wearing short. It wasn't the first one, and he doubted it would be the last either. Izel wrote death threats as if they were love letters—full of empty promises and foolish expectations—but Marius knew she would make good on the threat eventually if he didn't deliver on his vow to open a portal to Hell in Midgard.

In his other hand, he toyed with a silver coin, rolling it back and forth across his fingers, making it vanish and reappear. It was no ordinary coin, but a Charon's Obol blessed by Hades himself. This coin held the power to return a soul of the dead to the realms of the living. Marius could have easily used it to bring Izel to Midgard, but who wanted their boss breathing down their neck? He would give it to her eventually if necessary but on his terms.

Marius had been busy ensuring his reach spread far and

wide. Infiltrating various human organizations had been almost too easy. Not only was the Di Inferi gang under his thumb, but many government agencies as well. The only one that still proved to be problematic was the Inter-Realm Security Agency.

A few months ago, Colin Grayson, a spy who leaked information from the agency, had been outed. They arrested Grayson, and Marius doubted the others would be foolish enough to fall prey to one of his traps. However, there were other ways to neutralize the threat they posed. Sure, they were far more bloody, but he found those were often the most satisfying resolutions and the most permanent.

Marius had only been a young child full of grief and innocence when the Fae court damned him. He turned to Necromancy—the forbidden practice of death magic—out of desperation to resurrect his family. While too young to truly understand the significance of his crimes, there was still no mercy for the small and frightened orphan he had been. The streets of Hell had destroyed and rebuilt him so many times, but Izel had seen potential in him. She plucked him from the filth and whispered promises of revenge in his ear. He had idolized her and worshiped her like the Goddess she was, and in return, Izel showed him how to rise in the ranks of her political organization: the Demons. While he still desperately wished to please her, Marius knew that if he could offer the entire country on its knees when she arrived, it would be far more gratifying.

A knock on the door behind him stirred Marius from his thoughts.

"What do you want?" he hissed, not bothering to pull his eyes from the window.

Marius watched the reflection of the human as he stepped into the room. As a supporter of the cause, the man was technically a Demon as well—but a Lesser Demon, as he'd never been sentenced to life in Hell. He kept his head high and tried to look intimidating, but Marius knew that if he spun around to look at the man, his eyes would betray his fear.

The human cleared his throat. "Sir, I have news about the Elf."

"Well, spit it out," Marius muttered impatiently.

"We've confirmed she's out of the area—halfway around the world."

The Greater Demon straightened at that. "You're sure?"

"Yes. She's been spotted in Europe."

For the better part of a year, that meddlesome Elf had found ways to make his job infinitely more arduous. She was also frustratingly difficult to kill. Although, if she was gone, that left the rest of her team exposed.

"Sir, should we attack their office?" asked the human.

Marius turned to face him as his lip curled back. It was a look too cruel to call a smile.

"I've got a better idea. Find the strongest Supernaturals and tell them to prepare for a bloodbath." The Greater Demon's eyes glinted like steel as his malicious fantasies played out in his mind. "When we're done, there'll be no one for that Elf to return to."

CHAPTER 1

Erin skimmed the recipe on her cellphone again, trying to determine how much paprika was too much. The fajitas in her pan began to sizzle and fill the room with a deliciously spicy fragrance, suggesting to Erin that this might be her new favorite dish. Rather than using the stove burner, she opted to use her fire magic to heat the pan. It was getting easier for her to control spells, but she still lacked the ability to shift into her Dragon form—something that frustrated her to no end.

Frej, her Air Dragon mentor, stood a few paces away, stirring a pot of beans while he heated tortillas. The kitchen was large, but Frej's tall form always made it feel crowded. As a knight, she had seen him fight ruthlessly, and yet he was surprisingly delicate when it came to culinary arts. Erin glanced over at him. He might be a great chef, but Erin suspected she might surpass him someday.

Thanks to her sister's night off, the evening was proving to be pleasantly slow so far. Ali slept on the sofa, curled up next to her boyfriend, Mato, who flipped through their movie database. Not even the whir of the blender seemed to disturb her slumber. It was good, though, Ali needed all the rest she could get. She worked long hours to help cover for one of their friends who was out of town.

Lyn pulled back her curly bleached-blond hair and tied an apron over her cutoff jeans and crop-top. Aquatic tattoos curled along the surfer's dark skin, and piercings dotted her ears. She was Erin's roommate and a Witch who had lived in Los Angeles her entire life.

Lyn poured a batch of margaritas and gave Erin an amused look. "If I didn't know better, I'd say your sister was under some sort of sleeping enchantment."

Erin grinned. "At least she hasn't started snoring yet."

Mato carefully eased off the sofa, not wanting to disturb Ali—an effort almost as pointless as it was sweet. He wandered over to sniff the sizzling pan.

"Hey, I invited Henrik over for taco Tuesday. We've got enough food, right?"

She raised a brow. "That's the sort of thing you're supposed to ask *before* we start cooking."

Mato looked sheepish. "Well, he did offer to bring cannoli for dessert."

Frej paused his stirring to glance over his shoulder. "I've only been in this world a few months, but even I know cannoli don't fit the taco Tuesday theme."

"Yeah, but no one says no to cannoli," pointed out Mato with a sly grin.

Lyn chuckled. "He's got a point there."

Erin hid a smile as she stirred the pan of fajitas. Of course, she and Frej had already assumed Mato would invite Henrik over—the two were inseparable—but that didn't mean they couldn't give Mato a hard time.

The truth was, their house was anything but ordinary, and Erin liked it that way. She was Ali's adopted sister. It hadn't been easy being the only Dragon in the Fae capitol, and yet Erin wouldn't trade her Fae family for the world. Frej came into the picture six months ago as a mentor to help Erin work through her magical difficulties. The others were friends from Los Angeles, like Lyn, and while Mato wasn't a housemate, he stayed here often enough that he practically counted as one. He was a Shifter, or Were, who could transform into a massive grizzly bear. The only one missing from the household tonight was Laila.

They had rarely seen Laila in the past three months. She was on the other side of the planet undergoing special magical training. Even though it was necessary, it had been difficult for Ali, who had been trying to cover for the Elf. But with only three IRSA agents who could deal with Supernatural conflicts, some of their friends had to step in from time to time to help. Ali still insisted on shouldering the brunt of the burden as always. It was just the sort of person she was. Erin secretly hoped Laila would be back soon, but no one knew how long this training would last. The strain was starting to wear Ali down, and Erin worried it was too much for her sister.

A knock sounded on the door, and Mato left to answer it, expecting to find Henrik. Instead, a Vampire stood on the doorstep sporting spiky black hair and ripped jeans. Erin nearly caught herself drooling over his black leather jacket with wicked-looking spikes. His eyes were blood red and usually mischievous. Tonight a frown shadowed them.

"What's happened?" He shouldered past Mato and into the house, looking around frantically.

"What are you talking about, Darien?" Frej asked.

"We received a call from dispatch that there was a conflict here," explained a second newcomer. His entire being was various shades of grey, similar to an old black-and-white photo. Jerrik was a Svartálfr, or Dark Elf, and the latest official addition to the IRSA team.

Frej peered around at the group. "I'm not sure who called, but it wasn't us. Everything's been quiet tonight."

Erin waited for Darien to relax, but his demeanor turned more troubled than before. "I don't like this—wait, where's Ali?"

A groan issued from the sofa as Ali sat up. "Huh? What did I miss?"

Lyn walked over to a series of charms that sat on a side table. They looked like knick-knacks that you might find in a souvenir shop, but they were all complicated enchantments the Witch had created to protect the house.

"All of the protection spells are still active, and nothing out of the ordinary has happened tonight. Maybe it was just a prank?"

Darien gave her a look that said he wasn't convinced. "I don't like this. Something doesn't feel right."

Ali stretched and stood. "Then stick around for a bit. We're just about to have dinner."

Jerrik took a seat at a barstool and immediately a black ball of fur leapt into his lap. Mr. Whiskers butted Jerrik with his head as he meowed, demanding ear scratches. Jerrik chuckled and gave in. An ordinary-looking cat with silky black fur and bright green eyes, Mr. Whiskers was also a Bogey, a supernatural creature with the power to shift into any shape he desired. Currently, an enchanted collar kept him in the form of a cat, though, considering it was far easier to care for a housecat than a velociraptor or a tiger shark.

"How's the night going?" Ali asked them as she snagged an unclaimed margarita.

"Surprisingly slow, but I'm not going to complain." Jerrik eyed the fajitas. "Erin, you know that stove is off, right?"

"I'm cooking with Dragon fire," she explained, flames dancing across her fingers.

"Nice! And you're still taking Judo lessons?"

Erin beamed. "Every day!"

Jerrik gave an approving nod before turning back to Ali. "Have you heard anything from Laila? I would have thought she'd be back by now?"

Ali shrugged. "She's always vague about it. I think she's frustrated with how slow the training is going. She doesn't want to return until she's sure she can control her new powers. I think it's more complicated than she expected."

Erin could sympathize. Until recently, she hadn't been able to use magic at all. Others expected her to flip a switch and suddenly control fire or transform, but magic didn't quite work that way. As with any skill, it took time, dedication, and a lot of practice.

A car door slammed outside, and Darien's head whipped toward the entrance.

"Now that's got to be Henrik," said Mato, reaching for the door handle.

"Don't!" Darien shouted, eyes widening.

An explosion shook the house. The door burst open, bashing Mato in the face. Darien pulled the Werebear out of the way. *Wham!* A massive fist slammed into the wall where Mato's face had been a moment before.

"Take cover!" roared Darien, just as intruders swarmed through the door.

Erin stood frozen in horror as a Werewolf bolted through the door and lunged for Darien. Mato shifted into his bear form and plowed into the wolf, knocking it into the wall. A sorcerer of some sort attacked Lyn with a bolt of lightning, but Jerrik deflected the spell with a shield of air as he passed Ali his gun. He had elemental magic to fight with, bit Ali was unarmed.

"Get down," ordered Frej.

He grabbed Erin's arm and pulled her to the ground behind the kitchen island. Erin's heart pounded as the fight raged around them. She heard gunshots and screams but couldn't tell where they erupted from. She couldn't just sit there like a coward. She was a Dragon.

Erin stood and blasted the first intruder she saw with fire. He screamed as his clothes ignited. Another intruder moved to grab Erin from the other side, but she snatched the closest weapon she could find—the frying pan—and flung the Fajitas at him. The sizzling hot, oil-coated food hit him in the face, and he clawed at his burning flesh.

"Erin!" screamed Ali.

Erin yelped as someone large grabbed her from behind—the green tint of the skin telling her it was some sort of Goblin. She brought the frying pan down on the Goblin's knee. Unsurprisingly, he howled as bone fractured and his grip on her faltered. She dropped the frying pan and threw him over her shoulder. He hit the floor with a thud, and Erin followed up with a stomp to the collar bone. She felt a crunch as more bones shattered. He wouldn't be following her. She turned to find the others struggling against the intruders, but two more appeared through the door to replace them every time an attacker fell. Erin watched the chaos around her as sinking feeling erupted in her stomach. They were outnumbered.

Her sister screamed. Erin saw another Goblin thrust a wicked-looking knife into Ali's shoulder. The Dragon's vision went red as she charged. The Goblin's eyes grew round as Erin blasted him with fire.

She didn't let him recover before cutting across his face then kicking him in the chest. He tumbled backward over the sofa.

"Ali!" Erin knelt at her sister's side, pressing her hands against the bleeding wound.

Ali grabbed her sister's wrist with her good arm. "You need to go!"

"I'm not leaving!" Erin snapped. By The Morrigan, that was a lot of blood. It seeped through her fingers and pooled around them.

Ali's grip tightened. "Listen! You need to get Laila. Use the crystal!"

Erin realized what Ali was saying. Each of them had a crystal that could teleport them to the location where Laila was training.

Frej thrust his opponent across the room with a blast of air and pulled Erin to her feet. "Go! I'll cover you!"

Erin scrambled towards the hall that led to her room while Frej's shield protected her from the onslaught of attacks. She sprinted down the passage, her feet thundering on the wooden floor as something snarled behind her with a low, scratchy growl. Someone was following, but the Dragon didn't dare stop. Instead, she flung herself into her room and slammed the door shut. Even with the door locked, it would buy her mere seconds.

"Mert?" purred Mr. Whiskers. He rubbed against her leg.

Erin had no idea how the Bogey got there, but he had an unusual habit of appearing in locked rooms. She narrowed her eyes and remembered something Lyn had said when they first brought him home—Bogeys make excellent guards. Her fingers fumbled as she struggled to remove the collar. The wood of the door began to splinter behind her as someone attempted to kick it in. The door broke off the frame.

The wood struck Erin in the head, sending stars dancing across her vision. Dazed, she barely managed to unclasp the collar and free Mr. Whiskers from the binding spell. He was already shifting into something dark and massive. His claws grew to the size of daggers, and fur sprouted around his head in a shaggy mane. The hair on his tail morphed into sleek, serpentine scales, and he unleashed a ground-shaking growl as he pounced on the person reaching for Erin. She was morbidly fascinated but couldn't stop to watch. She needed to find the crystal—she needed to get Laila.

CHAPTER 2

Laila sat in the middle of a clearing blanketed in snow that glittered like diamonds in the early morning sun. She was bundled in layers of warm clothes to keep out the chill while she worked. Snowflakes settled on her auburn hair and brushed against her cheeks as a light breeze passed through the forest. Laila Eyvindr looked like an ordinary Elf, except for the faint blue shimmer that crept through the magical glamour she wore. A human might guess her to be early to mid-twenties, but as an Elf, she was far older. Elves aged more slowly than humans, but now that the divine magic had manifested itself in her body, she expected she would age even slower. It was one of the many changes she now faced.

She would have expected to be alone on such a chilly morning, but several creatures watched her from the trees and bushes. These were not ordinary animals like birds and squirrels, but whimsical, magical creatures. A dozen pixies perched in a nearby birch tree, while a large green stag with tangled brambles for antlers wandered nearby. She could feel other beings too, hidden from view. Perhaps her training was more interesting than their hibernation, or maybe they simply didn't have the urge to sleep through the cold of winter here in this enchanted sanctuary.

The area was protected by a magical barrier that kept wandering humans away from this remote part of the Blackforest in Germany. Arduinna, the Goddess who guarded this land, had declared it a sanctuary for creatures in need of a home. The result was a fairytale forest where Supernatural creatures were free to roam, undisturbed by humans. The seclusion also made it an ideal location for practicing advanced and potentially dangerous spells.

Laila took a deep breath and tapped into the newly acquired divine magic, her body glowing with an ethereal light as she closed her eyes and focused, allowing the barriers around her mind to lower. The process of opening her mind always left her uncomfortably exposed. While Arduinna insisted the only ones who could access her mind in this state were other divine beings, Laila always felt vulnerable—something she hated.

Nonetheless, she allowed her mind to open. Whispers seemed to drift around her as they floated along magical currents, but it wasn't her ears hearing them. These were prayers searching for the Gods. She was not a Goddess, and these prayers were clearly not directed at her, but Laila could still hear them. They were ethereal, and each prayer was connected to their originator by a gossamer strand of magic.

It felt like a violation of privacy to listen to these prayers, but Arduinna insisted it was an important skill to have. Not only could Laila locate a person by their prayer, but it allowed her to know when someone was in need. Even in total darkness, she could follow the magic to find the person if they were in need.

The prayers swirled around Laila along with the snowflakes.

HELP! A shout tore through her mind.

Laila scrambled backward. The watching creatures stirred and fled at her sudden movement—even the stag bounded away. She lay there half-buried in snow, her heart pounding with the realization of whose prayer it had been.

"Ali," Laila breathed. Dread gripped her. She clambered to her feet and sprinted back towards Arduinna's cottage, plowing through the snow. Branches whipped at her face as she wound her way past the trees. Something was happening in Los Angeles. She had to get back—she needed to find Ali.

Laila hurtled over a fallen beech then came skidding to a halt in front of the cottage as she found Arduinna speaking with a Centaur. They both frowned at her sudden appearance.

The words came tumbling from Laila's mouth. "Ali's in trouble. I heard her when I was listening in the woods—"

She felt a rippling in the magic of the forest, then a dark-haired figure appeared, stumbling from the shock of a teleportation spell. She wore an old Metallica t-shirt and a pair of grey sweat pants. Her bloodied hands clutched a crystal.

"Erin!" Laila rushed over, checking for wounds. "The blood—"

"It's Ali's. The house is under attack!" Her eyes were wide with fear, and she was trembling.

Laila turned to Arduinna, whose face looked nearly as ashen as the falling snow. The Goddess nodded and strode over. The second she grabbed their hands, the three women vanished.

In the blink of an eye, they were standing back in Erin's living room, which now looked like a war zone. Blood pooled on the floor and around Laila's feet. In one corner, Frej was doing his best to keep Ali shielded as she lay wounded on the floor, and three humans advanced on them with handguns. Mato was in his bear form and wrestling with two Werewolves while Jerrik and Darien endeavored to slow more Supernatural intruders attempting to enter the house. Darien with bullets while Jerrik used elemental magic.

Arduinna already had an arrow nocked in her conjured bow. "Erin, barricade yourself in your room."

"But—"

Arduinna's green eyes flashed. "That was not a request."

Erin must have obeyed since Laila heard footsteps retreating down the hall behind her.

Laila reached for her divine magic. It was eager to be unleashed, as restless as a caged lion. It didn't slip from her grasp as it once did but came to her call readily.

Laila dropped the glamour that masked her appearance. Her eyes shifted from forest green to glowing azure as blue flames licked at her hands. Arduinna could handle those already inside the house, so Laila strode towards the door directly into the line of fire. Bullets bounced off a crackling blue shield and melted on impact, earning her looks of shock from the attackers.

"It's her! It's the Elf!" One of the intruders tried to run.

"What's the rush?" The words were not her own as Laila spoke them.

Rage burned in the Elf's eyes as flames shot from her hand and incinerated the Vampire. All that remained was a wisp of sizzling blue ash that quickly dissipated. Laila watched in horror, unable to control her actions, and for a split second, she swore she heard a voice in her head chuckle. It was not her own. She had never noticed this feeling while training with Arduinna—as if she was no longer in control. The magic was always a little wild, but it felt as if it had a mind of its own in the heat of battle. Or that it was in control of her. She wrestled to regain control.

Gritting her teeth, Laila knelt until her fingers brushed the concrete. The walkway morphed into a liquid, rippling like water as it took on a life of its own. The cement quickly snatched up the rest of the intruders, wrapping around them, resembling the tentacles of a dozen sea monsters, trapping their arms and legs. A few intruders, mostly Vampires, managed to leap onto Mato's truck before the spell could seize them.

Abruptly, a massive form plowed into one of the Vampires. For a second, Laila thought it was Mato, but this creature looked more like a Chimera—a combination of a lion, a goat, and a serpent. She was pretty sure they didn't live here in Midgard. The Chimera swiveled its head to look at Laila.

"Mert?" it purred, looking at her with wide round eyes.

"Mr. Whiskers?" Laila gasped. Someone must have removed the Bogey's collar.

His serpentine tail swished back and forth in response. He seemed to be wondering what to do with the Vampires struggling under his massive paws. Then he turned and ripped a Vampire's head from its body, the skull crunching between his teeth before crumbling to dust.

"No! Don't eat that," Laila groaned.

"You won't win this war, Elf," hissed the nearest remaining Vampire as it backed away.

Laila kept her expression neutral as she examined him. With her divine senses, he stank of sulfur—he was clearly a Demon. "That remains to be seen. You are under arrest. You have the right to remain silent—"

"Execute," spat the Demonic Vampire.

Laila blinked, confused, but then a rune glowed red beneath his shirt, and Laila swore—it was an auto-death spell. The Vampire crumbled to soot. All around her, the others she had captured uttered the activation word too. Laila scrambled to counteract the enchantments, but there were too many of them, and the spell was too fast. Vampires crumbled to ash while the living Demons appeared to have their throats slit with an invisible knife. Laila grabbed the nearest and placed her hand over the rune on his skin, burning through it before the spell could fully activate. The Demon spat a string of curses at her as he struggled against the cement encasing him. Laila ignored it and rushed to save another.

"Laila! We need you!" called Arduinna through the doorway.

She lunged for the door, and Mr. Whiskers squeezed through behind her. Inside, she found the others gathered around Ali. Jerrik was doing his best to heal the wound, but he looked alarmed as Laila approached.

"She's not doing well. We need to get her to a hospital," Jerrik insisted.

Ali was losing too much blood, but something else felt off.

Laila could try a healing spell, but from the volatile way the divine magic was still fizzing in her veins from the fight, it could do more harm than good. Laila couldn't risk losing control—not with Ali's life at stake. She wouldn't be able to live with herself if anything happened to her friend.

"Meet me at Asclepius." Laila gingerly lifted Ali.

Before the others could respond, Laila vanished. In the blink of an eye, she was standing at the Asclepius Hospital of Supernatural Medicine's Emergency Room entrance. Her ears rang, and her knees buckled as a wave of fatigue from the teleportation hit her. Somehow, Laila stayed on her feet and kept hold of Ali.

"I need a doctor!" she shouted, stumbling down the hall with Ali, a trail of blood dripping on the white linoleum floor behind her.

The hospital staff rushed over and took Ali from her, loading the Fae onto a gurney. Laila followed them as they wheeled down the hall to a room. Doctor Elmerson, one of the Elves on staff, dashed in behind them.

He looked at Laila. "Agent Eyvindr? Your eyes!"

Oops. Laila hadn't bothered to mask her divine aura. She waved it off. "Ali needs help, but I'm afraid to heal her in this state."

He nodded hastily and returned his attention to assess Ali. "She needs a transfusion. The only wound I see is the stab wound."

She could feel his magic as he worked and stitched together the tissues Jerrik had tried to heal. Laila couldn't help but hover as he mended the wound. Something felt off about Ali's body. She was about to mention it when a nurse preparing a transfusion forced her out to give them space.

More footsteps pounded down the hall as the others appeared with Arduinna.

"Where's my sister!" called Erin, her voice cracking as she rushed towards Laila.

A nurse appeared in her path. "Woah there, we can't have this many people back here!"

A moment of tense discussion ensued, during which Laila convinced the nurse to allow Erin and Frej to stay while Laila returned to the waiting room with the others. The nurse tried to send Frej out as well, but the intense glow of Laila's eyes seemed to convince her otherwise. She was not leaving Ali without protection after an attack.

In the waiting room, Laila peeled off her thick winter coat and sank into a chair. The coat was far too warm and covered in blood. Next, she pulled off the thick sweater she wore and sat there in a t-shirt, the swirling blue markings on her arms glowing like her eyes. She took a deep breath and shoved the divine magic down, masking her aura until she resembled her ordinary self.

A nearby rustle of fabric drew her attention as Arduinna sat down beside her.

"Are you okay?" The Goddess asked.

Laila shook her head. She looked calm on the outside, but inside she felt somewhere between bursting into tears and screaming in frustration. She knew Ali would be okay. Doctor Elmerson was the best doctor on staff. It was her lack of control during the fight that left her distressed.

"Something was different back there. I lost control. I think the divine magic took over. It felt like it was sentient and manipulating me. I was so worried that it would lash out at Ali rather than save her." Laila ran her trembling, blood-caked fingers through her hair, pulling strands loose from her braid as she did. "I should have been there when they attacked. I was gone too long. I—"

"Enough, Laila. Stop blaming yourself. You've done what you can." Arduinna's voice was both commanding and calming, but her expression grew concerned as she continued. "I'm not sure why your magic lashed out like that. Magic isn't sentient."

"I'm telling you, it laughed at me." Laila sagged in her chair. Maybe she was losing her mind.

The Goddess frowned. "Really? I wonder if someone else is trying to possess you."

Laila felt the blood drain from her face. "Is that possible? I thought divine beings were immune to possession."

Arduinna hesitated. The Goddess was just as worried as Laila.

"I'm not sure. If that's the case, it would have to be a God or Goddess. How do you feel now?"

Laila shrugged. "Normal, I guess. I don't feel like a puppet anymore. But can I trust myself?"

"I don't know. I think it's time I returned to Asgard for answers. One of the other Gods are bound to know something about this."

Asgard. One of the seven worlds magically linked by portals. Midgard, or Earth, as the humans called it, was another such land. But while Midgard was primarily home to the humans, Asgard was ruled by the Gods. They lived there with other divine creatures that worked under them.

Despite being a Goddess, Arduinna preferred to avoid Asgard at all costs. She claimed that there was too much political drama and intrigue in that world that bordered on cruelty. If she was considering returning to hunt for answers, then she must genuinely feel at a loss.

Laila turned back to Arduinna and lowered her voice. "Something else happened. When I heard Ali, it wasn't just a faint whisper. It was like she was shouting. How can I hear a prayer like that?"

Arduinna's frown deepened. "That was a prayer meant for you, but that shouldn't be possible, not unless you actually are a Goddess."

Laila didn't know what to think about that. If true, it would complicate her life in ways she couldn't even comprehend. They still didn't know what she was, just that she was no longer an ordinary Elf.

Arduinna sighed. "I'm a Goddess of Hunting and Forests,

and my magic is very different from yours. You need someone who understands the nuances of your powers to guide you from this point. We don't have the luxury of time as most divine beings do."

Arduinna still hadn't been able to determine what Laila's specialty was supposed to be. While she seemed to have an affinity for fire, there was more to her powers than that. Still, Gods of Fire might be the right place to start.

Laila nodded, then glanced around and found Darien, Jerrik, and Mato standing in a corner.

"Hey," she mumbled as she joined them. She didn't know what else to say.

Mato nodded to her. "Lyn stayed back at the house with Mr. Whiskers and Henrik. He pulled up just after you left."

She could tell his mind was elsewhere, in that room with Ali.

"When do you think they'll let us see her?" he asked.

Laila peeked over her shoulder toward the hall. "Soon, I imagine. Once she's stable."

Darien huffed out an exasperated breath. "That was a premeditated attack. They wanted to ensure Jerrik and I were there in the house. We received a call and arrived only minutes before this happened."

Laila nodded and thought back to the Demons' initial surprise. "They didn't expect me to get there. One of them said as much. They also had auto-kill spells on them. I managed to keep a couple of them alive for now."

"Greater or Lesser?" asked Darien.

"Lesser, I think." Laila hadn't had the chance to compare the scent of the two types, but if there were that many Greater Demons running around Los Angeles, she imagined they would have heard.

None of the others seemed surprised about the Demonic involvement. Then again, the Demons were a constant threat.

Jerrik's expression was unreadable. "So, the Demons learn Laila is out of town and decide to launch an attack. Why?"

Darien sniffed. "They probably figured the rest of us would be more vulnerable then. We'll have to be more cautious. I'll arrange for a security detail. I should head back and check-in with the investigative team too." He looked torn, but as the new supervisor, Laila suspected he felt obligated to handle the investigation.

"I'll keep you updated," she promised.

Darien vanished through the door just as a nurse approached them.

"You came in with Alastrina Fiachra, right? You can see her now."

Laila breathed a sigh of relief and followed the nurse down the hall with the others. They were taken to a different location than before—a private room where Erin and Frej spoke with Doctor Elmerson. Ali was unconscious in the hospital bed, and Laila couldn't shake the feeling that something was still off.

Doctor Elmerson waited until the rest of them crowded into the room before speaking. "I'm afraid I have bad news."

CHAPTER 3

Doctor Elmerson surveyed Ali. "I was able to heal the stab wound that she sustained, but the injury was more complicated than I expected."

That explained the feeling Laila couldn't shake. Her new abilities must have been trying to tell her something was wrong.

"What do you mean by complicated?" she asked. Fear seeped onto her heart, chilling her to the bones.

The doctor shifted and ran a hand through his short blond hair. "We're trying a variety of treatments from human medicine as well as otherworldly healing, but I can't guarantee they will help."

"Why not? You're an Elven doctor. Why can't you heal her?" Erin demanded, her fists clenched.

"Because the blade is cursed," explained Arduinna as she rested her hand on Ali's head. She turned to look at the doctor. "That's why she's not waking up, isn't it?"

The doctor nodded. "Even though I can heal the wound itself, the curse acts almost like a poison. I've heard of these spells before, but I've never treated a victim. I'm afraid that none of the cases I've read about ended well."

The news hit Laila like a punch to the stomach. This couldn't be real. Ali had to be okay. Maybe Laila could save her. After all, divine magic was more potent than elemental magic. Yet as she looked to Arduinna, she saw the despair in the Goddess's eyes.

Erin stood. Tears welled in her eyes, and her voice trembled, "You can't give up! You can't just let her die!"

Doctor Elmerson's expression remained neutral, but Laila could see the pain in his eyes. "We will do everything we can, but I'm afraid all I can do is buy her time."

"That's not enough!" bellowed the young Dragon. Tears escaped from her eyes.

Ali was the only family Erin had. She already lost her birth parents and her adopted parents. Laila wasn't sure how she would cope if she lost her sister as well.

Laila pulled the teenage Dragon into her embrace. "We'll figure this out. We'll find a way."

Erin crumpled against Laila's shoulder and sobbed. "I can't lose her, Laila. I just can't!" She clung to Laila like a lifeline.

"I know. I'll do whatever I can to help her." Laila rubbed soothing circles on Erin's back and realized the Dragon wasn't the only one crying. Tears streamed down Laila's face as well, mixing with the dried blood on her cheeks. She should have been there when the Demons attacked. She would have stopped them and protected Ali.

The others stepped out of the room and into the hall to give them some privacy. She could hear them talking in hushed whispers.

Eventually, the tears ran their course. Laila left Erin sitting in a chair beside her sister's bed. She joined the others in the hall, feeling wrung out and helpless.

She turned to Arduinna, her voice tight. "There has to be something we can do."

The Goddess pressed her palms to her eyes, and Laila could

see she was fighting a similar battle on the inside. "I-I don't know. My strengths are with animals and nature. Healing, well, you know…" She trailed off. Healing was not one of her skills.

"What about my powers?" Laila asked.

"Given what happened earlier in that fight, do you truly trust yourself right now?"

Laila opened her mouth to speak but quickly shut it. She didn't trust herself. Not with something as important as this.

Mato, who had been quiet the entire time, finally spoke. "If we could find a cure, how long do you think you could keep her alive?"

The doctor shook his head and glanced back through the doorway. "A week, maybe? But again, I don't know of a cure."

"I do," said Jerrik softly.

They all turned to stare at him in surprise.

He took a deep breath. "Back in Svartalfheim, there is a flower that can cure any ailment, magical or otherwise. They're rare, but I know where to find one."

"You mean the Eirflower?" asked Doctor Elmerson skeptically. "That's just a legend."

Arduinna shook her head hastily. "No, they exist, but only two plants remain. They're heavily guarded. It would be impossible to get to them."

"I could do it, though. With Laila's help, I could bring back one of the blossoms," Jerrik insisted.

They all looked at Doctor Elmerson.

"At this point, anything's worth a try." Still, a skeptical tone crept into his voice.

As the doctor strode away, a spark of hope glimmered within Laila. It warmed her chest and kept the crushing grief at bay. If there was a chance the flower would save Ali, she would do anything within her power to get it.

Frej turned toward Jerrik. "I'll go with you. You know what will happen if you return to Svartalfheim."

Something unspoken passed between them. Back in the fall,

the two men had been at each other's throats in an absurd play for dominance, but something happened. Laila suspected they had reached an understanding. They had been oddly cryptic about it, though. She believed it had to do with Jerrik's past that he was so reluctant to reveal.

The Svartálfr shook his head. "Two Elves will draw less attention than a Dragon."

Frej glared at Jerrik. Laila hoped this wasn't a sign that whatever truce between them was crumbling. They didn't have time for arguments.

"Can I talk to you?" Laila asked Frej.

He nodded stiffly and followed her down the hall until she paused.

"I know that you don't trust Jerrik, but he's right. You're needed here." Laila thought of Erin's devastation. "Erin needs you now more than ever, and you're able to keep her safe."

Frej paced back and forth restlessly. "Laila, if you go with him, it places you in danger too. There's a lot that Jerrik's not telling you. He's the most wanted man in that kingdom!"

She narrowed her eyes. "What?"

He peered down the hall in Jerrik's direction. "It's not my place to tell you more, but it's the truth. The king put a massive bounty on his head. Even entering the kingdom is a major risk."

Laila had always known Jerrik's past was troubled. He rarely spoke of his life before Midgard. Even so, they had few options available to them. Trusting Jerrik shouldn't be a problem—she knew him well enough to know he was a good man. But if the portal guards were watching for him, they would have a difficult time getting through. Jerrik seemed confident enough, though. And it wasn't as if they had many options. If Laila went on her own, she would have no idea how to get the Eirflower. However, if caught, Jerrik wouldn't be the only one detained. She would, as well.

Laila placed a hand on Frej's arm. "It's a risk I have to take. I can't let Ali die."

Her voice hitched on the last word. This time, when Frej looked at her, he saw the fear she desperately tried to hide.

"I swore to Erin that I would do anything in my power to save Ali, and I meant it." Laila's eyes fixed on him, bright with unshed tears.

She could see something soften in the Dragon as he pulled her into his arms with a sigh. The familiar scent of paper and leather greeted her, and it felt oddly soothing.

"Laila, why do you always have to be the one that charges straight into a fight? Why can't you let me do this for you instead?" Frej's voice filled with a longing so deep it left Laila's heart fractured.

In the past months, Laila had thought about Frej often. He had admitted to still having feelings for his queen, Regina, back in the Dragon Kingdom. Regina had been married to the king for many years before her scandalous affair with Frej. It struck Laila harder than she would have imagined, but while she felt betrayed, she could hardly judge him. Not when she struggled with her feelings for Jerrik.

Frej was kind and honorable—the typical white knight. When she was with him, Laila felt like the center of his world and treasured in a way she had never experienced. He was both strong and gentle, but he wanted to protect her. She would never be the sort of woman to stay home and host dinner parties as the women of his kingdom did. It was her job to stop the Demons from taking hold of Los Angeles.

"You know I have to go," Laila whispered, her gaze flitting to Jerrik.

The Svartálfr leaned against the wall some distance away, doing his best to appear uninterested in their conversation. Jerrik reminded her of a fallen Angel—broken, lost, and burdened by troubles in his past that he did his best to avoid. Many months ago, the Demons had imprisoned the two of them. Gradually, they found a way to trust each other, and a bond formed that went deep. He would never ask Laila to back down from a fight.

Then there was the moment when Laila had died—stabbed by a Demon in tunnels below the city. Jerrik had been there and watched her die. The pain in his cry of anguish still haunted her dreams. She had returned, thanks to the divine magic, but she never told Frej about it. Perhaps it was time she changed that.

She pulled away and looked up into the Dragon's face lined with worry. It didn't make what she had to say any easier.

"Frej, I…I never told you this. But I died. It happened back when we were in the tunnels under the Old City. My powers brought me back, but for several moments I'd truly died. I didn't want to tell you, but you need to know that I was given these powers for a reason, and while I don't entirely understand it, this path isn't the sort of thing I can walk away from."

Frej's eyes widened.

Laila took his hands in hers and looked up at him. "If you are willing to try this relationship again, I have two conditions: you have to understand that I won't have anything resembling a normal life and, you have to be sure that I'm the one you really want."

Frej blinked then slowly nodded as he struggled to find words. "I-I don't know what to say. Even so, I don't think this burden is yours to shoulder alone."

Laila didn't respond. How could she when it would only draw out the same endless argument that had pushed them apart for months? Instead, Laila released his hands and strode away, her heart heavy. She didn't want to give Frej an ultimatum, and a part of her longed to run back to the Dragon and slide once more into his warm embrace. But what good would that do? She was a warrior, and he needed to learn to deal with it or let her go. If there was anyone he should be protecting, it was Erin.

Jerrik watched Laila as she approached. "So, what did you decide?"

She kept her expression neutral. "That I'm going with you. Frej will stay with Erin."

Jerrik nodded. "Good, then we'll leave in the morning."

"What about your situation back in Svartalfheim? How are we going to enter when the kingdom is hunting for you?"

He shrugged. "I'll make do with my IRSA credentials. I doubt they'll look closely. If necessary, I have false documents with a different name, though."

"Of course you do." Laila facepalmed.

His chuckle sounded half-hearted. "That should get us into the city. From there, we'll just have to keep a low profile."

"And you're sure we'll have enough time to retrieve the Eir-flower?"

His expression sobered. "I believe so. We'll have to pass through the city and to another portal, but it shouldn't take more than a few days if everything goes according to plan."

That didn't give them much time to spare. Laila wasn't fond of walking into a situation she wasn't familiar with, but she had placed her trust in Jerrik before. She would just have to trust that he knew what he was doing.

"Okay. I'll head back to the house and inform Darien."

He pushed off the wall with a nod. "We'll meet back here at dawn then."

She peered around but didn't see Frej. Laila supposed he needed some time to process her words. She checked the clock on the wall and realized she only had a few hours until sunrise. When she peeked inside Ali's room, she found Erin asleep. Mato and Arduinna were there too, looking troubled.

"I'll be back in a few hours. I've got to take care of some things before I leave for Svartalfheim."

Arduinna watched Ali's still form on the bed. "I'll be heading to Asgard soon as well. We need answers."

Mato sighed. "I'll be here. I'll…keep her company."

"Make sure one of the doctors checks you too." She indicated his broken nose and black eye. There were others with minor injuries as well.

He nodded. Laila squeezed his shoulder before teleporting out of the hospital.

CHAPTER 4

The metallic tang of blood replaced the sterile scent of antiseptics as Laila reappeared in the crimson-stained living room. Her arrival startled several members of the investigative team, who relaxed the moment they recognized her.

"Are you trying to give me a heart attack?" demanded Jenn, shaking her head.

As with the rest of the investigative team, she was human and wore a jacket with IRSA printed in bold letters across the back. Jenn's hair was pulled back from her face, and there was no trace of makeup on her dark skin. She was the definition of practical and had the exhausting job of managing the investigative team.

Two unofficial teams comprised the majority of the Inter-Realm Security Agency. The first were the field agents—a small group of specialized Supernaturals, including Laila, who could handle dangerous and magical conflicts. The second was the investigative team, which dealt with the crime scenes and whose members were primarily human. They were all technically agents but held different roles within IRSA.

Laila gave her a tired smile. "Sorry about that."

Jenn looked at the carnage from the fight. The gore didn't seem to disturb her, but then again, she was one of the toughest people Laila had met in any of the worlds. She had worked as a detective for the LAPD before the apocalyptic event that nearly wiped out humanity. After surviving an onslaught of Zombies raised during The Event, IRSA offered her a job. Much to Jenn's frustration, she was assigned to the investigative team with the other humans for safety reasons.

"I'm surprised there weren't more injuries considering all of this," Jenn said at last.

Laila cringed. Considering Ali was the only of their friends badly wounded, Jenn was right. It could have been much worse. "I think we all knew this was a possibility, especially after they attacked Lyn."

"Doesn't make it any easier to accept, though." She turned to Laila, her brow creased with worry. "I take it Ali's okay."

Others joined them, including Darien and Lyn.

She swallowed hard. "Ali's stable for now, but the blade transferred a curse. The doctor gave her a week to live without a cure."

Lyn gasped, and Darien sank onto one of the sofas. The investigative team stared at Laila. Shock etched across each of their faces.

Lyn motioned to the corner of the room where she had found Ali. "The blade's over there. I noticed the runes on it after you left."

"Can you look into it and see if there's a way to break the curse?" asked Darien, his voice unsteady.

Lyn nodded and folded her arms across her stomach. "Yeah, I'll get started as soon as you finish here. I'm sure Donald can help too."

Donald was a quirky member of their office who referred to himself as a Tech Wiz. He was a Witch but found "Tech Wiz" more accurate for his magical applications. He typically invented new magical technology for the team to use. While Lyn and Donald weren't overly fond of each other, they would have a better chance of understanding the curse if they worked together.

Laila crossed the room, her boots sticking in the coagulating blood that coated the floor. She found the blade and frowned down at it. "If you do find a way to break the curse, that would be the easiest solution. But be careful with that thing. A slip of the hand, and you could be in the hospital too."

The others nodded, still in shock. Laila paused to study each face. She didn't want to think that any members of their team could be spies. Yet, the unfortunate truth was that they already discovered one traitor amongst them—their old supervisor, Colin, who had given sensitive information to the Demons.

Laila motioned for Lyn, Darien, and Jenn to follow her down the hall to Erin's small office at the back of the house. Inside she found Henrik holding Mr. Whiskers, who was now bound once more with the enchanted collar. Henrik had been waiting for the team to interview him, and Laila allowed him to stay. Once they had crammed themselves into the room, she shut the door and quickly filled Henrik in.

"Jerrik is convinced a plant in his homeland can cure Ali. I'm leaving with him for Svartalfheim shortly."

Darien spoke, his voice strained, "Are you sure it's wise to leave so soon?"

Laila grimaced. "No, I'm sure it's not. That's why I need the rest of you to be vigilant. Arrange security details or stay in a safe house. Just make sure that you try to minimize the chance of being caught like this again. At least until I'm back. Then I'll hunt Marius and the rest of his Demons down and make them pay." A faint blue glow from the marks on her arms seeped through her glamour as she struggled to rein in her fury.

The breath hissed out of Darien's mouth. "I don't like this."

"I know. Hopefully, we'll only be gone a few days."

Jenn folded her arms and looked skeptical. "You know

they're probably watching us, even now. Won't they notice you leaving?"

"Not if I disguise myself." Magic slid along Laila's skin. When it faded, she could have passed for Jenn's identical twin.

"That's a new thing, right?" the real Jenn asked, brow raised.

Laila shifted back to her normal appearance and nodded. "Between that and the teleportation, I think I can slip out of the city unnoticed."

Silence settled amongst the group.

"How did things get so fucked up so fast?" muttered Lyn.

Jenn's shoulders sagged. "They've been fucked up for a while. We're just finally realizing the extent of it."

Laila watched Darien. His demeanor was unusually pensive. "Will you manage without the rest of the team?"

"No. But we don't have another choice." He lifted his eyes to meet hers. "Be careful. If the Demons are here, then there's a good chance they've made it to the other worlds too. Who knows what you're walking into."

"I will. Stay safe."

Laila left the others and climbed the stairs to her room. It remained untouched since her last visit, and a layer of dust had accumulated on the dressers. She cleared it away with a spell and started to gather anything she thought she might need for the journey ahead.

"Hey," called Lyn from the doorway. Mr. Whiskers was with her, rubbing against her leg.

Laila waved her into the room. "How are you holding up?"

The Witch took a seat on the edge of the bed. "I think I'm still in shock. I don't know how they managed to get past my security wards like that. The charms were all active, but after the fight, something had fried them. I've never heard of anything like that before."

Laila pulled a piece of armor from a drawer then paused. "I think we're all sailing into uncharted territory these days."

Lyn flopped back on the bed and let out a strangled cry.

"How do we stop them? We can barely save ourselves; how can we save the entire city?"

Laila knew Lyn was referring to the Demons, and Laila had caught herself thinking the same thing over the past months. The question plagued her in her waking hours as well as in her sleep. Visions of battlefields strewn with the dead had become a permanent part of her dreams.

She glanced down at the armor in her hands. It was some of the most extraordinary craftsmanship she had ever seen and incorporated materials from multiple worlds. Made of Dwarven steel from Svartalfheim, it was coated in Pegasus leather from Asgard and far more durable than anything created by human hands. The Pegasus leather helped to deflect magical attacks. It had been a gift from Queen Regina of the Dragons—a thank you for saving her husband, the king, from an assassination attempt.

"I think we need to stop looking at this like we're the only ones who can stop them. We can't do it alone." She looked up at Lyn as she tried to process the thoughts swirling through her mind. "We've kept this threat hidden to keep the rest of the world from panicking, but maybe we've backed ourselves into a corner. Maybe the rest of the world deserves to know that the Demons are here. It's hard to find potential allies when they're oblivious to this threat. How many others—Supernaturals and humans alike—would be willing to join us?"

Lyn bit the inside of her cheek as she stood. "You know what, I think you're on to something. There's someone I need to contact."

As curious as Laila was about Lyn's sudden revelation, she was running short on time. "Stay safe."

Lyn pulled her into a quick hug. "You too. I'll see what I can learn from that cursed blade. Hopefully, one of us can find a cure in time."

Laila hoped she was right. She was sure a cure existed, but each of them had their obstacles to face. Lyn would have to decipher the blade then figure out how, or if, it was possible to break the spell. While Laila's quest seemed straightforward, she wondered how Jerrik's past would come in to play. They only had a week or so, which wasn't much time, especially with the Demons growing bolder.

"Can you keep an eye on Erin? She's in a bad place. I know she's got Frej, but still…" Laila trailed off.

The Witch gave her a somber, understanding look. "He's got too much soldier in him to be comforting. Don't worry. I'll watch over her."

Once Lyn hurried off, Laila checked her reflection in the mirror on her dresser. Her pants were bloodstained, and patches of dried blood still clung to her arms. She pulled off the clothes and stepped into the shower. She could have used a spell to the same effect, but Laila found the warm water soothing. It helped ease some of the tension in her shoulders but didn't soothe the ache in her chest.

She leaned against the tiled wall as the tears came. They slipped out to mix with the hot water. When Laila first moved to Midgard, she felt so isolated. All she had to look forward to was work. Then she arrived in Los Angeles, and Ali offered her a place to stay along with an offer of friendship. Ali was so different from Laila—outgoing, extroverted, and fun-loving—but Laila knew that was what made her such a good friend. She never judged Laila and encouraged her to try new things. Ali had been there when Laila was in the hospital recovering from magic exhaustion, through heartbreak, and when Laila was struggling to accept her new powers. She never realized how much she needed a friend like that until she'd found one. Now Ali was fighting for her life. Laila couldn't lose her. She refused to let that happen. Laila would fight until her last breath if necessary. Ali was more than just a friend—she was family.

Laila stepped out of the shower and looked into the mirror. She could see the faint glow of the moonstone necklace she wore. The stone was the size of a thumbnail, set into a ring of woven silver, and threaded through a chain with no clasps. It had been given to Laila by the same anonymous Goddess that had gifted her with divine magic. It was supposed to help her tap into her powers. Unfortunately, she had yet to figure out who this Goddess was. Arduinna insisted she had to be patient, but time was not something she could spare.

In any case, the necklace seemed to be working. Laila's ability to access the magic had become far more reliable. At least it was until now. How the magic had possessed her earlier terrified Laila, and she refused to be forced down a path that left her devoid of sympathy for the lives she took, even if they were Lesser Demons. That just wasn't the person Laila was. She needed to find a way to regain control.

Laila pulled on a pair of jeans, a long-sleeve gray shirt, and the breastplate from Queen Regina. She also added a pair of black boots and a brown leather jacket that Lyn had given her for Winter Solstice.

The jacket had an incredibly useful enchantment in the pockets that would allow her to store things in a sub dimensional space. She could carry around a backpack's worth of items without the weight. In these magical pockets, she packed some extra clothes and the mystical dagger given to her by the unknown Goddess. It didn't matter if Laila packed the blade or not since she could summon it at will, but she might as well keep it close.

Laila picked up her IRSA badge before clipping it to her belt and tucking her credentials into her pocket. They might come in handy if the portal guards gave Jerrik any trouble. She just hoped his forged documents would be convincing.

"Meow," called Mr. Whiskers as he swatted at her boot.

"Hey, you." Laila picked up the Bogey and cuddled him. He purred and rubbed his face against her cheek. "Thank you for protecting the house, little buddy. I have to go again, but I'll be back soon. Can you guard the house while I'm gone?"

He head-butted her in response. Then he leapt from her

arms and prowled out of the room, his tail swishing back and forth. Laila felt a little better, knowing Mr. Whiskers would be here to protect her home. With one last check to ensure she had everything she would need, she left.

Laila appeared in the hall outside of Ali's hospital room, nearly colliding with a nurse who squealed in surprise. Laila muttered a hasty apology before stepping into Ali's room. Arduinna was already gone, and both Erin and Mato were sleeping now. Frej was still nowhere to be seen. Where in the worlds had he gone? It wasn't like him to leave abruptly.

The first rays of sunlight started to peek over the horizon through the window, but Jerrik wasn't there yet. She took a seat on the edge of Ali's bed and held her hand.

Laila's voice was little more than a whisper. "Hey Ali, I'm not sure if you can hear me or not, but I'm going to find a way to help you. Don't you dare die on me." Laila glanced over at Erin as she slept. "I know you don't need me to tell you this, but we need you. Especially Erin. You've got to keep fighting that curse."

The room's door eased open, and Frej stepped in with a paper bag and a cardboard carrier with three coffee drinks. He paused when he saw Laila and set the food and drinks on a table.

"I take it you're ready to go?" he asked.

"I'm just waiting for Jerrik."

He nodded and looked at the others snoring softly. "I want you to know that I think your conditions are fair. You don't deserve to be someone's second choice. You're too good for that."

It felt as though another fissure formed in Laila's heart. This sort of understanding is why she found it so hard to walk away from him. Even when he was hurting and upset, he was still caring and understanding.

His eyes met Laila's, and even in the gloom, the turmoil in them was visible. "I'll think about it and have an answer for you when you return. In the meantime, be safe and come back to us."

Laila nodded, not entirely trusting her voice. She looked back at Ali once more and prayed this wasn't the last time she would see her friend. Before more tears could form, Laila turned away and pulled herself together. It was time to go.

She stepped out of the room and eased the door shut behind her.

"Ready?" asked Jerrik, leaning against the wall beside the door. "I'll call a cab."

"That won't be necessary. I'll take us to the airport."

Laila concentrated for a moment, causing her appearance to shift. Rather than replicating Jenn's appearance as before, Laila made more subtle changes—transforming her eyes to blue, her hair to black, rounding out the tips of her ears, and making herself a couple of inches shorter. Laila looked just different enough to avoid unwanted attention as they entered the airport. If any Demons were watching the place, she hoped it would be enough to fool them.

She offered Jerrik a hand. "Let's go."

CHAPTER 5

This time Laila took more care when she selected her tele-portation destination, choosing a covered and seldom-used bus stop. Her knees buckled as they appeared in front of the In-ter-Realm Terminal at the Los Angeles International Airport. Jerrik grabbed her elbow to steady her.

"Are you okay?"

Laila tensed at his nearness and quickly pulled away. "Yeah, it just takes more energy to bring someone with me. That's why I can't take us directly to Svartalfheim. At least not yet."

They entered the terminal, which was surprisingly busy considering the early hour. Unlike flights, reservations were not necessary for portal travel. You simply arrived and stood in the cue. Security was also minimal for departures. It was the arrival portal that sent you through a rigorous round of customs.

Rather than standing in the long lines already forming at the check-in counters for the various cities, Laila approached a security guard and flashed him her badge. "We've got an urgent matter that requires travel to Svartalfheim."

The security guard nodded and motioned for them to follow him past the lines to a counter on the side. The man behind the Svartalfheim kiosk entered them into the cue. It was a bit of a challenge convincing the ticketer they needed to remain anonymous, but eventually, he conceded.

"Your departure time slot is in ten minutes," he said, passing them their tickets.

Laila nodded her thanks before she and Jerrik stepped into the waiting room.

Near the Svartalfheim portal, Jerrik set his backpack on the ground in the shadow of a pillar. Laila tried to keep her attention from wandering to him but failed. He had broken her heart last year when he vanished without a word. Now that she knew the truth—that her old supervisor was to blame for the miscommunication—she couldn't hold it against him.

"Since when can you use glamours?" Jerrik asked, tugging her from her thoughts.

"Divine magic gives me the ability to mask my aura and blend in."

It wasn't the same as Fae glamour that affected the way others perceived her. These changes were a physical manipulation of her body.

His brow rose in genuine interest. "What other new abilities do you have?"

Laila shrugged. "I'm still not entirely sure. Most of my abilities are sort of general, the sort any creature from Asgard would have. I think you've already seen those—teleporting, glamour, increased strength with elemental magic."

She knew Jerrik was about to pry further, so she switched the topic. "I know you're keeping things from me, mostly about your past. But I need to know if there is anything that could affect this mission before our arrival."

Jerrik studied the illuminated sign above the door that read: *Svartalfheim*. He appeared oddly withdrawn, but whether that was to do with last night's attack or the fact they were returning to his homeland, Laila couldn't tell.

"I have a lifetime of history there, far more than I can explain in a matter of minutes. None of it is relevant to our mission, at least not as long as we avoid the city guards. Plus, we won't even be in the city for long. The particular Eirflower plant we're looking for is in the temple of the Swordmasters."

That explained how Jerrik knew of the Eirflower's existence. He'd told her once that he'd been training with intentions of joining their mystical order of elite fighters. Unfortunately, his father disapproved of Jerrik's interest in the Swordmasters' Order. When he discovered Jerrik had continued his training in secret, he killed Jerrik's Swordmaster. It was hard to imagine Jerrik being labeled a criminal after that—instead of his father—but she heard rumors of corruption amongst the Dark Elves in recent years. His father could have bribed government officials and blamed the Swordmaster's death on Jerrik for all she knew.

Laila wished Jerrik would just open up and tell her the whole truth. What if her ignorance placed her in greater danger? But some wounds heal slower than others, and she imagined Jerrik was still recovering from his. She noticed he had a similar way of avoiding conversations about the Demonic fight rings as well.

Laila looked at him warily. "Isn't the temple of the Swordmasters in Jotunheim?"

"Yes, but the most direct route lies through a small portal in the tunnels below the palace in the city of Nidavellir. There were more portals, but the Swordmasters closed them over time. This one I know how to access."

"Just because it's the most direct doesn't mean it's the fastest," Laila pointed out.

He was still staring at that sign, lost in thought. The next moment he shook it off and flashed Laila a cocky smile. "Don't look so concerned. We can handle a bunch of grouchy old guards. I'm extraordinarily charming when I want to be."

Laila snorted.

He leaned a little closer. "I seem to recall it worked quite nicely on you."

She glowered up at him.

Jerrik laughed. "I've missed that look."

He chucked her chin playfully, and she swatted his hand away.

"Thor's hammer, this is going to be a long trip," Laila grumbled, trying not to think about the way her heart beat faster every time he leaned closer. It was probably just the anxiety of the situation and the pressure of finding the Eirflower. She couldn't afford to let emotions cloud her judgment, even if a part of her still wondered: what if she gave him another chance?

Laila shook her head as if it might rattle the treacherous thoughts from her mind.

"Two travelers for Svartalfheim," called a female voice on the intercom.

Jerrik gave her a little bow. "After you."

Laila ignored him and headed through the door to the portal hall, passing her ticket to the woman at the door as she went. On the other side of the door was a set of two portals leading to two of the cities in Svartalfheim: Deurgard, the capital of the Dwarven Kingdom, and Nidavellir, the capitol of the Svartálfr Kingdom.

Armed guards lined the walls, and more security watched over the portal hall from a room above, separated by a thick pane of bulletproof glass. It might seem like overkill, except there was no way to peer through the veil. No one could see who, or what, was approaching from the other side. If the creature posed a danger to the city—such as a Greater Demon—the guards would only have seconds to lock down the room and prevent the threat from escaping. Hence, the reason security was far more strict on the arrival side of a portal.

A guard standing by the portal to Nidavellir waved them forward, and they approached the veil that rippled with rainbow-colored strands of magic. It bathed their skin in its colorful glow as they neared, and Laila could feel the power resonating from the portal. Magic tickled her face like the touch of a thousand feathers as she passed through the veil.

As with all inter-world portals, the space between the worlds was dark. The only source of light was the mystical bridge of woven magic that connected one end of the threshold to the other. If you were foolish enough to step off the bridge and fall into the darkness beyond, it was said you would fall for eternity. It always made Laila a little nervous when crossing through these gateways.

She dropped her camouflage and crossed the bridge of rippling rainbow light with Jerrik. She wouldn't need it in Nidavellir. The bridge cast odd shadows that flickered across their faces, and the eerie silence that engulfed them was deeply unsettling. Laila avoided lingering in this space between the worlds. Her pace picked up, and she was about to charge through the other veil when she noticed Jerrik had stopped.

"Jerrik?" Laila caught a glimpse of uncertainty once more, but it was gone in a flash, replaced with a smirk. He stepped past her through the end of the portal.

The first thing Laila noticed was the shift in the magic. Svartalfheim had a completely different feel than her enchanting homeworld of Alfheim, let alone Midgard, which had little magic in its atmosphere. Here, the mystical energy of stone dominated, pulsing with a faint thrum. It whispered of lush secrets, ancient spells, and things best done in the cover of darkness. If she listened closely, she thought she could hear the pounding of a hammer on metal, although there was no forge in sight. There was a tantalizing quality to the magic, but also a cold harshness that reminded her of sharpened steel.

They stepped into a circular room of stone with three rows of balconies climbing up the walls. A dozen archers lined each platform, their crossbows trained on Laila and Jerrik. On the ground, more guards faced the Elves, their swords crackling with magical electricity. Laila's heart pounded in her chest, but she reminded herself that this was a typical reception in many kingdoms.

"Identification, please." A short, stout guard stretched his hand out with impatience.

Laila passed him her IRSA badge and credentials. He wrinkled his nose at the badge and frowned at the photo I.D.

"We're here on an assignment," Laila stated simply.

"What sort of assignment?" the guard asked.

Jerrik's expression had taken on a new level of arrogance. He rolled his eyes as if this was a massive waste of his time. "That's classified and far above your pay grade."

The guard centered his gaze on Jerrik. "You look familiar. Have we met?"

Jerrik tensed but flashed the guard his badge and credentials—quick enough that the man wouldn't be able to read the name. "I doubt it. We have approval from the Red Guard to conduct an interview, but you can call the captain down here if you don't believe me. I'm sure he'd *love* to be interrupted for such an insignificant matter."

Despite the smirk on Jerrik's face, there was a subtle hint of a threat. She wasn't sure who this Red Guard was, but from the way the stout man blanched, Laila had a feeling it was nothing good. She kicked herself mentally for not paying closer attention to her lessons in otherworldly politics back in Alfheim.

The guard quickly waved them on. "That won't be necessary. Enjoy your stay."

Jerrik scoffed as if staying in Nidavellir was about as pleasant as a trip to the sewers. They left the chamber and didn't speak a word as they walked through the Hall of Portals' branching corridors.

The halls were crowded with well-dressed Svartalfar coming and going. Vendors sold various goods from food to hats and other items that travelers might require. The smell of baked goods and candied nuts mixed with the heady perfume that rolled off the women dressed in heavy layers of silk and brocade. These women turned their noses up in disgust at Laila's plain appearance when she passed.

Laila's skin prickled. Someone was watching them. Glancing over her shoulder, she noticed another pair of guards weaving through the crowd after them.

"Jerrik, we're being followed." She placed a hand on his shoulder. "Hold on."

Laila teleported them away into an alcove some distance behind, startling Jerrik with the abruptness. She motioned for him to be quiet as the pair of guards looked around in confusion. Ignoring the ringing in her ears and wave of dizziness, Laila watched the guards. From this angle, she noted one of them clutched a wanted poster in his hand. It had Jerrik's face on it.

"Maybe I should've worn a disguise. I didn't think anyone would recognize me so quickly," muttered Jerrik.

Another moment and the guards moved on to search the crowd in a waiting room.

Quickly, they exited the Hall of Portals and stepped out onto a street. The air was oddly still and stale—heavy with the foul taste of smog. She glanced up at the sky and found stone far above them instead and stared in awe. The city was situated in a massive cavern. There was no sign of sunlight, but there was a faint colorful glow high above, dampened by a thick veil of haze drifting above the buildings. In front of them, a variety of carriages waited to carry visitors throughout the city. Cab drivers shouted to them as they passed, promising the lowest fares and most direct routes, but Jerrik ignored them. He led Laila across a busy street then down a deserted alley.

Once out of earshot from other pedestrians, Laila grabbed Jerrik's arm and yanked him to a stop.

"Why is there a bounty on your head? They identified you at the portal in under ten minutes." The look she gave him said she wasn't moving until she got an answer.

Jerrik checked to ensure no one had followed before lowering his voice until she could barely hear him. "After Master Kyvik's murder, I joined a rebellion here in the city that is determined to overthrow the king. I wanted to see an end to the corruption in this kingdom." He shook his head and, for a moment, appeared too frustrated to speak. "The king didn't like it when he found out a son of a highborn family had joined ranks with the rebels. He sent the entire Red Guard after me as well as every bounty hunter in the city. I couldn't make a move without someone discovering me, so I fled."

So, he was some sort of nobility. Laila expected that much, seeing as he had been training with a Swordmaster. What she hadn't expected was for him to be a rebel. But had it really been necessary to keep that from her?

"Those are the sort of things you were supposed to tell me beforehand," she grumbled.

"Would you have come?" A hint of a smile appeared.

Of course, she would have. But Laila hated walking into a situation unprepared. Surely Jerrik knew that. This wasn't some leisure trip; this was a mission, and failure would cost Ali her life. Laila would not allow Jerrik's discomfort to jeopardize the outcome.

He seemed to consider his next words carefully. "Look, I'm sorry. I'm just not used to opening up about this stuff. I've spent the better part of two years hiding from my past."

Laila bit her lip and debated how to react. She was raised as a soldier and knew how to place a mission before her own needs. But Jerrik was some sort of noble. Even if he'd forsaken that life, did he have the ability to detach himself emotionally from the situation? What if his insecurities compromised them?

"What is the Red Guard?" she asked.

Jerrik kept his voice low and motioned her to follow him down the alley. "The Red Guard is an elite group of fighters similar to the Royal Guard back in Alfheim. Only rather than simply protecting the royal family, they also enact King Oddvarr's will and deal harshly with those that oppose him. These guards are known for their cruelty and lack of mercy. Even the ordinary City Guards tread cautiously around them. There's no due process of law here, only the will of King Oddvarr."

Laila remembered hearing rumors that Nidavellir had been experiencing some sort of political turmoil. The other governments must have overlooked it when the Demonic threat became apparent a few years ago. Even so, she was surprised it had crumbled into this sort of fear-driven system. It left her deeply uneasy, and she imagined this wasn't the sort of place agents such as them would be looked on favorably. With each step, her uncertainty grew, and she regretted how easily she had dismissed Frej's concerns.

And yet, the truth was, there were far worse things than joining a rebellion, especially in a kingdom like this. Laila wanted to be annoyed with him for keeping this from her, but he had spent the last two years trying to avoid detection. He was just trying to protect himself.

Did he think that she would betray him? Is that why he hadn't told her sooner? Laila's heart sank. Just because she preferred to play by the rules didn't mean she would hand him over, especially under the circumstances. Regardless, they had a job to do. She might be frustrated with Jerrik, but he was the only one who could get her to the Eirflower.

Jerrik guided them back to the main roads, where they tried to blend in with the crowds. Although it had been early morning when they left Los Angeles, it appeared to be evening here in Svartalfheim. That the entire city was deep underground made it challenging to know what time it was, but they passed businesses closing up shop and restaurants preparing for the evening rush. Brick buildings towered above them, pressing in on the streets and obstructing her view of the rest of the city. Beyond those, that glimmer of colorful lights filtered through the blanket of hazy smog to illuminate the streets, supplementing the warm glow of enchanted lanterns that lined the sidewalks.

Almost everything was stone, with hardly any wood in sight. Even the tables and chairs were constructed from metal, bent into swirling artistic shapes. The lampposts were equally ornate, but no matter how many lights they crammed along the street and shop exteriors, the streets were dark and dingy. Soot collected on surfaces and blackened the buildings' windows. Shadows permeated the streets, feeling darker and deeper than felt natural.

The traffic around Jerrik and Laila rumbled deafeningly as motorized carriages and carts rolled down the street. The women seated in the carriages sported dresses of elegant fabrics and tightly laced corsets, while the men wore fine suits and top hats. Yet, those who traversed the streets on foot wore plain, worn clothing. City Guards in the same grey uniforms from the Hall of Portals patrolled the area, bowing to the gentry and scowling at the common folk.

It was so different from her homeland's open, airy streets where enchanted melodies drifted on gentle breezes. Here the air felt thick and heavy with pollution from the steam-powered carriages and grumbling machines in nearby factories.

A cart loaded with dust-covered men and women rolled in front of Laila. Their gaunt faces were grim, and their clothes were worn. She stared at the sunken, haunted eyes and shivered. These people appeared to be on the verge of magic exhaustion. A couple even looked unconscious.

"Are those prisoners?" Laila whispered to Jerrik.

"Those are miners. The kingdom's main sources of income are from the mines beneath the city and goods from the factories."

Laila's gut twisted in horror. Elderly men sat among them, and young children as well. One little boy watched her with sad, listless eyes.

"How is that allowed? Those people look worked to death!" Bile rose in her throat. What sort of monster would treat people this way?

Jerrik watched the cart rattle into the distance until the traffic swallowed it up. "The tunnels beneath the city have been over-mined. The workers are paid by what they can produce at the end of each day—not for hours worked. It's horrible, dangerous work down there, and nothing has been done to help the miners. The king just looks the other way. However, the city is overcrowded, and jobs are scarce. So, for many, it's their only option."

Laila's stomach tightened even more. As they continued, she noticed more people huddled in alleys and begging for coins. Many of them were missing limbs.

"From accidents in the mines," Jerrik said.

"I'm starting to see why you joined a rebellion." The hopeless expressions haunted her, and it took all Laila's willpower to keep from stopping—to try to help them in some way. She knew she couldn't linger, though, not with the bounty on Jerrik's head. They couldn't afford any delays.

"This isn't what I expected." She watched a carriage that was self-propelled like the cars in Midgard. An obscene amount of black smoke spewed from a tailpipe.

Jerrik choked and fanned away the fumes. "In what regard? The poverty? The lack of safe working conditions? The smog that requires an entire team of sorcerers to continually filter the air, so the whole city isn't poisoned?"

"All of it," she admitted with a sigh.

Jerrik paused on the sidewalk and stared up at a massive structure carved into the cave wall overlooking the city. Towers were reaching up like daggers, piercing through the natural face of the rock. It was a castle.

"Is everything okay?" she asked, studying Jerrik's torn expression.

"My mother's imprisoned in there," he said softly. His eyes remained fixed on the jagged cluster of towers.

Laila stopped. "What?"

"I found out a few months ago, during the Vampire investigations." His eyes didn't move from the palace.

She remembered some sort of news that had deeply disturbed Jerrik and caused him to lash out at the others—particularly Frej. But he never told her what that news was. No wonder he had lost it.

Laila felt a pang of guilt for being so harsh on him last fall. If only Jerrik had told her back then, she would have understood. She couldn't imagine how it felt for him to stare up at the palace and know he wasn't there to help his mother. The tumultuous look in his eyes tugged at her heart.

"What was she imprisoned for?" she asked gently.

"Because the king hasn't been able to find me. He's hoping I will surrender. I almost came back as soon as I received the message, but I knew I couldn't. There are too few of us with IRSA as it is. I think finding the Demons is more important."

"Oh, Jerrik. I'm so sorry." She pulled him into a hug. She had no idea how to make this easier or to help him. "Are you sure you want to help me with the Eirflower? You could stay here—"

He shook his head, tearing his eyes from the palace above.

"No, we have a mission. My mother is safe. The king favors her so he wouldn't dare harm her." For all the confidence in his voice, Laila glimpsed a hint of uncertainty in his eyes. It pained her to see.

Then a ghost of a smile appeared on his face, and he snaked an arm around her waist. "Although, if I knew that bringing up my unfortunate past was all it took to get you to embrace me again, I would've told you sooner."

Laila snorted and pushed him off. "Seriously? How can you joke at a time like this?"

He shrugged. His gaze flicked up to the palace once more, his expression distracted. "Because it keeps my mind off other things."

The guilt crept in. Of course, Jerrik was only distracting himself. He had done the same thing when the Demons imprisoned them. He had teased her until they both forgot about the danger they were facing.

"Come on. Let's go this way." He nodded toward a market only open to foot traffic.

Laila peered around in surprise. It was as if they suddenly stepped through a portal into another place. Here vendors continued to sell their wares along the street that snaked like a serpent through the city. Decorated in dark jewel-tones were rows of tents with strange, luscious scents lingering in the air, covering the stale odor of smog. Laila inhaled deeply as her stomach growled at the smell of a pastry stand. There were odd gadgets on display in some tents that ran off of magic and steam, while others contained items imported from the other worlds—everything from rare spices and herbs to fabric with enchanted dyes that would never fade. There were teacups charmed to keep your tea the perfect temperature and potions with magical properties. Laila eyed one of the bottles and wondered what Lyn would make of these. It was a whimsical feast for the senses.

She paused by one stand selling delicate lace made from magical spider silk that shimmered gold in the lantern light. As dismal as the main roads had been, this market felt vibrant and enchanting. The people here were spirited. The cheerful atmosphere was enough to keep their concerns at bay.

Jerrik smiled as Laila marveled at it all. "This was always my favorite part of the city. It's called the Twilight Market."

Laila could see why. It was like walking into a jewelry box.

A haunting, high voice floated through the market, and Laila spotted the singer standing between booths. Her pale, silvery skin was the color of moonbeams while her snow-white hair flowed about her shoulders. She wore a rich blue gown with embroidered silver stars that twinkled and glowed. All along the street, people paused to listen. It was tempting to stop with them, but there was no time to spare.

They wandered through the Twilight Market, where the occasional walkway led out to other streets where lovers tucked into corners to kiss in the shadows and illicit goods transferred hands. They were passing one such road when a commotion caught her attention.

"What do we have here?" sneered a guard with his back to

them. Judging by the crimson uniform he wore, this was a member of the Red Guard.

He had a Svartálfr man in plain, nondescript clothes cornered in the narrow street. Three other members of the Red Guard looked on menacingly as the man's eyes darted about looking for some means of escape.

One of the guards took a step closer to the man. "What a surprise to find a rebel wandering the marketplace alone. It's hard to believe your little resistance lasted this long!"

Laila glanced over at Jerrik, wondering if he knew this man. Jerrik looked as if he had seen a Ghost, confirming her suspicions.

One of the guards used a spell to pin the man to the brick wall as the others advanced on him. They began pummeling the man with their fists—four against one. The poor man grunted in pain as he doubled over and struggled to protect himself from the barrage of blows. Laila's blood boiled.

The Svartálfr man spotted Laila.

Help me! His silent prayer echoed in her head, eyes pleading with her. Laila's stomach twisted into knots. No one was coming to the man's aid. She had to do something.

Laila took a step, but Jerrik grabbed her arm. "You're not in Los Angeles anymore. You have to keep your head down!"

"I can't stand here and do nothing! They're beating him to death!" she hissed.

She tugged her arm out of his grasp and turned toward the conflict. Jerrik swore behind her.

"What is wrong with you!" she shouted and stormed up to the guards.

"Keep walking," the nearest one spat.

Laila used an air spell to freeze them in place. Her voice was cold as ice. "I don't think you heard me."

"Stay out of this, Elf, or you're next!" snarled one of them. People were stopping to stare at the commotion.

Laila ignored him. "Now tell me what crime this man has

committed."

"He's a traitor to the crown!"

"Then arrest him, don't beat him to death," her voice was harsh and threatening.

"Want to join him, Elf?" The guard broke through Laila's spell and raised a hand to strike her.

She blocked it and grabbed his wrist, then twisted it behind his back. Snatching up his other hand, she bound them together with the pair of cuffs dangling from his belt.

"See? How hard was that?" she cooed as the guard howled in rage.

The other two charged, and Laila tripped the first one, snagging the cuffs from his belt. She used the chain connecting them to block an incoming punch from the second guard before shoving him against the wall and restraining him as well.

A small crowd of bystanders gathered around them, watching with shock and amusement. Laila noticed Jerrik among them. He looked horrified.

The guard she had tripped climbed to his feet, shouting a string of profanity. Laila used her magic to summon another pair of cuffs from a detained guard's belt and caught them as they soared through the air.

The guard swung a baton at her head. She ducked. He lunged again and aimed for her stomach as she stepped back toward a wall. She flung the cuffs in the air, and they sped toward the guard. They magically clamped themselves around one wrist and then another, pinning his arms behind his back. Laila shoved him toward the others.

The crowd cheered.

The cornered rebel rushed to her. "Thank you! I owe you my life!"

"Just get out of here while you can."

"Damn it, Laila." Jerrik stormed up to her.

Recognition registered on the rebel's face. "Jerrik?" He faltered. "By the Gods, what are you doing here?"

He shook his head. "It's a long story. We need to get out of here before—"

Laila felt the buzz of electricity and threw a shield of air around them just as the lightning bolt struck. The guards had unlocked their cuffs and were rushing for them.

"I'm going to put your head on a spike!" one snarled, following up with another attack.

Laila's divine magic struggled to break free of her control, but she held it back. She wasn't sure she trusted it after last night.

"Laila, you've got to do something, or we're all dead," Jerrik said, shoving the crowd back.

Laila glanced around at the crowd of bystanders that was growing by the second. She didn't know how her magic would react. What if it lashed out and attacked them too? What if it killed one of the guards? All she needed was to disable them, not destroy them. Her elemental magic was predictable but had its limits, and they were outnumbered. If the Red Guard detained them, it would complicate matters immensely, and they would lose precious time.

Fine. Laila grit her teeth and reluctantly allowed the divine magic to come forth. Her eyes glowed along with the scars on her arms as she dropped the glamour, masking her aura. She sent a wave of blue fire towards the guard.

They managed to shield themselves in time, but her flames licked at barriers of air around them, weakening them and devouring their energy. Laila pulled up the path's cobblestones in front of her and levitated them in the air. Releasing the spell, she sent them piling on top of the Red Guards, burying them alive in their magical domes. It wouldn't stop them, but it would slow them.

The man she rescued stared in shock at the display of power.

Jerrik grabbed both of them and shoved them back toward the market. "We need to go. Now!"

Laila dimmed her glowing aura and plunged back into the

crowd with Jerrik and the rebel. People stared as they went. So much for keeping a low profile.

❖ 53 ❖

CHAPTER 6

They sprinted through the crowd, not bothering to apologize as they bumped into shoppers. Jerrik veered to the right, leading Laila and the rebel out of the Twilight Market along empty streets where they could cover more ground.

Laila could hear the sounds of pursuit in the distance. Over her shoulder, she glimpsed three guards gaining on them.

"Hold on!" She grabbed both men by the arms.

In an instant, they were back in the Twilight Market, standing in the shadow of a tent. Laila's legs gave out—the shock of transporting two people hitting her like a bus. Luckily, Jerrik caught her before she landed on the cobblestones.

"Thor's hammer, Laila. Now I know you're overdoing it," Jerrik grumbled through clenched teeth. He kept a hand around her waist to support her.

"I'm fine. I just need a moment."

"I'll be back." The rebel vanished into the crowd.

"What happened to keeping a low profile?" Jerrik snapped. "Was that really necessary?"

"Are you kidding me? You know that guy, and you were going to stand by and do nothing while guards beat him to death! What's gotten into you, Jerrik?" She glared at him. He would never hesitate that way back in Los Angeles.

Jerrik scowled. "How does picking a fight with guards help us? You should have let it be. Now they'll be looking for you too!"

Laila stared at him in disbelief. Sure, Jerrik wasn't the most selfless person she ever met, but she never thought he was this shallow.

The next moment, the other rebel returned, effectively ending the discussion.

"Here, eat this. It'll help." He passed her a small pouch he procured.

She opened the bag and found it filled with candied nuts—similar to chocolate-covered hazelnuts. They tasted divine, and after a few, she realized the man was right. She felt better.

"Thank you." She gave him a tired smile. "By the way, I'm Laila."

"I'm Hallr." He shook her hand enthusiastically.

Hallr was taller than Jerrik with broader shoulders and short hair. He was quick to smile and reminded her of Mato. They both had that same mischievous, boyish gleam in their eyes.

He turned to Jerrik. "And you? What the hell are you doing back here? I thought we told you to stay in Midgard!"

Jerrik's frown deepened. Laila could tell his patience was growing short. "It's a long story. Take us somewhere safe, and I'll explain."

"Sure thing." Hallr nodded back to the main street of the market.

Winding down a maze of side streets and alleys, he led them on a roundabout journey through the city to ensure no one followed them. Eventually, they arrived at a nondescript pub. Rather than entering through the front, he took them around back and down the steps toward a cellar. There was a door, but he paused and faced an old brick wall instead. From around his neck, he removed a small wooden talisman and pressed it against a worn brick. To Laila's surprise, lines of mortar disappeared as a panel swung open. It was a wonderfully disguised enchantment, and Laila doubted she would have found it on her own.

"Welcome!" said Hallr, waving them into the tunnel.

Jerrik conjured a light to illuminate a small passage that wound its way underground. The air was cold and stale, and slimy mold grew along the walls where filthy, brackish water dripped down from the streets above. It gave off an odd, rotting stench. Hallr and Jerrik covered their noses with cloth as they went. Laila followed suit, covering her mouth with a handkerchief to protect against mold spores. As they walked, Jerrik explained what brought them to Nidavellir.

Hallr groaned. "Please don't tell me you're planning to break into the palace gardens just to pick a flower."

Jerrik looked exasperated. "Of course not; that would be suicide. We'll go to the Swordmaster's temple instead."

"And you're sure they still have one of these Eirflowers in the Swordmasters' temple?" asked Hallr.

"It's been there for generations. One of my ancestors tasked them with protecting it."

Hallr didn't look reassured. "Well, it's not going to be easy to get to the portal. The Red Guard has been recruiting everyone they can. Between them and the city guard, they've practically got the city on lockdown. It's even worse than before."

"It's still possible, though, right?" Laila picked up her pace behind him.

Hallr nodded reluctantly. "I'm sure we can find a way."

Jerrik shot a look at Laila. "The trouble will be finding a route home. Now, they'll be searching for both of us."

She huffed out a frustrated breath. She hadn't thought about that.

Hallr paused in front of a steep set of steps leading upward. "Well, first things first. You both look like you could use a proper meal and some rest. I'll talk to the others and see if we can't come up with a way to smuggle you through the city."

The murmur of a small crowd echoed from above, and they emerged into what looked like a basic tavern, only there were no doors opening to the street. Svartalfar packed themselves around tables while more came and went from a variety of subterranean tunnels. They laughed and drank. Someone even played the fiddle in a corner.

Hallr gave Laila a reassuring smile. "Don't worry. This is one of the rebel hideouts. You'll be safe here."

No one seemed to pay her much attention, but when Jerrik emerged, the room fell silent. For a moment, everyone simply stared, some even bowed. Then at once, everyone bombarded him with questions.

"Wait! You're back?"

"How come no one told me?"

"Is there a new development?"

"Did something happen?"

Everyone seemed eager to speak to Jerrik. To avoid the crowd, Laila retreated with Hallr toward the bar.

"Wow, they seem quite excited to see him," Laila observed, watching the rebels fight for their chance to talk with Jerrik.

"Why wouldn't they be?" Hallr gave Laila an odd look.

"I don't know. I wouldn't think a noblemen's son would be so popular here, given the circumstances."

The rebel barked a laugh. "Is that what he told you? That he's the son of a nobleman?"

"Yeah. Why?"

Hallr roared with laughter, leaning against the bar. "Oh Gods! Hold on, let me order us drinks first."

He waved down a bartender and ordered two pints.

"Oh no, I'm fine," protested Laila.

"Trust me. You'll need it." He gave her a wicked look.

Laila eyed him suspiciously. The bartender plunked down two glasses in front of them, and Hallr passed her one.

"So, what has he told you?" he asked before taking a sip of

his drink.

"Not much, just that he's a wanted man and part of the re-bellion." Jerrik had been somewhat of an enigma since she met him. But he earned her trust, so she never felt the need to pry into his past until now.

Hallr watched Jerrik, who was still chatting with the other rebels. "Jerrik's the only child and heir of King Oddvarr."

"What?" Laila's jaw dropped.

There was no way that was true. Hallr had to be joking. Jerrik was, well...*Jerrik*. He had never struck her as diplomatic in any regard or even much of a leader. He went out to dive bars on his nights off with Henrik and Mato, and he lived in a dingy apartment in Playa Vista. This was the guy she had escaped from Demons with. Hell, they even had shower sex in a grimy, abandoned police station. No way. Jerrik couldn't be a prince.

Yet, somehow, it also made sense. His father had gotten away with murdering Jerrik's instructor because he was the king. Since he was the next in line for the throne, that also made Jerrik the king's greatest threat. No wonder there was a small army after him.

Laila grabbed the ale and took a large gulp, earning another burst of laughter from Hallr.

"I told you that you'd need it." Hallr patted her shoulder. "He never liked the title or how people fawned over him—he swore it was impossible to live his own life. He had no interest in the crown growing up, but fate has a funny way of making decisions for us."

"Are you talking about the death of the Swordmaster?" A part of Laila knew that Jerrik should be the one to tell her these things, but she had given him plenty of time to do so. She was finished waiting for answers.

"Master Kyvik was a part of it. I think it helped open his eyes to how corrupt his father had become. The king would do anything to hold onto power. Jerrik began to visit the mines and streets, where he realized how difficult life had become for the poorest citizens while the wealthy benefited. I was the son of a lesser noble, and we'd been friends for a long time. When he tried to persuade me to join the rebels, I was reluctant at first, but I knew it was the right thing to do."

"So, you're one of his closest friends, and he was still going to leave you to the Red Guard?" Laila could feel her anger flare again.

Hallr only shrugged. "He knows that I'd rather be captured than to have his life endangered. If he dies, our hope dies with him. I would never have looked to you if I'd realized who was with you."

Laila gulped down more ale, although it had little effect thanks to her divine magic. She thought of all the times Jerrik had put his life in danger back in Midgard, from the fight rings to the Vampire rebellion. What would Hallr think if he knew Jerrik hadn't exactly been playing it safe on Earth?

Hallr's gentle voice pulled her from her thoughts. "So, how did you meet Jerrik? I'm guessing it was in Midgard."

Laila nodded and launched into the story, omitting details where she deemed necessary. She told him about the fight ring and how Jerrik joined her team. It appeared that Jerrik hadn't had much contact with Hallr since his departure, only enough for Hallr to know he was still alive.

The rebel sighed and wiped his face with his hand. "Of course Jerrik wouldn't retreat to some quiet spot and take up a hobby. I should've known he'd go looking for trouble."

Laila shot him a sour look. "We don't go looking for it; it usually finds us."

She still couldn't believe what Hallr had told her. All this time, Jerrik had been a prince in hiding. Laila rested her elbows on the counter and placed her head in her hands. This was going to complicate everything exponentially.

"Really? You're already drinking without me?" Jerrik's playful tone rippled behind her.

Laila looked up at him, unsure of what to say. Her head was

still reeling, and not from the ale. Jerrik's gaze swung from her to Hallr, and he realized what they had been discussing.

"Damn it, Hallr!" Jerrik let loose a long string of profanity. "You had no right!"

Hallr's face grew serious. "Are you kidding me? You're the one who brought her here without telling her. How did you think that this would all play out? That you'd really slip through the city unnoticed?"

Jerrik threw his hands in the air. "Yes! That's exactly what I planned—until we found *you* getting beat to a pulp in the Twilight Market."

Jerrik turned to Laila with a desperate look. "I was going to tell you, I swear, I just…"

Laila pushed away from the bar and stormed past him. She had no idea where she was going, but she needed space. Laila climbed a staircase and reached the door to the roof. She stepped out onto a terrace overlooking the city, but it was odd to exit a building with no wind to greet her—just the still, heavy air of the massive cave.

She exhaled and sank to the ground with her back against the low wall that encircled the terrace. Why was it that every time she got to know someone, she had to discover some secret that completely shifted her understanding of them?

The fact that Jerrik was a prince shouldn't matter to her. He had already proven she could trust him. So, did a fancy title make a difference? Part of her reasoned that he wasn't any different just because he was born into a royal family. Yet, she still felt betrayed.

One thought stood out in her mind: why hadn't he trusted her?

The door opened, and Jerrik emerged. He hesitated as if he was afraid Laila might vanish. She considered it—to teleport somewhere else—but she was tired, and it had been a long day.

"Can I talk to you?" He took a hesitant step forward.

"That depends. Are you going to answer my questions, or

am I going to have to get my answers from Hallr?"

He flinched as if her words physically struck him. "Okay, I probably deserve that."

He crossed the roof and joined her on the floor. For a moment, he sat staring up at the glowing ceiling of the cave.

He waved to the stone far above. "Do you see the plants?"

Laila lifted an eyebrow, annoyed that was he changing the subject so soon, but she looked up all the same. She assumed the glow came from enchanted lights set into the stone above, but upon closer inspection, she realized the glow came from thousands of plants. They sparkled in the most vibrant shades she had ever seen. Some had large pointed leaves like emerald knives, while others had blossoms that glittered like rubies. There were creeping vines in turquoise and vast swaths of sapphire roses. They sprouted from the stone and clung to the cave walls and ceiling, bathing the city in their glow. How in the worlds had she missed them?

"I've never seen anything like it," Laila breathed.

"Even in the deepest caves and darkest spaces, beauty can grow and thrive." Jerrik stared at the spectacular plants above. "They only grow here in Nidavellir, and it's said that each family is magically connected to a plant. Have you heard the story of how the Svartalfar sacrificed their color?"

Laila shook her head. All she knew was that the Elves who established this kingdom left after a political dispute—something to do with a disagreement over tax funds.

"After leaving Alfheim, the Svartalfar became nomads, wandering the worlds in search of a new home where they could form their own government. A plague spread throughout the Dwarven Kingdom when they arrived, and the Elves were able to heal them. In return, they were given these caves. Although it was great to have land of their own, the Elves struggled with the oppressive darkness where no food could grow. They missed the lush forests of Alfheim, and many considered returning. One woman was determined to stay and thought if she could give a little bit of her magic to the cave that perhaps the cave would allow her plants to grow.

"She planted a single berry seed and transferred her magic into it, willing it to cultivate. As the magic seeped into the seed, it began to sprout rapidly, developing pale green leaves that illuminated the darkness. As the plant began to blossom, the Elf noticed something peculiar. The color was diminishing from her hands as her skin faded to grey. The price for this little miracle of life had been the color in her own body. It came as a shock at first, but the bush would provide much-needed food. Others soon tried the spell, and each created a new plant that glowed with magic until they had a whole garden. The Elves lost their vibrancy, but the sacrifice they made allowed for this kingdom to survive in the darkness. That is why we are referred to as Dark Elves—for our kingdom in the underground."

"Is it true?" asked Laila, still marveling at the glowing plants along the walls of the cave.

"I believe so. I know at least part of it is—that each family is connected to one variety of plant. The more populous the family tree, the more common the plant."

Laila looked around and noticed that some plants were indeed more common than others. "What about you? What flower is connected to your family?"

"The Eirflower. That's why I know so much about it, and since my father and I are the only two remaining in the bloodline, there are only two plants left." He pulled his gaze from the glowing foliage back to Laila. "I wish I could forget my past. Growing up in the palace, I never knew who I could trust—who was a friend and who was ready to stab me in the back. It was the same sort of environment that twisted my father into the man he is today. Few people took the time to get to know me like Hallr. Women flirted and tried to impress me, but they were always hungry for power. Well, at least those who weren't were too timid to come anywhere near me, thanks to my father's brutal reputation.

"When I joined the rebels, I thought it would be different. I was no longer dealing with courtiers, just ordinary men and women. I was wrong. Even though it was far different from the court, I always felt removed. I was a symbol instead of a person, but at least here, I felt like I was making a difference. Or at least trying to.

"Fleeing to Midgard felt like it wasn't just an escape from my father, but a chance to have a somewhat ordinary life. I swore not to tell anyone who I was for fear of changing that, and it worked."

Laila looked at him and saw the depths of the remorse in his eyes.

"I didn't want to tell you because I didn't want it to affect the way you thought of me," he continued. "I like being normal."

Laila recalled the incident last fall when Jerrik and Frej had fought and how they later reconciled their differences. "Does Frej know?"

Jerrik nodded. "He didn't recognize me at first, and it had been years since he and Regina had traveled here on business for the Dragon Kingdom. It wasn't until I revealed the truth of his affair that he remembered me. He knew how horrid my father was. I'd just found out that my mother, the queen, had been imprisoned. I told him everything when he confronted me then made him swear not to tell anyone."

And being the honorable man Frej was, he had kept his oath. Once again, Laila's heart wrenched at the misery in Jerrik's eyes. Frej had been the only confidant who knew the depths of Jerrik's struggles. If only he had told her sooner.

Jerrik started to reach for her hand before stopping himself. "I don't want this to change anything. I'm still the same person."

She stood, frustrated. "How can you say that? This changes everything. You have a kingdom. There are people counting on you!" She waved her hand toward the stairs.

Jerrik rose and folded his arms as he looked out over the city. "They're nowhere near making a move. They don't have the resources they need to stage a true rebellion, and until an opportunity presents itself, I can't do anything to help them. I might as well go back to Los Angeles. At least there I can help others."

She faced him, incredulous. "So, we get the Eirflower and return to Midgard like nothing happened?"

He took a step closer. "Yes. Here I'm stuck in hiding. At least there, I can actually do something. I can help you take down the Demons."

Laila sighed and studied him. She understood how he felt, to be desperate to help, but she realized his situation was different—he had other duties here. "I know that you're the only one who can make this choice, but are you certain it's the right one?"

"Maybe not, but I want to be there by your side when you send them back to Hell." He tucked a stray lock of Laila's auburn hair behind her ear, and his expression softened. "I've missed you, Laila. I wanted to tell you sooner, but…" he trailed off.

Laila's cheeks warmed as she held his gaze. He wore a black t-shirt that hugged the lean muscle of his chest and arms, and a lush, musky scent that reminded her of bourbon and autumn leaves clung to him.

His voice was low when he spoke again. "I stand by what I said back in October."

"Which was what?" Laila hated how her voice betrayed her nerves.

His hands rested on her hips, and while Laila knew she should pull away, she didn't.

"That Frej's a gentleman, but you need a warrior who will stand beside you."

A thrill ran through her at his words, and for a moment, she recalled the taste of his lips…

She swallowed and looked away. "This is ridiculous. You're a prince."

He tilted her chin until she was looking up at him once more. "You didn't fall for the Prince of the Svartalfar. You fell for Jerrik—a man with nothing to offer you but his sword." His fingers trailed along the edge of her jaw as his gaze lowered to her lips. "I've tried to walk away. I tried to be patient as you sorted through your feelings, but my heart still belongs to you. All I ask is that you give me another chance."

Her skin burned beneath his touch. His mouth hovered dangerously close. The temptation to give in to her desire and allow herself to be swept away by it was almost more than she could handle. How could something feel so frustratingly right yet so horribly wrong?

"Ahem," a cough sounded by the door. Hallr leaned against the doorframe with a growing smile as he looked from Laila to Jerrik. "I hate to interrupt, but your dinner is getting cold, and we still have much to discuss."

Laila stepped back, her face and neck erupting with heat. "Of course."

She didn't dare glance back as she followed Hallr into the building, but she could feel Jerrik a mere step behind her. Laila had been positive she could keep a level head while traveling with him, but they had only been gone a matter of hours, and he was already a distraction.

CHAPTER 7

Darien paced restlessly beside his desk and huffed a sigh. It was about an hour until sunset, and he had spent the entire day in the office trying to deal with the mess from the previous night. They arrested the few Demons Laila managed to save from their auto-kill spells, but none of them were talking. Laila assured him they were Lesser Demons, and he arranged to have them transported to the Supernatural Unit of the New Metropolitan Detention Center. He also set up a security detail at Ali's house for those staying there, but he feared that location was no longer safe.

He had been constantly interrupted with various calls throughout the day, but that was nothing new. The problem was there was no one left in the office that he could send on these calls. He was the only field agent in the office, and, as a Vampire, he was forced inside during the day.

He placed several urgent calls to the D.C. headquarters, hoping they would send temporary aid, but his messages had gone unanswered. Historically, they rarely sent help their way, but to ignore the calls was new. It left him unsettled as he wondered how many other cities were in similar situations. If he couldn't get help from the agency, he would have to find another way to manage. Thus was the struggle of post-apocalyptic life.

Feeling impatient, he stood and headed for the elevator. He took it all the way down to the morgue, where a tunnel connected IRSA's building to the hospital. Both structures had a special UV filtering glass that was nauseatingly expensive but protected Vampires from accidental exposure during the day. Since he couldn't respond to the calls until nightfall, he might as well check on Ali.

The two police officers who stood outside her room nodded to Darien when he approached. Inside, Lyn sat in one of the chairs, skimming through a page on her laptop with an enchanted staff beside her.

"Oh, hey," she said as Darien entered. "I finally convinced the Dragons to go home and get some rest."

"How's Erin holding up?" Darien took the chair beside her.

Lyn looked away toward the unconscious Fae. "Not well. She keeps blaming herself for what happened to her sister. Not that there's anything she could have done."

Darien looked at Ali lying in bed, the heart monitor beeping slowly. "Has she woken?"

Lyn shook her head wistfully. "I don't think she will unless we can counteract the curse. It's like the fairytale Sleeping Beauty. Only a kiss won't wake her. These curses are nasty, which is why they were banned by Witches eons ago. I guess that the Demons found an ancient Grimoire and used it to enchant the blade. I've been doing research, but not much is coming up."

"Leave it to Demons to unearth something like this."

A part of him had hoped the doctors had come up with some cure during the day, or that Ali was strong enough to fight it—that she would be awake when he walked in. But she was not.

Reluctantly, he turned to Lyn. "I don't want to pull you from your research, but I could really use some help in the office. I don't have any other SNPs at the moment."

SNP was an acronym for Supernatural Person used by their office to refer to any individuals who were otherworldly, had magical abilities, or fell into categories that would separate them from humans—such as Vampires. While Lyn wasn't an official member of IRSA, she had become a regular consultant on investigations.

She shut her computer gently and tucked it into her bag. "Sure, no worries. I've got some things to take care of this evening, but I'll call you once I finish." She paused and looked up at him, her dark eyes uncertain. "I might have a lead regarding Colin's connection to the Demons."

Colin. Darien was constantly receiving collect calls from their old supervisor, who was now awaiting trial. He had been feeding information to the Demons, although Colin swore he knew nothing about it. Darien knew that was a lie. You didn't just accidentally pass confidential government files to Demons. He had known Colin for years. He trusted Colin. And now he was simply disgusted. Darien wasn't about to haul his ass out to the detention center to listen to Colin's lies.

"What do you mean? What sort of lead?" he asked wearily, unsure if he had the energy to deal with Colin on top of everything else.

Lyn toyed absently with the frayed hem of her cutoff jeans. "I've got a friend. She's an SNP, and I think she's identified a potential Greater Demon in the city. The problem is, she's a little shy. I'm planning to meet with her this evening to convince her to speak with you."

That caught Darien off-guard. "That would be huge. Keep me updated."

They needed any lead they could get, especially if it led them to the Demons who orchestrated the attack.

Lyn nodded and gathered her things. "I'll be off then. Henrik and Mato were supposed to be here by now, but I've got to go. Can you stick around until they get back?"

"Of course." He still had a little time before dark.

Lyn left, and Darien sat there watching the gentle rise and fall of Ali's chest. He could smell her blood, but her pulse was far slower than expected. It felt strained.

He put his head in his hands. "Ali, you have no idea how awful this mess is. I've tried to be a good replacement for Colin, but I'm at a loss right now. I think this might be the first time I've realized we might not be able to beat the Demons." He rested his elbows on his knees and sighed. "I could really use one of your pep talks about now."

The doorknob turned, and in walked Henrik and Mato. Darien frowned as the strong scent of blood awakened his hunger, but he pushed the urge to feed aside. Mato and Henrik were covered in scrapes and bruises as if they had been in some sort of accident. Henrik's lip was swollen and split, and Mato had another black eye developing.

"Holy shit. What happened?" He rose and eyed their wounds.

Mato sank into a chair opposite the bed with a grunt of pain. "A fight broke out in front of the building. The human protestors are out there again, and one of them attacked an Elven nurse who got in their face. We jumped in and bought the nurse time to flee back into the lobby."

Darien groaned. "Okay, I'm going to go find her. You guys stay here. I'll see if I can send someone to patch you up."

Darien's teeth clenched so hard his fangs pierced his lower lip. The wound healed almost instantly, though. He found a nurse at the station at the end of the hall and explained what happened. The man grimaced and hurried to check the injured SNPs.

Darien found an Elf in scrubs leaning against the wall near the lobby, looking distraught. A bruise was starting to form on her jaw.

"Are you the nurse who was attacked by protesters?" he asked as he approached. "I'm Special Agent Pavoni with the Inter-Realm Security Agency."

She nodded. "I know who you are. I see you guys around pretty often. Yeah, I sort of got into it with the protesters. I know I shouldn't, but I just got off six days of twelve-hour shifts, and they've constantly been outside. I was fed up."

Darien opened a note-taking app on his phone. "I get it, trust me. Can you tell me everything that happened?"

The Elf explained how she had snapped at one of them. The protester struck her. Henrik and Mato were passing by and quickly intervened. She felt horrible for the two guys, but Darien assured her they were being examined. He made sure she had someone who could give her a ride home before heading outside.

The sun had just set, and the concrete path of the courtyard still radiated warmth. Jenn and a few members of the investigative team were already there with half-a-dozen humans in handcuffs.

She smiled as he approached. "Hey, I didn't expect to find you here."

"I was visiting Ali. Henrik and Mato told me about the incident, and I just spoke with the nurse too."

Jenn shook her head. "I figured it was Henrik and Mato by the description. We've got a more pressing matter, though. The body of an SNP was discovered in Santa Monica—likely a homicide."

"As if this day couldn't get any worse," Darien grumbled.

Jenn tipped her head toward the investigative team members. "They've got this handled. You coming?"

Darien followed her to the parking garage, pulling out the keys to his SUV as he went. He had a feeling they were in for a long night.

CHAPTER 8

Darien knelt by the remains of the man. With horns protruding from his skull, it was clear he wasn't human, but that was one of the few identifiable features left. The body was charred beyond recognition, and judging by the corpse's contorted pose, Darien had a feeling he had been burnt alive.

"Looks like he was doused with gasoline," said Jenn.

They were standing in an alley in Santa Monica—the most wealthy section of Los Angeles that had risen in popularity after The Event. It was known for its posh apartment buildings, designer stores, and opulent restaurants.

Darien rose and turned to the alley wall, where a message had been scrawled in spray paint: *Reclaim Earth*. In Darien's mind, there was no doubt that this murder was motivated by hate, but who committed the crime?

"Could it be a member of Di Inferi?" asked Jenn as she joined him. She referred to a human gang with known Demonic ties. They tended to escalate conflicts between humans and SNPs.

Darien considered this. "Could be, but Di Inferi likes to

make a statement. They'd have left him in some fancy bar rather than a back alley."

Jenn nodded. "Like when they trashed Club La Fae."

"It's more likely we've got a lone human who thinks he's some sort of vigilante." Darien scanned the surrounding buildings. "Are there any security cameras in the area? Or any witnesses?"

"I'm not sure yet." Jenn jerked her thumb at one of the buildings. "A couple of tenants heard screaming and called it in, but the alley is so narrow they couldn't see the crime. We'll have to talk to the business owners in the area to see if they noticed anything suspicious."

Police officers were already working to secure the location and keep back the curious bystanders. But even though the perpetrator was likely a human, the victim was an SNP, which meant the crime fell under IRSA's jurisdiction.

Darien clenched his fists. "We just don't have the agents to deal with this right now. Not when we've got Demons targeting our staff—"

His phone buzzed in his hand, and he swiped to answer the call. "Agent Pavoni here."

"We've got another report of a Supernatural badly beaten in Santa Monica near the pier," said a member of the support staff.

Darien fought the urge to snarl in frustration. "Okay, send me the location."

Jenn shook her head. "This is the fifth attack on an SNP today!"

"I know." He looked back at the body on the ground. "Why don't you stay here with the LAPD? I'd ask the officers if they can help take statements from the nearby shopkeepers. Take advantage of any help they're willing to give. I'll head over to the other location—"

The phone in his hand buzzed once more.

"God damn it! What now?" he hissed.

Jenn raised her eyebrows at his outburst.

He was about to ignore the call when he noticed it was Lyn. "Please tell me you have good news."

The Witch barked a laugh. "I guess I do. My friend's willing to speak with you."

Darien thought about the SNP who had been attacked. "I've got to deal with an issue in Santa Monica first, but I'll meet you as soon as we finish."

"No worries. Just come to my shop in Venice Beach. We'll be waiting out front."

"Sounds good." He ended the call.

To say he was feeling overwhelmed was an understatement. As a Vampire, he only needed a little rest, but it had been three days since he last took a nap. He had taken to working around the clock to deal with the casework coming in, but it didn't help. There was just too much to do.

Darien had never been a leader. He had no idea why he had been given this position or why headquarters hadn't sent a replacement. Anyone would have been better, in Darien's opinion.

Jenn snapped photos of the body for evidence. "I can see you're stressing."

"Gee, I wonder why," he growled, then immediately regretted it. "I'm sorry, Jenn, I didn't mean that."

She paused and gave him a pointed look. "You can't be everywhere at once, Darien. You've got to delegate."

"I'm trying to, but I don't have the agents—"

She scoffed. "You still have my team. We're not SNPs, but we're all experienced law enforcement agents. We are fully capable of dealing with these attacks on SNPs. A handful of murderers is nothing compared to the shit we'll be facing from the Demons. Go. Meet with Lyn and figure out how these Demons are taking over our city."

Darien ran his fingers through his hair, feeling worn out. "You should have this position, not me."

Jenn's expression softened. "I know you didn't ask to be supervisor, but you are nonetheless. My advice is to consider what assets *are* at your disposal and take advantage of them. Don't try to do it all yourself."

Darien took a deep breath for the first time in days. He didn't need the oxygen it provided, but it was still soothing. "Okay. You're sure your team can handle this?"

Jenn was already placing a call on her phone. "We've got it. Go."

Darien headed back to the SUV parked on the street, Jenn's words echoing in his ears. He had been trying to delegate, but maybe he was going about it the wrong way. They had a sizeable investigative team—far more extensive than his own team. Perhaps he needed to rethink their structure. Headquarters would not approve, but they also weren't responding.

He started his car, pulled onto the street, and turned back toward Venice Beach.

The rise in violence directed at SNPs had to do with the Governor, Fredrik Stacy. He managed to win the election back in the fall, using the fear generated by the Vampire rebellion. Since he was sworn into office, things had only gotten worse. There was a long list of laws he was trying to pass that would place restrictions on the SNPs—everything from banning Shifters from changing to prohibiting Vampires from feeding directly on the living, with or without consent. Stacy claimed he was trying to "level the playing field" for humans, but this was all oppressive in Darien's eyes. He had been around for hundreds of years, and he knew where this pattern led.

After The Event, Los Angeles was designated as the new state capital—mostly because the majority of California's population sought refuge here at the time. It still felt odd to Darien, but he supposed it made sense. Unfortunately, he suspected that it made the recent tension in the city all the worse.

It was still rush-hour, so traffic was terrible. Darien had to park several blocks away from the beach and continue on foot. Bars and restaurants overflowed with patrons. More people filled the sidewalks and walked along the beach, enjoying the moonlit surf.

When Darien reached the shop, Lyn was nowhere in sight. He peered through the window of *Lyn's Charms and Remedies*, but the place was dark. Her store should be reopened for business by now, but constant vandalism had slowed progress. Even now, there was a message scrawled across the window in red spray paint: *Die Devil Worshiper.*

Darien felt his lip curl into a hint of a snarl. Why were the people of this city so ungrateful? Did they even realize how much Lyn had done to save them? They probably didn't, but this was just despicable.

"Darien, over here!" Lyn waved from a nearby bench she shared with another woman.

He walked over, gesturing at her shop. "When did that happen?"

Lyn rolled her eyes. "Who knows? Sometime in the last few days. At least it's not another brick through the window."

Darin cringed. "I'm sorry."

"The Event fades away, and they forget that it was magic that saved them, but what can you do?" Lyn turned to the woman sitting beside her. "Darien, this is Ligeia—the friend I mentioned."

Ligeia was nothing short of gorgeous. Darien thought she might have been the most beautiful woman he had ever seen. She had olive skin and thick, dark hair that was loosely braided. Her large, brown eyes assessed him. There was something about her that felt hypnotic, but he couldn't put his finger on it. Under different circumstances, he might have made a fool of himself and asked her on a date right there on the spot. But that would be foolish. Not only because of his workload but because Lyn's scent was all over her.

This was Lyn's lover.

"Why the secrecy?" he asked, confused. The Supernatural and otherworldly communities had always been far more accepting of homosexuality than humans. That couldn't be why they hid the relationship.

Lyn watched the woman uncertainly. "Well, you see, she's not supposed to be here."

"I'm a Siren," explained Ligeia simply.

Darien's jaw dropped. Even amongst SNPs, the existence of Sirens had always been a point of uncertainty. The last traces of their civilization vanished thousands of years ago, along with Atlantis. No one was sure if they still existed, and no one had ever been able to locate their mysterious underground city, but here Ligeia was.

Ligeia's mouth twitched into a tight smile as she leaned over to Lyn. "Looks like you owe me twenty bucks."

Lyn pouted. "I was sure the Vampires knew you weren't a myth."

The Siren winked at her. "I told you, we're very good at keeping a low profile."

Darien shook himself out of his stupor. "Does Laila or Ali know?"

Lyn glanced at Ligeia. "We agreed that I could only introduce her to others if I kept her true identity hidden. It didn't feel right to lie to them like that, so I hadn't introduced them yet."

"So, what changed?"

The Siren shifted on the bench. "I believe I know the identity of a Greater Demon living here in Los Angeles. A Siren known as Lorelei. Many years ago, she threatened to expose our kind to humans. She'd begun to lure them to their deaths in a river after a human lover scorned her. When she refused to listen to our council, we called upon the Gods to damn her."

Of course. Darien had heard tales of The Lorelei before but never realized the woman in question was actually sent to Hell as punishment. Then again, he'd thought the Sirens were simply myths too.

"So, you think The Lorelei is here in Los Angeles?" he asked.

Ligeia wrinkled her nose. "We just call her Lorelei. And yes,

I'm fairly certain of it. Lyn told me what happened with the Werewolf, Colin, and I started to do some digging of my own. I believe you've met her."

Darien looked as if someone had struck him in the gut. "You mean Lorel, Colin's girlfriend."

Around the time that Laila had escaped from the Demonic fight ring, Colin had found himself a girlfriend. The woman, Lorel, had always confused Darien. He suspected Colin was still grieving for his wife. And even if he had gotten over her death, Colin was a notorious workaholic who had never expressed interest in dating. Darien never even heard how they met. It was as if she appeared in his life overnight. But Colin had seemed genuinely besotted.

If Lorel was Lorelei and had some sort of power to influence Colin's actions, she could have manipulated him to give over information to the Demons. Colin had sworn that he had no memory of leaking information, but what if that was because magic had messed with his mind?

To complicate matters, Lorel was also the governor's secretary, which meant that Fredrik Stacy could be under the same sort of spell. Every horrible word he spoke and action he took could very well be her doing. Hell, every human attack on an SNP in the last six months could be a result of her influence as she stirred up uncertainty and mistrust.

Darien sank onto the bench beside Lyn in shock. He certainly hadn't expected a revelation of this nature. This wasn't just a lead. It could change everything.

He swiveled his head to look at Ligeia. "Let's say you're right. How do we go about proving this? She's convinced everyone she's human."

The Siren seemed to expect that response. "I can confirm it if I see her, but I'm assuming you want some sort of evidence. That will be a little more complicated. First things first, I'll need to speak with the Werewolf and confirm we're on the right track."

Darien watched the people walking along the beach. "Why are you doing this? Why are you exposing yourself?"

The Siren grew tense. "We are powerful—far more powerful than most Supernaturals—with abilities that bewitch the mind and bend others to our will. History has shown us that our abilities bring nothing but turmoil to this world. Thus, we remain hidden for our sake as well as everyone else's. I convinced the council that we couldn't ignore the threat Lorelei poses, but in exchange, I'm supposed to wipe all memory of the Sirens from your minds." She turned to Lyn looking distressed. "Everyone's."

From the look of horror on Lyn's face, this was the first she had heard of this agreement. She sat there, speechless.

This just didn't seem right. But from the way Ligeia refused to meet her lover's eyes, he feared the Siren was not in a position to argue. Darien looked from Ligeia to Lyn, unsure of how to proceed. They were all making sacrifices, but he wasn't sure he could ask Lyn to do this.

CHAPTER 9

Back in the rebels' hideout in Nidavellir, Hallr led Laila and Jerrik to a smaller room where their dinner was waiting. A handful of others gathered around the table, dressed in sturdy but old clothes and well-worn leather armor. An elderly, grizzly looking man with a leather patch covering one eye had scars crisscrossing his hands. A smaller, grim-faced man dressed in black sat nearby. Laila spotted various knives strapped to his thighs and hilts poked out from beneath his jacket's sleeves. He was unusually still and quiet. Last was a young woman with an intense and unsettling gaze. Her eyes looked haunted from enough horrors to last a lifetime, but when they settled on Laila, the animosity was apparent. Laila bristled.

The young woman turned to Jerrik, her voice icy, "I thought we told you to wait until we contacted you."

The older man gave a short nod. "While it's good to see you again, Jerrik, Katla's right. Now is not a good time for you to return. The king is executing anyone suspected of aiding us."

Jerrik took a seat before one of the plates. "I'll only be here long enough to retrieve an Eirflower blossom and then return to Midgard. We're planning to use the portal under the palace to reach the Swordmasters' temple."

"How can retrieving a flower possibly be important enough to risk your life?" grumbled Katla. Her hand clamped tightly around a tankard of ale.

"One of our friends will die without it," Laila replied coolly. She removed her jacket and rolled up her sleeves while the others stared curiously at the blue flames wrapping up her arms similar to tattoos—magical scars from a fight with an Elemental last year. Ignoring the others, Laila took a seat beside Jerrik. She didn't feel entirely welcome, but she wasn't about to leave, either.

Katla's eyes narrowed. "A single life is not worth putting this entire rebellion at risk."

"Trust me, I had no idea what was at stake when we arrived." Laila shot a look at Jerrik. "Nonetheless, we're here now. Our friend is one of the few that is helping to fight the Demonic uprising in Midgard. There are too few of us to risk losing her."

"And who are you, Elf?" Katla's voice held a biting edge.

Laila wondered what her problem was. It was one thing to be wary, but another to be rude. "Special Agent Laila Eyvindr with the Inter-Realm Security Agency. I deal with Demons and other Supernatural threats."

"Sounds like a fancy name for a city guard," Katla sneered.

Laila clenched her jaw, irritation growing like a wildfire in summer. Laila reminded herself that if Katla had seen the things she had, she wouldn't be so quick to judge. She took a moment to swallow her ire. Still, that smug look ground away at Laila's resolve.

Jerrik cleared his throat and narrowed his eyes. "Laila saved me from a Greater Demon in Midgard. I've been helping her track them down ever since."

The smaller man in black chuckled. "Leave it to the prince to seek refuge only to stumble across Demons."

Hallr barked a laugh. "That's what I said. Laila, allow me to make the official introductions since I'm clearly the only one with any manners. This scrawny fellow here is Rune."

"A pleasure to meet you," said Rune, reaching out to shake her hand.

Hallr waved to the woman. "That prickly piece of work is Katla."

Katla stared at Laila and didn't bother with a greeting.

Hallr motioned to the oldest member of the group. "And finally, Folki, the leader of our little rebellion."

Folki extended a stiff nod to Laila.

Hallr lounged in his chair. "And Katla, I wouldn't piss off Laila if I were you. She humiliated a patrol of Red Guards and buried them under half of Tanner street. She certainly knows how to make an entrance."

Jerrik snorted and tried to cover a smile while Folki studied Laila.

"I don't suppose you have any interest in joining our rebellion, do you?" the leader asked.

Katla shot him a seething look.

Laila shook her head. "We're a little pressed for time, and I've got my own city to protect."

"Fair enough." He turned to Jerrik. "It's not going to be easy, but we'll get you to the portal. There's a harshly enforced curfew, but we find the early morning hours are the easiest time to navigate the city, so long as we avoid the patrols. We'll wait until then to move out."

Jerrik's shoulders relaxed a little. "Thank you, Folki. I appreciate it."

Hallr nudged Laila's arm and nodded at the plate. "Eat. Then I've arranged a room for you to get a few hours of rest. It's going to be a long trek on foot."

Laila gave him a half-smile before digging into the food. It was plain fare with gritty, flavorless bread and a weak soup primarily comprised of a starchy root similar to a parsnip. Still, it filled her stomach.

The others around her continued to chat. They filled Jerrik in on some of the changes that had occurred, and Jerrik told them about life in Midgard. Technology seemed to impress them in particular. Gradually, they all relaxed, and Laila could even see the ghost of a smile on Katla's face.

Katla's eyes lingered on Jerrik, and a hint of jealousy sparked within Laila. She tried to ignore it, but it chafed her. Then there was the way they all laughed and joked as they recounted stories from the past. Laila felt a little awkward—as if she was intruding on their reunion. Finally, she excused herself and asked Hallr if he could show her to her room. He obliged and led her down the hall.

"Thank you for doing all of this. I really appreciate it," Laila said as they reached her door.

He waved off her comment. "It's nothing. You saved my life, remember?"

Her expression sobered. "I'm sorry for bringing Jerrik back here. I wish I'd known all of this before."

"Eh, Jerrik's pretty stubborn like that. I think that living in Midgard has been good for him, though. He's happier than when he left. I think I have you to thank for that too." He winked.

Laila turned to cover the blush that heated her face. Of course, he would jump to conclusions after what he saw earlier. She opened her mouth to explain, but he was already heading back down the hall. Shaking her head, Laila entered the room.

It was sparsely finished with a rickety cot in one corner and a washbasin on a table in the other. Laila flopped onto the cot and stared up at the ceiling. She was physically exhausted, but her brain buzzed with activity.

She thought of the others down the hall. From the way they watched Jerrik, she knew how much they relied on him and the hope he represented. Even if Jerrik couldn't see it, Laila knew deep in her heart that this was where he belonged. His people needed him.

The memory of Jerrik holding her on the roof slid into her thoughts. He looked at her as though she was the only thing that mattered. Why hadn't she pushed him away? Nothing good would come of this attraction, especially now that she knew he was royalty. But Laila still struggled to turn her back on it.

She pulled her phone from her pocket and switched it on. Of course, it wouldn't work here, but on the lock screen was a photo of Laila, Erin, and Ali from the holiday party they had last month. Ali had pulled them close to snap the selfie, and all three of them were laughing. Laila switched it off as her eyes clouded with tears. She couldn't allow Jerrik to come between her and this mission. Not when Ali's life hung in the balance. How could she even think about her feelings for Jerrik at a time like this?

Laila closed her eyes and pressed her palms to them. She knew that, as horrible as she felt, it was nothing compared to the terror Erin was feeling. She just hoped Frej would be able to keep her safe in the meantime.

Izel leaned against the throne room wall and watched from the shadows as the Red Guard gave their report. Apparently, some Elf created quite a disturbance in the Twilight Market. She would have dismissed the incident, except one detail caught her attention.

"Did you say blue flame?" she asked.

The guard shifted nervously under Izel's gaze. "Yes, your Greatness. She also had glowing blue eyes. I've never seen anything like it."

She wondered if this might have been the same Elf that Marius was after. But what would she be doing in Nidavellir?

"And what of her clothing?" Izel cocked her head and watched the guard intently.

He swallowed hard. "Um, they were odd. Blue canvas pants that were form-fitting and a rather plain shirt and coat."

"Midgardian fashion," mused Izel.

She didn't bother requesting the king's permission to leave

the chamber. He was nothing to her, just an angry, paranoid puppet. Instead, she swept out the door and returned to her chambers. The shadows that clung to the dark, heavy fabric in the room seemed to shift in greeting as she entered. She took a seat at a vanity that doubled as a large scrying glass.

"Marius," she murmured and pictured his face in her mind.

Mist swirled across the surface before fading. In the glass, Izel could see Marius standing in a room of some dreary, abandoned building.

"Really, Marius, it's like you try to find the most miserable accommodations," she mocked.

He frowned. "I'm working around the clock planting our people in every corner of this world. Redecorating seemed low on the priority list." He watched her suspiciously for a moment. "You seem to be in an oddly pleasant mood, and you haven't called in months. What's happened?"

Izel folded her arms smugly. "When was the last time you saw that Elf? The problematic one?"

"She was sighted last night. She cost me over a dozen Lesser Demons," he grumbled.

She watched him closely, feeling smug. "What if I told you she was here only hours ago?"

Marius gaped at her. "What? How? I've had spies watching the house and hospital."

Izel shrugged. "Well, I suppose she slipped past them. You're disappointingly incompetent, Marius. I expected more from you. In any case, I'll deal with her. I just thought you'd like to know."

She loved gloating, especially when Marius was involved. He might be her right hand, but he was always easily frazzled. It was like teasing a child. Even now, she delighted in the lovely shade of scarlet his face was turning.

"Fine. You handle the Elf. I'll handle the rest of the agents." He opened a drawer and removed a glass vile and a syringe.

She gave him a wicked grin. "Are you sure you're up for it?

If not, I have a long list of Greater Demons eager to take your place in Midgard. I've tolerated your ineptitude for too long already."

His hands clenched and trembled, but rather than waiting for a response, Izel released the spell on the mirror.

According to her spies, Marius had been far moodier lately. She wondered if the strain was getting to him. As much as Marius craved power, Izel wasn't sure he honestly had what it took to seize Midgard. He was ambitious and scheming, but he wasn't a leader or a warrior. Marius hid in the back while others got their hands dirty. The only reason he made it this far was due to her protection and favor. But Izel could easily revoke that.

She sat at the vanity, drumming her pointed nails on the polished wood. Izel may not know what the Elf was up to, but she had a feeling the woman was working with the rebels. Rumors of the missing prince's arrival had already reached her, and she suspected it was more than just a coincidence. But if the Elf was involved with the rebels, she would catch her. Izel had eyes everywhere in the city.

CHAPTER 10

The heart monitor beeped a slow and steady rhythm, the only sound breaking the heavy silence in the hospital room. Frej glanced up from his book to study Erin, curled up in a chair. Erin watched her sister with her arms wrapped around her knees as she listened to the music playing in her headphones. He took her home for a few hours in the afternoon, but around nine o'clock, she insisted on coming back. It was probably for the best, considering the rough shape Henrik and Mato had been in when Frej arrived.

Even in the time since he arrived in the city, Erin's look had grown darker and edgier. The teenager wore ripped jeans and chunky combat boots. Her shirt was torn and worn, but Erin insisted that it was a style here in Midgard. He didn't quite understand it, but Darien seemed to have a similar taste in clothing. Erin's messy black hair was shorter too—a pixy cut, as she called it. She almost looked like a boy.

Back in the Dragon Kingdom, young women her age would be wearing elegant dresses and attending social gatherings. That sort of formality seemed normal to Frej. Then again, when he thought back to his adolescent years, he remembered having little interest in formalities. He joined the army to escape the city and have his own adventures. Queen Regina had been the same way. As a girl, Regina had been even wilder than him. Nonetheless, a time came when they returned to the capital and accepted their places in society.

Erin would inevitably have to do the same. She was a Dragon and belonged with her own kind. As much as she loved this world, Frej knew it was far too dangerous to stay with the Demons targeting them. Ali would want him to take Erin to safety. They had spoken about it once. Ali had insisted he take Erin and return to the Dragon Kingdom if anything happened to her. He held the role of Erin's guardian in the Dragon Kingdom, and Ali knew that she would be far safer with him than in a city plagued with Demons.

As he sat there watching Erin, he knew she wouldn't leave. Not now, when Ali's life hung in the balance. She was fiercely stubborn, even for a Fire Dragon, and loved her sister more than anything. He couldn't fault her, though. Frej was orphaned at a young age. If he had any surviving family, he imagined he would be equally protective.

Most of his friends had settled down and were starting families, but Frej had never given the idea of fatherhood much thought. Now he had a teenage charge to care for. He wasn't sure he was ready for that responsibility. Training Erin had been one thing, but how was he supposed to counsel her through the possibility of losing Ali?

Then there was the problem of Laila. How could he leave when there was so much left unsaid? He had been upset by her ultimatum at first, but he quickly realized she was right. He wanted to dedicate his heart to her entirely, but was he ready to let go of his first love? He knew he needed to move on.

He sat there deep in thought and staring out the window at the faint glow of the city beyond. The door opened, and he spun around to confront the intruder, but it was just a nurse. She was human with honey-colored hair. He didn't recognize her.

She pulled a syringe and a bottle out of her pocket, and he frowned.

"What's that for?" he asked suspiciously.

"An experimental treatment the doctor would like to try," she explained, extracting the liquid from the bottle.

As she moved to inject the substance into Ali's I.V., Frej leapt to his feet. He slammed her against the wall with his air magic and quickly crossed the room to face her.

"What the hell are you doing?" she shrieked.

"I don't know much about hospitals here, but every other person has confirmed her identity—thoroughly. You didn't even bother to check her name. So, who sent you and what's really in the bottle?" he growled.

Erin snatched up the vial as it rolled across the floor, then quickly typed something into her phone.

"This would slow her heart rate. That would kill her!" She looked up sharply.

"Guards!" Frej bellowed, not relinquishing his hold on the woman.

Two police officers rushed into the room. Their eyes widened at the sight of the nurse pinned to the wall.

"I think this was an assassination attempt. Can we get a doctor to check this medication?" He inclined his head to Erin, who showed them the vial.

One of the officers nodded. "I'll ask at the nurse's station—"

The assassin muttered something under her breath, and suddenly Frej's spell on her broke. The woman wasn't just a human; she was a Witch. She reached into her pocket and pulled out a second vial etched with runes.

"Don't move, or I'll blow this whole room to pieces." She waved the bottle for emphasis.

One of the police officers took a tentative step forward. "Easy now, we just want to talk."

She wasn't interested. She threw the bottle to the ground. Luckily, Frej trapped it in an orb of air before it shattered.

The woman lunged for the door, but the officers tackled her to the ground. "You're under arrest—" began one of the officers.

Inside Frej's orb of air, the bottle began to crackle and fizz as the spell seeped from the loosened stopper. He swore and reinforced the magic surrounding it as the explosion erupted, but the enchanted bomb was strong and tore through the shield.

"Frej!" Erin screamed.

She reached out and took hold of the fire from the explosion, then wrapped it around herself and redirected the force of the blast through the window, shattering the glass. Above them, the sprinklers switched on, and the fire alarm sounded.

The assassin broke free of the officers' grasp and sprinted out the doorway and down the hall. Frej was after her in an instant, forcing her to the ground with a blast of air. The officers caught up to her and slapped a pair of handcuffs on the assassin's wrists.

"Execute," muttered the woman. A deep cut appeared along her throat as if being slit by an invisible blade and blood poured over the linoleum tiles. It was the auto-kill spell Laila had mentioned. The Demons had sent this assassin.

One of the officers tried to apply pressure to the wound until a group of nurses rushed in. They attempted to stop the bleeding, but the injury was too deep. Within moments the assassin bled out.

Frej's mind raced. How did she make it past the guards? What would have happened if he hadn't caught that misstep?

He returned to Erin and checked her for wounds. "Are you okay?"

She nodded and glanced around as water continued to rain down on them, dripping from Erin's shaggy hair. "They're still coming after her. What are we going to do?"

"I don't know, but we can't stay here. I'm going to call

Darien." Frej conjured a shield overhead to keep them dry as he pulled out his phone and placed the call.

Darien swore and hung up as Lyn and Ligeia stared at him.

"That was Frej. There's been an assassination attempt at the hospital." His head spun as he tried to determine the best course of action to take. He needed to get them somewhere safe—to a place where the Demons couldn't find them.

Lyn let out a long string of curses. "Is anyone hurt?"

"No, except for the assassin who took her own life with one of those auto-kill spells." He looked from Lyn to Ligeia. "I want the two of you to return to the office with me. Frej and Erin are going to meet us there. We need to regroup."

Lyn gave the Siren a questioning look, and Ligeia nodded in response. They followed him back to his SUV as Darien pulled out his phone once more and scrolled through his contact list.

The phone rang twice before his sire, Talen, answered. "Good evening Darien."

"I need your help. Demons attacked my colleagues and I last night, and now there's been another assassination attempt. I need somewhere safe for them to hide until we can get to the bottom of this." He realized how fast he was walking in his agitation. The two women were jogging to keep up. He forced himself to slow down.

"What? Why didn't you call me last night?" Darien could hear the concern in his sire's voice.

Darien swallowed his pride. "I thought I had it under control, but I don't. I need help."

"Where are you now?" Talen asked.

"Heading back to the office."

"Good. I'll meet you there with an escort shortly. You can use one of my safehouses."

Darien breathed a sigh of relief as he ended the call. It

wounded his pride a little to go running to his sire for help, but he knew Talen would be happy to give it. Darien's team had helped prevent a Vampire rebellion from taking control over the city in the fall. They worked with some of the other Vampires on the council to stop it. Not only would Talen do anything to help, but he wielded a great deal of power in the Vampire community. Perhaps this was what Jenn was talking about when she said to work with what resources he had.

He sped through the city using his emergency lights and siren to get through what remained of the traffic. Lyn and Ligeia clung to their seats with white knuckles, but he didn't apologize. He just wanted to get back. Frej's call had been brief, and Darien needed to know what happened. As he drove, he had Lyn text the others to meet in the conference room at the office.

He pulled into the parking garage and quickly found a spot before taking the elevator up to his floor. When they reached the conference room, several people were already there. Erin and Frej sat at one end of the table, looking like they had just come in from a rainstorm. Donald, the Tech Wiz, sat with a large black case and a backpack resting beside him. Henrik and Mato were still on their way, as was as Jenn, who was leaving the crime scene from earlier.

"I sent the Giant over to guard Ali," Frej said when they entered. "I told him the only one allowed in would be Dr. Elmerson."

The Giant was a fellow named Benning, who worked as a security guard at their front desk. He had accidentally been summoned to this world and decided to stay. Lyn had given him a charm to shrink his size. He was still massive, but at least he could fit through most doorways now. Ordinarily, Benning had the gentlest demeanor, but he was known to fend off threats when his friends and colleagues were in danger. He would do for now, at least for the duration of the meeting.

Voices echoed down the hall as Mato and Henrik rounded the corner with Jenn.

"I found these two downstairs. They said they were looking for you," Jenn said as they approached.

Darien nodded. "Yes. Everyone, go ahead and find a seat."

Once settled, he asked Frej to recount the details of the assassination attempt. Darien realized how close this call had been. Erin seemed quiet and withdrawn, which was unusual. She was probably in shock.

Darien resisted the urge to fidget with the hem of his leather jacket as he spoke. "I don't think any of us are safe here now. I spoke with my sire, and he's making arrangements to take you to a safehouse for now until we can figure out what move to make next. Luckily, it sounds like we have a lead." He glanced at Ligeia, who nodded before returning his gaze to the others.

"What about Ali? I won't leave her." Erin glowered from across the table.

"Ali would want you to be somewhere safe. I'm going to request a security detail of Talen's mercenaries and limit the staff with access to the room."

That didn't seem to satisfy her. "I'm staying."

"You're going." Frej shot her a look that dared her to argue. Erin seemed as if she might but must have thought better of it.

"Donald, did you pack your gear?" he asked.

The Tech Wiz patted the box beside him. "I've got everything I need."

"Good. Then let's head down to the garage."

He stood, and the others followed him toward the elevator.

Jenn pulled him aside to hiss, "You're not locking me up in a safehouse. You need me here."

"I know, but I want you up to speed. I also want you to know that the option is available for you and the rest of your team. Just because the Demons haven't targeted them yet doesn't mean they won't."

She relaxed slightly. "Okay. What do you need me to do?"

"Deal with the human attacks on SNPs for now and keep an eye on Ali while I'm gone." He watched Lyn as she stepped into the elevator. "I think that lead Lyn mentioned is going to pan out. I'm going to make an appointment to visit Colin as soon as possible. I want to find the Demons at the heart of this and bring the fight to them."

A thought occurred to him, and he waved for Donald to join them. "Donald, weren't you working on some protective gear?"

He nodded. "I've got some things assembled. I was going to show you, but you've been so busy."

"Can you show us now?"

"Of course."

Darien turned to the others. "Head downstairs to the garage. We'll meet you there."

Donald led them on a detour to the workshop he inherited from Torsten, the inventor he used to work with. Torsten had died fighting a group of Vampires during the raid last fall. Darien knew Donald still hadn't recovered from the loss.

The workshop was like something out of a sci-fi movie. In addition to the more usual assortment of potions and charms that Witches worked with, there was an odd array of weapons and gadgets with special enchantments. There were workbenches crowded with partially-built inventions and stacks of papers with diagrams and spells. There were several rows of shelves stocked with enchanted gear and other devices.

Donald selected a metal wristband and passed it to Jenn. "Here, try it on."

Jenn hesitated then obeyed. Donald pressed a button on the band, and a glowing orange shield appeared.

"This shield will protect you from physical and magical attacks, although the spell will eventually break after so much damage, and the power source will need replacing."

"What's it run off of? Crystals?" Jenn waved the shield around experimentally.

"Nope, lithium batteries. Here try this as well." He passed her a helmet and showed her how to switch it on. "These are embedded with a detection spell. It allows you to detect any kind of SNP in the database."

"Woah." Jenn looked from Donald to Darien. "Here, you try."

Darien took the helmet from her and slid it on. There was a screen embedded in the protective glass covering his eyes, and when he looked at Donald, a digital script appeared that identified him as a Witch. He turned to Jenn, who was identified as a human.

"It also should detect Demonic energy, but I haven't been able to test that function yet," added Donald proudly.

"How many of these do you have?"

"Six of each that are finished." He indicated a shelf behind him.

Darien turned to Jenn. "Use them if you need to, especially during the day when I'm unavailable."

She nodded. "You guys be careful too. I know your sire is trustworthy, but I have a feeling the Demons are watching the building."

Darien had been thinking the same thing. They headed down to join the others, hoping Talen had kept that in mind.

CHAPTER 11

Talen was just pulling up as Darien stepped out of the elevator and into the parking garage. The agent buzzed him through the gate, and six black SUVs pulled up, similar to the one Darien drove. Talen climbed out of the first.

Although Talen was literally ancient, he only looked to be about thirty, with long brown hair that fell past his shoulders and a black designer suit with the top few buttons of his shirt casually undone. He approached the group and scanned them, taking stock of those missing.

"What about the others?" he asked, his voice tight. Even though he had only worked with the team briefly, Talen had grown fond of Darien's coworkers.

Darien pulled Talen aside even though he was all too aware Erin was still listening. "Ali was stabbed with a cursed blade and is in critical condition, and the Elves are away on a mission looking for a cure. The Demons made another attempt on Ali's life this evening, but she's in no shape to be moved—"

"I'll leave three of my mercenaries," he said before Darien could finish. He waved over three of the Vampires from the

SUVs. They wore black suits and had sunglasses on to conceal their red eyes. "I want you to stay and guard a Fae woman. She risked her life to help us, and it's our time to return the favor."

"I'll fill them in on our way to the hospital. I want to speak to the hospital staff anyway," offered Jenn.

Darien gave her a grateful look before she left with the mercenaries, then returned his attention to Talen. "I suspect the Demons are watching us. We'll have to be careful."

Talen shot him an amused look. "You know you can trust me. I've already planned a route with decoys."

Even as they spoke, Vampires were removing the license plates on the SUVs. With the dark tinted glass, there would be no way to tell them apart.

Talen turned to the others. "Load up in the last two SUVs. It'll be a little tight, but we'll make do." He turned to Darien, bemused. "It's a good thing I picked the large safehouse. I didn't expect this many."

Darien shrugged. "They've all been targeted or are working on sensitive research."

The Vampires waited until the others seated themselves in the SUVs before climbing into the last one.

"We're good to go. Head out," Talen said into his coms.

The engines rumbled to life, and the line of SUVs exited the garage like clockwork. Talen's mercenaries were nothing if not precise. He was extremely thorough in his recruitment process. Many were conscripted and turned after leaving special operations teams from various militaries around the world. He paid them each handsomely, but it was a risky job with absurdly high expectations.

Darien knew he would never belong among them. He was a little too wild and reckless, not to mention he enjoyed having a personal life. Talen knew this all too well. Instead, Darien served him as a sort of assistant for many years. When Darien heard about IRSA, Talen gave his blessing to apply, although his sire still called on him from time to time.

He was fortunate to have such a causal relationship with his sire. Vampires were all about hierarchy, and many sires ruled over those beneath them harshly. Talen preferred a different approach of mutual respect, but even so, he was far more lenient with Darien than he was with others. Perhaps it was all the years he spent as his sire's right hand that brought them together—those long nights of tense negotiations with rival bloodlines and their narrow escapes. Whatever the case, Darien knew Talen would always come through.

Everyone in the vehicle was anxious and silent as they drove through the dark streets of Los Angeles—out of the Westside and into the mostly abandoned Old City. SUVs branched off in various directions as they wound their way deeper into the city's abandoned sector. Darien watched the dark streets and ruins of Beverly Hills through the windows, periodically peering behind them to see if anyone followed. He saw no trace of other cars, but that didn't mean they were in the clear. Drones or SNPs in flight could be watching from the skies.

At last, the SUV pulled into an old parking structure. In the back was a massive steel door that opened for them. The tunnel they entered was of newer construction, and beyond that, they pulled into another, smaller garage. This one was mostly full, hosting a variety of classic cars and sporty vehicles—all belonging to Talen, of course. There was a doorway with four more mercenaries armed with automatic weapons.

Darien breathed a sigh of relief and climbed out of the SUV. The second one pulled out from another tunnel. Henrik and Mato piled out of the vehicle and ogled at the automobiles surrounding them.

"This way." Talen beckoned them through the doorway.

The others followed him into a luxurious building. The interior was sleek and modern, in shades of black, white, and grey with pops of crimson—Talen's usual style. The safehouse hub was a massive kitchen and living area with various bedrooms surrounding them on two levels. There were no windows since they were underground. Darien had only been here once before when Talen got into a nasty confrontation with another powerful Vampire. The place was basically a lavish underground bunker with the best security and planning money could buy. This was possibly the most secure location in the entire city.

Talen gestured around the safehouse. "Go ahead and make yourselves at home. I've stocked the refrigerator, and there should be enough rooms for all of you. You can rest assured you're safe here."

The others appeared relieved and wandered off to check out the rooms while Donald claimed the dining room as his temporary workshop. Erin flopped on one of the sofas—her face as stony as the Guards outside. He knew she was furious about leaving the hospital, but it's what Ali would want.

"You should get some sleep. Or, if you can't sleep, Talen has a large database of movies," Darien suggested.

Erin didn't move.

"If they kill her, I'll kill you." Her words erupted so coldly they sent a shiver down his undead spine. Most people would scoff at her for being an overdramatic teen, but the hard look in her eyes promised she would make good on her threat.

Before he could reply, Erin abruptly stood and walked off in search of the nearest bedroom. Darien watched her and knew she was justified in her concern. If he could bring everything they needed here, including Ali and the doctor, he would. But Ali needed the hospital's resources. He wouldn't risk moving her unless absolutely necessary.

"You look like you could use this." Talen passed him a glass of blood, Elven, by the sumptuous scent. Then he nodded to an office off the main room where they could talk freely.

Darien collapsed into an armchair as Talen shut the door.

"How did all of this happen?" his sire asked, joining him.

Darien explained while Talen's expression grew more troubled. By the time he finished, Talen was refilling both of their glasses.

"So, you think they are targeting you because Laila is not around?" he asked.

"One of the Demons practically admitted it. Erin is livid, and rightly so. Hell, she even threatened me! What kind of a kid does that?"

Talen chuckled. "I remember the stories from the tunnel raid last fall. A number of my men and women owe her their lives. She's a tough one. Then again, she's a Dragon."

"Don't even think about recruiting her. The kid's got enough problems as it is," grumbled Darien.

Talen twitched his hand dismissively. "In any case, what do you plan to do now? They are free to stay as long as they need, but we both know that's not realistic."

Darien swirled the thick red blood in his glass. Talen must have remembered Elf's blood was his favorite—not that he would ever drink from his coworkers. Laila forced him to do so once, and her blood had unusual side effects from the divine magic.

He wished she had stayed, not only because she was powerful, but because she was his partner. They kept each other out of trouble. They were a team. Jerrik was okay, but he didn't have her sharp observational skills. Now they were both gone, and he had to find a way to manage without them.

"Laila and Jerrik will hopefully be back soon, but in the meantime, I've got a lead. Lyn's girlfriend suspects a powerful Greater Demon called Lorelei is behind much of the chaos in the city."

Talen froze. "The Lorelei? Shit."

Darien watched his sire stand and pace. "What is it?"

Talen shook his head. "I should have guessed it. Hell, it should have been obvious!" He turned to face Darien. "So, the new woman, the one with Lyn, she's a Siren too, right?"

Darien nodded.

"I thought I smelled it, but it's been a long time. The scandal Lorelei created was unlike anything the Supernatural community had dealt with before. Those of us old enough to remember avoid speaking about it. Her actions placed all Supernaturals in danger by exposing herself to the humans. I should have known that woman was too vindictive to resist a chance to return."

Darien wasn't surprised Talen knew of the Sirens. After all, as one of the oldest Vampires on the continent, he had seen centuries come and go. "Well, if Ligeia's right, we may even know where to find Lorelei. We need to meet with Colin first, to confirm her suspicions, then we'll go from there."

Talen's expression remained grim. "That will be easier said than done. Even if you find her, you'll have to kill her immediately or send her back to Hell. Otherwise, you'll fall under her spell too."

Darien knew he was right, but at least this lead gave them something to go on. He was sick of playing games. If the Demons were looking for a fight, he would bring them one.

CHAPTER 12

Laila sat at a table in the nearly deserted pub, picking at a chunk of bread. It was early morning, probably around three o'clock, and Laila suspected she had only gotten a couple of hours of sleep at the most, but it was better than nothing. At least she had mostly recovered from the magic used the previous day.

"Mornin'!" called Hallr, his eyes bright. He looked eager for the journey ahead.

Jerrik rolled his eyes in disgust. "I've always hated that you're a morning person."

Hallr mussed Jerrik's hair and earned himself a scowl. "Hey, I'm still alive. That means it's a good day!"

Jerrik cracked a smile. Laila had the feeling he missed Hallr during his time on Earth.

The others filtered into the room, dressed in dark colors, and armed to the teeth. They had knives strapped to thighs and sheathed in boots, and swords and crossbows slung across their backs. Katla carried a staff that hummed with an enchantment, and Folki carried a machine gun. He must have had it smuggled in from Earth because Laila doubted they were legal here.

Jerrik and Hallr both sported hand-and-half swords buckled to their sides, as well as a couple of knives. Laila had her magical dagger strapped to her thigh. They offered her a sword, but she declined. It would only slow her down. Besides, her divine magic was more deadly than any weapon—if she dared to use it.

"Ready?" asked Folki. He peered around the room at them with his one good eye.

They replied with a host of sober nods.

Rune moved toward the largest of the subterranean exits. "Stay close and quiet. There will be patrols throughout the city."

Laila followed Jerrik over to a ladder that descended into a tunnel. Rune had conjured an orb of red light to illuminate the passageway before them. Folki, Hallr, and Katla fell in line behind Laila.

Hallr passed Laila a scarf to tie around her mouth and nose. "For the mold. Prolonged exposure will make you ill and disoriented. This tunnel is much longer than the other one."

Laila thanked him and secured the scarf.

As they walked, Laila could feel Katla's eyes boring holes into her back. She seemed even more hostile than yesterday. She also noticed Jerrik stayed close and periodically cast a warning look at the rebel, giving Laila the distinct impression she missed something last night. She was tempted to ask Jerrik about it, but not with the others in such close proximity.

The rebels remained silent and exited the tunnel through a hidden door disguised as a factory's back entrance. Workers had extinguished the lanterns, darkening the streets. The only remaining light was the faint glow of the magical foliage far above. It filtered down like the light of a full moon, providing just enough illumination for Laila to see.

Aside from the Twilight Market, Laila had found the city to be dismal by day, but it was positively foreboding at night. An odd mist clung to the cobblestones and seeped up through holes in the street. Jerrik quietly explained it was steam from equipment in the mines below. It drifted through vents and cooled when it reached the streets and created a fog. It played tricks on her eyes, and Laila kept turning her head to look for nonexistent shadow figures. She couldn't shake the feeling that someone followed them just beyond the edge of her vision, yet no one approached. But what would be trailing them? She suspected more than a few Ghosts wandered these streets, blending into the mist and wandering aimlessly. Most Ghosts were harmless, but not all. Laila's own experiences had taught her to be wary of them.

The group clung to the shadows and crept through side streets and narrow alleys, their boots hardly making a sound as they hurried over the cobblestones. They had several miles of the subterranean city to traverse before they reached the tunnels where the portal was located. With any luck, they would be able to find it before the rest of the city stirred for the morning. Then they would have more guards to deal with.

The first patrol they encountered consisted of twelve City Guards. They were easy enough to avoid, seeming half-asleep where they stood. After that came two patrols of Red Guards. They emerged from the mist as though they were bloody specters, causing the rebels to duck down a side alley to escape their notice. The Red Guard seemed far more eager to track down those breaking curfew.

Laila walked for what seemed an eternity through those eerie, dark streets, jumping at every little noise. Katla snickered when a cat startled Laila, but she ignored the woman and refused to lower her guard. Laila wasn't the only nervous one. Folki and Hallr seemed equally on edge.

"We're almost there," Folki whispered after several miles.

Just as the tension in Laila's gut started to ease, a horrid stench assaulted her nose. She swore. "Demons are here, Jerrik."

Katla snorted behind her. "How the hell would you know—"

There was a flash of movement in the corner of her eye. Laila spun around and lunged for Katla, shoving her against the wall as a black crossbow bolt sliced through the air precisely where Katla's head had been. Katla's face was pale as a Ghost, but she quickly recovered, searching the gloom for the crossbow's wielder. Laila released her and peered down the street where a dozen figures emerged from the mist. She noted the variety—Vampires, Elves, and even an Ogre. None of them native to this world, but all were Demons from the strong smell of sulfur. She gagged. The scent assailing her nostrils was even worse than it had been with the Lessor Demons in Los Angeles. These were Greater Demons.

Laila released the glamour that masked her aura. She was a pale blue beacon in the shadows. The divine magic clawed at Laila, demanding to be let free, and this time she relented. There was no redemption for a Greater Demon. A sentence to Hell was worse than death and reserved only for the worst crimes. Demons that managed to claw their way out of that prison left nothing but pain and destruction in their wake.

Blue flames swirled around Laila's hands as she took a step forward. Another crossbow bolt whizzed through the darkness, but she disintegrated the arrow mid-flight. In a flash, she teleported behind one of them and slit the throat of a woman covered in scales. The Ogre turned and grabbed for Laila, but her blue fire wrapped around him and consumed his flesh. His cry of agony echoed through the streets.

The staccato beat of a machine gun echoed through the street as Folki unleashed a round of bullets. Laila barely noticed the others plunge into the fray. The magic had taken over, delighted to be free once more. Laila teleported again and thrust her dagger into the chest of a Vampire, piercing his heart. A thrill ran through her that felt utterly foreign to her mind, and Laila faltered. An ancient-looking Elf took advantage of Laila's momentary distraction and blasted her with a wall of air that slammed her against a building. She groaned as stars danced in her vision, and a sharp pain erupted from her shoulder. Bones broke, but the divine magic was already mending her body. She shook off the agony and unleashed a divine inferno that tore through the wall of air, then took the Elf down with a bolt of lightning. The resounding crack was deafening, and when her eyes recovered from the intense light, the charred remains were unrecognizable.

Two Goblins lunged for her, but she spun, grabbing them by the throats and blasting them with more fire. Flesh sizzled, and hair burned. Their screams lasted mere moments before their bodies crumbled in the divine flames.

Laila glanced around at the others. A decapitated frost creature lay on the ground near Jerrik, who pulled another Vampire off of Hallr. Jerrik shoved the Vampire back with a kick to the chest and thrust his sword into the undead woman's heart.

Folki had taken two of their attackers down with his machine gun while Katla and Rune dispatched the rest. A wounded Elf tried to crawl away to the darkness of a nearby alley, but Laila slid a strand of magic around him and pulled him back across the cobblestones. She pinned him to the ground in front of her.

"How did you get here? How did you escape?" she demanded, magic crackling around her.

His eyes grew wide. "She was right. You're the one."

"Who?"

He shook his head and sneered. "You can't defeat her. My mistress will destroy you and everything you care about. The time for us to rise from Hell is nearly here!"

"Stop screwing around!" she warned. The magic around her flared.

The Demonic Elf only chuckled. "Execute."

"No!"

Blood spurted from the sudden cut on his throat, and he began to choke. Laila cursed as he died. She should have seen that coming. Who was this woman? Was it the same person who ordered the attack on her home?

The divine magic still crackled through her being, hungry for more death. A tendril of magic reached for Rune, but Laila pulled it back, turning down an alley to give herself space. She could feel the magic tugging at her the way a leashed dog struggling to free itself.

"Enough," she growled.

She shoved the magic down, suppressing it within her until the urge to destroy no longer overwhelmed her. It was restless, but for now, under control. She took a deep breath to steady her nerves. She hated that she couldn't control this magic and still couldn't shake the feeling it was somehow possessing her. She hoped Arduinna found some answers in Asgard. Fighting Greater Demons was one thing, as she had little remorse for them, but the divine magic tried to lash out at one of the rebels—Rune. She couldn't allow that to happen again.

She joined the others.

"Well, this is a mess. We better get moving before reinforcements arrive," grunted Folki.

They jogged with him down the street. Already Laila could hear voices in the distance.

"What are you?" asked Rune as they ran.

Fire was a part of the elemental magic skill set that both Elves and Svartalfar had, but it was nothing compared to the raw power of the divine flames Laila now wielded. They were all-consuming and devastating.

"I have abilities gifted to me by a Goddess," Laila explained simply. There was no use in denying it—not after what they had seen.

He cringed. "I don't envy you. As amazing as those powers are, I'd rather not get mixed up in Gods and their antics."

Laila agreed. She tried her best to ignore these powers, but it eventually became clear that she had a role to play, whether she liked it or not.

Katla still watched her, but with less malice and more fear. Laila hoped Katla would think twice before sticking a knife in her back now that she knew Laila could vaporize her with a single spell.

"How did they follow us?" asked Jerrik, bewildered.

Laila mulled over the possibilities. "I don't think they followed us. It's more likely they were already here. They probably caught wind of the incident in the Twilight Market and came to hunt us down. One of them mentioned a mistress who's set on destroying us."

Laila had only encountered one Greater Demon in Midgard—Marius. He had been the Master of the Games and was the suspected ringleader of much of the Demonic activity in Los Angeles. That they encountered a dozen Greater Demons here on the street made her suspect they had found a portal out of Hell to Svartalfheim.

As she thought about Marius, she remembered a letter she found addressed from someone named Izel. They assumed she was some sort of high-ranking Greater Demon from the way she threatened Marius. Could that be the woman who was after them?

"Did you know about this?" Jerrik asked Folki.

He exchanged a glance with Hallr. "Strange things have been happening lately. I've heard rumors that the king hired a sorcerer versed in odd magics. More foreigners walk the streets and the halls of the palace too. I suspect it's linked."

Jerrik frowned. "When did they arrive?"

"Around the time Oddvarr imprisoned your mother. We don't think it was a coincidence."

Rune stopped abruptly and motioned for them to be silent. They retreated to the shadowy stoop of a building as another Red Guard patrol passed. They pressed in close, Laila leaning against Jerrik's chest as he pulled her deeper into the gloom. Katla's jaw clenched, and she frowned at the hand he rested on Laila's arm.

Laila wondered if they had once been lovers. That would explain a lot. She wanted to tell Katla to take him—to save her from her confusing feelings. And yet, another part of her felt smug. She pushed such thoughts from her mind, noting Jerrik seemed oblivious to Katla's attention. Or perhaps he simply ignored it.

No one dared to breathe until the last guard faded into the distance.

Folki was the first to cautiously emerge, his gun at the ready. "The tunnel entrance is just ahead."

They reached the edge of the city, where the cave wall descended downward. The glow from the magical plants shone brighter here, and in the distance, Laila could see a dark fissure in the rock.

She assumed they would be heading into a magically carved tunnel, but this was a natural opening barely wide enough for two people to walk abreast. They hurried into the dark tunnel, conjuring lights as they went.

Jerrik examined the black stone jutting up like broken glass around them. "This is one of the old entrances to the mines. The portal we're looking for is located just above them in a remote part of the castle. A cave-in several years back breached the palace's basement and exposed it to the tunnels below. That level of the palace is sealed off now and mostly forgotten."

"In other words, we shouldn't meet anyone down here, but keep your eyes open," warned Rune.

The ground sloped sharply then the tunnel opened up into a large cavern. The team stood on a stone ledge that hung over a pit so deep Laila couldn't see the bottom. Carts on pulley systems crisscrossed above the chasm, leading to other ledges and platforms. Massive crystals jutted from the walls and glowed with a dull orange light to illuminate the chamber.

"Are these the mines?" Laila asked.

Folki nodded. "One of them. This particular section isn't mined as much anymore since the palace is carved into the rock above, but deep in the crevasse, you can still find veins rich in sapphires. The other mines contain veins of coal or metal ore we smelt in our factories and trade with other kingdoms. It's filled the king's coffers, but…well, I'm sure you saw the miners in the city."

Laila nodded, remembering their gaunt, fatigued faces.

Rune reached for one of the hanging carts and opened the rusty metal door. "After you."

The others climbed in, but Laila hesitated. The idea of climbing into a rusty metal bucket suspended over an endless pit wasn't ideal. She could teleport herself, but not a group of six. She needed to conserve her strength in case they encountered another patrol or a new threat. Reluctantly, she stepped in.

Rune shut the door and latched it into place as Folki switched a lever. There was a grinding of gears and a mechanical screech. The cart began to creep at a steep angle along one of the cables spanning the crevasse. They made it about halfway when the motor shuddered and ground to a halt.

"Damn it!" Folki uttered. He examined the gears.

"Can you fix it?" Jerrik asked.

Folki shook his head. "I don't have the tools. These machines are too old. We should've split up—"

There was another noise, a metallic screech as the cables protested under their collective weight. The others froze.

"That's not all that's wrong with these old carts," muttered Rune.

The sickening moan of metal straining left the hair on the back of Laila's neck standing. That was not a good sign.

Crack. Laila's stomach dropped as the cart lurched. She grabbed the rusted side to keep from tumbling into the darkness below. The steel edge of the cart bit into Laila's hands. She turned to look back at the platform behind them, and her heart pounded in her chest. Years of neglect had left the cables brittle from rust, and one of the three anchors tethering the line to the stone wall had snapped. The sudden weight was too much.

The others began arguing behind her, but Laila couldn't tear her eyes from the anchors. Already she could see the metal of the second cable fraying. With a sharp twang, it snapped too. She braced herself as the cart jolted to the left. It swung wildly, giving them a sickening view of the crevasse looming below. Only one anchor held them in place.

"We've got to get off this thing!" Katla yelled.

Laila grabbed the cable and felt along it with her powers. She sent tendrils of magic out to reinforce the metal, but the entire line was unstable along with the rock where the remaining anchor was mounted. Cracks were beginning to appear along the stone. They would have to think of something quick or plunge to their deaths in the pit below.

CHAPTER 13

Laila struggled to bind the cable and stone together before their cart plummeted into the darkness. Around her, the rebels frantically searched for a means of escape. The other platforms were far. She could teleport them, but she had never moved more than two others at a time. Plus, the second she released her spell on the cable, it would give out and plunge them into the pit below.

"Start climbing," Folki ordered.

Rune went first, then Katla and Hallr, all of them hanging upside down as they shimmied along the cable towards the far side of the cave.

"Laila, you're next," called the rebel leader.

She shook her head. "I'll hold the line together. Go on without me. I'll catch up."

Jerrik looked ready to argue, but Folki stepped in. "You heard her. Keep going."

Jerrik grit his teeth in frustration but obeyed, hoisting himself up to hook his legs around the cable. Folki was just behind him, and Laila watched them inch their way toward safety. She strained to adjust her grip on the line she held together. It was difficult at this distance, especially when the rock was so unstable too. It took all of her concentration to bind the metal and stone together.

Rune made it about a hundred yards to where another cart rested on a lower cable. Laila sucked in a tense breath as he released his hands and dropped ten feet into the cart below. It swung but held. Katla followed suit, taking the time to calculate the jump. The cart swayed, and cable bowed as Hallr joined them, and Laila worried that the other line would be unable to support the weight as well.

Jerrik hesitated when he prepared to make the drop to the new cart. Laila tensed, and for a split second, lost her focus on the stone wall behind them. A crack resounded in the rock, and Laila's cart lurched as the cable broke free.

For a sickening moment, she felt the cart falling beneath her. Above, Jerrik and Folki both lost their grip on the cable. Rune was the first to react—something shot from his hand and coiled around Jerrik. The new cart pitched violently to the side as Rune struggled to maintain his hold on Jerrik.

Folki was still falling along with Laila, tumbling deeper into the darkness. Suspended cables rushed past them at a frightening speed. A collision would break bones if not kill them. Laila reached out to Folki with her magic and pulled him through the air toward her. The moment he collided with her, she managed to grab hold. The sensation of falling vanished as Laila teleported them to a ledge above. They both tumbled to the ground, trembling in shock.

Neither of them spoke. Laila didn't know if she should laugh or cry in relief.

"Laila!" bellowed Jerrik from somewhere below.

"I'm okay. We're both okay!" She crawled to the edge of the platform. "We're up here."

She looked down at the cart below and saw Jerrik relax. Rune and Hallr must have pulled him up into the cart. Unfortunately, it was on a cable leading to a different platform.

"Great, now how are we going to get up there?" grumbled Katla.

"Rune, do you have a rope?" Hallr asked.

"Not long enough to span that."

Laila dropped her gaze to examine the rock face below. Even if they made it to the other platform, it would be too far to climb.

"Hold on. I'll get you." She abruptly appeared in the cart, causing it to sway. "Hold onto me."

The others didn't question—they clung to her hands or arms. She made the return trip to the ledge above, but even as she traveled along the magical pathways, she could feel the others' weight slowing her. Her feet touched the stone above. The shock of magic hit her even harder than it had the day before, but they made it to the safety of the ledge. Her legs buckled, and this time she blacked out before she hit the floor.

Voices reached Laila through the darkness first, distant as though they were speaking from the other end of a tunnel. It was hard to make out who they belonged to.

"I don't think healing her will do anything."

"Well, what do you suggest?" That voice she recognized. It was definitely Jerrik.

"I'm fine," Laila muttered more faintly than she intended.

Gradually, Jerrik's face swam into focus. He was looking down at her. "Easy now."

Laila sat up with a grunt and was promptly greeted by a wave of nausea—a residual effect her body had to the overuse of divine magic. She turned to the side and retched. Her whole body ached, and she could still feel the electrifying buzz of magic arcing through her. Fatigue from divine magic was even worse than from the elemental kind. Jerrik's hand rubbed soothing circles on her back as she continued to expel her breakfast.

"Are you okay?" he asked once the heaving subsided.

Laila nodded and accepted a water bottle from him. An ache began to creep into her back and head—the magical equivalent of a hangover. "I'll be fine. I just need a minute or two."

Jerrik helped her move away from the ledge and lean against the rough stone wall. The others stood nearby, looking shaken.

"I'm surprised you're not in a coma after that," Jerrik said.

He referred to what happened after the escape from the Demonic fight ring. She used so much magic that she slipped into a coma for days. It was how most sorcerers reacted when they had pushed themselves too far.

"My new abilities help me recover faster, but the physical effects are still awful." She couldn't stand the sour taste in her mouth. She reached into an enchanted pocket of her jacket and pulled out the pouch of candied nuts Hallr had given her yesterday.

Laila gave her body another two minutes before deciding she was ready to continue. She sincerely hoped there wouldn't be any more chasms to cross. Luckily, the rest of their journey was on firm ground through a series of tunnels. Some of the passageways had partially caved in, and she wondered how stable the rest of them were. They proceeded cautiously until they reached a dead-end where rubble sealed the entire passage. The only way forward was a small gap near the top of the debris.

"This is where we part ways," declared Folki.

Rune pointed up at the rock. "Once you squeeze through there, you'll be able to access the portal."

"You're not coming with us?" Laila glanced at Hallr.

He looked conflicted. "As much as I'd like to, the Swordmasters are a little particular about who they allow into their temple."

Folki pulled out a map of the tunnels to examine with Rune. "We'll have to find another route back to the city. I'm guessing you can find your own way back."

Laila nodded. With just the two of them, she would be able to traverse the old mineshaft magically.

"Good luck," Katla told Jerrik brusquely. She folded her arms across her chest.

Hallr placed a hand on his shoulder.

"I should've asked earlier," Jerrik said to his friend, "but has anyone managed to find a way to help my mother?"

Hallr ran his fingers through his short dark hair. "We've been trying to find a way to break her out of the palace, but don't have the resources to risk an attempt. Not with the new sorcerer in the palace. There are too many unknowns."

Hallr lingered a moment longer before he waved goodbye and followed the others down the passage.

Jerrik turned to stare up at the small opening, and Laila noticed the uncertainty in his eyes. Despite the turmoil she sensed, Jerrik hoisted himself over the rubble and climbed through the narrow gap. Laila followed, moving cautiously in case any of the boulders shifted loose. The hole was snug, barely wide enough for Jerrik's broad shoulders. Once he emerged, he helped Laila through the gap and into the passage above.

Laila dusted herself off and examined their new surroundings. The walls were reinforced with brick that arched above them in the places where the roof remained. They picked their way through the rubble that littered the abandoned passage and following a deserted corridor with an arch that led to a small chamber.

Crumbling statues lined the chamber's sides. They were severely damaged and marred beyond recognition. It appeared as though someone had blasted away at their faces and robes. Chunks of rock covered the floor, and cracks ran along the brick walls.

Jerrik paused before one of the sculptures. "These were statues of my ancestors—the ones who achieved the rank of Swordmaster. My father did this after their order rejected him."

Laila stared at the wreckage, feeling uneasy. "Why was he

rejected?"

"He didn't have the proper training. No one took him on as an apprentice, but he thought he could pass the trials anyway. Or maybe they sensed how wicked he was. They turned him away at the temple gates. In his youth, he didn't have anyone to look after him. An assassin killed my grandmother and grandfather when he was a boy. He was essentially raised by the court, who groomed him to put their desires over that of the kingdom. There was no one with a level head and fair heart to guide him as my mother did with me."

Jerrik looked around at the destruction and shook his head. "I can't leave my mother here. I thought Hallr and the others would find some way to help her, but they can't—not when the Red Guard has them cornered this way. I can't let my father destroy her. What choice do I have, though?"

He sagged against a broken statue looking far more defeated than she had seen in a long time.

Laila didn't know what else to do, so she asked, "Would you tell me about her?"

Jerrik's eyes were hollow as he spoke. "My mother is the gentlest person I've ever known—the sort of person who would release a spider into the garden several floors below rather than see it crushed. When she smiles, the entire mood of the room lifts. She not only knows the names of every servant who's ever worked for her, but she would sneak them little gifts for their birthdays or holidays—bundles of coins tied in handkerchiefs with enough gold to feed their families for a month. My father would've been livid if he'd found out, but she continued to do it anyway."

Jerrik's mother sounded far different from what Laila had heard of King Oddvarr. "Why did she marry your father?"

Jerrik rubbed a hand along the back of his neck. "When the king wants something, it's foolish to refuse him. That's what she always told me. I don't think she wanted to, but my father had a bloody reputation even at a young age. She convinced herself that life as a queen wouldn't be so bad. I think she thought she could make a difference somehow."

"Did she?"

He shrugged. "In her own little ways, but my father was careful not to give her too much power. He's always been paranoid. When I came along, she was like a buffer between my father and me. She didn't want me to become like him. She told me stories of her grandfather, a valiant Swordmaster who traveled the worlds, helping others in need. Then, when I was old enough, she took me to Master Kyvik for lessons."

So that was how the Swordmasters factored into all of this. They were his mother's hope for Jerrik's salvation. Laila had a feeling that when his mother realized she couldn't help her people directly, she hoped Jerrik might someday have that chance.

Jerrik continued. "I suppose my father has always loved her in a way. He could never punish her like he did others. It was her saving grace all these years. That's why I was so angry when I found out he imprisoned her."

His mother clearly had a plan when she introduced him to the Swordmasters. Even though they had set out on this journey to save Ali, Laila couldn't help but feel Jerrik had his own journey that needed to be completed here in Nidavellir.

She may not have a way to save his mother, but she could fix one thing his father had destroyed. Laila reached out to the stone around them, and the rock began to move.

Jerrik looked over. "What are you doing?"

"Repairing the one thing I can right now."

The stones shifted and rolled back into the forms they had once taken as she pulled them back into place, the magic in the rock guiding her as she pieced the stone together once more. She stood and walked over to a statue, examining the fine cracks and wondering if there was some way to repair them. If she released the spell now, they would simply tumble to the ground once more. She brushed her fingers along the surface, and a blue light shot from her fingers through the stone, running along the cracks and filling them.

Stepping back, Laila cautiously released her hold on the rock. The statues retained their forms, with the faint blue lines running throughout them like veins. Another wave of fatigue hit her, and spots appeared in her vision, but she managed to hide the toll from Jerrik.

The prince examined the statues, his expression filled with wonder. He paused in front of each one to look into the faces of his ancestors and predecessors. Then he pulled Laila into his arms.

"I'm not sure how you did it, but thank you," he whispered against her hair.

"Thank you for letting me in."

He finally opened up to her and let her understand something about his past. Something so deep, so raw, and so emotional. He bared a part of his soul. As with the statues, he was so broken, yet no one but Frej had any idea of the turmoil he had been through. She wished he had found a way to tell her before but now was better than never.

"Jerrik, it doesn't matter whether you are a prince or the poorest man in the kingdom. All I've ever wanted is a chance to get to know you."

His thumb brushed her lips in a feather-light line. "I'm sorry I didn't sooner."

His lips lowered. They hovered a moment and then met her own. Gentle. Cautious. Laila leaned into his embrace and tipped her head back, allowing their kiss to deepen. Perhaps it was wrong of her to savor him and enjoy the way he held her close. But there had always been something that drew her to him—as if some bond of fate linked them. No matter how much she longed to, she couldn't walk away from him.

They surfaced for air, and Laila realized how heavy she was breathing. She was putty in his hands and feared what would happen if they lingered here in this forgotten hall, alone.

With reluctance, she pushed aside her desire and stepped

away from him. She swallowed and refused to look at him, star-ing at the portal instead. "Are you ready for this? To go to the temple?"

Jerrik watched the portal's rippling surface. "I believe so. We don't have another choice."

Laila glanced back up at him. "Perhaps they'll have some idea of how to help your mother. We already know there are Demons loose in the city. Perhaps they'll even be willing to help us in some way."

Doubt shadowed his features, but he nodded all the same.

With a deep breath, he stepped toward the portal.

CHAPTER 14

"They took out a dozen Greater Demons? Ha! See, the Elf is harder to kill than a cockroach." Marius sneered at Izel's reflection in the small scrying glass he held.

She glowered, and the shadows that drifted around her darkened, resembling storm clouds. "I needed to ensure you weren't exaggerating. I'll kill the Elf myself. I have another plan in motion now that I know the prince is with her."

Marius shrugged. "Good luck."

She cast him a venomous look before ending the spell. Marius chuckled and tucked the scrying glass into his pocket.

"Sounds like Izel has her hands full," Lorelei said as she sipped her iced coffee. They were sitting in a secluded corner of a rooftop café in Santa Monica, enjoying lunch. It was a welcomed change of scenery for Marius, even if it was a bit risky.

"It's nice to watch her struggle every now and then. In any case, I want an update from you. I would've thought you would find a way to immobilize those agents by now."

Lorelei was his secret weapon and worth more than an entire army of Demons. He fought for her to join him, knowing the chaos she was capable of unleashing. She could be cruel and devastatingly cunning, but she worked slowly—single-handedly turning many humans against the Supernaturals, which generated enough disruptions to keep the agents off his trail. Still, she hadn't brought IRSA to heel yet.

It was maddening. What was taking Lorelei so long? The governor was her lapdog, or worse, her puppet. She held this crumbling state in her perfectly manicured hands.

She offered up a feline smile. "Patience Marius. They're federal agents. It complicates things. Don't worry. I have this under control. By this time tomorrow, the agents will no longer pose a threat."

"What do you mean?"

"You'll have to wait and see." She finished the last sip of coffee and winked. "Thanks for picking up the bill, darling."

She stood and sauntered away, her hips swaying as she headed for the door. Marius sighed and pulled out his wallet. Of course, she would leave the bill for him. He didn't mind, though, not as long as her plan worked. He had other cities and spies to see to. He would have to trust Lorelei.

When Laila stepped out of the portal to the Swordmasters' temple in Jotunheim, the first thing that struck her were the colors. Here, the earth jutted up around them in various shades of purple, from the lightest shade of lavender to dark eggplant. Ivy crept over the rocky landscape with leaves the size of shields, and instead of blue, the sky swirled in shades of pink and purple with faint, shimmering stars swirling above them. It could have been twilight, yet the ambient light filled the sky with no identifiable source. It felt as if she stepped into a psychedelic dream.

"Woah." Jerrik's tone mirrored her own awe.

This world's magic also felt different, weaker, similar to Midgard, with almost a sluggish quality. It added to the feeling that this place hung suspended in time.

Laila had never been to Jotunheim, but she always thought it would be similar to Midgard or Alfheim. She never imagined an alien landscape, such as the one before her. Laila and Jerrik looked out from a rocky outcropping where several other portals stood—or had once stood, since many of the archways were now empty. Where worn paths ought to lead to ten other portals, only three remained. They faced the peak of a mountain upon which a forsaken stone temple covered in ivy stood and balanced on the edge of a cliff that overlooked the ocean far below.

"You sure this is the right place? It looks sort of abandoned." There was no sign of life. Had the Swordmasters moved to a different location?

The grinding noise of an earthquake shook the ground beneath them, and the Elves struggled to maintain their footing. Two massive boulders shifted and began to move. Laila blinked and realized they weren't rocks but creatures of stone. The boulders rose to three times her height and had a vaguely humanoid look. Their fists were disproportionately large and rested on the earth as the stone monsters towered over them. Laila peered up at their faces in wonder. They were fossilized dinosaur heads— the mouths filled with massive stone teeth and empty sockets. She wasn't quite sure if they were living creatures or some sort of complicated spell.

When the one closest to Laila spoke, its voice was rough and gritty, "Be wary visitors, those who bear ill-intentions will not be allowed further into this land. Speak your intention toward this place. We will forcibly remove those who lie."

Jerrik nudged Laila, urging her to speak.

"We seek aid and guidance from the Swordmasters."

The rock creatures remained still for a tense moment, then the second spoke. "Your intentions are pure. You may proceed but beware. Everything comes with a price, even knowledge."

The two figures resumed their original positions as unassuming piles of rock.

Jerrik remained quiet and pensive as they climbed the path toward the mountaintop. Gazing down the slope, Laila noted a few oversized trees and shrubs dotting the landscape in bold shades of azure and sapphire. Beyond them, the cliff fell away to a vast, churning ocean the color of blood. It made for an unsettling sight, with waves large enough to swamp a battleship. She wondered what strange beasts lurked beneath its surface.

They approached the temple, which was far more extensive than it appeared at a distance. A pair of massive doors creaked open, and a trio of robed figures emerged. They wore white robes with hoods so deep that Laila was unable to discern their facial features.

"Welcome to the temple of the Swordmasters," called the one in the middle. "I am Grandmaster Zorion. What business do you have here?" Their voice vibrated unearthly, with both high and low tones intertwining.

Jerrik held his ground. "We are searching for the Eirflower. A friend of ours has been wounded with a cursed blade. We need the flower to cure her."

"Are you certain the flower is the cure?" The Grandmaster asked.

Laila faltered. Dr. Elmerson had been skeptical, and the truth was that they didn't know if this would break the curse.

"No, but we have to try. There are few options left," Laila said.

"We have been tasked with protecting the Eirflower. We cannot allow one of its blossoms to be so easily taken. A price is required."

Laila and Jerrik exchanged a glance.

"What sort of price?" asked Jerrik warily.

The robed figure cocked its head. "Our numbers dwindle, and few seek to follow our path. We require you—Jerrik, son of Oddvarr—to complete the trials. If you can join our order as so many of your forebearers have, then you will be allowed a single blossom. Hopefully, that is enough to revive your comrade."

The hair on the back of Laila's neck stood. How could this Swordmaster possibly know so much? They hadn't spoken their names since they set foot in this world. And what would joining the Swordmasters' order entail? Would he be required to remain at the temple?

Jerrik was shaking his head. "I'm not ready. Not now. There has to be another way."

The robed figure remained still. "That is the only offer I have for you. Make your decision."

Laila silently pleaded with him. They needed that flower. How could they return without it? How could they face Erin and tell her they had failed because of this request? She waited for Jerrik to respond.

"Very well, I will do it," he replied at last.

"Good. You may enter the temple."

They both moved towards the door, but the Grandmaster lifted their arm and blocked Laila's path.

"None may enter while in disguise. Remove your glamor and show your true face," the Grandmaster asserted. Even from this proximity, Laila couldn't see the face beneath the cowl.

She relented and dropped the spell that dimmed her aura, allowing her eyes to shine. Her swirling scars shimmered as well, and her entire being became wreathed in a pale light radiating from within her.

The figure retreated and bowed. "Forgive my insolence. Please be welcome, divine one."

Laila ignored the look Jerrik gave her and simply nodded before stepping through the doorway. The robed figures followed them in and closed both doors behind them.

"The others will show you where you may rest from your journey. We will discuss preparations for the trials tomorrow after you've recovered from your journey." With that, the Grandmaster departed with a bow.

The remaining two lowered their hoods to reveal their faces. One was Fae, like Ali, with violet eyes and long, dark hair streaked with white. He wore it braided back from his face, where faint lines framed his eyes and mouth. He looked to be near the same age as Laila's father. The other had pale scales that glistened and were almost translucent. His blue eyes were so light they were nearly lost in the whites of his eyes. While he had no hair, a ridge of short, grey horns adorned his head like a crown. Laila suspected he was some sort of Merfolk that dwelled in the oceans of Alfheim. He bowed eagerly.

"Welcome! You both look worn out. We'll show you to your rooms to wash up. Then you can join us in the dining hall. By the way, I'm Master Okaenos, and this is Master Manach."

Master Okaenos chattered excitedly as he showed them deeper into the temple complex.

"We have guest quarters at the far end of the temple near the dining hall. You are free to roam the outer halls during your stay, but the sacred inner garden is off-limits. Only the highest of our order may enter." From the wistful look on his face, Laila suspected the Grandmaster did not permit him access either.

The hallway was large, with arched ceilings far above set with glass panels to allow natural light to filter into the space. They passed a series of colorful stone mosaics lit by torches along the walls. Each depicted various scenes from peaceful forests and castle ruins to bloody battle scenes that reminded Laila all too much of the nightmares that often plagued her sleep. Others portrayed Gods and Goddesses.

When they reached the end of the hall, Master Okaenos pushed open another oversized door and beckoned them inside. Laila entered a large hall with a massive stone fireplace at its center. Sofas and chairs upholstered in plum-colored fabric were arranged in front of the hearth, and a variety of lanterns set into the walls and placed on the tables filled the room with a soft orange glow. Laila counted eight alcoves with draping curtains one could shut for privacy, and each held beds large enough to accommodate Supernaturals of various sizes.

"There's a bathroom through a doorway at the far end of the room. Feel free to make yourselves at home. We'll be back to take you to the dining hall shortly," explained Master Okaenos.

The Elves thanked him as he shut the door.

Laila wandered over to the nearest bed and pulled off her jacket before unbuckling her dagger's scabbard from her thigh. Then she wandered to the back of the guest quarters to look for the bathroom, which she found through a smaller archway with two branches—one that led to a toilet chamber and sink with running water, and the other to a massive stone pool filled with steaming water. Tree trunk-shaped pillars reached up from the water's depths to support the roof above, and the sound of running water echoed throughout the chamber.

As inviting as the massive tub looked, she didn't want to leave the others waiting. Instead, she splashed water on her face and arms to rinse off the flecks of dried blood and dust from their journey.

She looked at her reflection in the mirror, the faint glow of her skin shimmering. It felt as though she was looking at another person. That was why she preferred to mask her aura—at least that way, she looked more like her usual self. Or was that her old self? She didn't know anymore. The uncertainty of the path before her left her stomach in knots. All she could do was take it day by day. At least for now, her task was straightforward—retrieve the Eirflower. Yet beyond that, what? She needed to find a way to stop the Demons, but how? Especially now when she knew their presence reached across the worlds. That she felt as though she was drowning in her own powers didn't help either.

She pulled herself away from the mirror and returned to the room. Jerrik had claimed the bed in the alcove next to her own.

"Well, I'll admit this is a little more luxurious than I was expecting," he declared with a cocky smile. He lounged back on the mattress. "Far more spacious than my tiny apartment in L.A. I could get used to a place like this."

Laila nodded behind her. "Wait until you see the bathroom."

He stood and vanished through the arch. It was good to see a bit of his normal self returning.

"Are you ready?" called Master Okaenos. He stuck his head through the door to the chamber moments later.

Jerrik reappeared, and they followed Okaenos into the hall, but this time his silent companion was nowhere to be seen. He led them down the corridor, where voices echoed toward them. The dining hall was large enough to seat more than a hundred, but there were maybe two-dozen people at most. They all wore white robes and had plain scabbards buckled to their waists. There were both men and women amongst their ranks, as well as creatures from a variety of worlds. The Swordmasters came in every shape, size, and race—from a female Dwarf with pale hair to a large Troll close to twelve feet tall. Some creatures had dark obsidian scales, while others had bright blue skin.

Master Okaenos motioned for them to join him at a table. Master Manach was already there with a man who had a furry face and cat eyes. His tawny fur was streaked grey, and his body bent with age.

"Welcome! I'm Master Bas, please join us!" the man chirped.

"It's a pleasure to meet you. I'm Laila." She bowed.

"And I'm Jerrik," the Dark Elf beside her added.

Master Bas nodded. "You are the one who will go through the trials. Best of luck to you! I know it's what Master Kyvik would have wanted."

Jerrik started in surprise. "You knew him?" He seated himself beside the older man.

Master Bas nodded. "He was trying to arrange for you to undergo the trials before his death."

Laila took a seat across from Master Manach as another Swordmaster brought a tray of food to their table. It was a basic stew, but Laila's mouth watered. Her stomach growled.

Master Okaenos passed her a bowl. "So, what news do you have of the outside worlds? It's been a long time since I left the temple grounds."

"That may be a blessing for you then." Laila picked up her spoon. "The worlds are more chaotic, and we are experiencing the most Demonic activity since The Event. I live in Midgard now, where I've been trying to track down the escaped Demons. I thought it was just Midgard, but we were attacked by a dozen Greater Demons in Svartalfheim on our way here."

Both Master Manach and Master Okaenos froze.

"How could they possibly escape Muspelheim?" Master Manach asked at last.

Laila bit her lip. "We're not sure. Some were probably summoned in rituals, and others might have tricked the ferryman in Styx. I suspect there's an open portal to Hell somewhere in Nidavellir, given how many we saw."

The Fae cringed. "That's disconcerting. I'm not surprised Asgard sent one of their own to deal with it."

"Oh no, I'm just an Elf. I'm not sure what is happening to me." She motioned to the markings on her arms. "The power is a gift from a Goddess to help me, I suppose. I'm still struggling to understand it."

Master Okaenos's eyes lit up. "I've never heard of anything like it! You know, we each pledge ourselves to a God or Goddess when we pass the trials, but I've never seen a God gift anyone with power such as this."

The Fae Swordmaster sipped his stew thoughtfully. "I wonder if there is any mention of it in the records."

"Do you think there could be others like me?" If Gods had gifted Swordmasters with powers in the past, maybe there would be some information that could help Laila understand how to keep her magic under control.

The Fae nodded. "You should speak to the records keepers and the librarians. I'm sure they would permit you to view relevant materials."

"Thank you." Laila studied his violet eyes. They were so similar to Ali's that it brought a pang of anguish. How was she doing? How was Erin? Was Darien managing on his own? She needed a distraction to keep those fears at bay, at least until she was alone.

"Is it inappropriate to ask which Gods you pledged yourselves to?" She looked at the others.

Master Okaenos put down his spoon. "Not at all! I pledged myself to Poseidon. I visited his temple from the time I was young, so it just felt right."

The Fae chuckled. "Not a usual choice for a Swordmaster, though."

The Merfolk shrugged.

"I pledged myself to The Morrigan. Most Fae do," explained Master Manach.

"Have you ever seen them?" she asked, curious.

Master Manach nodded. "Once, long ago in a vision. The Morrigan gave me a task to help the Fae Queen in a time of need."

Laila desperately hoped she might finally find answers to some of her questions here, especially since there seemed to be an innate divine connection. If she was going to search for answers in any mortal realm, this was a decent place to start.

While they ate, the two Swordmasters explained they were essentially a nondenominational order of monks who aid the worlds in times of need and maintain balance. The Gods they pledged themselves to helped to inform their individual path. When they weren't away on assignments, most of the Swordmasters remained at the temple studying, training, and meditating. Still, others lived in various cities to provide counsel and guidance, such as Master Kyvik. Occasionally, nobility and royalty trained to join their ranks, although their responsibilities took them in a different direction. In those instances, their training would help them to serve their kingdoms better.

Someone from another table pulled out a stringed instrument and began playing a cheerful tune while others moved to gather around a hearth. Laila grinned at the pleasant, joyful bunch and their eagerness to chat with the newcomers. But she was also exhausted.

Jerrik still sat engrossed in his conversation with Master Bas, who offered him advice for the trials ahead. Knowing the information would be invaluable, she didn't want to pull him away, so she quietly excused herself from the others and returned to her room.

Back in the guest quarters, she retreated to the massive tub and removed her clothes. She sank into the blissfully warm water and wondered if it was fed by a hot spring. The past two days had been trying, both physically and emotionally. While Laila was used to Arduinna pushing her boundaries in her training, this was another level of exhausting. At least tonight, she would be able to get a full night's sleep. She rested her head on the rocks at the edge of the pool and shut her eyes.

"I was wondering where you snuck off to," a voice murmured behind her.

Her eyes flew open. Turning, Laila found Jerrik leaning against the arch, watching.

"Seriously? Is privacy a foreign concept to you?" She conjured a thicker mist to obscure the water's surface.

He chuckled and pushed off the wall. He strode over to the side of the pool where he knelt, amused as Laila continued to glower at him.

He started to remove his shirt.

"What the hell do you think you're doing!" she howled

He smirked. "I thought I'd join you. It looks relaxing."

"Don't you dare!" she snapped, earning a round of laughter from Jerrik.

Except he didn't stop. Laila debated what to do. She retreated to the far end of the pool, grumbling as she swam.

"You stay on that side, or I'll freeze you into a block of ice." She made sure to avert her eyes, trying to maintain some shred of dignity.

The water rippled as he climbed into the pool. "Now, where's the fun in that?"

There was a velvety quality to his voice that left her aching, but she ignored it. Instead, she sent an icy current in his direction. He swore as it reached him and countered with a mist so heavy she could hardly see her hand in front of her.

They didn't have time for distractions, yet she also couldn't deny a part of her liked this. She enjoyed Jerrik's playful flirtations and felt a thrill every time he came near. Yet, at the same time, the guilt plagued her. Ali's life was in danger, and every moment they were away brought her closer to death. Not to mention the rest of their team was at risk as well…

"We're on a mission," she reminded him, keeping her distance.

"So you've said, but there is nothing we can do until tomorrow." His voice bounced off the walls making it all but impossible to locate him in the fog.

A splash behind her was all the warning he gave. Jerrik spun her around and pinned her wrists to one of the pillars. She gasped, and her heart skipped a beat. All too aware of his closeness, Laila knew she should move away, but her body ached for his touch.

His eyes lingered on her bare shoulders as she sank deeper into the water. "Oh, Laila, you make it so easy to tease you. It's not as if there's a part of you I haven't seen, remember?"

He winked, and her face ignited with heat. Gods, she was ready to throttle him. She pulled her arms from his grasp and swept his feet out from under him as she shoved him under the water. The moment he surfaced, it was her turn to pin him to the pillar.

She narrowed her eyes. "I thought princes were supposed to be charming."

"And I'm not?" he gloated.

She hated how much he seemed to enjoy the way she trapped him.

She huffed out a breath of hot air and moved away, only to realize her mistake too late. The second she turned her back,

Jerrik grabbed her in a headlock, pinning her arms above her as he laced his fingers behind her neck. He was so near that she could feel his chest brushing against her spine.

Jerrik leaned in until she could feel his breath on her skin. "Tell me you don't want me, and I'll stop."

The feel of his skin on hers was maddening. Laila recalled the sensation of his lips as they kissed back in the tunnels, and a sudden heat flared between her legs that had nothing to do with the water's temperature. She should resist, but the aching in her core betrayed her.

Jerrik released her only to brush his lips along her earlobe. When he gently nipped her skin, a soft moan escaped her lips.

"What was that?" he whispered, the length of his body pressing against her.

Her self-restraint evaporated. She leaned into him, enjoying the way her body fit perfectly against his as Jerrik's hands roved along her skin, lingering over her taunt breasts before traveling down further.

"Just for tonight," she murmured as he kissed his way down her neck. "Just for tonight."

He flipped her around to face him, and the frenzy of her hunger took over. Damn the consequences. She couldn't resist him—not when she wanted it so badly. And not when every fiber of her being was begging for more.

CHAPTER 15

Laila stared up at the dark ceiling far above. Although exhausted, sleep still eluded her. She felt inexplicably restless and envied Jerrik, who soundly slept on the other side of the bed. Then again, he needed the sleep more than she did, especially with the upcoming trials. The Swordmasters hadn't told her what it would entail, but she imagined it would push him to his limits.

She tilted her head to the side to look at him. When they finally collapsed on the bed, their bodies spent and limbs entangled, Laila tried to tell herself it was just a fling. This romp had been a way to distract themselves from the harsh realities they weren't ready to face. Yet, as her breathing slowed and Jerrik drifted off to sleep with his arm wrapped around her bare waist, she already knew that was a lie. She had never stopped caring about him or wanting him. Each kiss and every touch only confirmed that.

It seemed crazy to think he was truly a runaway prince. Part of her wanted to reject the idea and simply return to Los Angeles as if Hallr had never revealed the truth—exactly as Jerrik wanted. But was that right? Not when his kingdom was struggling on the brink of starvation and Demons prowled the streets.

How had the Demons gotten to Nidavellir? There had to be an open portal for that many to get through. It was safe to assume Demons were involved in the government. If Jerrik's father was harboring Demons, then Laila wasn't sure she could turn a blind eye. But if she stayed, how would she get the cure to Ali?

Ali. She had been there for Laila ever since she moved to Los Angeles. Ali was her closest friend. They were like family. No matter what happened and how uncertain Laila felt, Ali always knew how to cheer her up. In the past months, she missed their movie nights and shopping trips. She even missed their nights out clubbing and dancing. Arduinna was good company, but Ali was…well, Ali.

Laila? I don't know if you can hear me. I don't know what to do, echoed a voice inside her head. It was just as Ali's had done before, only this time it was Erin.

Laila slipped out of bed and pulled on her clothes. Laila had never tried replying to a prayer before, but it made sense that she should be able to respond somehow if she could hear them. She wrapped a blanket around her shoulders and took a seat on a sofa in the sitting area.

Erin? Can you hear me?

Yes! I can! But how? Laila could feel the relief in her voice.

I'm not entirely sure, honestly. But how are you? How is Ali? Laila asked.

About the same, but getting weaker. Do you know when you'll be back?

No, not yet. We made it to where the Eirflower is located, but it will take some time to get it and then make it back to Los Angeles. There have been some complications.

Here too, Erin said. *The Demons attempted to assassinate Ali.*

"What?" Laila said out loud. Her throat tightened with dread. She peeked over her shoulder in hopes she hadn't disturbed Jerrik. *What do you mean? What happened?*

Frej and I were there. He noticed something was off. We stopped the assassin, but Darien's really freaked out. He's taken us to a safehouse his sire owns, but Ali's still at the hospital. He's got Vampires guarding her now, but I wish I could be with her.

Laila could feel Erin's distress through whatever connection they had established.

She made a fist. Now was not a time to be away, but she had to get that flower and return before the Demons harmed anyone else. *Talen is a good man, and his Vampires will keep Ali safe. She'd want to ensure you're safe too, though. Maybe they could bring Ali to the safehouse? Did you talk to Darien about that?*

No. I don't think he wants to move her away from the doctor.

That made sense. *Has Lyn translated the blade yet?*

Lyn and Donald are here with me. They're trying to decipher the cursed blade, but I don't think they're making much progress.

There went Laila's hope that Lyn would beat her to a cure. Their hopes hung on the Eirflower alone, now.

How are you? Are you doing okay? she asked the Dragon.

I don't know. I feel so angry and helpless. I just want to punch something or burn it to a crisp. I know it won't help, but I just hate feeling so useless. I want to help instead of sitting around doing nothing.

Can you help Lyn? Laila suggested.

Maybe. I guess I could ask.

Laila wished she could hug the poor girl. *Hang in there, okay? Can you keep me updated on Ali?*

Yeah.

Okay, I'll see you soon.

Erin went silent, and Laila suddenly felt terribly alone. She was used to following orders—it was how the Elves had trained her. Now there was no one to give her orders or tell her what path to take. Should she rush home and help the others? Or should she stay and deal with the Greater Demons in Svartalfheim before they spread to other realms?

CHAPTER 16

The sun would be rising shortly, so Talen talked Darien into sheltering in the bunker for the day. Darien agreed reluctantly. He didn't even have his computer with him. Cursing himself for leaving it at the office, he resorted to using his phone to address the growing list of emails in his inbox.

As soon as the offices of the Supernatural Unit of the New Metropolitan Detention Center opened, he scheduled a special after-hours visit for that evening. He also checked in with Jenn so many times she started ignoring him.

Henrik and Mato had gone to sleep long ago, and no one had seen Erin since they arrived. Lyn, Ligeia, and Donald had finally wandered off to their rooms, exhausted. Talen convinced Darien to take a nap. While only a few hours long, it was the most sleep he had in days.

When he awoke, Lyn and Ligeia sat gathered around the dining room table with Donald once more. They had the cursed blade in a plexiglass case. A pile of old books lay open around them alongside their computers.

He joined them. "Any luck deciphering the curse?"

Donald shook his head. "I'm not familiar with the language. We've been looking into other spells with similar effects, but they're all quite different in their composition. There's no mention of how to break them, so I can understand why Witches banned them millennia ago."

Ligeia flipped through the pages of a book. "We'd have better luck with the libraries in Atlantis, but it was hard enough for me to get permission to leave this time. If I go back, the elders may not allow me to leave again. It's not worth the risk. Not when we have Lorelei to deal with."

"You're sure you haven't seen this language before?" Lyn asked the Siren.

"I'm positive, but languages have never been my strong suit."

Darien turned at the sound of approaching footsteps and found Erin entering the kitchen. Deep circles lurked under her eyes.

"Were you able to sleep?" he asked.

"A little." She grabbed an apple from the refrigerator and took a bite then wandered over to the table. "What are you doing?"

Donald leaned back in his chair and took a large gulp of the energy drink beside him. "This is the cursed blade Ali was stabbed with."

Erin leaned over Lyn's shoulder to examine the knife. "Can I see that magnifying glass?"

Lyn handed it over, and Erin took a closer look at the tiny markings etched into the blade.

"Weird. This blade looks modern, but the markings are Sumerian cuneiform. That was used over four thousand years ago."

The others stared at her, dumbfounded.

"You can read this?" spluttered Donald.

She snorted. "*Read* wouldn't be the right word, but I know enough about the language to stumble through it with a translation table."

"How?" Donald stared at the Dragon as if she sprouted a second head.

"I was bored before Frej showed up, so I studied dead languages through online classes. Earth's got some pretty cool ones." She pulled up a chair and munched on the apple.

Darien shook his head. Who would have thought Erin's hobby could be the missing link to deciphering the spell? If nothing else, maybe it would keep Erin's mind off Ali's condition.

He turned to the Siren. "I've got a visit scheduled with Colin this evening. Are you still up to it?"

She nodded. "Of course."

Lyn frowned at the blade. "I'm going to stay here. As much as I want to help, I think I'd better continue my work on this with Donald."

Darien nodded. "Don't worry. We'll be fine. I'm going to find a ride. The sun will be setting soon, and I want to get an early start."

He left the others to look for Talen, who was still sitting in his office. As Darien waited for him to finish a call, he examined the artifacts on the shelves, all of which appeared to be ancient. They were certainly older than he was.

Talen set his cellphone on the desk. "I just organized another shift of Vampires to watch Ali tonight. They'll be arriving at the hospital shortly after sundown."

"Any issues?"

Talen shook his head. "No, at least not yet. I've reached out to some of my connections around the world. It appears there is suspected Demonic activity in a variety of countries now, but the governments are trying to keep it under wraps. It's not going to help though—not at this point."

"I haven't been able to get through to D.C. in weeks," admitted Darien. He didn't like to think about what that could mean.

The ancient Vampire drummed his fingers against the desk.

"We need a way to unite people against the Demons. They need to know what's going on."

"I agree, but how? The government hasn't felt this fragmented since The Event." He had thought it over for hours on end, but none of them had the type of influence that would be required. Talen might, but only within the Vampire community, and there was still a lot of mistrust between humans and Vampires.

Talen looked equally troubled. "I'll think on it. You're heading to the detention center, right?"

Darien nodded. "I was hoping to borrow a car."

Talen waved towards the garage. "Take your pick. Do you want an escort?"

"No, I don't want to draw unnecessary attention."

Talen stood and followed him out. "Then, be careful."

Darien gave him a sardonic smile. "I'm always careful. Don't you remember all the times I had to haul you out of fights?"

"We were never up against Demons. Vampires are predictable. Demons aren't. They've been rotting in Hell too long."

Darien appreciated the sentiment all the same.

He left the office and nodded to Ligeia to follow. It was tempting to take one of the sleek sports cars, but that would attract too much attention. He opted for one of the SUVs instead, seeing as they were the least conspicuous. They made it out of the labyrinth of the Old City and took the 405 south towards the Los Angeles International Airport.

"Were you serious when you said you were going to wipe our memories?" he asked to break the silence.

"I don't want to, but yes. Maybe there's a way around it, but I don't know for sure. Yet." She watched out the window, intrigued by her surroundings.

"Is it necessary to maintain your isolation? The worlds are a very different place now."

Her brow creased in a frown. "Maybe not, but it's not my place to make such decisions. I could end up damned like Lorelei if I disobey."

He cringed. Vampires didn't tolerate disobedience, but he hadn't heard of a Vampire being damned in centuries.

"Do your kind come to the surface often?" he probed out of pure curiosity. Ligeia would wipe his memory anyway, so he couldn't see any harm in asking.

"No, just those of us who are scouts. We report on the rest of the world, sort of like journalists. We're supposed to avoid interaction, but one day I stumbled across Lyn at the beach. She was so easygoing and relaxed—so different from my kind. She was surfing when she spotted me. I think she could tell I was a Supernatural. Spending time with her was fun. It was nice to escape for a while. I've been visiting her for two years now." She smiled sadly and gazed off into the distance.

Darien felt a pang of sorrow. It had been a long time since he had been in love, and women had hurt him so many times that he often felt it was hopeless. Fate always seemed to find a way to tear you apart.

They were silent for the rest of the drive past the airport and south towards Manhattan Beach. This wasn't a part of the Old City, but it was still mostly abandoned. A large plot of land had been cleared for the Supernatural Unit of the New Metropolitan Detention Center a few years back.

Darien and Ligeia checked in. The fact that she had no form of identification didn't seem to be a problem. The guard just smiled and waved her through. Darien knew it was her charm magic, but it was disturbing how effortless and subtle she worked it. It was far more potent than Ali's.

A guard showed them to a private visiting room that attorneys typically used. They waited on one side of a thick and magically reinforced pane of glass. After a few minutes, Darien watched a guard lead Colin into the room on the other side. The Werewolf looked as though he aged a decade with gaunt cheeks and haunted, sunken eyes. They widened when he saw Darien. Colin scrambled to pick up the phone receiver that would allow them to communicate. Darin reached for his receiver as well, but with far less enthusiasm, and held it so both he and Ligeia could hear.

"You came!" Colin whispered.

"We came to ask you a few questions about your girlfriend." Darien kept his face emotionless.

Colin frowned. "I haven't had any communication with Lorel since my arrest. I figured she was trying to distance herself for political reasons with the election and all."

Darien figured as much. Colin was no longer useful to her. "Did she tell you what she was? Or did she exhibit any Supernatural abilities?"

The Werewolf looked surprised. "What? No, she's human."

"How do you know? Did she tell you?" asked Ligeia.

"Well, sure. That and Lorel works for Fredrik Stacy. I can't imagine him hiring an SNP." Which, in Darien's mind, had made her disguise all the more convincing.

"Yet, here she was dating an SNP," Darien pointed out.

Colin eyed them. "Why does it feel like you're interrogating me? And who is she?" He jerked his thumb at Ligeia.

Darin glanced at Ligeia, unsure how much she wanted to tell Colin.

She leaned closer to the glass. "I'm the one who believes the Demons tricked you into handing over information, and I'm certain that the woman you know as Lorel was the one to do it."

"No." Colin shook his head. "That can't be possible. She… cares about me."

The Siren arched an eyebrow. "How do you know? Can you tell me why you care about her so much?"

Colin opened then closed his mouth several times as he tried to come up with something, anything.

"What about Karina?" asked Darien, referring to Colin's late wife.

"Karina?" For a moment, Colin didn't seem to recognize the name, but then his expression turned to horror. "Oh, God!

How could I forget about her? How—"

He dropped the receiver and cradled his head in his hands as his grief crashed back around him. It was as if he had suddenly awoken from a dream to remember that his wife had died.

Darien lowered his voice. "What do you think?"

Ligeia looked thoroughly disturbed. "I'm certain he was under her spell, but it's concerning that she had him under so deeply. It's extremely difficult to make someone forget about the sort of love and grief he's experiencing right now. She would have needed assistance, something to lower his tolerance to her charm."

Darien recalled Colin had been suffering from strange headaches. He had been taking some sort of medication. "He was taking pills. Do you think she could have laced them with something?"

Ligeia nodded. "That's a possibility."

She tapped the glass to get Colin's attention once more. Reluctantly, the Werewolf picked up the receiver.

"I'm sorry, I don't know what just happened." Colin's voice sounded raw. Darien felt horrible for dredging this up, but perhaps it was for the best. At least Colin could remember his wife now.

Ligeia gave him a sympathetic look, her features softening. "Don't be too hard on yourself. This is what I was talking about. I think Lorel had you under a charm spell that made it difficult for you to remember certain things and allowed you to commit these crimes that, under normal circumstances, you wouldn't."

Colin nodded, but her words didn't ease his guilt. It didn't reduce Darien's either. Colin had been right all along. Even if the Werewolf was technically a Demon and his aura stained from contact with Lorel's hellish energy, he became one unwittingly.

Darien pulled himself from his thoughts. "Hey man, don't worry. We'll get to the bottom of this. How have your headaches been? Are you still taking those meds?"

Colin shook his head. "They offered me something different in here, but I haven't needed them. I guess cutting back on screen time helped." Or the fact he wasn't being charmed out of his wits.

"Do you know where we'd be able to find a bottle of the medication? I want to get it tested to see if Lorel tampered with it."

Colin thought a moment. "There should be a bottle at my apartment if it wasn't confiscated as evidence."

"Do you mind if we go there and look around?"

Colin shook his head. "No. Go ahead, especially if it helps. And… I'm sorry. I don't know what happened, Darien. I never wanted to betray you. You know I would never do anything like that."

Darien gave him a sad nod. "Hang in there, Colin. I'll do what I can."

CHAPTER 17

The air was cold and foggy as Darien drove away from the detention center and back into the city's inhabited zone. Colin had a small apartment near the office, which is where they were headed now.

Ligeia was certain Lorel was indeed Lorelei, and any doubts Darien had regarding it cleared the moment he saw Colin's devastation at the memory of his late wife. Darien had known Colin for years, and he couldn't fake something like that. Even now, the memory of Colin's pained expression haunted his thoughts.

Pushing aside his guilt, Darien parked the SUV in a spot reserved for guests then stepped out of the vehicle.

"Are you coming?" he asked the Siren.

"Sure." She joined him on the sidewalk.

Colin had a second-floor apartment with an exterior entrance. Darien scanned the area for security cameras. Luckily, there were none. He wasn't about to wait around for an irritated landlord to arrive with a spare key. And with Colin's permission, it technically wasn't breaking and entering.

Darien removed the lock picking tools from his belt and

started to work the lock, carefully manipulating the pins with a small rod. If Laila were here, she would probably disapprove and ask where he learned such an illicit skill. He smiled. Darien missed messing with her and hoped she and Jerrik were doing okay.

The lock clicked, and the door opened. Darien and Ligeia stepped into the apartment. It was in disarray from the search last fall, and adding to the mess was a layer of dust that accumulated. The disorder aside, there was something lonely about the space. It was sparsely furnished, and nothing hung on the walls, as if he had just moved in. Knowing Colin, it was more likely he never felt the desire to decorate. He hardly spent time here anyway. It was just a place for him to sleep between shifts. Before Lorel, Colin's career had been his life. Although considering the amount of work Darien had, it was no wonder.

They wandered through the apartment in search of the bottle of meds. Darien found it in the medicine cabinet of the small bathroom. He pulled on a pair of nitrile gloves and opened the container to find half a dozen pills inside. It had an ordinary prescription label for painkillers, but Lorel could have easily swapped the drugs within. He stuck the bottle in an evidence bag before tucking it away in the pocket of his leather jacket.

He returned to the living room to find Ligeia holding a small picture frame.

"Is this the woman you mentioned earlier?" she asked, showing Darien. It was a photo of Colin and Karina at the beach on their honeymoon.

"Yeah, that's his late wife. She died during The Event. It was pretty traumatic for Colin, and I don't think he was ready to move on."

She nodded toward an open drawer. "I found it inside. Lorelei probably hid it from him so as not to remind him of his true love."

Darien snapped his head up. "Wait a minute, that's why you're doing this. Why you're willing to help us even if it means wiping Lyn's memory, you're hoping her feelings will overcome the spell, and she'll remember you."

The Siren was quiet for a long minute as she shut the drawer and carefully placed the photo on the table. "Yes, you're right. It's a gamble, though, since there's a risk she still wouldn't remember me. Her feelings might not be strong enough to overpower the spell, or she might only remember that she was in love with someone, but not who. Many things could go wrong, but there is still hope it might work out." Her eyes lingered on the photo.

"For what it's worth, I hope it works. I truly do." But unfortunately, life had taught him that fairytale endings were just that—fairytales.

Darien locked the apartment, and they returned to the SUV.

"Do you mind if I stop by the office? I want to check on a few things. I want to see how Ali is doing too."

Ligeia nodded.

Darien turned the car around toward the IRSA building and wove them through the late evening traffic. The parking garage was empty when they pulled in—only his work car remained. The others were probably on calls.

They stopped by the hospital first. When Darien arrived at Ali's room, he found two Vampire mercenaries waiting outside the door. They tipped their heads as he approached, recognizing him. Inside he found two more. All four were fresh mercenaries Talen had sent over.

"Is there any change in her condition?" he asked the one nearest.

The mercenary shook her head. "No. The doctor stopped by right after we arrived. He said to tell you he's been able to keep her alive, but her condition is still gradually deteriorating."

Darien watched Ali while the guard spoke. He could sense the effects of the curse slowing wearing the woman's body down little by little—her blood moving sluggishly. At this rate, he wondered if Jerrik and Laila would return in time. Darien thanked the mercenaries before leaving with Ligeia for the office.

When they arrived, he motioned at the door of the conference room. "You can wait there if you'd like. I just need to check my computer. It shouldn't take long."

She nodded and took a seat.

Darien headed back to his office and switched on his computer, then pulled out the evidence bag with the bottle of pills. Pulling up the file from Colin's case, he scrolled through the documented evidence, but it appeared no one had been particularly interested in the pain meds.

There had been two agents investigating Colin. Of course, Ali was in no condition to answer his questions, but perhaps the other was. He flipped through the contacts in his phone until he found the one he was looking for—Special Agent Adam Johnson. He had flown out from D.C. to aid Ali in the investigation.

Darien wasn't optimistic anyone would answer, considering he hadn't been able to contact headquarters in weeks. He was surprised when a voice came over the line.

"Agent Johnson here, how can I help you?"

"Hey, this is Darien Pavoni from Los Angeles."

"Right! Of course! What can I help you with, Darien?"

The Vampire picked up the evidence bag and examined the bottle's label again. "I have an investigation that's tied to Colin Grayson. I have reason to believe he was possibly under the influence of a powerful Greater Demon with the ability to manipulate his mind. I also have reason to believe that the medication he was taking for his headaches had something to do with it. Did you happen to send any of those pills to a lab for analysis?"

"Give me a second..." Darien heard the clack of a keyboard on the other end of the line. "No, I don't believe we did."

"Okay, don't worry about it, I'll send them in." He set the bottle down with a frown.

"You said you suspect a Greater Demon was influencing his mind?" clarified Johnson.

"Yes, I have a witness who came forward and made the connection. If it's true, then the entire state has also been affected by this Demon. I've been trying to contact D.C. for reinforcements, but I can't get through."

A grinding noise appeared on the other end of the line that sounded suspiciously like a pencil sharpener. Darien could barely make out the agent's voice over it. "You can't count on H.Q. to back you up. Things are bad here. Information is being leaked left and right. I think Demons are watching me, too. I'm trying to find a way to deal with it, but there's a good chance they're on to me."

"What? How?" Johnson had just voiced Darien's worst fears. The Demons had already infiltrated high levels of the government.

"I don't know. I came back, and shit started hitting the fan."

"You should come out here."

"Maybe. I'm not sure I can leave, though. I need to stop these Demons if I can."

Darien passed a hand over his face. "You should know Ali's in critical condition. It's not looking good. Laila and Jerrik left to find a cure, so I'm the only field agent left in Los Angeles."

Johnson swore. "I'll see what I can do. In the meantime, be careful."

"Thanks, you too." Darien hung up and stared at the phone.

What was happening? How had the Demons made it into the headquarters of IRSA? What about the President and Congress? Both had been oddly quiet over the last several months. How could he fight a foe that controlled the government?

He tried Jenn, but her phone went straight to voicemail. The fact that he hadn't received any alerts led him to suspect she had them redirected to her phone instead. He wasn't sure he liked that, but it allowed him to focus on Lorelei. He left a message asking Jenn to call him as soon as possible. Then he packed up his laptop and any other gear he thought he might need. He would return Ligeia to the safehouse and go from there. He needed time to gather his thoughts anyway.

CHAPTER 18

When Darien arrived at the safehouse, the building was bustling with activity. The Witches still worked at the dining room table while Frej and Henrik cooked in the kitchen. Mato flipped through news stations while deep in discussion with Talen, and Erin appeared to be finished with the translation because she played chess in the corner with a woman who hadn't been there earlier.

Darien froze in the doorway, causing Ligeia to bump into him and swear in her own language. He barely noticed. His entire focus was on the dark-haired woman playing chess with Erin. She had a clean bob and wore a sleek black suit. The black stilettos with metallic spikes for heals looked positively lethal, and, knowing this Vampire, she probably *had* used them as weapons. The woman grinned broadly as she noticed him and wiggled her fingers in a wave. It was Sarnai, a member of the Vampire council, cold-blooded killer, and Darien's psycho ex-girlfriend.

He strode over to Talen. "What the hell were you thinking bringing her here?"

Darien indicated Sarnai, not caring that the entire room was staring at him. Granted, welcoming Sarnai into a safehouse was akin to inviting a pit viper into your home—no sane person would consider it.

Before Talen could reply, Sarnai rose and sauntered over to them. "Aw, and here I thought you would be glad to see me."

Darien didn't believe her disappointed pout for a second.

Talen clamped his hand on his shoulder and shot him a meaningful look, reminding him of his place in this hierarchy. "I called Sarnai because you need help, and I knew she'd be willing and able."

"*You* are help. Frej and Mato are help. She's a walking hurricane!"

Sarnai's smile only grew. "Don't worry, I missed you too, babe."

Darien looked at Talen and willed him to say something, but his sire's expression said Darien was on his own. He scanned the room and realized everyone was still staring at him. Whatever Frej was cooking was beginning to burn on the stove.

Darien clenched his jaw and turned to Sarnai. "Can I speak to you privately?"

Talen rolled his eyes but inclined his head towards his office. "Just try not to break anything."

The others gradually resumed their previous activities as he headed to the office. Darien planted his feet and crossed his arms, his jaw still clenched as Sarnai brushed past him and seated herself in an armchair as if it were her throne. She was enjoying this. He shut the door and turned to face her.

"You know, I like that little Dragon," she said in a voice smooth as silk. "I was wondering where you found her."

"Leave Erin alone." He glowered at the councilwoman.

She propped her chin on a perfectly manicured hand as she lounged in the chair. "Then what about the big one? He's easy on the eyes. I bet he's tasty too."

Darien knew she was goading him, but he fell for it anyway. "Stay away from them. All of them!"

"Is that a hint of jealousy I detect?" Her eyes sparked.

He took a deep breath and tried to rein in his temper. He reminded himself that Sarnai was one of the most powerful Vampires on the continent and could easily kill him for his insolence. Not that she would—she was far too fond of irritating Darien to kill him.

He met her while on assignment for Talen about a hundred years ago. Darien had no idea who she was, and beautiful women had always been his weakness. He didn't stand a chance when she seduced him. He believed he had found the most incredible woman in the world and followed her around for years until he realized the truth. The woman was a cold, heartless bitch. Talen had tried to warn him, but Darien wouldn't listen. Eventually, Darien came to his senses and realized how cruel she was, but Sarnai wasn't ready to give up her plaything.

Yet, despite their messy past, Talen did have a point. Darien needed help. He didn't have to worry about Sarnai's safety since she was harder to kill than a goddamned cockroach. She was also incredibly strong and deadly in a fight. The issue was that she was also a loose cannon.

Sarnai sat there waiting for him to organize his thoughts while she continued examining her nails with disinterest. Darien knew he had to say something.

Gritting his teeth, Darien said at last, "Look, I'll admit, we need help. Things are…bad. But you have to follow my lead."

Her grin widened to show her fangs. "You know you're so cute when you try to order me around."

Darien kept his expression neutral. "I mean it."

She stood and closed the distance between them. "Very well, I'll help you, but for a price." She lifted a hand to caress his face.

Darien resisted the urge to pull away. "Which is what?"

"A kiss," she purred, pressing one of her pointed nails into the skin beneath his chin.

He made a sound of disgust and shouldered past her. He felt as if the air in the room was growing thin. No matter how much he hated her, she always had an affected on him.

"What's the matter? You're not afraid, are you?" she taunted.

He felt more inclined to rip her throat out, but he needed the help. She could ask him for anything. A kiss was so simple...

He spun around and grabbed her roughly. His lips met hers for what should have been a moment, but her intoxicating scent washed over him, he was unable to pull away. He shouldn't be doing this. He was about to shove her away when one of her fangs pierced her lower lip. Darien growled as the taste of her blood hit him—there was no flavor more divine. It was just a single drop, but it was potent. He backed her to the wall, and her legs wrapped around him, driving him into a greater frenzy. More—he needed more.

He shoved away from her and nearly stumbled over a chair as he shook his head to clear the blood-induced haze. He should have known she would do that. It should have been obvious it was a trap.

She was like a drug—her body, her scent, and especially her blood. It was how she controlled Darien. For years he avoided her and distanced himself. He tried to forget that taste for decades, but it still haunted his dreams.

"That wasn't a part of the deal!" he hissed.

She tossed him a malicious look as she straitened her designer clothes. "That was just a bonus. Don't worry. I'll hold up my end of the bargain." Sarnai winked and left the room.

Darien sank down into a chair, his head in his hands. Why had he done it? Why did she always have to draw him back in? Darien witnessed her commit unspeakable crimes. She slaughtered villages on a whim and tortured prisoners for sport. The only reason she hadn't been damned was that she was too smart to get caught. It made him sick, so why was he still attracted to her?

There was a click as the door opened, and Darien looked up to find Talen.

Darien fought the growl creeping in his throat. "I know you did it because I won't feel guilty about placing her in danger. But was that really necessary?"

Talen folded his arms and leaned against the door, his expression unreadable. "We're fighting monsters, Darien. At least this one's on our side. You know as well as I do she could easily be tempted to flip sides, and we can't afford to have another member of the council turn on us."

Darien hadn't thought of that. The reason the Vampire rebellion had managed to grow so large was that a local councilman named Dagan had been covering for them. Once the other councilmembers found out, Dagan had been punished and stripped of his status. Talen had ascended in his place, joining the council and immersing himself in their politics.

Darien shook his head. "But why me? She could choose any other person on the face of the Earth! Why does it always have to be me?"

Talen barked a laugh. "Because you're the only one with the balls to say no." Then his expression sobered. "You're stronger now, Darien—strong enough to resist her lure. I would not have allowed her in here otherwise."

That was true. Despite tasting Sarnai's blood, Darien didn't feel the same urge he once had to please her. He was no longer under her control. It still left him craving her, but the desire was manageable.

Darien rolled his eyes. "Fine, I'll put up with her, but only because I'm running out of options. I received confirmation the Demons have infiltrated the higher levels of the agency. This isn't just about Los Angeles anymore—it's about this entire country, and maybe even the world."

Talen frowned at the door. "All the more reason to keep the rest of the council close. If this turns into a free-for-all, we'll need them."

They left the office, and Darien crossed over to the table where the Witches worked. Both Lyn and Donald were pouring over books with the cursed blade resting inside its case before them.

"Anything new?" he asked, taking a seat.

Lyn shook her head, her gaze bleak. "Erin was able to translate the inscription, but we still can't find a way to break the curse." She lowered her voice and glanced at Erin. "I think it got her hopes up, but she's more miserable than ever. We're trying to keep her distracted."

He looked over his shoulder toward Erin, who watched the television. "What do we do now?"

Donald shut his book. "Honestly, we're better off applying ourselves elsewhere."

Lyn nodded. "I'm going to speak to Ligeia about any spells that might help us deal with Lorelei."

"And I've got some more prototypes that might help," added Donald.

"Any chance you could analyze these? I think Lorelei tampered with them." Darien held up the evidence bag with the pill bottle. It was lighter than before since he had sent a couple of the pills off to a lab, but it wouldn't hurt to have the Witches take a look.

Lyn pulled on a pair of gloves and removed a pill from the bottle. "I'll see what I can find, but unless there's something magical in them, I'm not sure we'll be of much help."

That was good enough for him. He figured the Siren would be able to help as well. He went over to the sofa where Erin sat and gave her an update on Ali, emphasizing that she was safe with the new security detail.

"I'll check on her again before sunrise," he added.

Erin avoided his gaze. "When can I go back?"

"I'm not sure. Maybe I can arrange something for tomorrow."

"And what about Mr. Whiskers? He's still at the house."

"I'll be sure to stop by and feed him."

She gave him a small nod. He didn't know what else to say,

so he turned to the two Vampire elders watching the television with grim expressions. Fredrik Stacy was on, hosting a press conference.

The Governor stood behind a podium onscreen. "California is in a state of crisis. I cannot stand by while more and more violence breaks out across the state. To cope with this chaos, I have decided to establish a new division of state law enforcement. Starting tomorrow, my California State Troopers will take to the streets to ensure the safety and protection of California's residents."

Darien scowled. This was the first he had heard of these state troopers. The state disbanded the California Highway Patrol after The Event since its resources were needed in the cities. No one had established a new form of state police until now.

"Mr. Stacy, are you implying you would be willing to declare martial law in order to deal with the Supernatural conflicts in the state?" asked a reporter off-screen.

"Yes. Yes, I am, if that's what it takes," declared the governor. Behind him lurked Lorelei, studying him attentively. Darien wondered how much of this speech was the Demon's. The State Troopers were probably her idea as well. He feared they were up to something.

Darien stood. "I'm heading back to the office for a few hours. I want to make sure everything is under control with the other team while I can."

"What about the Greater Demon?" Talen asked.

Darien shrugged. "I'll have to wait until morning to call the judge for a search warrant for her house. I'm certain she tampered with Colin's medication, but I need proof that she's a Siren. Until then, I might as well make myself useful."

"Great! I'll grab my purse, and we can go!" Sarnai announced.

Darien gave Talen a look. It was going to be a long night. He strode to the garage to wait for Sarnai, grumbling as he went.

CHAPTER 19

The next morning, the Grandmaster summoned Jerrik to a meeting regarding the trials. While he was gone, Laila poured over the ancient tomes in the hall of records where a group of elderly Swordmasters maintained detailed accounts of the order's history. They had been gracious enough to allow her to read through their archives. Together, Laila and the record keepers had spent hours digging through any entries that mentioned divine and mortal interactions but unfortunately came up blank. There were records of Gods gifting magical swords, charms, and other objects of power to mortals, but nothing close to Laila's abilities.

She eventually gave up and decided to sit with Master Okaenos by a large, arching window overlooking the garden in the center of the temple complex. She stared down at the variety of plants, from the large species native to Jotunheim to smaller plants from the other worlds. There were glowing purple lilies the Fae used to honor the dead and several other plants from her homeworld, but much of the vegetation was unfamiliar. She wondered which one was the Eirflower.

"Now you're certain you're not a Demigod? Both of your parents were truly Elves?" Master Okaenos propped his head in a hand as he stared up at a mosaic depicting the Valkyries flying into battle. He still seemed determined to help Laila find answers.

"Yes, quite certain. This change came on recently."

But was she? Only a few months ago, Talen had asked her the same thing. Was it possible that she had a divine ancestor? How could that be possible, though? She couldn't imagine her mother having an affair. Perhaps the magic came from an older forebearer? But if that were true, why was she the only one experiencing these abilities? The whole thing didn't make sense.

The Swordmaster tilted his head. "Any items involved or magical substances consumed that could trigger these changes?"

She shook her head. "Not that I know of. After my first encounter with the Goddess, I had a wound on my back heal miraculously. A few weeks later, I used the powers for the first time and accidentally conjured a dagger. Over time, the power grew, and eventually, I had to work with Arduinna to learn how to wield it. Unfortunately, I don't seem to have mastered it—at least not to the degree I would like. It's too unpredictable, and I don't trust it."

He nodded, scrutinizing the necklace she wore. "What about that?"

Laila ran a finger over the faintly glowing moonstone. "The same Goddess who gave me the powers gave me this. She said it would help me control them, but it doesn't seem to help. If anything, I feel less in control of the outbursts now."

Master Okaenos seemed at a loss, and it wasn't long before his duties called him away. With his departure, Laila decided to explore the halls. The clash of steel echoed through the corridor where she wandered. She paused when she caught a glimpse of a familiar figure. Jerrik faced Master Manach in the center of the training room. They cut and parried in a whirl of steel as the Swordmaster barked notes to Jerrik. The prince breathed heavily, and sweat soaked his tunic. Master Manach certainly wasn't taking it easy on him.

In Laila's opinion, there was nothing quite as entrancing as watching two skilled warriors fight. It left her in awe and drew her in. She leaned against the doorframe, caught up in the fight unfolding. She was used to rough and dirty skirmishes, and it had been a long time since she watched a bout such as this.

In one elegant move, Master Manach slipped past Jerrik's guard and brought the edge of a blade to rest against his exposed neck.

"Not bad, but you could use more practice," declared the Swordmaster. He sheathed his sword and inclined his head. "That's enough for today. I don't want to exhaust you before the trials tomorrow, although I suppose we could make this more interesting and add Laila to the exercise."

Laila realized she had intruded and felt her face warm. "Sorry. I couldn't help it."

Master Manach chuckled. "Well, maybe tomorrow then. It's almost time for dinner anyway."

Laila hadn't considered the time or how hungry she was. All that research had taken longer than she had thought. They entered the dining hall, where a few Swordmasters laid out the meal. Laila offered to help one of the Swordmasters who passed her a stack of baskets filled with freshly baked bread. She distributed them amongst the tables while Jerrik set out pitchers with some type of ale.

Word of Jerrik's identity and intentions of undergoing the trials must have spread. The people chatted excitedly and were eager to give him advice. After a dinner of roasted fish and vegetables, they gathered around to laugh and drink. Laila's magic burned through the alcohol, counteracting its effects. It was probably for the best, though. This was perhaps one of the safest locations in the worlds, but there was always a chance that more Demons could track them here and launch an attack.

Jerrik had been pulled away by a group of Swordmasters

telling stories of their trials. Laila remained with Master Manach, who seemed more withdrawn than the others.

"What exactly do these trials entail?" she asked the dark-haired Fae.

"They are a series of tests designed not only to test a person's skill but their judgment and character. There's a panel of masters—typically the oldest and wisest amongst us—that will assess him. The trials are different for each individual, and their performance in one area will typically influence the trials to follow. Some are physical, while others are more abstract."

"Am I able to watch?" she asked, intrigued.

He shook his head. "Only the Masters administering the trials may observe. I won't even be allowed in."

Laila nodded. Such secrecy wasn't uncommon among orders such as this. Even the elite Royal Guard that her father belonged to had secret rites of their own. "Do you think he's ready?"

The Swordmaster paused and stared into the depths of his tankard. "I'm not sure. He's well trained, but his weakness may be his resolve. He's been running from his past for too long. As royalty, he will have to prove that he can take charge and rule. I have no idea how the Grandmaster intends to test him in that regard."

That was worrisome, not only because Jerrik needed to pass these trials to obtain the Eirflower, but because there were many people in his kingdom counting on him to step up and take the throne someday.

"Which one is the Grandmaster?" She looked around at the others.

"Grandmaster Zorion isn't here. Both Master Bas and the Grandmaster are preparing for the trials tomorrow," he said, then sipped his ale. He noticed Laila was no longer drinking hers. "Does something have you on edge?"

She fidgeted absently with her necklace. "I'm just worried about my friend—the one who needs the Eirflower. So many things seem intent on distracting me from that task—my powers, the turmoil in Jerrik's kingdom… I have to get the Eirflower back to Midgard, but how can I leave his people to suffer? I know it's not necessarily my problem, but I can't shake the feeling I still need to act."

Master Manach chuckled. "You have the opposite problem of Jerrik. You realize that, right? You feel obligated to protect everyone."

She shook her head. "I don't think he's running from his responsibility. He simply doesn't know how to proceed. The rebels don't have the resources needed to make a move, and it was their idea to send him away. In Midgard, it was obvious he could help protect the people by joining IRSA. He likes it there for the same reason I do—we can help others. In Nidavellir, he felt powerless."

The Swordmaster studied her. "You know, you would make an excellent Swordmaster. You have the mind of one."

She gave a soft laugh. "I think I already have more than enough on my plate, but I appreciate it."

He shrugged and watched the others laughing by the fire. "If you want my advice about your dilemma, I'd say you should find a way to help Jerrik. His people may not have the ability to start a revolution, but I suspect you do. I don't believe it was a mere coincidence fate took you to Nidavellir—your quest is just the catalyst to show where your help is needed."

Laila eyed Jerrik joking with the Swordmasters. Perhaps fate had brought them together so that she could help his people in their time of need. It didn't ease the tight feeling in her chest when Laila thought of Ali, though. She excused herself and returned to the guest quarters.

Flopping down on a sofa before a crackling hearth, Laila kicked off her boots and pulled her knees up to her chin. There had to be a way to fix all of this. What if she could just teleport back to Midgard? She had never attempted an inter-world teleportation, and there was no one here to walk her through it. If anything went wrong, she could be trapped in that endless space between the worlds. The thought sent a shiver down her spine. Maybe she could sneak through the portal back to Los Angeles and return to help Jerrik after she took the flower to the hospital. Alone, it should be easy enough to sneak through in disguise. That was probably the most logical solution, but then she would have to leave Jerrik behind.

The door opened behind her, and Jerrik walked in. He wavered slightly on his feet, and his grin was a little too broad. Clearly, he hadn't shied away from the ale.

"There you are! I was looking for you." He leaned over the back of the sofa to peer into her face. "Did you know you are far more beautiful than any of the Ladies of my father's court?"

Laila wrinkled her nose at the sour stench of ale on his breath. "Jerrik, you're drunk."

"They have all the intelligence and strength of a bouquet of flowers, but you're practical and deadly, like a knife." He climbed over the back of the sofa and plopped down beside her.

Laila rolled her eyes. "Wow. How romantic."

"You should be flattered! A knife blends in, and you can easily conceal it, but it's also fast, graceful, and lethal. Far more arousing than frills and petals if you ask me." He leaned blissfully against the cushions as if he didn't have a care in the world. The light from the fire cast a warm glow on his silver skin and strong, angular face.

"Jerrik, your trials are in the morning," she chastised. "How could you get drunk the night before?"

"That ale is excellent. You know, I think I'm going to go get a little more—" Jerrik started to rise.

Laila grabbed his sleeve and pulled him back down. "Oh no you don't. You are going to bed and sleeping this off."

He acquiesced and sat on top of her—something he didn't seem to mind at all. Laila grunted under his weight and shoved him off of her.

"Very well, I'll stay." He shifted until his head was in her lap with his long black hair draping over her legs. "Besides, I'd rather stay here with you."

She scowled. "I'm not your damned pillow."

He ignored her. "You can try to deny it all you want, but I know you can't stay away from me either. We're connected. What I don't get is why you're so determined to fight it."

Laila opened her mouth but found all valid arguments had evaporated. Yes, he had hurt her before, but she couldn't even use that against him. She could use her relationship with Frej, but she wasn't sure he would ever be able to love her in the way he loved Regina. Was it just her stubbornness that cautioned her?

Jerrik sat up on the sofa beside her as he took her hand in his. He suddenly seemed far more sober, and she wondered if it was all just an act. "Are you afraid I will hurt you again?"

Laila needed room to breathe. She hastily stood and started to walk away, but Jerrik jumped up and caught her waist.

"Stop running from me, please? Just tell me what you're thinking. Talk to me," his eyes pleaded with hers.

She looked up and stopped fighting. "I don't know what to say. We belong to two different worlds."

"Maybe you should stop worrying about that. A war is on the horizon, and we don't even know if we'll survive. All I want is a chance for us to be happy. Is that too much to ask?"

His words caught Laila off guard. She was the sort of person who planned contingencies, but Jerrik had a point—none of their futures were certain, not even hers. It was impossible to know what the next year would bring. She had to find a way to stop the Demons, and there was so much she still needed to learn. Her task seemed impossible, and if she failed, the price would be unimaginable. Who knew if there would be a safe haven left by the time the Demons finished their conquest?

"You're right. We don't know what the future holds," she whispered.

That same overwhelming uncertainty that plagued her

dreams crept back. Death, destruction, the desolation of the worlds: those were the premonitions that haunted her nightmares. The Demons would wipe everything and everyone she cared for from the worlds. Her greatest fear was that one day she would be left alone standing in the middle of the battlefield as lifeless faces stared up at the heavens and crows leisurely picked at their flesh. It was a fate she was desperate to prevent, but how?

"But I'll be here with you. You don't have to face this alone." He brushed stray strands of auburn hair from her face and tucked them behind her ear.

"I'd like that." A hot tear rolled down her cheek as she kissed him.

Maybe he was a distraction. Maybe Laila was playing into the Demons' hands, but she couldn't do this alone.

CHAPTER 20

The harsh scent of antiseptics and blood clogged Laila's nostrils as she sprinted through the hospital. Blood splattered the walls and soaked the floor, her feet splashing through it as she ran. It appeared to be the sight of a massacre, but there was not a single body in view. What in the worlds had happened here?

Laila didn't have time to think about it. She was running out of time. Ali was dying, and Laila had to get the Eirflower to her. She searched the empty rooms but found no sign of the Fae.

"Ali!" Laila screamed. The hospital was eerily silent.

She rounded another corner and nearly slipped as she came to a halt. Ali stood in the middle of the hall.

"Thank the Gods you're okay!" Laila's legs wobbled from relief.

Her respite was short-lived as she noticed the cursed blade in Ali's chest. Tendrils of sickly grey magic wrapped around her friend's body, and old, dried blood stained the hospital gown. The scent of decay hung heavy in the air.

Ali cocked her head to the side, her face blank and pale.

"You did this. This is your fault."

"What?" Laila asked uncertainly.

"You abandoned us. You let the Demons kill me!" she shrieked.

Behind her, others emerged from rooms—doctors, nurses, patients, even her friends. They moved slowly at first, stumbling in odd, disjointed ways. Laila thought they were injured, but they seemed to feel no pain as they shambled forward. There was no blood seeping from their wounds either. Laila's skin crawled—they were Zombies.

Ali took a step forward, then another, snarling as she picked up momentum. The other Zombies followed. Laila backed away, only to trip over a mass and tumble to the ground. It was another corpse crawling along the floor. The bloated hand twitched, then lashed out and wrapped its fingers around her ankle.

Laila kicked at the Zombie to free herself, but the weight of another body collided with her as Ali pinned her to the ground. Her cracked nails dug into Laila's skin as Ali's hands wrapped around her throat.

"You let me die! I died because of you!" Ali wailed.

Laila tried to speak, but the blood surrounding her pooled deeper. She opened her mouth to scream, and the blood poured in, filling her mouth and nose. Ali continued to pin her to the ground, forcing her to drown, while the other Zombies piled on top to tear at her hair and limbs—

With a gasp, Laila bolted upright. She searched her surroundings but saw no blood, no hospital, and no Zombies. She was still at the Swordmasters' temple.

She took several deep breaths to steady herself. The dreams were getting worse and more vivid. In each one, she tried to save Ali, but she was always too late. The Zombies were a new twist, though. Perhaps her mind was struggling to come up with new ways to torture her. It certainly worked.

Jerrik slept deeply, utterly unaware as Laila crept around in her alcove. She pulled on a fresh tank top before donning jeans and boots. Laila hoped she would feel better after a walk, so she eased the door open and snuck out of the guest quarters.

The Swordmasters had magically dimmed the lanterns lining the hall for the night. She walked along the silent corridor back toward the empty dining hall, then beyond it to the hallway where arches opened to the garden at the heart of the temple. As she leaned against a pillar, she realized the garden was far more massive than she had thought. It appeared smaller from the floors above, but it seemed as thick and dense as a forest from here. Earlier she spied a building at the center, but it wasn't even visible through the foliage now.

Above, the sky had shifted to the darkest shade of plum, with a pale pink moon that bathed the courtyard in an ethereal light. The sweet scent of night-blooming flowers beckoned to her through the arches, drawing her in. The Swordmasters had told her this inner part of the temple was off-limits, but surely she could admire the garden's beauty from here. Slowly, she meandered the hall along the arches, savoring the tranquility.

"I told you she'd come," whispered a smug voice.

Laila spun, blue flame crackling at her fingertips. A part of her was expecting Demons to emerge. Instead, two figures in white stepped from the shadow of the arch leading to the garden.

The shorter Swordmaster was Master Bas with his cat-like face. The other was tall and lean. There was no hair on their chin or head, and they had no discernable gender. It occured to Laila that they could be non-bianary. This Swordmaster's eyes shone the same solid blue as polished lapis lazuli, and their skin was pale blue with patches of green.

The Swordmaster cast a cool look at Master Bas before turning back to Laila. "Allow me to introduce myself properly. I am Grandmaster Zorion, the head of our order."

"A pleasure to meet you, but why did you think I would come here?" She looked from one Swordmaster to another.

The Grandmaster motioned for her to follow them into the garden along a rambling path. "Merely a hunch. Master Bas tells me the worlds outside grow chaotic."

Laila nodded. "The Demons grow stronger. At this rate, I'm worried Midgard will fall to them. Svartalfheim too."

Master Bas shook his head. "Jerrik mentioned the Greater Demons. I find this to be extremely concerning. We should be out there helping to right the balance instead of staying in the temple's safety."

A muscle twitched in the Grandmaster's jaw. "It is a necessary precaution. Master Kyvik was proof of that."

Master Bas flinched and looked away.

"What do you mean? What's he got to do with this?" Laila asked.

The Grandmaster halted on the path. "I made a difficult decision after King Oddvarr killed Master Kyvik. I chose to have the Swordmasters return to the temple. They had experienced varying degrees of mistrust, and it became clear the worlds did not value our wisdom as they once did."

Laila's eyes grew wide. "You mean, you've all been living in here for years?"

Master Bas nodded. "And clearly the worlds have spiraled deeper into chaos. It's time for us to return and help."

Laila thought of the oppression she had seen in the streets of Nidavellir. "Many of the lands get by as best they can, but the corruption I saw in Jerrik's kingdom was chilling. I'm not sure how many other kingdoms are suffering the same fate."

"The prince is one of the topics we wished to discuss with you," admitted the Grandmaster as they resumed walking. "I faced King Oddvarr long ago and denied him access to the temple. Even back then, there was a treacherous streak in him born of mistrust and misguidance from a childhood in the hands of the court. Master Kyvik and the queen groomed Jerrik to take his place and to ensure he wouldn't follow in his father's footsteps. But unfortunately, Jerrik seems to have strayed from his path."

Laila wasn't sure she liked where this conversation was going. "Shouldn't you be speaking to Jerrik about this directly?"

The Grandmaster nodded. "All in good time. But as someone with great power, you know there are consequences for those who run from their destinies. If the prince does not make a move against his father soon, it may be too late. I fear the Demons will all too easily exploit King Oddvarr's hunger for power."

"That's assuming it hasn't happened already," added Laila.

The two masters nodded grimly.

Laila pondered this as she brushed past a large fern. "Is this why you want Jerrik to join your order. The trials have nothing to do with the Eirflower, do they?"

"You're correct. I could simply give you the flower, but Jerrik needs to remember who he is. The trials will reveal that and so much more."

"*If* he passes. It has been years since he had any guidance," pointed out Master Bas.

Laila's stomach knotted with unease. She didn't like keeping secrets from people. She couldn't quite argue that they were wrong, but whether or not Jerrik chose to challenge his father's rule was Jerrik's choice to make.

The Grandmaster passed beneath the branches of a tree with leaves red as blood. "There is something else we wanted to bring to your attention. Our predecessors built this temple thousands of years ago to provide us with a sanctuary, but also to safeguard objects and knowledge of great importance."

They reached the edge of a pool. At first glance, it appeared to be an ordinary pond until Laila noticed the hum of magic surrounding it.

"This is known as the Well of Knowledge. It reaches far below to a root of Yggdrasil—the magical tree of life that binds our worlds together. It is said the God Odin gave his eye to the well in exchange for the knowledge it contained. Its waters are too powerful. None of our order are permitted access. Thus, why access to this garden is restricted."

"I'm honored to have glimpsed it," said Laila.

Master Bas chuckled. "That's not the only reason we brought you here. Look up."

Laila followed his gaze to a massive mosaic inlaid along a wall above the Well of Knowledge. In the image, a lone figure seemed to be fighting a mass of shadows. Her auburn hair flowed behind her as she charged. Both her eyes and the markings on her arms were bright blue.

The Grandmaster stared at the mosaic. "There is a prophecy regarding a divine being who would visit this temple in search of knowledge."

Laila surveyed her likeness, her hands trembling. This was all too much. "How is this possible?"

Master Bas answered, "Some stories are foretold by fate many years before they're set into motion. All we know of yours is that a time of such great imbalance will come that the Norns themselves will deem it necessary to intervene."

The Norns—Goddesses of Fate. The Goddess that gave her these powers had never identified herself, but she had been incredibly powerful. Could it be that she was a Norn? The stone in Laila's necklace seemed to pulse in response.

Laila scanned the image again, looking more closely. She noticed her likeness held a sword with a pale stone embedded in the pommel. Upon closer inspection, it appeared the rock was a moonstone, just as the one in the pommel of her dagger.

A pale light shimmered in the well's depths, drawing her attention.

"What's that? Is something down there?" Laila asked, leaning in.

The Grandmaster frowned. "I've never seen this happen before. Perhaps you should step back—"

It was as if an invisible hand gabbed Laila by the front of her shirt. She lurched forward and cried out in shock. There was barely time to gasp for breath before she was plunged into the Well of Knowledge and pulled down into the depths toward the glowing light far below.

CHAPTER 21

Laila was pulled deeper into the Well of Knowledge, speeding towards the light far below. Her lungs screamed for air, and she feared she would drown. Suddenly, the water vanished, and Laila found herself kneeling on a stone floor gasping for air. She was no longer in the garden but in an old stone temple surrounded by massive pillars made of trees carved from stone. They reached overhead, the branches forming a system of arching supports.

There was no sign of the Well of Knowledge or the Swordmasters' temple. From the shift in the overwhelming amount of magic radiating from her surroundings, she suspected that she was in another world, but which one? And how could she pass through a portal without stepping between the worlds unless she managed to teleport somehow? She didn't think it was a coincidence she had been brought here, but who had summoned her and why?

Laila studied this new temple searching for clues. The images on the walls contained a wide array of Supernaturals. They were organized in a variety of scenes carved into the walls along horizontal bands. It occurred to her these represented each of the worlds. At the bottom layer was Muspelheim or Hell, and at the top Asgard, where the Gods looked down at the other worlds. Everything was covered in moss and vines as if the care-takers abandoned the temple long ago.

Water dripped from her clothes, creating a puddle around her boots. She dried herself with a spell then wandered through the temple, which was as silent as a crypt in an unearthly way. No birds chirped, no bugs hummed. It was a deep and eerie silence. Only the sound was that of her footsteps.

"Hello?" she called. Her voice echoed off the stone. There was no response.

Where in the worlds was she?

Laila continued through the pillars until she reached the end of the temple. Three women in billowing gowns were carved into the stone above a large dais. Beneath the carvings sat three empty thrones. Was this a temple of the Norns? It made sense that it would be, yet there was not a soul in sight.

Laila continued her search and found a staircase that spi-raled upward. With nowhere else to go, she climbed up and, at the top, encountered an unlocked wooden door. It opened into an apartment.

She took a hesitant step forward. "Hello?"

Before Laila was a sitting area crowded with so much stuff that it had been heaped in stacks on any available surface. Books piled high above her head on tables, and the chairs contained mounds of blankets, clothes, and boxes overflowing with a whole manner of objects. There was everything from mundane items such as teacups and frying pans to opulent tiaras dripping with jewels. Clocks ticked, and gears whirled on odd little ma-chines. A skull from some sort of creature had been upturned and used as a makeshift vessel to hold a bouquet of dead flow-ers.

Amidst the junk, Laila spotted a woman in a frumpy orange sweater who practically defined the term ancient. Her white hair hung so long it pooled on the ground around her feet. It almost mixed with the fibers she spun into thread with an old drop spindle. She grinned up at Laila with bright, child-like eyes peering out of her wrinkled face. They were such a dark shade of blue Laila thought they could be black.

Had she stepped through a portal? Or was this woman a caretaker of the temple below?

The older woman cackled and sat up straighter in her chair. "Haha! Well, what do you know, the girl decided to show up after all! Verdani! Come here!"

From the other room entered a middle-aged woman with long dark hair trailing past her hips. She was clad in a simple but worn gown with patches in a few places. Her eyes were shrewd and gave the impression she was slightly irritated.

"What's all the commotion about? Don't tell me you ran out of fiber already—" she stopped short as she noticed Laila. "Huh. I guess I owe Senere that ring. The Elf actually showed up."

"What's going on? Who are you?" asked Laila as she looked from one woman to the other.

She did not think they were humans, but they didn't look like any other creature she had met. They felt divine, but she had a hard time imagining a pair of Goddesses living in such a horrible mess. Or in such a rustic, modest apartment, for that matter. The old stone bricks were already starting to crumble in places.

The older woman chuckled. "Oh dear, I don't think she knows, does she?"

The younger one sniffed. "Of course she doesn't. Senere! Your Elf is here!"

"Oh! While you get Senere, can you also water the plant? The poor thing is probably parched," requested the elderly woman as she returned her focus to spinning.

The younger muttered something under her breath as she vanished through the piles of books.

"Um, excuse me?" called Laila. She followed the woman

into a kitchen where she stuck an old bucket into a grimy sink and switched on the faucet. "I don't mean to bother you, but I'm not sure how I got here."

"Patience girl, Senere will explain. She gets grumpy when I do her work for her. She's sort of particular about that sort of thing. Senere! Hurry up!" she bellowed.

The woman switched off the faucet and hauled the bucket out of the sink with a grunt of effort.

"Here, let me help," offered Laila, taking the bucket from her.

"Ah, good. I'm too old to be hauling buckets anyway. Just dump it out the window there, would you?" She waved to a window at the other end of the room.

Laila did as she was told and carried the bucket over to the window. She set it on the windowsill and started to tip the water out when she noticed the enormous tree. This tower was nestled in the trunk of a tree with wide branches spreading out above. Laila looked down and found the roots stretched so far below that a thick mist obscured them. The tree was easily the size of a mountain if not larger, and as she tipped out the remaining water in the bucket, she wondered what good a measly bucket of water would do for a tree of this size.

"Quite a sight, isn't it?" The woman seated herself at the cluttered table. "Few from your world have ever laid eyes on Yggdrasill."

Laila froze. Yggdrasill was the legendary tree of life that was said to connect the various worlds. It was tended to by the Norns—or Fates as some called them. But if this woman was watering the tree...

"You're a Norn," said Laila in shock.

The woman cracked a smile. "Well, I suppose you're not entirely ignorant, are you?"

According to legend, the Norns were the most powerful beings in all the worlds—even the Gods bowed to them. They were known by many names, and their purpose was to weave the tapestry of life, which controlled each individual's fate.

Laila looked around at the mess of a kitchen and found it hard to believe these were indeed the Norns. She expected beings of such exalted status to live in a grand palace with dozens of attendants—not a small tower apartment in desperate need of a deep clean. The Norns didn't dress like bag ladies and medieval peasants, did they?

"What in the worlds is all the fuss about?" A young woman swept into the room. Her appearance was far different from the others. Her long white gown billowed around her as she came to an abrupt stop. Her skin was as flawless as a fresh blanket of snow on a winter morning. Her pale hair was the color of moonbeams, and she held herself with all the elegance of royalty. But of all her beautiful features, it was her eyes that Laila focused on—they were a bright electric blue. It was not the first time she had seen these eyes, but each time they vanished, she had been unable to recall them. There was no blinding light or epic display of power, but Laila knew with certainty that the woman who stood before her was the mysterious Goddess who visited her.

"Ah, there you are, Senere! This is your pet, isn't it?" asked the dark-haired woman.

The Norn—Senere—looked Laila over. "She's the one I've chosen if that's what you mean. I told you precisely when to expect her, so it shouldn't come as a surprise—" She narrowed her eyes at the bucket in Laila's hands. "Verdani, please tell me you didn't give her access to the Well of Fate!"

Verdani held up her hands in surrender. "Relax, she was just carrying the bucket for me."

Senere marched over to Laila and snatched the empty bucket from her hands. "Rule number one: don't go near the Well of Fate—it's dangerous for your kind."

Just as the Well of Knowledge was of legendary significance, so was the Well of Fate the Norns used to water the tree. From the stories she heard as a child, the well possessed incredible magical properties shrouded in mystery.

Laila glanced at the grimy sink incredulously. "You mean *that's* the Well of Fate?"

Verdani shrugged. "You didn't really think we'd haul the water out of the well by hand, did you? Plumbing is not just for mortals, you know."

This was all too much. Was it some kind of joke? Was it a test the Swordmasters arranged? There was no way any of this was real.

"Oh dear, she looks a little ill." Verdani eyed Laila with concern.

Senere shot Verdani a look, then snapped her fingers. The room around them vanished, and Laila and Senere stood alone in the old temple below.

"Please excuse my sisters—their ages have addled their brains. This wasn't how I expected this encounter to go, but I suppose the tapestry had other plans." She shook her head.

The Tapestry of Fate. It was a record of every life—past, present, and future.

Laila looked at the images carved into the wall above the dais. "The other woman, Verdani, said you were Norns."

Senere nodded. "We are. Wyrd—the eldest—deals with the past. Verdani handles the present, and I the future. Our accommodations may seem a little unusual, but that is mostly because of the other two. They insisted that humble accommodations and clothing were more comfortable. It's absurd as if they've completely forgotten the significance of our positions. They can't even tidy the place. I suppose that's what happens when you spend an eon locked away in an apartment."

Laila watched the haughty Goddess with uncertainty. This was not what she expected, especially after their previous encounters. These Norns seemed so…ordinary.

"Don't be ridiculous. You are equally capable of cleaning," snapped Verdani as she appeared beside the other Norn.

Wyrd appeared as well, her long hair trailing on the ground.

She wrung her hands, clearly upset. "Oh, I hate this dismal place! Why would you bring her down here? You can't even enjoy a cup of tea."

Senere was clearly irked by the intrusion. "I brought her here for some peace and quiet, something you are both oblivious to. Besides, this hall was our original home."

They started to argue amongst themselves, and Laila worried they had forgotten she was there. She cleared her throat. "Why am I here? I take it you have something to do with these powers I've acquired, but I don't understand what you expect me from me."

A voice in her head reminded her she should be more careful. If she was actually speaking to the Norns, they deserved a great deal of respect. But it was hard to take them seriously. Senere seemed the most dignified, but with the constant interruptions, it ruined the effect. This was like watching a bad sitcom.

Wyrd clasped her hands and turned to Laila. "Sorry, dear. Many millennia in isolation seems to do a number on our manners. Senere, would you like to explain?"

The youngest Norn nodded stiffly. "As my sister just mentioned, we have been in isolation for thousands of years. We can see much from our tower, but we rarely leave since there is always so much work to do. But recently, we've been faced with a difficult conundrum."

She snapped her fingers, and the surroundings shifted again. They now stood in another large chamber lit by a variety of lamps. Hanging in the center of the room was a rippling, multicolored fabric. It looked similar to the rainbow bridges of magic that connected portals, only far more intricate.

"This is the Tapestry of Fate—woven from the magic of Yggdrasill. Each thread corresponds with the fate of an individual as it intertwines amongst the others. Ordinarily, the path is clear, and the tapestry is woven easily without disruption, but lately, this has been happening." She strode over to one edge where the tapestry had begun to fray. "We noticed this a few years back and have done our best to repair it, but to no avail."

Wyrd eased herself into a chair and conjured a cup of tea. "You see, the problem is that we are stuck here, and the source of the disruption is in the other worlds."

Senere nodded. "We are the guardians of this tapestry. We do not leave our tower unless the situation is dire. So, it has become clear to us a champion is needed to handle this situation. That is what you have been chosen for—to enact our will in the worlds and correct the imbalance created by the Demons."

Laila shook her head. "Why not tell me sooner? Why not explain this in the beginning when we met rather than giving me cryptic messages?"

The youngest Norn cast her a stern look. "Then was not the time. There was more you needed to see and experience before you were ready to hear the full truth. You've known the Demons were a threat, but not the full scope of the matter. Their influence has spread far, and their schemes cause the tapestry to unravel faster than ever. If their path continues unchecked, the tapestry will unravel entirely."

Even as Laila watched, she could see the strands of the tapestry slowly untangling themselves. Some of them even blackened and crumbled. "What happens if the tapestry unravels?"

Verdani cocked her head at the tapestry. "No one knows for sure, but lately, I've noticed branches of Yggdrasill growing sickly as well, and the two are magically connected. If the tree dies, I suppose the magic that stems from it and flows into the worlds will die as well. Life would be destroyed, and the worlds left barren."

"And at the center of it all stands one woman," added Wyrd, shuffling up to the tapestry. She grasped a grey thread in between two fingers. It writhed as if trying to free itself as Wyrd wrinkled her nose in disgust. "This is the lifeline of a woman called Izel, who was supposed to die long ago but cheated her fate."

Laila frowned at the grey strand, struggling to free itself.

"I've heard the name. Who is she exactly?"

The older woman released the thread and watched it slither back into the tapestry. "She was a human once, but her quest for power took her on a dark and twisted path. She discovered a spell that would give her the powers of a Death God. Thus, the first strand tugged loose. Naturally, the Gods sent her to Hell, but there, her powers and influence grew like a cancer. By the time we discovered the hole, it was already too late to intervene."

Senere seized the opportunity to regain control of the conversation. "Luckily, I had planned for an unforeseen danger such as this. I found a way to ensure a warrior would rise in our time of need to be our champion in the worlds. We have given you a portion of our abilities to provide you with the strength you will need to fight Izel and her Demonic army." She waved to the moonstone necklace around Laila's throat. "That necklace is your link to us. It helps you control your powers and allows you to communicate with me as needed."

Laila brushed her fingers over the necklace. "I can't control the power, though. It lashes out and causes destruction."

"Only of those who oppose us," insisted Senere, unconcerned.

Laila wasn't sure she accepted that answer. The other two Norns exchanged subtle glances, but didn't speak up. She was missing something, but there were so many questions surfacing in her mind she didn't know where to begin.

"Can you teach me how to use these powers? Perhaps how to travel between the worlds?" she asked, looking around at the three Norns.

Senere sighed. "We already have more work than we can handle as we struggle with the tapestry, but we have another servant. He's worked for us for centuries."

In a whirl of wind and feathers, another figure materialized beside Senere. He was handsome with dark hair and glowing silver eyes. His dark clothing was unadorned, aside from the silver insignia of Yggdrasil embroidered on his chest. At his hip hung a sword of similar craftsmanship as her dagger, and he had a pair of massive white wings tucked behind his back. He was an Angel.

Senere motioned to the Angel. "Luc, I'd like you to meet Laila. She's our chosen emissary in the mortal worlds. Luc is our messenger in Asgard. He'll be able to guide and teach you how to control your powers fully."

Luc eyed Laila with a distinct lack of enthusiasm. "If I must. Are you certain she is prepared, though?"

The Norn appraised Laila. "We don't have much time left, but she'll manage."

"Very well, I'll seek her out as soon as I finish with my current assignment." Luc bowed to the Norn.

There was something about Luc's dismissive attitude and emotionless face that left her on edge. He was cold and robotic. Was that how they expected her to be?

"That's enough for today. We'll be in contact with you soon, Laila." Senere started to turn away.

Laila knew she was being dismissed, but she couldn't go yet. "Wait, I have one more question: If I help the Svartalfar in Nidavellir, will I still have time to save Ali?"

Senere's expression remained blank. "Such things are not for me to reveal, but not all wounds can be healed. There are limits to the magic of the mortal worlds. The Demonic threat is more important. If you do not stop the Demonic plight in Nidavellir, then that entire world will be forfeited. Izel is there already and preparing for her next move. Individual lives are meaningless when the balance of the worlds is at stake."

Before Laila could blurt out another question, the air around her shimmered. The next thing she knew, dark water surrounded her. Laila started to panic until she noticed the light above. Frantically she swam and breached the surface, gasping for breath. As she clambered out of the Well of Knowledge back into the temple of the Swordmasters, she noticed something weighty appear in her hand. She glanced down to find the sword with the moonstone pommel from the mosaic. It glowed faintly with a pale blue light as she held it.

"I take it you found the answers you've been searching for." Master Bas rose from a nearby bench and helped Laila to her feet.

"Some, but not as many as I need." She studied the blade. It was the same exquisite quality as her dagger.

"Such is the way of the worlds, but having questions means you always have something to look forward to. May I?" He motioned at the sword.

Laila passed it to the older man, who carefully inspected it and tried a couple of maneuvers.

"This is a weapon fit for a God. If I'm not mistaken, it was forged in Asgard. I have only seen a weapon of similar make twice before—one carried by a Valkyrie, another by an Angel. I trust it will serve you well." He offered it back to her hilt-first, and she accepted. "Now, I'm off to bed. I have a feeling tomorrow will be rather eventful."

Laila dried herself off, then followed him out of the garden and back into the building. She returned to the guest quarters and set the sword on a table beside her bed. For a time, she sat there staring at it, thinking over what she had learned.

It was now clear why she had the powers, but there were so many more questions. She supposed more answers would come in time. It seemed that her next task would be to save Nidavellir, but she couldn't let Ali die. She was determined to find a way to do both. Ali was still clinging to life. If she could just hold on a little longer, then Laila would be able to deliver the cure.

CHAPTER 22

Darien sat in the driver's seat of his SUV, parked across the street from a posh house in Malibu. This was the address where Lorel—or Lorelei—lived.

Sarnai watched the house through a pair of binoculars. "Hell, she's got excellent taste. Do you think she bought all that or charmed the shopkeepers? Even *I* don't have that many designer handbags."

"Seriously? We're trying to catch a Greater Demon, and all you care about is her closet?" Darien rolled his eyes.

"Well, it's not like we can see much else," she pouted. Sarnai passed the binoculars back to him.

She was right about that. From the street, all they had was a view of the empty bedroom. Her car was in the driveway, so he was sure she was home, but so far, this night had been a waste of time.

He called a judge first thing that morning, but they refused to give him a search warrant without substantial physical evidence. Without the test results from those pills, he had nothing but suspicions to back his claim. He thought staking out Lorelei's house would give him some ideas, but so far, he had come up blank. All of her paperwork indicated she was human, but if he could prove she had forged the documents, it could go a long way towards helping him prove she was also a Greater Demon.

Then there was Sarnai. She had been relatively quiet, but he knew this was all just part of some game. Maybe she was waiting to see how long Darien could tolerate her presence before he lost control. Another part of him wondered if she was genuinely interested in the case. Sarnai had been fascinated when he filled her in and explained what he believed the Siren was up to. Perhaps she was genuinely interested in catching the Demon, or maybe she was appreciating Lorelei's work.

Sarnai rested her feet on the dash. "I'm still surprised that the Greater Demon is Fredrik Stacy's secretary."

Darien frowned at her feet. "Yeah, but it explains a lot."

"You know this is pointless." Sarnai waved at the house. "You're not going to learn anything like this."

"Yeah, but if I break in and discover evidence, how am I supposed to explain how I found it? The only other option is to find some way to expose her publicly."

"Exactly! That's what you should be doing."

Darien stared at her. "How? The majority of the time she's in public, it's with the governor."

A scheming glint shone in Sarnai's blood-red eyes. "Even better. It's far more scandalous that way."

Right. Except Darien still had no idea how. It's not as if he could tap her on the shoulder and ask her to reveal her powers. He would have to provoke her somehow—to make her feel threatened or cornered.

His phone rang, saving him from further conversation. It was Jenn.

"So, you're finally responding to me now?" he asked.

"Yeah, well, shit really hit the fan. There's a small army of state troopers at the front door with arrest warrants for all of our staff—for the whole damn building."

"What? Why?"

"Some bullshit about endangering the city. This whole thing stinks of Fredrik Stacy," she fumed.

Darien unleashed a string of profanity. So this is why the governor had established the state troopers—to stop IRSA from interfering with the Demons. Without IRSA, there would be no one to apprehend Lorelei.

Darien started the car. "I'm on my way. I suspect there's Demonic involvement at play. Ask those willing to go quietly to buy us some time. Those who wish to stand against the Demons can meet me in the morgue. Bring any equipment you can carry from Donald's workshop."

She barked a laugh. "And how do you suppose you'll get in here?"

"Trust me. I'll find a way. Just keep the troopers occupied."

Darien sped off into the night as she hung up. He made it there in record time but slowed when he saw the small army of state troopers posted in front of the office blocking his path.

Sarnai watched him, an eager grin spreading across her face. "So, what's the plan?"

Darien parked around the corner in the hospital's parking structure. "There's another entrance to the building underground. They use it to transport bodies to our morgue. I use it to access the hospital during the day."

He led her inside, watching for any sign of the troopers. A couple of them were on the first floor of the hospital speaking to a doctor. Darien and Sarnai slunk around the corner and took the stairs down to a tunnel on the basement level. They needed to act fast if they were going to get the others out, including Ali. He wasn't going to leave her here, especially since he feared Lorelei was onto them.

They hurried through the small tunnel below the hospital. As usual, the passage was deserted, but the sound of voices echoed through the tunnel when he reached the morgue. Darien came to a halt. The room was absolutely packed. The majority of the investigative team was there with Jenn and a few members of their support staff. The two medical examiners looked positively bewildered. He doubted they ever had this many bodies in their morgue at once—living or dead.

"Quiet!" Jenn barked when he entered. "He's here."

The room fell silent as everyone turned.

"Has the Governor made any mention of this to the public?" Darien asked.

A member of the support staff nodded and held up her phone. "He made a statement denouncing IRSA a few minutes ago."

Jenn snorted. "I believe his exact words were 'a bunch of Supernatural-loving delinquents.'"

That sounded like him, all right. "Okay, well, I have reason to believe he's working with the Demons. We all have a choice here, and I won't fault you either way. You can go quietly with the troopers, which is probably the wise choice. Or you can come with me and find a way to stop the Demons, but know that you will be a fugitive. This could put your career and life in jeopardy if my suspicions are wrong, so choose carefully. If you wish to go, then now is the time."

The others watched him solemnly as his words sank in. Some of them left, apologizing as they did. He didn't hold it against them, though, considering what the rest of them were about to do was downright insubordinate. He wasn't exaggerating about the potential repercussions since this could be viewed as a criminal act.

He looked at the dozen or so left in the room. "As you know, Ali is still in the hospital. If they move her to another location, there's a good chance we won't be able to get her the cure she needs, and she will die. If she stays, we won't be able to protect her. We need to move her to safety."

The others nodded.

"Do you have a plan?" asked Meuric, one of the medical examiners. He was also the only SNP left aside from the two

Vampires. He was an Abhartach—similar to a cross between a Vampire and a Svartálfr.

Darien indicated the equipment around them. "I do. Do you have extra scrubs by chance?"

Darien walked down the hall with a surgical gown covering the majority of his clothing. Jenn and Meuric both wore scrubs. The three of them pushed a gurney with a body bag down the hall in the direction of Ali's room. Similarly disguised, the rest of the team had branched off towards the ambulance bay down below.

Darien paused next to a nurse who eyed them. "I need you to find Dr. Elmerson immediately. Tell him to go to Alastrina Fiachra's room."

The nurse looked skeptical but nodded all the same.

"Hey, you sanitize these things, right?" called a voice from within the body bag. They had cut slits into the sides for airflow.

"Sorry, I can't hear you," replied Darien smugly.

He knew a disguise wasn't necessary for Sarnai. After all, the state troopers were looking for the IRSA staff. Still, the opportunity to shove her into a body bag had been too good to pass up.

The Vampire mercenaries looked nearly as confused as the nurse when they saw Darien approaching. He nodded for them to follow as the others wheeled the gurney into the room. Jenn unzipped the body bag, and Sarnai sat up from within, looking annoyed. She hopped off the gurney just as the guards recognized her and bowed.

The door opened again, and Dr. Elmerson and the nurse entered.

The doctor looked bewildered. "What the hell is going on? First, the state troopers are beating down your door, and now this?"

Darien pulled him over to Ali. "Look, the Demons have infiltrated the government. We've got to move her while we still can. Do you think Meuric can handle her care?"

Dr. Elmerson glanced over at the medical examiner. "I don't know, I suppose so. Just counteract the damage of the curse." He turned back to Darien. "I'm not sure she has much time left. Possibly only a matter of days."

Anxiety gripped Darien, but he shoved it down. "Still, I want to give her a fighting chance. The governor has decided to arrest my entire office."

"What? Why?" The doctor asked, surprise breaking through his Elven composure.

Sarnai gave him a toothy grin. "Because the nutcase has a Greater Demon manipulating him. I suggest this hospital prepares for what's to come. As the largest Supernatural organization in the city, I have a feeling he'll go after you next."

The Elf blinked in shock, then nodded. He and the nurse got to work preparing Ali for transport then carefully placed her inside the body bag.

Darien clapped Doctor Elmerson on the shoulder. "Be careful."

The Elf frowned. "You too. These are disturbing times."

Meuric and Jenn wheeled the gurney from the room, and the rest of them followed.

"We'll meet you downstairs," said Sarnai, the mercenaries flanking her.

They split up to avoid drawing unnecessary attention. Sarnai and the other Vampires would leave through the front doors while the agents headed to the ambulance bay. Meuric led them toward an elevator. They rounded a corner and nearly ran into a group of troopers.

"Oh, sorry there," said Meuric.

The troopers ignored them and continued on their way. Darien was suddenly glad he insisted on the body bag and disguises. They made it to the elevator before the shouts erupted behind them.

"What do you mean she's gone?" someone bellowed.

Jenn punched the button for ground level, and the doors shut. "And that's our cue to get out."

The elevator doors opened at the ground floor, where they quickly wheeled the gurney toward the emergency room's ambulance bay. They had only gone a dozen yards when an LAPD officer rounded the corner. He was an older man with a handlebar mustache and greying hair. Darien thought he recognized the man from past investigations. The officer did a doubletake as they approached.

"Jenn? Is that you?" He blinked at her.

Then it clicked. Jenn had introduced them before. He was her old sergeant from her days with the LAPD.

For a tense moment, no one moved.

"We have to go. We've got a wounded agent that needs special care," explained Jenn. Her voice was steady, but Darien noticed her body tense.

Darien thought the police sergeant was going to stop them, but instead, he stepped aside. "Jenn, I don't know what's going on or why there's a warrant for your arrest. But I do know you, and this city would be a mess without IRSA. Go now. I never saw you."

Relief washed over Darien. "Thank you."

Darien and the others rushed towards the ambulance bay. The double doors slid open, and Darien found the rest of their group waiting beside an ambulance while one of them argued with a confused paramedic.

Meuric unzipped the body bag once more as they prepared to transfer Ali into the vehicle. Darien couldn't believe the plan had actually worked, but his optimism was short-lived.

"That's them!" hollered a state trooper from inside the hospital.

Darien swore.

"Load up!" Jenn ordered, facing the troopers.

Darien obeyed and lifted Ali from the body bag.

"Freeze!" shouted one of the troopers as he drew his gun. He aimed at Jenn.

"Easy now," said Jenn, her hands in the air.

More troopers in tan uniforms poured out of the hospital, but Darien remained focus on loading Ali into the ambulance. He passed her up to the other agents as Meuric climbed into the back.

"You don't want to do this! You know these arrest warrants are sketchy," Jenn said to the troopers.

"On the ground, Supernatural!" the lead trooper shouted.

"I'm human!"

"Jenn, we've got to go!" Darien shut the back doors of the ambulance.

Jenn nodded and turned towards the driver's side of the ambulance.

"I said, get down!" ordered the trooper.

Darien saw a muscle twitch in the man's arm. "No!"

Using every ounce of undead speed his body possessed, Darien launched forward as the trooper fired at Jenn's back. A bright orange shield sprung up from the band on his wrist as he intercepted the bullet.

He snarled at the trooper, but a figure in black appeared behind the man. Sarnai wrenched the gun from the trooper's grasp and shoved the man aside. He flew ten feet before skidding along the asphalt.

"I told you not to hurt them!" hissed Darien.

"My bad, but he was about to put a bullet into your friend," said Sarnai unapologetically.

Talen's mercenaries held the other troopers captive.

"Don't harm them! Only restrain them," Darien command-ed.

The Vampires nodded.

He turned to Jenn. "You okay?"

"A little shaken, but yeah. Thanks."

"Good. Let's go."

Jenn shoved aside any lingering shock and hurried to the ambulance, where she climbed into the driver's seat. Darien climbed in on the other side of the rig.

"Here," Darien tossed the keys to his SUV to Sarnai. "I'll meet you there."

She winked and sauntered off, waving for the mercenaries to follow her. They finished restraining the state troopers in their own handcuffs before fading into the darkness.

"Step on it," Darien said, tearing off the surgical gown.

Jenn obliged. She stomped on the gas pedal, and the tires screeched as they sped off into the night.

CHAPTER 23

Talen emerged from the safehouse as Darien and the others climbed out of the ambulance.

"What the hell is this?" he snapped, looking at the small crowd.

Darien ran his fingers through his hair. "What remains of IRSA. The governor dispatched the state troopers to round us up. We had to break Ali out of the hospital, and I didn't know where else to take them."

Talen pursed his lips and sighed. "Well, bring them in. We'll figure something out."

Meuric and Jenn wheeled Ali into the safehouse and settled her in Erin's room. Talen showed the agents into the living room while he sorted out sleeping arrangements. Sarnai showed up eventually, sauntering through the door as if the whole ordeal had merely been an invigorating night out.

"Hey, you guys better listen to this!" shouted Henrik over the chaos.

He switched the volume of the television up so everyone could hear. They fell silent when they saw the governor in another press conference.

"I am shocked by the horrific actions of those at the Inter-Realm Security Agency here in the city of Los Angeles. Their violent reactions today only emphasize the volatile nature that Supernaturals are said to possess. One of the brave state troopers is recovering from injuries sustained in the confrontation with the former IRSA Agents."

Jenn leapt to her feet from the sofa. "Seriously!?! He tried to shoot me! I had my back to him!"

The governor continued, "We believe the actions of the IRSA agents were orchestrated by their acting supervisor, Darien Pavoni." An image of Darien at a crime scene flashed on the screen. "Pavoni is to be considered armed and dangerous. If you have any information regarding his whereabouts, I urge you to contact the state troopers immediately. Effective now, all Supernatural-related conflicts will be handled by the California State Troopers."

More faces of the other agents from the investigative team and Meuric flashed across the screen. Darien shook his head in disgust. In his pocket, his phone buzzed. It was Adam Johnson from D.C. Darien was tempted to answer and explain, but he couldn't risk it being traced. He waited for the voicemail instead.

"Hey, it's Johnson. I don't know what happened, but it looks like you've become rather popular. I'm going to try to smooth things out, but the entire agency is crumbling. I'll contact you soon." The message ended abruptly.

Darien wondered if Johnson would be able to do anything. If not, this was going to make his task even more difficult. He would hardly be able to move around the city now.

It took Darien a moment to realize the room had grown silent, and all eyes were on him.

"So now what?" asked Jenn.

Darien rubbed his chin. "Look, guys, I know things seem pretty bleak, but we still have a pretty substantial force here. We don't need badges to stop the Demons, not when it's clear that law and order have been compromised in this city. It's time we stop chasing after the Demons and confront them."

Sarnai nodded her approval. "So, where are we going to make our stand?"

Darien studied the television screen where the governor was answering questions. "In the most public place possible—during one of his press conferences. We're going to take Fredrik Stacy and the Demons down in front of a statewide audience. We need the public to understand how the Demons have been playing them, so we unveil the truth live during a broadcast."

Jenn's expression remained grim. "Those press conferences are crawling with security. We can't exactly walk through the front door."

"Maybe not, but it's the best chance we've got of exposing them." Darien pulled the wristband with the shield spell off and passed it to Donald. "Do you think you can come up with more of these in the next day or two?"

Donald nodded. "Probably, if I have help. I'd also need supplies."

"Just let me know what you need," said Talen.

Darien turned back to the group. "Rest for now. Tomorrow we'll figure out where we go from here."

With that, Talen started to assign rooms and showed the newcomers where they could get cleaned up. Mato and Henrik volunteered to help cook a big batch of pasta to feed them all while Lyn and Donald tackled the discussion over how to produce more equipment on such short notice.

Darien left the room to check on Ali.

Meuric held his hands above Ali as he worked his healing magic. "It's been a while since I've dealt with the living, but she's in pretty bad shape. The doctor was right. All we can do is try to keep her alive long enough for the cure."

Erin studied her sister, her fingers glowing red-hot as flames started to crackle. "I know she would disapprove, but I want to help. Hate sitting around and waiting like this. I can help. You know I can."

Darien looked down at her beseeching eyes. Ali would never approve, and Frej wouldn't either. But right now, they were shorthanded. "I think Donald and Lyn could use a hand with the gear. As for the rest, we'll see. That's the best I can offer for now."

She nodded, and the glow surrounding her hands faded. She looked entirely worn out. The stress was taking its toll on her.

He left the room to find Talen and Frej waiting for him.

"Have you considered the possibility that Laila may not return in time?" Talen asked quietly.

Darien shut the door behind him. "Laila knows what she's doing."

Frej shook his head. "Look, there is more to Jerrik's story that not only complicates the journey but places Laila in grave danger. They should've been back by now, and I'm worried something went wrong."

Talen gave him a meaningful look. "You know there's a way to save her, Darien. It's within our power."

Darien paused. They could turn her. Ali would become a Vampire, but she would live. He massaged the bridge of his nose and exhaled. The change was not to be taken lightly, especially if the person in question couldn't give their consent. He wasn't sure if Ali would even want that. "I don't know. Let's give Laila a few more days. If she still isn't back, then we'll consider it."

They nodded, and he had a distinct feeling they felt equally conflicted on the matter.

Darien stared down at the floorplan he printed off from the capitol building's website. It wasn't exactly a detailed layout. He had been puzzling over it with Frej and Talen for the better part of an hour. It was nearly seven o'clock in the morning, and most of the others had gone to sleep long ago. Only Donald and Erin were still up as Erin stumbled her way through an enchantment spell. Apparently, Dragons could learn enchantments. Sleep eluded Erin, but helping Donald with his workload provided her with a much-needed distraction. Darien knew she was desperate to help in some way.

"The problem is we don't know enough about the security detail," Frej pointed out. Frustration crept into his voice. "We won't know what to prepare for until we get inside."

Darien wasn't going to sit around and wait for the Demons to track them down. He wanted to act within the next few days before the city spiraled further out of control. Preferably Friday, when the next press conference was scheduled. It only gave them two days, but that would have to do. Each day they wasted was another day the SNPs of the city were left unprotected. There was no doubt the attacks on Supernaturals would only worsen now that IRSA was not there to help maintain the peace. He just hoped the LAPD could handle those issues and keep the troopers in check in the meantime.

"According to the morning news, that's not our only obstacle," Sarnai said from the sofa next to them. She nodded at the screen.

A news reporter in a blue suit spoke. "New orders were released this morning from the governor's office. A curfew has been established for Supernatural residents of California effective immediately. All Supernaturals caught out past dusk will be subject to a fine and possible jail time."

"What? He can't do that!" Donald hissed as he joined them.

The reporter continued. "While the Governor's official statement insists he established the curfew in reaction to an increase in Supernatural-related crime, this comes only hours after a Vampire and former IRSA agent fled the state troopers in a violent confrontation."

The screen switched to another reporter. "Speaking of that confrontation, new footage from a security camera at the hospital has been released to the public. Let's have a look."

They cut away to a video from the previous night of Jenn with her back to the state trooper as she moved towards the ambulance.

"It appears this woman in hospital scrubs had her back to this state trooper when he opened fire. Fortunately, a companion shielded her from the shot." As the reporter spoke, Darien appeared on-screen, darting in front of Jenn with the shield. "It looks like a moment out of an action movie. And there's more. Another woman appeared out of nowhere to attack the trooper. It's unclear if she was simply a pedestrian passing by, but she does not seem to be affiliated with IRSA."

The broadcast cut back to the first reporter. "Wow, that's quite a scene. It's pretty shocking the way the trooper opened fire on that woman." She paused to listen to her earpiece. "This just in, it looks like the victim in this footage has been identified as Jennifer Holt, one of the IRSA agents. While she's worked for the organization for the past several years, it appears that she is actually a human, and originally a detective with the LAPD."

Jenn's photo appeared on the screen. Darien watched as the reporters continued to discuss the topic before they switched to another story. He wondered who had released the security footage. Had it been someone from the hospital?

His thoughts turned to the state trooper. Was he under Lorelei's control too? Or was he simply fueled by a fear of Supernaturals—believing them to be as dangerous as Frederik Stacy claimed? Once Darien cleared his name and resumed his work with IRSA, he would be confronting the governor and the state troopers.

Now there was this new curfew to consider as they moved forward. While it affected the Supernatural community as a whole, this attack was directed at the Vampires, trapping them in place. Either Lorelei was growing power-hungry, or she was aware they were on to her. Darien suspected the latter. She likely remembered how much support he had access to among the local Vampires.

His determination was renewed by the bleak news. Darien returned his attention to his notes on the capital building.

"I can do it. I can get into the state building," said Erin from behind the sofa. She must have wandered over at some point during the newscast.

"What?" Frej's tone was incredulous.

She continued. "They have school tours during the day, so it wouldn't be so strange for me to be there. Not to mention that I can blend in like a human."

"You're not going anywhere near there," declared Frej.

Erin glared at him. "Why can't you give me a chance? I've been in far worse situations than this!"

"This is not up for discussion."

Erin turned away, grumbling under her breath as she stormed off to Ali's room.

Darien placed a tentative hand on Frej's shoulder. "I know you want to protect Erin, but I think it's time we let her help. I think she really needs that right now. You saw her back at the house. She can handle it."

Frej bristled. "Absolutely not! She's a child!"

Darien jerked his thumb at the closed door. "You know that's just an excuse. She's older than every human in this bunker, she's got magic, and she can fight. You know she'll just find a way to sneak out and join us anyway, so we might as well involve her in our plan."

Frej looked livid. He opened and closed his mouth but was apparently at a loss for words.

Sarnai lounged on a sofa. "For the record, Darien, I agree with you wholeheartedly. By the time I was fifty, I'd already helped a warlord conquer two nations." She looked rather cheerful, all things considered, but Darien knew this was her twisted idea of fun.

"I don't think you're helping our point," muttered Darien.

She smirked and took a sip of blood from her martini glass. "Considering I'm around five thousand years old, you'd do well to trust me on this. The only way you survive in a world like this is to prove you're the real monster."

Darien ignored her and turned back to Frej. "Look, we don't have to send her in alone. What if we send Ligeia with her? We need this information, and you have to admit she's the best chance we've got."

The Dragon still didn't approve of Erin entering the building, but they eventually wore him down. His one condition was that he would be in a van nearby with Henrik and Mato in case something happened. Only the living could take part in this mission since the sun would be up.

Frej left to speak with Erin and the Siren, while Donald and Talen went to the garage to prepare a van. Darien headed for Talen's office to get some much-needed sleep. With all the rooms full, he claimed a sofa for a few hours. He needed a clear head, and there wasn't much more he could do until the others returned.

CHAPTER 24

It was only a few hours later when Laila awoke. She let Jerrik sleep and went to take a bath and dress. By the time she finished, Jerrik was awake and warming up in the guest quarters.

"Hey, how'd you sleep?" She joined him in the sitting area.

"Alright, I suppose, but I noticed you left last night. Is everything okay?" He kept his tone even, but his expression revealed his concern.

Laila ran her hand over the blue flames on her arm. She didn't want to trouble him, especially not when his focus should be on today's trials.

"Just restless. Are you ready for the trials?"

He frowned at the sword in his hand. "If the Swordmasters would just give us the Eirflower, we could return to Los Angeles and get back to work. I'm not sure what my ability to pass the trials has to do with it."

She thought back to the conversation she had with the Grandmaster. "I think it's more important than you realize. You were on this path for many years until your father got in the way. I think it's time you prove to yourself you're worthy."

He still seemed uncertain.

Laila offered a small smile. "Come on, let's go get some breakfast."

After their quick meal, footsteps approached from the hall. The dining chamber fell silent as three robed figures appeared in the doorway, their hoods concealing their faces.

"Prince Jerrik, it is time. Please follow us."

Jerrik nodded, and Laila gave him one last reassuring look. They led him to the garden, and Laila watched Jerrik vanish down the path and into the foliage. Despite her words of encouragement, her stomach twisted in knots.

The trials would take a matter of hours, but Laila was already impatient. Master Manach must have noticed her pacing in the hall because he convinced her to join him in his morning training.

They faced each other in a training room as sunlight filtered through the windows and bathed the space in the unnatural reddish light. Laila's entire focus was on her opponent, assessing him. She watched his body for a tell-tale twitch of a muscle. He feinted right then cut left. She moved to parry the cut when she realized it was a feint too. She quickly adapted and retreated a step, bringing her point down in an arc and catching his blade on hers. She didn't linger but followed through with a cut to his head, stopping the sword inches from his cheek.

He nodded appreciatively as he took a step back and returned to his guard position. "You're much faster than an ordinary mortal. That's good. Again."

She obeyed, and this time she noticed how slow his reactions seemed. Despite his skill, she was able to beat him with timing. Laila hadn't realized how fast she had become, but then again, she was used to Arduinna and Darien, both of which were faster than most mortals. Even so, the Swordmaster had an endless stream of feedback for her.

"Watch that angle. Ease up and let the blade do the work. You don't need that much force..." On and on the notes continued, and occasionally he paused to make adjustments. Finally, they stopped to rest. Laila's breathing came a little heavy, but not as much as the Fae.

He sank down onto a bench, sweat soaking his brow. "That magic gives you one hell of an advantage, but don't rely on it too much. Eventually, you'll meet an opponent who's your equal in speed and strength. That's where technique will save you. I take it you were trained by the Royal Guard?"

She nodded. "They wouldn't permit me entry, though. I was too young. Hence, why I ended up in Midgard."

"Well, they didn't reject you for lack of skill. That much is obvious. I bet they're regretting the decision now. Have you considered reapplying?" he asked.

Laila made a face and joined him on the bench. "I was knighted and offered a position in the Dragon Kingdom, but I turned the offer down. I think I would turn down a position with the Royal Guard, too, now that I know how much Midgard needs help. Not that it matters. It seems the Norns have their own plans for me."

There was a commotion down the hall, and a bell echoed through the corridor.

Laila leapt to her feet. "Are they finished with the trials?"

The Swordmaster furrowed his brow. "That's the sentry's bell. Someone came through a portal."

Laila's stomach lurched. Had the Demons tracked them down? She followed Master Manach through the halls at a jog, heading for the temple's doors. They hung back as a pair of hooded Swordmasters stepped through to intercept the new arrivals. Laila peered over the small crowd that had gathered and recognized the two travelers. It was Hallr and Rune.

Jerrik stood in the middle of a dark room. Sweat soaked his clothes and burned his eyes, and the only source of light fell from a circular window far above. It pooled around him and his opponent, whose face remained concealed by a hood. The only sound came from the clash of steel and their heavy breathing. The other Swordmasters formed a ring around them and watched like Ghosts in shadows.

After one opponent yielded, Jerrik scarcely had time to catch his breath before another would step forward to launch a fresh attack. He won some bouts but was miserably outmatched in others. He lost count of how many Swordmasters he faced so far, but he could feel the fatigue setting in. Even though his legs trembled and the sword grew heavy in his hands, Jerrik refused to back down. He would not fail.

The current opponent cut to his exposed side. Jerrik reacted on pure instinct and caught the blade with his own. With a roll of his fingers, he expulsed his adversary's blade to the side, wrenching it from the Swordmaster's grasp. The sword clattered on the wood floor as Jerrik leveled his tip to his rival's chest. They bowed their head and accepted defeat.

Jerrik retrieved the blade and offered it to them hilt-first. The Swordmaster took it with a second bow before melting back into the shadows.

Jerrik's chest heaved, and he wiped the sweat from his brow. He watched the circle, but no one stepped forward. Fear gripped him. Had he done something wrong?

"Despite the disruption of your training, your skill is worthy of a Swordmaster. You have passed the first trial." The Grandmaster's words echoed on the stone walls through the chamber.

Jerrik's shoulders sagged with relief and exhaustion, but he feared this was only the beginning. The trials were different for each individual, and Jerrik wondered what sort of challenge was next.

One of the Swordmasters entered the circle of light.

"Kneel." The voice reverberated off the stone walls.

Jerrik obeyed, and the Grandmaster stopped before him.

"You may find this disorienting." There was a rustle of

movement as the Grandmaster raised an arm and placed a pale hand on Jerrik's forehead.

Jerrik blinked, and his surroundings suddenly shifted. It wasn't like when Laila teleported—where he felt the ground pitch from under him. This was some sort of illusion. He stood alone in a forest shrouded in mist that swirled and shifted, playing tricks on his eyes. A small boy with dark, shaggy hair sat on a rock in front of him, whittling a piece of wood.

"Hello. Who are you?" asked Jerrik.

"I am Liam." The boy looked up, and Jerrik suppressed a shiver. He had never seen a child with eyes so cold and detached. They were almost robotic.

Liam snapped his fingers, and Laila stepped from the mist with her wrists bound, led by a man with long white hair and violet eyes.

"Marius," Jerrik snarled.

"You've always known I'd find her." The Demonic Fae grinned. He pulled Laila closer and pressed a knife to her throat, breathing in the scent of her hair as he did.

Illusion or not, Jerrik nearly lost his mind. He lunged for the Demon.

"Wait," The small boy held up his hand.

Jerrik wanted to shove that knife into the Demon's chest and tear out his heart, but he reminded himself this was another test. An illusion. Even if the blood trickling down Laila's throat looked all too real.

Two more figures emerged on the other side of the boy. Jerrik's father led his mother through the mist, the tip of his sword at her back. His mother's eyes lit up when she saw Jerrik, but her elation was short-lived.

"Kneel!" King Oddvarr barked.

He shoved the queen to her knees and leveled the sword to her neck. Jerrik forced himself to remain in place, although his clenched fists trembled.

The boy continued to whittle away with disinterest as he

spoke. "You can only save one. Choose wisely."

Jerrik swore and swept his gaze from his mother to Laila. How in the worlds was he supposed to do that? He suspected the Swordmasters would want him to pick his mother. She was the queen, after all. But Laila had a much larger role to play in the fight with the Demons. So, perhaps Laila was the correct choice.

Could he really allow his mother to die, though?

"Have you made your choice?" the boy asked blankly.

Jerrik remained silent as his heart and mind battled within.

CHAPTER 25

Laila watched Hallr argue with the Swordmasters, who blocked his path.

"Hold on, I know them." Laila turned to Master Manach. "They're rebels from Nidavellir. They escorted us to the portal."

The Swordmaster scrutinized the Svartalfar through the doorway. "Come on then, let's see what they're doing here."

The others parted, allowing them through.

"Please, we need to speak with Prince Jerrik. It's of dire importance!" insisted Hallr. He was growing agitated. Something was wrong.

The Swordmasters seemed skeptical.

"Hallr, what's going on? What are you doing here?" Laila asked, joining them.

His relief was apparent, but he remained tense and on guard. "I need to speak to Jerrik."

"He's in the middle of the trials. Did something happen?"

The Svartálfr huffed a frustrated breath. "Yes. King Oddvarr made an announcement last night—his mother, Queen Birgitta, will be executed in a few days' time."

Laila froze. "What?"

No wonder they had been so desperate to find their prince. Jerrik adored his mother. It was bad enough that Oddvarr imprisoned her, but this…

"Can they come in?" Laila asked Master Manach.

"Can you vouch for them?"

She nodded.

"Then, yes. At least until they can speak with Jerrik." He motioned to Rune and Hallr. "Come, we'll find you some refreshments while you wait for the prince."

He led them to the dining hall, where Laila seated herself with the newcomers.

"What happened?" she asked.

Hallr shook his head. "My best guess is King Oddvarr knows Jerrik's back and intends to lure him out of hiding."

Laila ran her fingers through her hair and groaned. Jerrik wouldn't take this well.

"He'll want to attempt a rescue," Hallr said, clearly thinking along the same lines.

"Is there any possibility of success?"

Rune fingered the hilt of a knife nearly hidden in the cuff of his jacket. "We'd be walking straight into a trap. Which is obviously what the king wants."

"So, it would be suicidal." Laila massaged her temples. The timing could not be any worse.

He chuckled. "I didn't say that. We'd simply have to be on our guard. Sure, it'd be risky, but not necessarily impossible. Not with your abilities."

Hallr wasn't as optimistic. "We can't risk it. Even if we succeeded, where would the queen go? She'd be stuck in one of our hideouts."

Laila drummed the table with her fingers as she thought. "Maybe not. The Elves in Alfheim might be willing to take her in. I have some connections in the court. They might be willing to shelter her, given the circumstances."

Master Manach took a seat beside them and passed mugs of tea around.

She offered him a quizzical look. "Do you think the Swordmasters would be willing to aid us?"

He was quiet a moment. "I don't believe the Grandmaster would permit it unless the circumstances were dire."

That wasn't reassuring. Laila hoped a few of them would be willing to help, but she supposed they would obey the Grandmaster's orders.

She went to reach for her tea when a flash of light blossomed in her vision. She blinked, but it didn't fade. *What in the worlds?*

"Are you okay?" someone asked.

She was unable to respond. She was caught in a trance as snapshots of Jerrik passed before her eyes: a dark room, a misty wood, and Jerrik kneeling before the Grandmaster.

What was going on? Why did she see this? She was unable to stop the images flooding her mind.

Jerrik looked back and forth between his mother and Laila as his hands clenched.

"Well?" asked the boy. He peered up from his carving.

"I would choose my mother," he said at last.

The boy cocked his head. "Why?"

Jerrik looked at her frail body as she trembled on the floor. The sight made his heart crumble. "Laila can protect herself. My mother cannot. If I am not there for her, she will have no one to save her."

His mother looked at him through the grateful tears welling in her eyes. The sight made his chest ache.

He turned to Laila—the woman who captured his heart. The one person in these worlds he desired to be with. The woman who reminded him of the good in the worlds. His light in the darkness.

He dipped his head in apology. "Laila is strong. I believe she would be able to save herself. I've seen her rise from the dead before. Her power is beyond my understanding, and I know that there are some battles she will have to fight on her own."

He looked up and saw Laila nod. Then the scene dissolved around him, and once more, he was standing in the dark chamber, surrounded by the white-robed Swordmasters.

The Grandmaster took a step back and lowered their hood. "Interesting. I wondered whether you would be willing to separate your desires from your duties. You have shown us you can. You do not rush through difficult decisions and made your selection based on the individual who needed your help the most. I could see into your mind, and there was no deception. You have passed the trials."

"I have?" Jerrik paused, a little in shock.

He honestly hadn't thought the Swordmasters would accept him. His life had been nothing but a mess since Master Kyvik's murder, and he had changed a lot in ways he wasn't sure were for the better. Those events opened his eyes to the cruelty of his father, but also of the Demons. He had seen what they could do—how they could destroy his own kingdom. He had been through ordeals that broke his resolve but found others who helped him build it back up. Now he understood what it felt like to be a part of a team that selflessly protected others. For the first time, he realized how everything he learned in Midgard had not only prepared him for the trials but to face his father too.

Jerrik bowed his head. "I am deeply honored that you find me worthy."

A faint smile appeared on the Grandmaster's lips. "Have you chosen the God you wish to serve?"

The Gods could be treacherous to mortals, whose short lives were meaningless and insignificant. However, Jerrik knew he was not the only one who would be affected by this decision. Laila was the pawn of a Goddess, and if she ever earned the wrath of the Gods, they could use him against her. With this binding oath, the God he chose could order him to capture her, lie to her, or worse. He wouldn't allow them to use him as a pawn in their political games. There was only one clear choice.

He nodded. "I have."

"Good, then kneel." The Grandmaster retrieved a sword from the shadowy corner of the chamber. "This sword belonged to Master Kyvik. I went through a great deal of trouble to retrieve it, but I believe he would want you to have it."

Jerrik's eyes pricked with tears. "I am honored."

The Grandmaster offered him the sword. "Now, you may take your vow."

He held the sword before him in his upraised palms. "I, Jerrik, Prince of the Svartalfar, swear to uphold the values of this sacred order. I swear to uphold justice wherever the path takes me, to let wisdom guide my actions, and to fight for those who cannot defend themselves. I pledge my life and sword to uphold these virtues and to protect those in need. With this oath, I dedicate my life to serve and follow the will of the divine being of my choice. I pledge myself to Laila Eyvindr."

Magic crackled and rippled around him as a murmur of shock swept through the room.

"Are you certain?" the Grandmaster asked.

Jerrik looked up as he spoke. "Laila may not know what sort of being she is, but she is divine nonetheless. The rules state that I only need to pledge myself to a divine being—not specifically a God. I have given this much thought, and she is the one I trust."

"Very well, then it is done. Just be warned—there may be repercussions. Now rise, Master Jerrik, and welcome to our order."

Jerrik stood, and the rest of the Swordmasters removed their hoods. They echoed the Grandmaster's welcome and offered approving smiles; then, the Grandmaster motioned towards the door.

He followed them into the garden and along the path until they reached the gate. A small crowd had gathered, but the only face he searched for was Laila's.

"Welcome the newest member of our order," announced the Grandmaster.

The group cheered, and Jerrik offered a gracious nod as the crowd pulled him into their midst. The Swordmasters clapped him on the back and cried their praise. Then, between the robed Swordmasters, Jerrik found himself face to face with Laila.

He snaked his arm around her waist and kissed her, earning a fresh wave of cheers from the audience. But when he pulled away, he realized his mistake. Jerrik had expected her to be elated, but instead, she was livid.

"What in Thor's name did you do?" she growled, her eyes glowing in rage.

It appeared she already knew about the pledge.

CHAPTER 26

Jerrik stared at Laila in surprise. Around them, Swordmasters cheered and shouted by the edge of the garden, but Laila blocked them out of her mind as fury gripped her. Why in the worlds would he pledge himself to her? Had he completely lost his mind?

Perhaps she was a little harsh on him, but she couldn't believe he would do something so rash without consulting her.

Laila had been deep in discussion with the rebels when the visions began until one image emerged sharper than the rest. It was as if she had been standing before Jerrik, entirely unseen, as he pledged himself to her. With the wave of magic that sealed the oath, a bond had materialized and connected them. Even now, Laila could feel the magical connection as thin as a strand of spider silk.

She wanted to confront him here on the spot, but it would be inappropriate to make a scene in front of the other Swordmasters. Instead, she swallowed her irritation for now. She would face him later, in private.

"Congratulations!" boomed Hallr, pulling Jerrik into a

bone-crushing hug.

Jerrik gaped at him. "Hallr? What in the worlds are you do-ing here?"

"We, um, just wanted to be here to congratulate you." He forced a smile.

Rune bowed beside him. "Congratulations, Your Highness."

They decided to keep the news of his mother's approaching execution a secret for the time being. They would give Jerrik a chance to revel in his success.

Laila sighed as she sat on a bench overlooking the garden and let the crowd sweep Jerrik and his friends away to the dining hall.

Laila? A voice whispered in her head.

Erin? Is everything okay?

I don't know. The city is losing its mind. The Governor tried to shut IRSA down and arrest everyone in the office. Darien and Jenn managed to get Ali and some of the others back here to safety, but I don't know what to do. There's a new group of state troopers that Fredrik Stacy created, and he's using them to do his dirty work.

Thor's Hammer! How did this happen? Things were bad when they left, but this was insane. *How is Darien managing?*

He's convinced that Colin's girlfriend, or ex, or whatever she is, must be behind this. They believe she's a Greater Demon who's got crazy mind-con-trol powers. Like, they supposedly put Fae magic to shame. Anyway, he's going to try to reveal her true identity publicly.

Laila's mind swam with questions. She wanted to talk to Darien, but she didn't know how to do so unless he contacted her first. *How is Ali?*

Worse than the last time I saw her. One of the Medical Examiners monitors her, but it looks like she's only got a few days.

A few days wasn't much time. Not enough to deal with the Demons in Svartalfheim.

You're going to make it back in time, right? The hesitation was apparent in Erin's tone.

I'll find a way. I promise.

Laila knew she shouldn't make assurances, but she was not ready to give up on Ali. Demons be damned, she would make it back to Midgard.

Even so, she told the rebels she would find a way to help Jerrik's mother. While they were enjoying the celebration, she could at least start making arrangements.

She returned to the guest quarters and entered the bathroom. Standing before the mirror, she ran a finger over the surface and murmured a spell. The mirror rippled as the scrying enchantment took hold. Her parents still didn't know about her divine powers, so she took a moment to shift her appearance until she looked ordinary and mortal.

"Ragna Eyvindr," she said.

Mist clouded the mirror before revealing her mother's face as she walked down a hall in an opulent dress. Laila guessed she was at some sort of court function.

"Laila? Is everything alright? You haven't contacted us since the solstice." Her brows knitted together in concern.

"A lot has happened in the last couple of weeks," Laila admitted before launching into a brief explanation of everything since the Demons attacked the house. She made sure to omit anything relating to her new powers. She wasn't sure how to break that news to them.

Ragna was shocked by the time she finished. "You mean to say that you've been working with the prince the entire time?"

"Yes, and I'm certain that his father is involved with the Demons. I need to come up with a way to save Queen Birgitta. I thought that if I could help her escape, I could take her to Ingegard to seek refuge with the Elven Royalty. Do you think they would allow it?"

Ragna frowned. "I'm not sure. I could speak to them and see."

"Something has to be done. King Oddvarr is a tyrant. His people are worked to death in the mines and starved in the streets. The rebels hope to make a difference, but they don't have the numbers. I also fear the Demons' influence will only spread from here if they are left unchecked."

"I agree. This situation is truly concerning. If Demons have taken Nidavellir, then the security of the other worlds is also compromised. Who knows how many Demons have already crossed through the portals?" Laila heard her mother drumming her fingers against a piece of wooden furniture anxiously. "I'll speak to the Royal family and see what they have to say on the matter. In the meantime, plan to bring the queen here. If nothing else, she could help us to understand the full extent of this threat. I should be able to arrange some sort of accommodations for her. There isn't a direct portal from Nidavellir, so take the one to the Dragon Kingdom. I'll arrange an escort from there."

Laila breathed a sigh of relief. Perhaps the Elves would step in and help, buying her time to return and save Ali.

"Thank you, mother. We leave tomorrow and are short on time. We'll have to act quickly to save the queen if I'm going to save Ali too. Expect our arrival by the following morning."

Ragna nodded. "I will. Be careful. I've not had any dealings with the Svartálfr King in many years, but he's as cunning as he is cruel. Stay on guard."

"I will. Give father my regards."

Laila ended the call and removed the mirror's enchantment, silently thanking Arduinna for showing her that trick.

Her plan was starting to take shape. She needed to speak with the others and determine how they could break the queen out of the palace. She also had to find a way to tell the news to Jerrik—and to confront him about his oath.

She was on her way out of the guest quarters when the door opened, and Jerrik entered.

"Where have you been? I thought you'd join us." He shut the door gently behind him and cut off the echo of boisterous singing down the hall.

Laila folded her arms. Her eyes bore into him with an icy

look. "What the hell were you thinking? Have you completely lost your mind? Why would you pledge yourself to me?"

He stopped in his tracks. "That's why you're sulking in here? You're upset about that?"

"You had no right! You should have spoken to me first!"

He shook his head, incredulously. "I have every right. I can pledge myself to whomever I please. I did this for you to show you that no matter what, you will never be alone."

Laila couldn't believe it. "That's not what I meant! You wasted this oath on me! I'm not a Goddess!"

"Yet it worked, didn't it?" He sighed and leaned against the back of a sofa. "Look, I get that you're upset I didn't speak to you about it first, but I know it's for the best. You're walking into a game of Gods. I would have been a pawn for any of them to use against you. I'd be unable to resist their command. The only way I could be certain I would never be used to betray you was to bind myself to you."

Laila hadn't thought of that. She felt a twinge of guilt, but she still wished he had spoken to her first.

He approached and placed his hands on her shoulders. "Look, this doesn't have to change anything between us. I only did it to ensure I couldn't hurt you."

And yet, it *would* change things. Even so, there were other, more pressing matters. "We'll figure this out later. There's something I need to tell you. The true reason Hallr and Rune came to the temple is that your mother's in danger."

He stiffened. "What do you mean?"

"The king announced last night that he would execute her publicly for treason." Jerrik's expression crumbled as she spoke.

"When?" his voice was a whisper. Laila could feel his internal battle struggling to keep his emotions in check.

"In three days."

A growl escaped his throat and grew into a cry of anguish. He turned and sank onto the arm of the sofa. Laila had never seen Jerrik so broken. He was always cool and cocky. This pain was so raw, so deep, that it seemed as though his heart had been torn in two.

"This is what my father does. He destroys everything he touches." His voice was rough and gravelly from the sob he fought to keep back. "I can't let him destroy her too."

With his back to her, Laila couldn't see his face, but perhaps he didn't want her to. Not with his emotions so bare. Laila took a tentative step closer and placed her hand on his shoulder to let him know she was there.

"I'm so sorry, Jerrik." She snaked her arms around him until she was hugging him.

He didn't react. After a moment, Laila released him, worried that he needed space.

"Wait," he said.

She leaned against the sofa beside him. "I know this is a lot to take in, but I'm working on a plan to free her. I've already contacted my mother, and she'll ensure there is a safe place for the queen in Ingegard."

He looked skeptical. "Are you sure that's wise? Our peoples haven't exactly been on the best terms throughout the centuries."

Laila nodded. "Trust me. She'll be safe there. They've got bigger problems than old grudges to worry about."

Jerrik still seemed uncertain, but Laila knew his mother would be safer with the Elves than anywhere in Midgard.

Laila continued. "We'll speak with Hallr and Rune tonight and figure out a plan to free her. They mentioned something about using the passages below the palace. I've got a little more research to do first."

He seemed reluctant, but Laila eventually convinced him to go back and join the others. Perhaps the Swordmasters would have some advice as well. In the meantime, there was one, in particular, she needed to speak with.

Leaving him, Laila wandered through the halls of the temple in search of the Grandmaster, but they were nowhere in sight. Finally, she found them waiting at the garden entrance.

"I was about to take a walk. Care to join me?" asked the Grandmaster.

Laila nodded and followed them into the garden. "I've been looking for you. I learned that King Oddvarr will execute Jerrik's mother in a few days. We're planning a rescue mission, and I was hoping you'd permit a few of the Swordmasters to join us."

The Grandmaster paused beneath a large, turquoise fern. "I'm afraid it is not yet time for us to return to the worlds. Jerrik is a prince; thus, he may leave the temple, but the rest of us will wait."

Laila frowned. "Wait for what? The Demons are already out of control. We need all the help we can get."

"Until I am given a sign, we will remain here." The Grandmaster's voice was harsh, leaving no room for debate. "Come, I have something to show you."

They wandered deeper down the winding path to where the cobblestones encircled a single plant. It had long slender leaves, and atop the delicate stalks sat creamy white blossoms. It glowed with warm, inviting light as the last rays of sunlight vanished over the walls of the courtyard above.

Laila leaned in to examine it. "Is this the Eirflower?"

"It is. I have guarded the plant for many years. I'm not sure if the legends surrounding its powers are true, but I hope it will help your friend. Remember, though, not all ailments can be cured."

The Norn had mentioned something similar, but Laila wasn't going to give up. The Eirflower had to work. They were out of options.

The Grandmaster plucked a single blossom and tucked it into a square of gold silk before passing it to Laila.

"Thank you."

She was relieved to have found the Eirflower at last, but unfortunately, there was now a new obstacle blocking her path home.

They made their way back up the walkway toward the temple, passing the mosaic. That image of her looked far more powerful and confident than she felt. She still couldn't believe Jerrik picked her. She understood his reasoning, but she also didn't feel worthy. If anything, she felt as if she was some sort of imposter.

"You look disturbed," commented the Grandmaster strolling beside her.

Laila blinked and pulled herself from her reveries. "I'm not sure I agree with Jerrik's choice. I'm not a God. I just work for one."

The Grandmaster's face was stoic. It was the same neutral expression that always seemed to linger on their face. "Perhaps that is the case, but you are a creature of divine abilities. I believe that qualifies you enough. I can't say for certain, but I'm inclined to think he chose you because you would not lead him down the same destructive path his father has walked, but one he would be proud of."

Maybe the Grandmaster was right, but it still made Laila uncomfortable. She disapproved of the idea of someone serving her. It made her sound superior, but that wasn't true. It didn't matter if she had all the magic in the world; she was just Laila. She didn't want anything more than that.

The Grandmaster paused as they reached the entrance to the garden. "If it still troubles you, think of it this way—you only have to call upon him in this capacity if you wish it."

Laila bit her lip. Hopefully, she would never have to resort to that.

The Grandmaster bid her goodnight before disappearing through a doorway. Laila followed the sounds of music and merriment through the corridors to the dining hall, where the celebration was still in progress. She wondered how Jerrik was coping.

CHAPTER 27

Darien awoke from a disturbing dream involving riots in the street where the buildings burned around them. He desperately hoped it wasn't some sort of premonition. He sat up with a grunt and ran a hand over his messy hair.

"I don't remember you talking in your sleep so much."

He snapped his head to the side to find Sarnai lounging in an armchair.

"What the hell! Didn't anyone ever tell you it's creepy to watch someone while they sleep?" he snapped, his mood turning sour. The fact he was ravenous didn't help. He couldn't remember the last time he had fed. It was probably the day before yesterday.

Sarnai closed the book in her lap and set it on a side table. "I was reading in here because it was too loud out there with all those humans chattering. Not everything revolves around you, you know."

If it were anyone else, he might have felt guilty, but he knew the sentiment was wasted on her. Instead, he watched the elder Vampire warily.

"What are you really doing here, Sarnai? You could leave whenever you want, so why spend the whole day trapped in here with us?"

She took her time answering, her expression thoughtful. "I suppose I just felt like staying. I wasn't lying when I said I missed you, and I have a feeling that underneath all that hate and mistrust, you miss me as well." She batted her eyelashes.

"What did you say last night? 'The only way you survive in a world like this is to prove you're the real monster.' Well, at least you admit you are one." Darien scoffed as he pulled his boots on and stood.

Sarnai leaned over the edge of her armchair and scowled. "Monsters endure when heroes die."

He leaned over the chair far enough to let his lips brush her ear. "But who kills the monsters, darling?"

If Sarnai was determined to mess with him, then he would give as good as he got. He pulled away just enough to see the smug look on her face.

"I've killed thousands of 'heroes.'" Her gaze settled on his lips, and he wondered if she struggled to resist as well.

"And yet someone always steps up to try again." God, he craved the taste of her mouth, and the hunger was making it harder to think clearly.

"Is that what you think you are? A hero?" Her chuckle was deep and velvety, floating around him like smoke.

He had never thought of himself as heroic by any stretch of the imagination, but he had a conscience, and he wouldn't let this city fall or abandon its people. Did that really make him a hero? He didn't think so. It only made him a decent person.

He cupped her chin in his hands and brushed his thumb over her lips until her breath stilled. "If I am, that means I have to kill you, doesn't it?"

Her eyes flashed with a wicked thrill. "Perhaps. Or maybe you can tame me instead."

Darien tipped her chin up and brought his lips dangerously

close to hers. "I'd take an irritable crocodile over you any day, darling."

Before he gave in to temptations, he straightened and strode for the door. Sarnai probably watched him with her dark delight, knowing he ached to turn around, but he wouldn't let her draw him back in. Not this time. Yet, even as he left the room, he couldn't shake the feeling he was still playing directly into her hands.

He found most of the agents gathered around the television in the living room, flipping back and forth between evening newscasts. He hadn't realized how late it was, but Frej had already returned with the others. They gathered around the counter where Erin jotted notes on the building's plans. Talen and Jenn stood with them, listening as Erin briefed them on the details of the building.

"Well, I take it the mission went off without a hitch," Darien said. No one seemed battered, which was a good sign.

Erin nodded and motioned toward her phone. "I've got the notes here."

He scanned over the notes she made on the layout regarding the building's security. She marked locations where she had observed the guards and cameras. Henrik offered more information on the exterior. He had done a little snooping of his own and found most of the staff used a back door to access a couple of cafes down the street. With the information collected, they now had a better idea of what they were up against.

Darien grabbed the pencil and began to add notes of his own. "So, here's what I'm thinking: we swap out members of their security team with our own people. The press conference is at five o'clock. We send in the humans before sunset, maybe around four o'clock, and then send in the Vampires. We'll need colored contacts for them, though, so they don't draw attention. More of us will enter from the front with the press, but we'll be unarmed because of the security screening."

The others nodded, and he glanced at Ligeia. "After the

conference starts and the cameras are broadcasting, you'll confront Lorelei. I think she'll try to make a run for it, so the rest of us will be on hand to stop her."

She agreed. "I think I'll be able to goad her into revealing herself."

Lyn grew concerned. "Are you sure?"

The Siren nodded. "It's my task to bring Lorelei to justice. However, all of you who enter will need protective charms; otherwise, you'll be at Lorelei's mercy."

"I think I can come up with something." Lyn returned to her stack of books on the table.

Darien turned to Donald next. "Do you think you can find a way to ensure the news station continues to broadcast? I don't want them shutting it down when they realize something's up."

The Tech Wiz examined his supplies on the table. "I think I can. I'll see what I can come up with. I've got more equipment that should be ready by morning too."

"Are you planning to address the public?" Talen asked.

Darien shook his head and surveyed the current news broadcast on the television. It was the video of the trooper nearly shooting Jenn. News stations across the country were reporting on it. Jenn had become the topic of much debate.

"No. The people of Los Angeles don't want a Vampire telling them what to do, especially after the uprising last fall. We need someone they know—someone they can identify with. Jenn should be the one."

She blinked. "What? No way. I don't do speeches or cameras. Have one of the others do it."

Darien indicated the screen. "Thanks to this video, the public not only knows your face, but they sympathize with you. You're human. You understand Supernaturals. You've worked multiple jobs in law enforcement, and you've lived in this city your entire life. Not only that, but you are strong, honest, and direct. That's the kind of person they need right now."

A hush fell over the room while Jenn thought. "I don't

know. I don't even know what I'd say."

"You give one hell of a pep talk, but we could script it," offered one of the agents.

Others joined in voicing their agreement.

She held her hand up. "Fine, but just this once. Then someone else needs to step up."

Darien nodded. He understood. He was just grateful she was willing to do it.

Another problem remained—their lack of proper clothing for the state building. Most of the agents still wore scrubs or wrinkled work clothes. Thankfully, Sarnai offered to deal with that. She took down everyone's sizes then placed orders at a couple of shops. Talen called an optometrist who used to supply him with colored contacts before The Event when Vampires needed to disguise themselves. He arranged to pick them up before dawn. The others discussed how they might be able to contribute or where they might be able to help.

Darien felt better knowing they had a plan in motion, but he was also aware of how much could go wrong. If they had weeks to plan and more information, maybe he would feel better about it. However, as it stood, they would have to be flexible and adapt.

He noted the others looked far more hopeful.

His gaze fell to Lyn and Ligeia. The Witch had her arm casually draped around the Siren's shoulders. What would happen to them? Would Lyn's feelings overpower the Siren's magic, or would she forget, just as Colin had? He was not envious of that situation. Darien watched the tender way they treated each other, with Lyn lacing her fingers through Ligeia's. He truly hoped their love would find a way. This world needed more happiness.

He realized Erin had vanished and found her seated on her sister's bed. Ali's skin had taken on a sickly pale tinge, and her condition was worsening despite Meuric's care. There was still no word from Laila or Arduinna. They were running out of time, waiting for a miracle cure.

Erin looked up when he entered and gave a half-smile. "Thanks for giving me a chance today. I know you were the one who convinced Frej."

Darien shrugged. "Well, I just wanted to say you did a great job, so thanks."

The Dragon looked back at her sister, and her smile vanished. Darien didn't want to intrude, so he quietly left. Outside, Sarnai watched with a peculiar expression from the doorway. He thought it might be sadness, but the look was so foreign on her.

She spoke low, and he could barely hear her. "You know, I was raised by my older sister too. A group of warriors raided our village. They raped and murdered her in front of me. One clean cut to the throat, and she was gone forever. I thought they'd do the same to me, but they took me back to their camp instead.

"It was years before I managed to get away. When I did, I fled to the blood-drinking monster that lurked in the mountains. I begged him to turn me so I could destroy my sister's murderers." Her eyes glazed over as she lost herself to the memory. "When I finished tearing them apart limb from limb, I looked for others like them to exact the revenge their victims deserved."

Her face was withdrawn and haunted as her gaze settled on Erin. He never heard this story before. This was a completely new side of her. It could have been an act, but there was something so raw and pained in the way she watched Erin that he couldn't help but believe.

"Careful, that almost makes you sound like a hero," he whispered.

She shook her head. "We both know there's no redemption for me at the end of this life. I've made my peace with that. I probably belong in Hell. But the one thing that kept me going is the knowledge that I can avenge those who deserve it. Earlier, you asked me why I'm still here—that's why."

Sarnai looked up at him, and for the first time, he saw her with no shields and no armor—just the lost and broken girl who fled from her captors so many centuries ago. He thought back to all the people she killed over the years—particularly the ones he witnessed. He had seen her slaughter an entire village once, but now that he thought about it, she hadn't killed the children or mothers. He never actually saw her harm a child. There was no doubt she was cruel and seriously screwed up, but maybe she wasn't as despicable as he thought. Even monsters had their limits.

CHAPTER 28

As the celebration wound down and the Swordmasters drifted back to their bed chambers, Laila found herself sitting at a table by the fire with Jerrik, Hallr, and Rune. Before them lay two maps Hallr had brought: one of the city and the other of the palace. They sat there with tankards of ale and mugs of tea, debating the best course of action.

As tempting as it was for Laila to teleport into the palace and retrieve the queen, there was no telling what sort of magical traps were in place. Not to mention that she was unfamiliar with the palace. Teleporting to a location that she didn't know posed a variety of dangers since she could find herself trapped between walls or furniture. It would be safer to traverse the palace on foot.

"Do you have any contacts within the palace?" Laila asked the two rebels.

Hallr wrinkled his nose. "Sort of. I have a few contacts amongst the nobility. They're okay with passing on court gossip and the odd tip, but I don't think they'd be willing to risk themselves with a task like this. Discovery would mean death for all involved."

Laila turned to Rune. "How about you?"

He stared into the dregs of his tankard. "I do, but I suspect they'd be too afraid in this case."

Laila could understand that. "Well, I suppose that just leaves the four of us then. I've already spoken to the Grandmaster, and the Swordmasters will not leave the temple."

Hallr made a disgusted noise as he shoved the map of the castle across the table. "I don't like this. We have to cross the entire palace. The chances of us even making it to the royal wing aren't good."

Rune clicked his tongue. "I don't know. I think we could do it. There is a minimum of four Red Guards watching the sealed entrance to the tunnels. We'll have to deal with them anyway. If we take their cloaks, no one will bother us. I've done it before with good results."

Jerrik nodded in pensive agreement. Hallr shot a silent plea to Laila, willing her to talk sense into the other two.

She studied the palace map. "The king will be expecting this. I don't think there is an ideal time. I suppose we might as well attempt it tomorrow."

Hallr groaned. "Fine, but on one condition: if we're compromised, Laila takes Jerrik and teleports away. You get one attempt at this, Jerrik, and if it fails, you leave Svartalfheim. We can't lose you. Period."

Jerrik nodded reluctantly. "Well then, I guess we better make this one count."

As the fire burned low, they chose their route and finalized their plan. Laila didn't approve of this any more than Hallr, but she knew Jerrik wouldn't walk away from his mother. She thought of the stories he told her back in the caves. She was a kind and compassionate person—one of the few who truly cared for Jerrik in his old life. How could Laila dissuade him from helping his mother? It wouldn't be right.

They returned to the guest quarters as the last embers died

in the fireplace. The two rebels chose beds for the night and pulled the curtains of the alcoves shut. Laila carefully tucked the Eirflower away in a magical pocket of her jacket. She decided to return to Midgard after delivering Jerrik's mother safely to the Elves. She would take the flower to Erin and ensure Ali was okay, then return to help Jerrik with his father. There was no need for her to stay in Svartalfheim until the rebellion was ready to attack. Perhaps Jerrik would even come with her.

She found him leaning against the sink in the bathroom, staring at his reflection. His gaze flicked in her direction when she approached.

"How are you doing?" she asked, coming to a stop by his shoulder.

He shrugged. "I don't know. I should've gotten my mother out of the palace years ago. I never thought it would come to this."

Laila looked into the haunted silver eyes of his reflection. "She chose to stay, though, didn't she?"

"She did." He spun to face Laila. "Thank you for helping with this. I'm not sure what I would've done if you weren't here. You have a way of making the impossible achievable."

Laila gave him a half-smile. "Well, we haven't pulled this off yet. Come on. You'd better get some sleep."

Jerrik placed his hands on her hips before she could move. "You haven't told me if I'm forgiven." A ghost of a smile tugged at his lips.

Laila regarded him smugly. "Let's put it this way: you are now bound to me. Thus you must obey my orders. Keep that in mind next time you attempt something idiotic."

"So, I take it that's a yes," he purred and pulled her closer.

Laila rolled her eyes.

Jerrik chuckled and gently tilted her chin up. "In all honesty, though, there is no one I trust more than you, Laila."

He lowered his mouth to hers, and she melted into his embrace. Jerrik may be a fool, but he was a well-intentioned one.

She didn't want to use this power over him, but she already decided she would make an exception if it meant saving him during their rescue mission. He may hate her for it, but she knew how much his people needed him. She would not allow him to throw his life away.

The next morning Laila rose early and quickly prepared for the journey back to Nidavellir. Jerrik and the others were grim and silent as they checked their weapons and headed to the dining hall.

Master Okaenos nervously ate his breakfast on the other side of the table. "Are you certain it's wise to return to Nidavellir? Perhaps you should allow the situation to calm first?"

Jerrik nodded as he stared down at his plate. He had hardly eaten a thing. "My mother will be executed in a couple of days. If I don't act now, it will be too late."

The other man nodded. "I see. Well, in that case, I wish you luck. I hear the Grandmaster will see you out."

Laila finished her breakfast and stood. "It was a pleasure to meet you."

He nodded enthusiastically. "It was an honor! I hope to see you again one day!"

Jerrik said his goodbyes to the others before their group strode toward the doors. There waited Master Bas, Master Manach, and the Grandmaster.

The Grandmaster inclined their head ever so slightly. "Prince Jerrik. Remember what you have learned here. We hope you find time to visit the temple soon."

He nodded.

Master Bas took a step forward.

"I have a gift for Laila." He presented her with a beautiful black scabbard embellished with silver. "I found this in our treasury. I believe it will fit your newfound sword nicely. Even if you can summon it, I imagine it would be nice to feel its weight at your side."

She thanked him and donned the scabbard, conjuring the sword to test the fit. He was correct. It was a near-perfect match. It was different from the Swordmasters' plain scabbards and had a series of metal stars set into it.

Master Manach pushed the doors open. "Take care, and know that we are here for you, should you ever require our guidance."

They thanked the Swordmasters once more before stepping out of the temple with Rune and Hallr. The doors swung shut behind them, and the group made their way back to the portals. The wind whipped past, carrying with it a salty tang from the ocean. The stone guardians did not appear as the team stepped through the portal back to Nidavellir.

They arrived in the stone passage deep within the bowels of the palace. The recently repaired statues looked down on them and pulsed with magical blue light, illuminating the chamber with their glow.

"You're sure about this?" Laila asked Jerrik.

He nodded, already heading toward the passage beyond.

Hallr gave her a stern look, reminding her of their deal. She would stay close to Jerrik and keep him from harm.

The others led her through the abandoned tunnels beneath the palace. Old furniture and other discarded items littered the passage, but there was no sign of palace staff or guards.

They reached a massive stone doorway sealed with magic. It had a faint green glow to it as Laila examined the spell.

"There's an alarm system connected to the door. If we open it, we risk setting it off. That's why I've never used this entrance before," Rune explained beside her.

"You can get us through, right?" Jerrik turned to Laila.

She frowned at the glowing symbols. "Yes, since it is such a short distance, but I need an idea of the layout beyond. It's never a good idea to teleport to a location you haven't seen before, but I think that's our only option."

"There is a staircase about fifteen feet beyond that ascends to the next level, where the storerooms are." Jerrik looked to Rune for confirmation.

The small man unsheathed a knife. "That is correct. The four guards are typically stationed just on the other side of this door. So, when we appear, be ready for a fight."

Laila offered them her arms. The others unsheathed their weapons before grabbing hold of her. Laila reached out with her magic once more and felt around the stone doors, assessing the space on the other side before teleporting them. For such a short distance, it only took a millisecond.

The guards let out startled cries when Laila's group appeared. As Rune had said, four guards flanked the door. The team dispatched them without hesitation, attacking to disable and render them unconscious, but not to kill. They were members of the Red Guard, but Laila found her opponent sorely lacking in skill. All it took was a simple spell to drop his blood pressure, and he collapsed.

Next, they hauled the guards up the stone staircase and into one of the kitchen storerooms before removing their red cloaks. Jerrik found a rope to bind them with since they didn't want the guards escaping and sounding the alarm. Eventually, the kitchen staff would discover the men, but hopefully not before Laila and the rebels had a chance to escape. They donned the guards' cloaks and pulled their hoods up to conceal their faces. There were undoubtedly many in the palace who would recognize Jerrik and Hallr otherwise, and Laila could only use glamour magic to disguise herself, so that wouldn't help the others.

They left the storeroom and strode through the level, only passing the occasional servant dressed in grey uniforms. The palace staff paid them little attention as they hurried about their business.

They climbed a flight of stairs, and Rune led them down a hallway into a more populous part of the palace where nobles in colorful clothing milled about.

"It will look too suspicious if we take the servants' passages. Guards never use them. We'll hide in plain sight," Rune explained when Laila hesitated.

Laila felt more inclined to take the servants' passages, but she knew she ought to trust Rune's judgment on this. He snuck into the castle often to spy for the rebels. She focused on keeping her pace unhurried and casual.

Despite the risk they were taking, Laila couldn't help but stare at the nobility she passed. They wore opulent gowns and suits that were nothing short of gaudy and bordering on the absurd. One woman had a hat with a massive stuffed bird tucked between crimson lace and silk flowers, and her skirts puffed out as colorful as a circus tent, layered in enough fabric to clothe an entire family. Laila spotted another pair of women and gaped in morbid fascination at their waists, clinched to half their natural size. Laila wondered how they could possibly digest their food. There were similar corsets in parts of Alfheim, but not as extreme as this. She had thought the Dragon Kingdom was opulent, but this was a whole new level. It felt as if she was walking through a carnival or a strange costume party. Even the men wore thick layers of heavily embroidered suits in vibrant colors, with large, flashy gemstones adorning their fingers and ears. She wondered if Jerrik had once dressed that way too. She found it hard to believe, considering his love for jeans and plain black t-shirts.

Yet again, no one seemed to mind them. More guards nodded to them, but otherwise, they went unnoticed. They reached a winding staircase that led upward to the palace's higher floors and toward the royal family's wing.

Hallr leaned in close. "I can't shake the feeling that something's off. I know Rune is used to sneaking in here, but this seems too easy."

"You think this is a trap?" she kept her voice low.

He nodded to the arch in front of them. "Back when Jerrik

and I lived in the palace, there were always guards stationed here, but their posts are deserted."

They passed under the arch into another stairwell. Laila was on edge, carefully examining each floor they passed as they climbed higher. There were no guards in sight. In fact, this part of the palace was entirely deserted. Something was definitely off.

Laila grabbed Jerrik's arm. "I don't like this, something's not right. We should go."

"No, not until we find my mother. Not when we've made it this far." His eyes were desperate.

"It's only a little farther," urged Rune.

Laila and Hallr exchanged uncertain glances, and Laila moved closer to Jerrik to keep him within reach.

She paused by a hallway lined with portraits of past monarchs. The faint scent of sulfur lingered in the air.

"What is it?" whispered Rune impatiently.

Laila frowned and watched for movement down the hall. "Demons. I think they're nearby."

Jerrik looked around nervously and urged her up the stairs. "Come on. We don't have time. If my father finds us, we're screwed."

Laila was just pulling her eyes away from the hall when the doors nearest opened and out sprang a pair of Demons—one a grizzly-looking Dragon and the other a creature of shadow. They lunged for Jerrik, but Laila stepped between them. She blasted the Demons with fire, but the shadow creature threw up a wall of darkness.

A gasp erupted behind her, and she turned to find Rune lunging for Jerrik—knife raised. Before she could move, Hallr sprang and tackled Rune to the ground.

"What are you doing?" Hallr snarled.

The shadow creature attacked, and Laila lost track of her friends. Massive talons extending from the shadow creature's fingers clawed at Laila. She ducked and attempted to thrust it away with a wall of air. It dodged and snaked shadowy tendrils from their hands to wrap around Laila's body.

As she struggled, Jerrik fought with the Dragon, and Hallr grappled with Rune by the stairs. There had to be reinforcements on the way. They needed to get out of there.

Laila grabbed the shadow tendrils with her glowing hands and sent a blast of fire along the coils, consuming them and destroying the shadow creature. Beside her, Jerrik decapitated the Demonic Dragon. Its blood sprayed across a painting on the wall.

"Get him out of here!" bellowed Hallr, still trying to wrestle the knife from Rune's grasp.

A glint of steel flashed as Rune palmed another knife in his free hand.

"No!" Jerrik shouted.

Too late, Hallr's eyes grew wide in shock as Rune pulled the knife across his throat. Crimson blood poured down his chest and stained his pale shirt. Rune grinned, but it was short-lived. Jerrik roared and impaled Rune on a spike of ice, pinning him to the stairwell wall. Blood gurgled from his mouth.

"Hallr!" Jerrik moved to help his friend, but Laila blocked his path.

"Jerrik, we have to get out of here." She glanced back at Hallr. He was Jerrik's oldest friend. How could they leave him here to die?

Go, mouthed Hallr, the light fading from his eyes. It was too late. There was nothing she could do for him now. They had to go.

Laila reluctantly turned to Jerrik. "I'm getting you out of here."

"No, not when we're so close! I won't let Hallr die in vain." Jerrik's voice cracked, and angry tears welled in his eyes.

Laila could force him to leave. She had power over him now that he was pledged to her. Yet Laila couldn't bring herself to. Reluctantly, she agreed and sprinted up the stairs with him, leaving Hallr's body below.

Jerrik froze at the top of the stairs. "This is it."

Still, no guards. Laila bit back a groan as Jerrik pushed the door open, and they stepped into the hall beyond. Rows of cells lined the walls. A shiver crept down her spine at the sight. She still had nightmares of being trapped behind bars. Just seeing them left her anxious.

"Mother!" Jerrik whispered as he reached her cell.

An older woman in a tattered gown sat within. Her long obsidian hair was streaked with silver and partially veiled her face. She was terribly thin, and her cheeks were hollow. Had the king been starving her? At the sound of Jerrik's voice, her body went tense, and her head turned sharply.

Her dark eyes grew wide. "Jerrik? Oh Gods no!"

"Don't worry. We're going to get you out of here."

She shook her head and stumbled to the bars of the door. "No! You can't be here!"

The reek of brimstone assaulted Laila's senses, causing her to gag as two figures appeared at the end of the hall. There was a scraping sound as the door locked behind her. Laila swore. They were trapped.

CHAPTER 29

The two figures approached through the shadows at the end of the tower prison. One was a tall man in an opulent blue suit. Gold accents decorated his coat, and a crown rested on his brow. If the crown wasn't a dead giveaway, the resemblance to Jerrik would have been. King Oddvarr. He had the same angular face, but the malice in his eyes was unlike anything Laila had ever seen in Jerrik.

Beside the king stood a woman with long dark hair. She didn't wear the Svartálfr court's fashions, but rather a plain silk dress in the deepest shade of black. The shadows seemed to lean in around her. Not only was she a Greater Demon, but Laila could sense divine magic in her aura. It was different from her own—distorted and volatile. This was Izel, the leader of the Demons.

"We have to go!" Laila hissed at Jerrik.

She reached for his arm but grabbed nothing but air. Jerrik's body was pulled across the room as if he was a marionette on an invisible string. He came to a jarring stop on his knees before his father.

Izel grinned viciously at Laila. "You can't leave. The reunion's only just begun!"

A pair of guards stepped out of a cell behind Laila and leveled their swords to her throat. Laila regarded them coolly as she struggled to form a plan.

"I told you I would kill you, boy," sneered the King while Jerrik fought the magic binding him.

Jerrik looked up into his father's eyes, calm but dignified. "This is precisely why the Swordmasters rejected you. They saw your spite, but they never imagined you would stoop so low as to fraternize with Demons."

Jerrik choked as Izel's magic clamped around his throat.

"Stop!" Laila screamed.

Izel cackled, but she released Jerrik. "You're that mettlesome Elf Marius told me about. You're more pathetic than I expected. It was all too easy to catch you. I honestly expected more of a fight."

Laila glanced at the two guards flanking her. Clearly, Izel underestimated her if she thought a couple of guards and a locked door were enough to stop her. The problem was Jerrik and his mother. If she was going to get them both out of here, she would have to choose her next moves carefully.

Laila gave the king a disgusted look. "How could you threaten to kill your own son? What sort of a twisted bastard are you?"

The king's eyes flashed. "Silence! Guards, dispose of her."

Laila watched as the sword swung toward her throat. In the last second, she vanished. Amidst the confusion, she appeared beside Jerrik and reached for his arm—

Wham! A blur in black silk slammed into her. The air was forced from Laila's lungs with the strength of the impact as she collided with the wall. She gasped as Izel sank her talons into Laila's arms and pinned her in place. There was a disturbing intensity in the Demon's eyes.

Laila recalled something Master Manach had said: that one day she would meet her equal in speed and strength. She had lost the element of surprise; now, she would have to find a way to outmaneuver Izel.

Laila's eyes flashed blue, and the markings on her arms roared to life—burning Izel's hands. The woman screamed and released her as the skin on the Demon's hands blistered. The spell holding Jerrik broke, and he drew his sword on his father.

"Protect the king!" a guard cried and rushed toward his monarch.

Jerrik thrust them back with a blast of air then charged his father, who waited with his sword at the ready.

Laila sent a blast of blue flame at Izel. The Demon hauled a guard in front of her as a shield, and he screamed. The fire incinerated the man before Laila could release the spell. She barely had time to conjure a shield as Izel blasted her with an obsidian spear of dark magic. She grunted as Izel attacked the barrier from all angles. Blow after blow pelted the shield. Laila's powers were strong, but Izel had been honing her abilities for centuries, if not longer.

Laila looked for an opportunity to reach Jerrik, but his focus was on fighting the King and three guards. If Laila grabbed him now, Jerrik would cut her to ribbons.

"Laila, go!" he cried, unable to pull his attention away from the fight at hand.

"No!" She struggled to hold her shield. "I'm not leaving without you."

"You have to. Please. Save her." The clash of steel echoed through the room as Jerrik disarmed a guard and nearly decapitated him. "Go!"

Tears clouded her vision. She wouldn't leave him to die. She couldn't. With a cry, she unleashed a massive blast of fire, but Izel contained it with her shadows.

"Is that all you've got, little Elf?" she mocked.

Laila couldn't do it. There was no way she could beat Izel. She simply wasn't strong enough.

"GO!" screamed Jerrik.

Laila grit her teeth and vanished in the darkness reappearing in the queen's cell. She reached for the woman just as she saw the guards tackle Jerrik to the ground.

"NO!" Laila screamed, but there was no way to get to him—not with Izel between them. She grabbed Jerrik's mother instead and vanished into darkness.

Her feet hit the ground, and she collapsed on the floor with the queen in the middle of the rebels' dining room. People around them gasped and scrambled from their seats.

"No! You have to go back! You have to save him!" the queen wailed.

Laila's body shook with a sob.

"I can't…I can't…Izel…" She trailed off.

Laila thought she would be able to get him out of there. She should have listened to Hallr and fled with Jerrik when she had the chance. Now he was trapped by his father, possibly even dead. Laila held the distraught queen and wondered how she could have let this happen.

CHAPTER 30

"They've killed him! They've killed my son!" The queen sobbed.

Laila could feel the shock and grief dragging her down as well. She left Jerrik behind. She had been so damned afraid to let him get close—that he would hurt her again. Now, he was in danger because of her.

Laila searched for the thread that formed when Jerrik bound himself to her. It was still there. She clung to it and focused on the other end.

Jerrik? Jerrik, are you okay? she asked desperately.

Laila? he replied.

Are you okay? What's happening?

Yes, at least for now. My father locked me up. Izel is keeping watch.

I couldn't stop her—

Shh, it's okay. I know. It's okay.

She felt along the thread for reassurance that he was okay. In her mind, she saw an image of Jerrik sitting in a cell. His lip bled, and bruises were starting to form across his face, but otherwise, he appeared alright.

I'm going to get you out. I'll find a way, she insisted.

Help the others, Laila. Make sure my father falls. He sounded resigned to his fate.

Damn it, Jerrik! Do not give up on me!

He didn't answer, but she could sense his presence.

Laila turned to the queen. "He's okay. At least for now."

"What are you talking about?" The queen sniffed.

Laila wasn't sure how the queen would react to learning her son had bound himself to her. "We're magically linked. I can communicate with him and see him."

The queen gave her a confused look.

"Your Majesty!" called Folki. He bowed to the monarch before helping her to her feet. "What's going on? Where's Jerrik?"

The queen peered around. "Where are we?"

Laila got to her feet, assisted by the crowd of rebels that had gathered around them. It was the only safe place she knew of in the city. Katla appeared from the group as well, examining the newcomers with a frown.

"I think it's best if you both come with me," said Folki as he motioned towards the stairs.

The queen glanced at Laila, who nodded reassuringly. Together they followed Folki upstairs to a makeshift war room with a hand-drawn map of the city spread out on a worn table. Katla joined and shut the door behind her.

"What happened? Where are the others?" Folki asked Laila roughly.

"We were returning from Jotunheim, and Jerrik insisted on attempting a rescue mission. I didn't like it, and neither did Hallr, but Rune was confident we could pull it off. Rune must've been a double agent, though. He led us directly into a trap."

"What?" Katla narrowed her eyes. "That's not possible."

Laila hardly acknowledged her. "I watched him slit Hallr's throat."

Her words hung heavy in the air as their meaning sunk in. The others seemed at a loss for words.

The queen collapsed into a chair. "Hallr is dead. Oh Gods, no. He was always such a good boy. He always watched Jerrik's back."

"What happened next?" asked Folki.

"The King was waiting with a powerful Demon sorcerer—a human turned Goddess named Izel. I couldn't…" She shut her eyes to maintain her composure. "I failed. I couldn't reach Jerrik to get him out."

A silence fell over the room.

"Where is he now?" whispered Folki.

Laila sagged against the back of her chair. "Imprisoned but still alive."

He paced back and forth. "Knowing the king, he will hold a public execution. Probably in place of her Majesty's."

Katla slammed her fist on the table. "You shouldn't have let him do this! He was our hope!"

Laila flinched. She had no retort since the woman was right.

"He's not dead yet; we still have a chance to save him." Folki looked around the table.

The queen spoke up. "How? They'll be ready and waiting for you, just as they were before."

Folki placed a silver marker on the map before them. "Then we wait until the execution itself. They will be the most vulnerable in the courtyard."

The queen shook her head. "You'd never be able to fight your way past the guards."

"We won't have to. It's a public event, so we can walk right in with the crowd." He pointed to the courtyard where he set the marker. "We won't have weapons aside from magic, but that may be our only chance."

"Izel will be there too, though, as well as dozens of guards. How can you hope to get close enough to free Jerrik?" The queen stared at Laila. Her eyes were mournful with an undercurrent of anger.

Laila had to find a way to make this right.

She took a deep breath. "We won't be alone. I think I can convince my people to send aid. I've made arrangements to take your Majesty to safety in Alfheim. I'll need to smuggle the two of us through the hall of portals, though."

Folki rubbed the back of his neck and examined the hall of portals on the map. "Katla knows a guy who can forge travel documents. We used him to get Jerrik out of here last year. You'll need disguises too."

"Only the queen will need a disguise. I can change my appearance," she reminded him.

Over the next hour, they debated the best approach for handling the situation. Laila's greatest concern was Izel. There had to be a way to beat her. Still, she came up blank over and over again.

It grew late, and the queen was exhausted. Folki showed the woman to her room for the night while Laila remained to stare at the map as the room emptied.

The cold bite of a steel blade pressed against her throat.

"If we didn't need you, I'd slit your throat," Katla hissed into her ear.

Laila didn't so much as blink. "You're not the only one who cares about him, you know. Yes, I made a mistake, but what would you have done in my position? Jerrik is your prince. Would you disobey his command?"

A soft growl escaped the woman's throat. "Even so, you should have found a way to bring him back."

In a flash, Laila disarmed the woman and plunged the knife deep into the table. She turned to Katla. "Jerrik's a big boy. He can make his own decisions. His choice was to sacrifice himself to save someone he loves. That is the kind of person he is, not the kind of person who hides in the shadows. For years he's been dying to take action and help others, and this is how he chose to do it. Who are you to question his decision?"

The Svartálfr narrowed her eyes but didn't find a retort, which was fine with Laila. She wasn't in a mood to talk, especially not to Katla. Laila brushed past the woman and left in search of something to drink.

She sat in the corner of the dining hall, and one of the rebels brought her a mug of tea. She sipped it and ignored the eyes of the others upon her. Rumors were already spreading about Jerrik's capture.

Folki sank into the chair opposite her. "I found Katla struggling to pry one of her knives out of the table. I take it you two had a confrontation."

Laila gave a half-hearted shrug. "If you could call it that. She's justified in her anger, though."

Folki shook his head. "She's impulsive and hotheaded. That's how she got on the wrong side of the Red Guard in the first place. Don't take it personally."

"Will she get the documents?" Laila asked, wondering how far the woman would go to spite her.

"Yes, she's just left to meet with her contact as we speak. I don't expect she'll be back for several hours, though."

Laila nodded. She figured it would take time to fabricate the papers. "I suppose the streets are crawling with guards. We'll have to be careful when we leave for the Hall of Portals."

"Probably, but I imagine that's not what you're concerned about." He studied her from across the table. "That Izel person really has you worried, doesn't she?"

Laila gave a reluctant nod. "I don't even know how to prepare for a fight with her. She thwarted every one of my attacks effortlessly. How can I hope to defeat an opponent like that?"

"Every opponent has a weakness. What's hers?"

Laila thought for a moment, recalling the magic she witnessed in the palace. "There was a moment when I teleported into the queen's cell that I froze. She could have easily followed, but she didn't. It makes me think that she can't teleport. Otherwise, why would she let me get away? I've been nothing but a nuisance for her and the Demons."

Folki's mouth quirked into a smile. "See? Now was that so

hard?”

“Even so, I’m not sure how to use that against her.” She stared down at the leaves swirling in the bottom of her mug, too ashamed to meet his gaze. “I’m so sorry about Hallr. I should’ve seen it coming—”

“How? I’ve been working with Rune for years, and I never suspected he would turn on us. He knew every move we’ve intended to make. Now I wonder how long he had been working for the enemy.”

Laila understood. She felt that way when she discovered Colin had been working for the Demons.

Folki shook his head and watched the rebels at the other tables. “The people in this city have grown restless. Rumors of Jerrik’s return have spread like wildfire. All over the city I’m seeing messages painted on walls announcing his return and calling for the people to rise up. It’s not our doing, but others in the city. We’re not alone, and I suspect they would be willing to join us and fight. Change is coming, Laila. It’s finally time to make our stand.”

The Norns had insisted she help the people of Nidavellir. She wondered how much they had known and how different things would have been if they warned her that Izel had set a trap.

CHAPTER 31

Laila pulled on the clothes the rebels found for her journey to Alfheim. No one wore jeans here, so they lent her a pair of light brown pants that gathered at the knees. She also wore a simple cream blouse beneath her black breastplate. Corsets were the fashion, but the breastplate looked similar enough and was far more practical. She kept her boots and leather jacket. They wouldn't look too out of place, and the jacket had the magical pockets, which she would need to store the Eirflower.

As she pulled on the clothes, she thought through the plan once more. Laila would teleport the queen to a location near the Hall of Portals, and they would enter with the morning rush-hour traffic. Hopefully, the guards would be more preoccupied with the crowd. There was no direct portal to the Elven city of Ingegard, but there was a portal to Schonengard in the Dragon Kingdom, where an escort would be waiting.

It was close to dawn, and Laila had spent the majority of the night helping the rebels prepare in whatever way she could. Her mind was troubled, and sleep eluded her, so she fletched arrows for archers and assembled little potions in glass vials that acted similar to a smoke grenade. These would be used by archers on rooftops to provide the rebels with cover along the escape route. As much as they hoped the plan would succeed, they had to be realistic. If the plan failed, they would have to retreat or face death. As she worked, she listened to their stories, and many of them were similar. The majority of these people had labored in the mines and lost friends or family to the dangerous conditions. Others told stories of the city guards who had seized their businesses and accused them of sympathizing with rebels. Ironically, they had been given shelter by the rebels when they had nowhere else to go. A few were scholars from wealthy families who had seen the other kingdoms and knew there was something better worth fighting for. Few of these rebels were trained fighters, though, and that fact alone concerned Laila.

She pulled on her jacket and left the room. She found Folki waiting.

He handed Laila two envelopes. "Here are the documents you'll need to get past the guards."

Laila pulled out the papers from the first envelope. These were the documents for the queen, who was to be an elderly widow named Helga.

Laila frowned. "This image doesn't really look like her."

"Katla is taking care of that."

Laila examined her papers next. Her name was Jax, and she worked in a shop in the Twilight Market. The Svartálfr woman in the photo was plain, middle-aged, and had dark hair starting to grey at the temples. She looked as though she could be the daughter of the woman in the other documents. Laila concentrated on the image and shifted her features to match.

Folki watched with mild interest as Laila checked her appearance in a mirror. "Looks good. They'll never know."

A door opened and out stepped Katla with an older woman dressed in a simple black gown and shawl. Even Laila was caught off guard. Katla must've applied a prosthetic nose and makeup, so the queen's thin, wan face appeared much older. Her hair had been pulled back into a simple bun and tucked under a small lace cap.

"Who is this?" the queen asked, eyeing Laila.

"It's me, Laila. I've magically altered my appearance." She explained with a bow. "Are you ready, your Majesty?"

"I'm not fond of the idea of fleeing," said the queen. Laila suspected it was mainly due to Jerrik's imprisonment. She couldn't blame her.

"I understand, but Jerrik was convinced this was best." Laila stowed their documents into a pocket then offered the queen her hand. "This may be a little disorienting like before."

The woman nodded. Laila kept a firm grip on Queen Birgitta as she teleported them out of the building. They arrived in one of the alleys across the street from the Hall of Portals.

Laila paused as a small wave of fatigue hit her. She was getting used to transporting others, although it was still far from easy.

"What manner of creature are you?" the queen asked as Laila led her towards the main street.

"I'm an Elf, but I was given divine powers to protect the mortal worlds." Laila scanned the busy street then ushered the queen across during a break in the traffic.

"The others told me my son has been working with you in Midgard." The queen watched the large crowd before the Hall of Portals as they waited for the doors to be unlocked.

Laila kept an eye out for any guards or nobles that might recognize the queen, which was unlikely. It was a pretty convincing disguise. While they waited, she told the queen how she met Jerrik. By the time she finished her story, the doors had opened, and the crowd began to move.

"So, no one in Midgard knew his true identity?" the queen sounded surprised.

"Only the Dragon Knight, but he didn't tell anyone. Jerrik preferred it that way. He enjoyed the freedom."

Queen Birgitta dipped her head, and Laila caught a glimpse

of a sad smile. "I tried so hard to give him a happy childhood, but somehow I always knew a conflict like this would arise. I don't think Jerrik was ever happy here. I'm not surprised he prefers Midgard."

Laila stuck close to her side as they waded through the crowd, blending in with the other travelers. "Do you think he'll make a good king?"

The queen nodded. "I don't think he'll be popular amongst the court since he would make many changes. But the people will approve. He may not want it for himself, but it's what the kingdom needs."

Laila spotted a pair of guards ahead. "Avoid making eye contact with them."

The queen did as Laila instructed, and they made it past without drawing attention. They followed the signs and took a branch of hallways leading to the Alfheim portals. Travelers crowded this branch, and more guards patrolled the area. They stood in line for the portal to Schonengard. Through the portal chamber's doorway, Laila could see rows of archers stationed in tiers along the walls. She didn't dare speak, not with this many sentries surrounding them. Instead, she pulled out their documents and payment as they waited.

"It wasn't always like this, you know," said the queen in a hushed tone. She looked around at the guards scrutinizing the travelers. "When I was a child, there were only a few sentries at each portal. There was no need for documents and no fee collected."

A passing guard turned his head sharply. "What did you just say, old woman?"

Laila placed herself between the queen and the guard, giving him a nervous smile. "My deepest apologies, sir. Please forgive my mother. She's just a delirious old woman. I'm taking her to live with her sister in Alfheim, where she won't be able to cause trouble."

Laila didn't dare to breathe as the guard snatched their documents from her hand and roughly flipped through them. He paused to scan Laila's information.

"Be sure she minds her tongue. It'd be a shame if anything were to happen to that shop of yours. You know what happens to rebel property." He shoved the papers back at her.

Laila fought to keep her expression neutral. She bowed and uttered a string of apologies through grit teeth. This abuse of power was disgusting, but she had to go along with it for now. It wasn't worth exposing herself or the queen. With a sick sensation in her stomach, Laila prayed she hadn't placed a target on some poor shopkeeper's livelihood.

She cast the monarch a warning look as they stepped up to the front of the line, where another guard waited to inspect their papers.

"What is your reason for traveling?" The woman skimmed over the paperwork.

"My mother's mind is starting to go. I'm taking her to live with her younger sister in the countryside where she'll be less of a disturbance."

The guard snorted as she counted the coins Laila gave her. "Some daughter you are, but if it keeps her from creating trouble here, then who am I to deny your request?" She handed Laila the papers and waved them through.

That was a relief. Laila walked towards the portal with the queen beside her. They had nearly reached the rippling veil of magic when a voice called out behind them.

"Wait just a minute!"

Laila spun as the same guard advanced upon them.

"Where is your luggage? If you are truly moving your mother, then where are her belongings?" demanded the guard.

The queen looked at Laila with wide, worried eyes.

Laila faced the guard calmly. "I sent her belongings ahead. I didn't want to haul everything through and keep an eye on her at the same time. She'd only find a way to sneak off and cause a scene in one of the halls. As for myself, I'll be returning later today or tomorrow. It seemed unnecessary to bring anything."

The guard eyed her suspiciously for another moment, but without proof of anything incriminating, she had no reason to stop them. "Very well. Be on your way."

Laila turned back to the portal and offered the queen her arm. Together they stepped through the veil. She didn't dare pause to relax, not yet. They hurried across the bridge and through to the other side. Laila dropped her disguise as she went. There would be no use for it in the Dragon Kingdom.

They emerged in a chamber where a small group of sentries greeted them.

"Welcome to Schonengard. Will you be staying here or making a connection?" asked one of the men who stepped forward.

"I'm not sure yet. Did an Elven emissary arrive here?"

Understanding dawned on his face, and he bowed. "Ah, yes, of course! You're Sir Eyvindr. I've been instructed to take you to them. Right this way!"

"Sir Eyvindr?" asked Queen Birgitta as they followed the Dragon down a hall.

"I saved the king last year. It's an honorary title the Queen of the Dragons bestowed in thanks."

Jerrik's mother watched her with an unreadable expression, but Laila didn't have time to think about it. They reached a door, and the guard knocked.

"Your majesty, the knight, has arrived," he announced, waving them into the room.

Laila relaxed the moment she saw her mother. She wore the sort of formal flowing gown most of the women in the Elven court preferred. Her mother stood beside a man a little older than Laila. She had never met him personally, but she had seen him at a couple of court events. It was Haraldur, Prince of the Elves. Laila bowed.

"Queen Birgitta, I see you arrived safely. Do not worry, you will be a welcome guest in my kingdom," said Prince Haraldur.

The queen drew herself up in her peasant attire and nodded. "You have my sincerest gratitude."

Laila straightened and noticed one of the guards standing behind the prince was her father. She had the strong urge to rush across the room and hug him, but that was not the way of their people—especially not in the presence of royalty.

Her mother took a step forward. "If I may, this is my daughter, Laila."

The prince turned to examine her. "I've heard many interesting tales of your exploits. It is a pleasure to finally meet you in person, Miss Eyvindr."

"Sir Eyvindr actually," corrected a woman behind her.

Laila spun around to find Queen Regina of the Dragons leaning casually against the wall beside the door. She wore pants and a tunic shirt that revealed the obvious bump of her stomach. She had just announced that she was expecting during Laila's last visit, and now she was showing.

Laila thought of how Regina had strung Frej along—seducing him despite her marriage to the King of the Dragons. Laila hadn't known this during their previous encounter. Fury smoldered like coals in her stomach, and for a moment, she nearly lunged for the queen. However, her years of discipline and training took over, and Laila maintained her composure. As much as she wanted to strangle the queen, she couldn't afford to lose allies, especially not at a time as tense as this.

Shoving her personal feelings aside, Laila forced herself to bow to Regina. "It's good to see you again, Your Majesty."

"I'm glad to see you've put my armor to good use." Regina gave her an approving grin—completely oblivious to the anger simmering within Laila. The queen sauntered smugly over to the Elven Prince. "Haraldur, you screwed up when you refused her for your royal guard. I would have taken her in a heartbeat. I offered her a position, but she declined to tend to her duties in Midgard." She sighed dramatically.

The Elven Prince allowed a brief flicker of surprise to break through his composure.

Laila was grateful she hadn't accepted the position, especially now that she knew more about the Dragon Queen.

"Don't forget about her abilities. I never thought I'd meet one of the divine in my lifetime." Queen Birgitta removed her prosthetic nose and scrubbed the makeup from her face with a handkerchief.

Everyone turned to look at her.

"What?" Laila's mother's voice rose an octave.

Laila chuckled nervously and looked away. She wasn't sure she wanted so many people to know the truth of her abilities. "I've been given the power to right the imbalance in the worlds. That's partially why I'm here. You see, King Oddvarr is working with Izel—the leader of the Demons. She and many of her people have made it to Nidavellir. If I can't remove them from this foothold now, the entire world will be forfeit. Likely, the other worlds as well. There are rebels in Nidavellir looking to rise up, but they can't do it alone. The prince, Jerrik, is imprisoned, and King Oddvarr will execute him tomorrow if we don't save him. I implore you to send aid."

Prince Haraldur turned to Ragna with a frown. "You did not mention anything about the prince's capture or that the leader of the Demons is involved."

"Oddvarr captured my son during my rescue," explained the Svartálfr Queen.

"Which was when I encountered Izel," added Laila.

Regina stepped forward. "I think we need to help. We've both known the situation in Nidavellir was volatile for years now. It's time we intervene and help those rebels before things get worse."

Prince Haraldur nodded slowly. "I agree that something must be done, but the portals are heavily monitored. I don't see how it would be possible to transport aid without drawing suspicion."

Laila's eyes fell on the sword at his hip. It was similar to the one Jerrik had been given by the Swordmasters.

"Excuse me, Your Highness, but did you train with the Swordmasters?" she asked.

He nodded. "Yes, it is a tradition in my family. Why?"

"There is an unsupervised portal beneath King Oddvarr's palace. It leads to the Swordmasters' temple in Jotunheim. If you could transport your soldiers to the temple, they could sneak into the city."

The prince nodded eagerly. "There is still a portal beneath our palace as well. It would be easy enough."

For the first time in days, Laila allowed herself a spark of hope. She was starting to make progress. "Excellent. I'll send guides to get you through the caves. Do you think your soldiers could be ready by tonight?"

"Yes, it's possible. I'll give the order to prepare."

Laila turned to Regina. "We could use aerial support if you'd be willing to lend it."

"I never back down from a fight," said the queen enthusiastically.

"Good. Then perhaps you can send your soldiers to join the Elves." She gave the prince a questioning look. She wasn't sure how he would feel about leading another army's soldiers through the bowels of the palace.

To her surprise, he inclined his head. "I will arrange it. We will need to learn to work together against this growing Demonic threat."

Laila discussed other details with them, including how they would reach the courtyard and the supplies the rebels required. Jerrik's mother offered to fill the prince in on additional information later.

Prince Haraldur thanked them both. "Now, if there isn't anything further to discuss, we should be going. I'll need to prepare the soldiers."

He turned to leave, but Laila's mother, Ragna, stepped up beside him. "Excuse me, Your Highness, might I have a word with my daughter?"

He nodded. "I'll meet you at the portal."

Ragna hung back as he swept out of the room. Laila caught her father's eye, and he gave her a warm smile before hurrying out with the king.

Jerrik's mother paused before Laila. "I want to apologize for my hostility last night. My son is fortunate to have you watching over him. Please save him. I can't lose him."

Laila bowed. "I swear I will do everything within my power to save him."

"Thank you," Queen Birgitta whispered before following the prince.

"Your father sends his love," said her mother gently as the door shut. "Why didn't you tell us about these powers?"

"I don't know. I just didn't want to worry you." She looked down at the edge of the blue scar that poked out from under her jacket sleeve.

"We will always worry; that's what parents do. But we will also be there to support you, even if it is on a path where we cannot follow." She gave Laila a tender look.

Laila couldn't help it. She pulled her mother into a hug. "Thank you."

Ragna's eyes widened at the sudden display of affection, which was shocking by Elven standards, but she relented and hugged her daughter. "Be careful tomorrow."

"I will. I have a favor to ask, though." Laila reached into her pocket and pulled out the silk pouch with the Eirflower. "This is the cure my friend Ali needs. Do you think you could have a trusted messenger deliver it to Los Angeles?"

Ragna looked down at the pouch mournfully. "I'm sorry, but Los Angeles has suspended all arrivals. No one can get through. The consulate tells me the governor gave the order yesterday. Even if a messenger took it through, they would not be allowed to deliver it."

"What?" Laila's heart plummeted. How was she supposed to deliver the flower now? The only option she had was to go herself and teleport the moment she arrived in Los Angeles, but she didn't have time. Not when she had so much more to prepare.

The price of one life cannot compare to that of an entire world. The voice of the Norn echoed in her head.

"It's okay. I'll find another way." Laila gave her mother a sad smile as Ragna bid her goodbye and left to join the others.

Queen Regina stepped forward. "Can I offer you anything before you return?"

They were now alone in the room, and as Laila turned to the woman, she thought of Frej and the drama his queen had caused in his life.

"I know about what happened between you and Frej," Laila said, ice creeping into her tone.

The queen blinked. "He hadn't told you before?"

Laila shot her a hard look. "No, and he's still struggling with his feelings for you. I don't approve of your actions or treatment of him, but for the sake of the threat the Demons pose, I intend to put our differences aside."

The monarch's cheeks flushed, her guilt apparent. "I under-stand. You are a better person than I am. I would fight you on the spot if our positions were switched. You should know that I've vowed not to let history repeat itself—for the sake of my family and for Frej."

There was so much more Laila wanted to say, but she feared she would lose her composure. Now was not the time for pet-ty squabbles. There was far more work to be done before the morning.

As she returned to Nidavellir, Laila was confronted once more by guards, but they allowed her passage. Laila wandered through the crowd that headed toward the exit and found a cor-ner hidden from view. She teleported to the chamber below the palace, where the statues of Jerrik's ancestors watched over the portal to Jotunheim.

It was strange how much had changed since she passed

through here the day before. She certainly hadn't planned on returning so soon, but she needed all the help she could get. With a deep breath, she stepped through the portal and into the space between the worlds.

❖ 257 ❖

CHAPTER 32

The wind whipped at Laila's hair and face as she made her way to the Swordmasters' temple in Jotunheim. The clouds above were dark and foreboding, and in the distance, the rumble of thunder echoed over the crashing surf. As she approached the temple, two figures in white lowered their hoods—Master Manach and Master Bas.

"Laila, what brings you back so soon?" Master Bas asked.

The words tumbled from her mouth faster than she intended. "Jerrik's been captured. He'll be executed in the morning. I need your help to save him."

The Swordmasters exchanged horrified glances.

"Come, we'll take you to the Grandmaster," said Master Manach, as he waved her into the temple.

Laila nodded and followed them through the halls to a door on the top floor of the temple complex. Master Bas knocked, then they entered a small study with a large wooden desk. Beyond it, massive windows overlooked the raging ocean, creating a foreboding backdrop.

The Grandmaster looked up from a thick tome. "Laila?

What are you doing here?"

"Jerrik has been captured by his father and Izel, ruler of the Demons. Oddvarr will execute him in the morning. We need the Swordmasters to help us rescue him and to deal with the Demons who've invaded Nidavellir."

The Grandmaster frowned and slowly closed their book. "I'm sorry, I truly am, but I told you before that we will not leave the temple grounds—not even for one of our own. We will not risk losing what remains of this order."

Laila planted her hands on the desk and leaned in close as she stared down the Grandmaster. She didn't have time for this.

"How dare you sit in the comfort of your temple while the rest of us struggle against the Demons! Your order was established to keep the balance—the same task the Norns gave me. A war is coming that will decide the fate of all the worlds. This isn't about politics and court drama; it's about saving people. The Demons will destroy countless innocent lives, but you're willing to look the other way. If you have one shred of honor left, you will arm yourselves and help us remove the Demonic presence in Nidavellir." With each word she spoke, her anger grew, and with it, her aura until she filled the room with her glow, and her voice echoed through the chamber. "What good will your order be when there is no one left? When the Demons have conquered the mortal realms, and the very fabric of our worlds unravels!"

Lightning forked across the sky beyond the window, and thunder shook the building as if punctuating her statement. The Grandmaster stared at her, stunned.

Laila straightened. "Make your choice. The Dragons and Elves will be here soon to use your portals. Come with them if you're ready to return to the worlds. You told me you were waiting for a sign, well, here it is."

With that, Laila stormed out of the room, leaving the shocked Swordmasters behind. She left the temple and returned to the portal as flashes of lightning lit up the sky. The decision was in their hands now, and regardless, there were preparations to be made.

The cold, rough stone dug into Jerrik's back and gradually sapped the heat from his body. Far from the warmth and comfort of the palace below, the tower prison was dark and dreary. He heard stories of prisoners becoming ill and dying, leaving their Ghosts to roam these halls. As a boy, he exchanged those wild tales with Hallr, each more gruesome than the last, until they scared themselves silly.

Hallr. A terrible sense of helplessness gripped Jerrik as he recalled the moment Rune drew his blade across Hallr's throat. The sight of crimson rivulets pouring down his shirt and dripping down the stairs below was seared into Jerrik's mind. The light that danced in Hallr's eyes slowly fading for eternity. Hallr was dead.

He had been Jerrik's constant companion for most of his life. Hallr had given up everything—his title, his name, his inheritance—to follow Jerrik into the rebellion. He never once lamented the fact but took to life in hiding with a sense of purpose, knowing he was fighting for a cause greater than himself. Amongst the rebels, Hallr never acted as though he were superior. Any rank and respect he earned came from his hard work and dedication. He was quick to laugh and charismatic but also genuine.

Jerrik rested his face in his hands. He had been such a fool to lead the others into the palace. They tried to warn him, but he refused to listen. It was his fault they had walked into this trap, and Hallr had paid the price.

A clack of delicate boots upon the stone floor signaled Izel's approach. She had hardly left Jerrik alone since his capture. He was certain she waited for Laila.

Keys jingled, and the door of his cell creaked open.

"Here. Clean yourself up." Izel plunked a bucket on the floor of the cell. The water sloshed over the rim as she locked the door once more.

Jerrik ignored the Demon.

She clicked her tongue in disapproval. "You know, I'm the only one with the power to spare your life now. It would be wise to show some respect."

"How long has my father been your puppet?" Jerrik remained where he was. He didn't care if he was caked in blood. He would ignore the bucket out of spite if it irritated Izel. It was one of the few freedoms he had left.

She scraped one of her claws along an iron bar of his cell, and Jerrik involuntarily winced at the shrill sound. She chuckled.

"Not long, I admit. Fate has done a good job of driving him to madness without me. Vengeance and fear are the breeding ground for suspicion. His actions in his youth set the stage. Has he ever told you how it felt to kill his father? I imagine it was quite daunting for one so young." Her wicked glee was tangible.

Jerrik looked up. His grandfather died at the hands of an assassin when his father was a boy. At least, that's what Jerrik had been told.

"So, you didn't know then?" Izel's eyes shone like polished steel. "As a boy, your father grew weary of your grandfather's disdain. He poisoned the man in hopes of rising above the misery and mockery the court had made of the angry boy. I'm not sure it worked that way, though. Now he's grown to fear history will repeat itself—that you will be the one to end his life."

"Sounds like a self-fulfilling prophecy," muttered Jerrik.

"Indeed. Those are always the most tantalizing, in my opinion! Such a shame you seem so uninterested. Otherwise, I'm sure I could help you find a way to remove him from power." She watched him eagerly as the shadows floated and twitched around her.

Jerrik wasn't interested. He had no desire to kill his father—not unless absolutely necessary. His father wasn't a good person by any stretch of the imagination, but Jerrik knew Izel would only prey on his dark thoughts. She didn't care who ruled this country, so long as they were within her grasp.

She leaned in. "Don't tell me you think that Elf is still going to save you. Even if she does return, I will be waiting. And even with the Norns backing her, she is still not strong enough to kill me."

Laila was working with the Norns. Since when? His face must have betrayed his surprise because Izel's grin widened.

"I see she kept that from you. How interesting. Perhaps she doesn't trust you quite as much as you thought." She looked positively delighted as she knelt to his eye level and cocked her head to the side. "You see, this is why I turned my back on the Gods. They pretend to care about the lives of mortals while ignoring their pleas on a whim. I knew I was the only one I could trust to save my people. The Gods only claim I'm evil because I chose to defy their treachery."

Her words wrapped around him in the dark. He knew she was trying to break him down and to turn him against Laila. Yet, despite his best efforts, he couldn't help but feel there was some truth to her words. After all, what had the Gods ever done to help the people he cared about? Even Laila, who followed him on this absurd mission, had left him behind.

Jerrik shook his head. No, he told her to go… Or had he? He couldn't remember now.

Izel continued to watch him as her shadows shifted around him, resembling a thousand beetles crawling about the cell and sowing seeds of doubt in his mind.

A ring of fire erupted around him, burning bright enough to disrupt the shadows and send them fleeing into the deepest recesses of the cell. The poisoned thoughts suddenly evaporated like mist on a hot summer morning.

He glared at Izel through his flaming circle. "You will not break me. You can try your little mind tricks all you want, but I know Laila. She will not abandon me."

Izel sneered through the bars of the cell. "You better hope she does because if I see her again, you can be sure I'll destroy her. There are some deaths even the divine can't return from."

The malice in her eyes chilled him to the bone. He couldn't breathe. His flames wavered, and the shadows seemed to lean in closer. Could he allow Laila to risk herself that way? How could he let her walk into yet another trap for his sake?

Laila? He sent his thoughts out, hoping she would hear him.

I'm here. Your mother is safe. I've found a way to rescue you too.

Don't. It's a trap. Please, Laila—

I'm not leaving you, Jerrik.

Gods damn her stubborn streak.

Izel peered at him, fascinated. "You're communicating with her, aren't you? Interesting. Send her my regards, won't you? Tell her I'll be waiting."

With that, Izel stood and faded back into the shadows. Jerrik couldn't see her, but it didn't matter. He could still feel her lurking in the darkness—a spider watching its web.

"Your Highness." Laila bowed as Prince Haraldur of the Elves stepped through the portal deep in the tunnels of Nidavellir.

He inclined his head ever so slightly. "So, what is the plan here?"

Laila guided him through the collapsed passage to the mine tunnels. "These mines are abandoned due to safety concerns, but there are shafts through the main channel that lead to platforms high above the city."

They reached the main shaft where Laila and the others had nearly tumbled to their deaths. Now, Dragons in their scaled forms stood on the ledges, waiting for orders. The Fire and Air Dragons had wings and were able to fly up to the tallest platforms. The Earth Dragons, with their strong talons, could climb the walls and clear away debris.

She motioned to the Dragons. "They will help transport the Elves into the city and provide aerial support. In the meantime, our people will wait in the caverns above until I give the signal. The palace is built into the cave's stone wall almost directly above where we stand, and a long, winding walkway climbs from the city up to a courtyard. It will be far easier for reinforcements to drop in from above than to scale the stone below the palace."

The prince nodded. "I take it you will be with the rebels in the city?"

"Yes. We'll make our way up to the palace courtyard on foot and stop the execution. From there, we will try to take the palace and capture the king and Izel. If a retreat is necessary, we'll fall back to the Hall of Portals. It's the second-largest building aside from the palace and the most defensible. It would also allow us to retreat to the Dragon Kingdom if necessary. We'll send some of our reinforcements to secure the building."

It would also ensure she had a clear route to Los Angeles after the battle.

The prince called orders to the soldiers filtering in behind him while a general from the Dragon Kingdom started assigning Dragons to transport them to the upper levels. A handful of rebels with experience in these mines were on hand to act as guides since the tunnels above were nothing short of a labyrinth. The rest of the rebels waited down in the city, making preparations.

Laila noticed the prince watching her.

"What do you plan to do when this is all over? Will you stay here?" he asked.

"I must return to Midgard. I have pressing matters to attend to there. A dear friend will die if I don't return with a cure for her." She swallowed and watched an Air Dragon take off with three Elves on his back.

"You are torn between staying and leaving."

Laila shrugged, forgetting for a brief moment she addressed

royalty. "I've been commanded to dispatch the Demons here. I cannot leave until I accomplish that."

His face remained calm and emotionless—the epitome of Elven composure. "No leader ever wants to be in that position. I believe you are doing the right thing, but that doesn't make it easier. You have my sympathies."

"Thank you, I appreciate that. If you'll excuse me, I should check on the portal." Laila bowed and took her leave. She returned to the portal as the last of the Elves entered and directed them to follow the others. However, before she could turn to follow them, another figure emerged from the portal.

"Hello Laila!" Master Okaenos waved.

Laila stopped in her tracks. "Wait, what are you doing here?"

More Swordmasters emerged from the portal, including the Grandmaster. Instead of their usual white robes, they wore armor emblazoned with a single sword pointed skyward.

The Grandmaster approached and bowed. "I determined you were right. Now is a time for action, and I would be a fool to refuse the Norns. We are here to aid you in any way we can."

Thank the Gods! She knew they would need all the help they could get.

Master Bas stepped up to Laila, examining her with a frown. "Where is the rest of your armor?"

All Laila had was the breastplate. She hadn't wanted to pull from the rebels' resources. The Swordmaster turned and stepped back through the portal as Laila ran through her plan with the Grandmaster.

"If we can acquire robes from the local temples, we would be able to enter without being searched," the Grandmaster pointed out.

"That could make things a lot easier. You'd be able to enter with the rebels," mused Laila as she looked down at a map. They still had a few hours before curfew was lifted and the city awoke. "I'll see what I can do."

Now that the Elves and Dragons were nearly in position,

she had time to return to the rebel headquarters. Hopefully, Folki would have some resources or connections in local temples to draw from.

Even if the Dragons were swift, there was still a window of time where the rebels would face the guards on their own. It was a risk since most of them lacked training, but if the Swordmasters were there as well, it would give them a better chance of survival.

As reckless as this plan had seemed last night, Laila began to feel a glimmer of hope. She wasn't alone. Her allies were here to help. Perhaps they actually had a shot at success after all.

CHAPTER 33

The sun was setting along the horizon when Frej leaned against the wall of the state capital building in Santa Monica. He stood by a backdoor leading out to a small street lined with cafes and restaurants. Yesterday, Mato had seen a group of people exit the building from this door—presumably on their breaks. He waited with Henrik and a man from Jenn's investigative team, Rob. Close to forty, he had sandy blond hair colored brown with temporary dye. Jenn had assured Frej that the agent would be able to get them into the computer's security system.

They each wore suits and held cups of coffee. To anyone passing by, they would appear to be a group of employees on break. A short distance away, other agents sat inconspicuously at cafes. Many of them had also altered their appearances slightly, hoping the pedestrians wouldn't recognize them.

"Frej, what's going on? Do you need a charm to get through the door?" Lyn asked through his enchanted com device.

A second later, the door opened with a click, and two men in suits exited the building, deep in discussion. They hardly acknowledged the others. Frej caught the door with a spell of air before it shut, and they quickly entered the building.

"We're in," Frej whispered as he and the others walked down the hall.

They passed a couple of custodians, but no one seemed to question their presence. They reached a door labeled security. Frej nodded to the others before tugging it open and stepping into the room.

Two security guards seated at desks glanced up. Before they could react, Frej grabbed the first and looped a necklace with a carved piece of wood over the man's head. He dropped to the ground asleep, with Frej cushioning the impact. Henrik and Rob soon rendered the other unconscious as well, and the three of them dragged the sleeping men into a closet in the corner of the room.

"How long will these charms last?" Frej asked Lyn. He locked the closet for good measure.

"I tested them on an IRSA agent yesterday, and she was out for hours. It wasn't until I removed it that the effects wore off."

Henrik shook his head. "That's a strong spell."

She barked a laugh. "Yeah, I came across it when we were researching cursed blades. I guess that reading wasn't all for nothing."

Rob pulled out a thumb drive inscribed with runes. "Okay, Lyn, I'm inserting the USB stick now."

He placed it in the computer at the first desk. For a moment, the screen flickered. Then the runes on the USB stick began to glow.

Lyn's voice came through the com device. "I've got access. I can see you from here on the security cameras. Just don't remove the thumb drive."

Henrik and Rob stayed back in the office while Frej returned to the back door. "Okay, team two, I'm coming for you now."

He reached the back door and swiped an access card he had taken from the security guards. Three agents stepped in.

"Careful Frej, you've got two more guards heading your

way," cautioned Lyn.

"Thanks for the warning." He pulled out another charm, as did one of the agents.

They found the security guards rounding a corner. Frej generated a barrier of air to dampen the noise while the IRSA agents grabbed the guards and slipped the charms over their heads. Together they carried the guards back to the office and stowed them with the first two.

That was four security guards down. From what Frej could see on camera, they had about ten more in the building, including the three guarding the front door. All they needed to do was to pick them off before the journalists arrived in an hour for the conference.

"Okay, team two is in. Team three, what's your status?" asked Frej.

"We've got five more minutes until sundown. We'll notify you when we're on our way," said one of the Vampires.

"Okay, what about team four?"

"We're still in position." They were the ones waiting at the cafés and in a couple of cars. Their mission was to help the others get out in case something went wrong.

"Team five?"

"Good to go." Team five consisted of nearly a dozen armed Vampires who would enter as their backup after Darien and Ligeia made their presences known.

So far, everything seemed to be going according to plan. The Demons they dealt with thus far seemed to rely on brute force, but Lorelei relied on her magic. Meaning, while it had been easier to break into this building than the Vampire rebels' underground complex, they would have to steer clear of Lorelei or risk falling prey to her spell. Lyn had painted enchanted runes on the back of their necks, which should deter the Siren's magic. Still, this seemed far too easy, and Frej worried they were forgetting something.

Darien finished combing his hair in the bathroom mirror and stared at his reflection. Gone was the denim and leather, replaced by a suit the color of steel with a black shirt and crimson tie that Sarnai had provided. He also wore a pair of polished dress shoes far nicer than his usual boots.

He opened the case with his contacts and paused. He hadn't worn contacts in five years, and he suddenly remembered how much he hated them—mostly because he hated hiding. If this mission failed and he still survived, he wondered if he would have to go back to wearing them to move about the city freely. If Lorelei killed him, what would happen to the other SNPs? Who would be there for them?

He put the contacts in and looked at his reflection. The man staring back at him was an entirely different person, but wasn't that the idea? He would sneak in, right under the governor's nose.

He gathered his regular clothes and returned to the living room. The safehouse felt empty, with the majority of the team already gone. Only Talen, Ligeia, and Sarnai remained. They waited by the door for him.

"I knew you'd look good in that suit," Sarnai said, pleased.

The other Vampires wore contacts as well. They were dressed in business attire with the press passes Talen acquired from a local newspaper called The Supernatural Times.

"They're loading Ali into the ambulance," explained Talen as he handed Darien a pass.

Darien nodded and entered the garage. The ambulance's back doors stood open, and Meuric was securing Ali in the back of the rig. Her condition had deteriorated rapidly, and Erin insisted they stay close.

Erin stared through the doors at her sister and watched as if sheer will might be enough to save the Fae. Mato was there as well, climbing into the driver's seat. Meuric had informed them that despite his healing, Ali was barely clinging to life. Without a miracle, this would be her last night.

"You look really different," said Erin quietly as Darien approached.

"Yeah, I haven't worn a suit in a while." He peered at Ali inside the ambulance. "I wanted to tell you… there's a possibility we can save her by turning her. I'm not sure how it would work given the curse, and there would be side effects from the change, but I wanted you to know that it's an option."

Erin nodded slowly. "I'd thought about that. I know she wouldn't be crazy about being a Vampire, but I also think she wouldn't want to die. Not when there is so much more to do. Still, it's part of the reason I want us to be nearby."

"And the other part?"

"Because Laila is on her way. She won't be able to find us here in the safehouse, but she'd find us at the capitol building." There was an unusual amount of confidence in her voice—certainly more than he felt.

Darien shook his head. "Why do you think she's going to make it?"

"Because she can hear my prayers. I've been keeping her updated, and she knows Ali's running out of time. She told me she'd be here tonight." She clenched her phone in her hand tightly as if expecting Laila to call at any moment.

Darien wasn't sure how to react. Was it true, or just the wishful thinking of a girl who was losing her sister? "Okay, but you call me if anything changes with her condition, okay?"

She nodded.

He walked around the side of the ambulance to where Mato sat in the driver's seat. "Did you grab the equipment?"

The Were patted the duffel bag beside him. "I've got the helmet and other gear in here."

Darien nodded. "Good. I want you to keep a low profile and park in one of the alleys. The helmet will allow you to communicate with us and identify anyone who approaches."

"Got it." His expression remained hard and unreadable.

Darien had never seen Mato so grim and withdrawn. He was uninterested in the confrontation with Lorelei and refused to leave Ali's side. But Darien knew the Werebear was fighting an internal battle of his own. Mato had been through Hell before and always managed to stay optimistic, but he cared deeply about Ali.

Darien stepped back as Erin climbed into the ambulance and pulled the doors shut. He followed the others into a car. The faint glow of sunset was still on the horizon as they pulled out of the garage with the ambulance behind them.

As they drove, Talen explained that the majority of their people, human and Vampire alike, had made it into the building. They would be able to communicate to the others via Donald's enchanted earpieces once they got closer.

Donald wasn't on site. He had chosen to park over at the news station and attempt to hack into the computers from there. Jenn was with him and ready to make her live broadcast speech. She still wasn't crazy about the plan, but Darien knew she was the right person for the job.

The tension was thick as they drove. Ligeia was a woman of few words, but he noticed the nervous way she wrung her hands in the back seat. In the last few days, she had spent every moment she could with Lyn. He knew she not only worried about confronting the Siren, but what would come after.

They pulled into the parking lot of the new state building.

"Okay, Lyn, we're heading in," he said into his com device.

"Just a heads up, none of our people are at the security checkpoint," she replied.

That meant they would have to enter unarmed, but fortunately, he planned for this. They entered the building and stepped in line with the reporters. He recognized many of them from various news stations, but no one appeared to give him a second glance.

When they reached the front of the line, Darien showed the

security guard his press pass for The Supernatural Times.

"Really? That rag? I'm not even sure it qualifies as a newspaper!" The man sneered but waved them through the metal detector.

Darien, Talen, and Ligeia passed through with no problems, but an alarm sounded on Sarnai. Two of the security guards approached. She rolled her eyes and kicked off a pair of pumps with metallic heels, and handed them over.

"Sorry, I tend to forget I'm wearing these."

One of the guards passed the shoes through the metal detector, setting off the alarms once more.

"Sorry, ma'am, we're still going to have to search you."

Ligeia walked over and looked up innocently at the guard. "Is there a problem here?"

Both guards blinked as her charm magic hit them. "Um, no. Of course not. Please go ahead."

Sarnai slipped on her shoes, and they continued to the press conference. "That's quite a skill you've got there, Siren."

Ligeia shrugged. "It comes with the territory."

They followed the journalists toward the press room. When they entered, Darien noticed Frej standing to the right. Henrik was there as well, plus the majority of their backup who stood along the edges of the room. They made no sign of acknowledgment as the group took their seats. Everything had gone according to plan so far. A camera crew was busy setting up in the back, and Darien hoped Donald would take control of their broadcasting system before his team made their move.

By the time the rest of the journalists entered, the room was near full capacity. The Governor walked in and stepped up to the podium. Lorelei entered as well, but she hung back by the door.

Darien leaned over to Ligeia. "Is she the one?"

The Siren gave him a stiff nod. "Yes, but she's much stronger than I expected. I can feel her. She wasn't this powerful the last time I saw her."

That wasn't reassuring.

"Do you still think you can provoke her?" he asked.

"I hope so."

Darien's doubt seeped through his confidence as well. If they failed to prove the Demon's identity, not only would she remain in control, but any chance of clearing their names and returning to the agency would be gone as well.

They sat in silence as Fredrik Stacy addressed the crowd. "Good evening, we are going to go ahead and get started. I know there's been a lot of talk about the former IRSA agents still at large, and I've been informed that the California State Troopers are following up on leads as I speak. I have full faith in them, and I'm certain it is only a matter of time before the rogue agents are apprehended."

The irony of the situation wasn't lost on Darien, but he kept his expression neutral. As much as he wanted to act and get this over with, they were still waiting on Donald. They needed to ensure they had control of the broadcast feed before making a move.

"Donald, how's it going?" asked Lyn through the coms.

"Still working. I just need a little longer."

They had time, but only another twenty minutes or so at the most. It would have to be enough.

Jenn watched Donald work away on his computer. She could tell he was beginning to panic, and while Donald was the awkward, nervous sort, she had rarely seen him frazzled like this—especially when he was working.

"Hey, you've got this. The press conference is just getting started. There's plenty of time."

He grunted in response.

"Is there anything I can do to help? Is there another one of those thumb drive things I can plug into their system?" she offered.

He shook his head. "The one I gave the other team is a prototype. I have to do this the old-fashioned way."

Jenn gave him some space and crawled to the back of the van, where they had set up a recording area for her. She double-checked the laptop she would use as a teleprompter for her speech the team had prepared. Jenn skimmed through it, but something about it still seemed to miss the mark. It just seemed too formal. It didn't feel right, or at least it didn't feel like her.

She still didn't think she should be the one to do this. Not only did she have a raging case of stage fright, but this was just too public. Jenn was a private person. Hell, she didn't even have a social media account. The others had a point, though. She had grown up in this city. She was a bridge between communities—the sort of person who should be able to bring people together. It was a lot of pressure, though, and words could easily be misinterpreted.

"Yes!" cheered Donald, pumping his fist in the air. He spun around as he spoke into his com device. "I'm in. We're ready whenever you are, Darien!"

Jenn settled herself into position, her heart pounding as Donald prepared the camera for the live broadcast.

CHAPTER 34

Laila watched the crowd as she entered the palace gates. Some of the people looked fearful, while others were disturbingly excited. Bile rose in her throat as she remembered the fight ring. It just went to show that no matter what world you were in, there would always be those who got a thrill out of violence.

She picked out the faces she knew in the crowd. The rebels were dressed in plain clothes and lacked their weapons since the guards searched everyone entering the courtyard. Laila had lent her jacket with the enchanted pockets to Katla to store knives and other smaller weapons, plus the rebels still had their elemental magic. It would have to be enough.

A pair of monks in drab, grey robes from the Temple of Loki shuffled along next to her. Their hoods were drawn so close Laila could barely make out their features. Master Bas and Master Manach nodded to her in acknowledgment.

"We are ready," Master Bas uttered as his cat eyes scanned the crowd. More Swordmasters dotted the crowd, dressed in robes from various temples around the city that Folki managed to procure.

"Good. Our friends will be waiting," Laila replied. They kept their conversation vague since there was no telling who might overhear.

Laila wore a robe from the Temple of the Norns, made of dark blue fabric with Yggdrasil embroidered in pale blue thread. Beneath, she wore her breastplate from Regina. Master Bas had given her armor from their own stores, including bracers to protect her arms and a gorget to protect her throat and neck. She hadn't brought her weapons, but she would be able to summon them. One item she did carry with her was the Eirflower—carefully tucked into a pouch at her hip.

Laila, please hurry! Ali's running out of time. Erin's voice echoed in her head.

I'll be there soon. I'll let you know as soon as I make it through the portal. Laila hoped Ali could hold on a little longer. She just had to secure Jerrik's safety and deal with Izel, and then she could leave. Unfortunately, it wasn't going to be that easy.

She walked with the Swordmasters towards the gates, where a pair of guards stopped them.

"All who enter must be searched," the nearest guard announced.

"We are holy men and women. Surely you wouldn't offend us so," hissed Master Manach from the depths of his hood.

"This is an offense not only to our orders but to those we serve! How dare you disgrace us!" snapped Laila.

One of the other sentries intervened—likely fearful some angry God might smite them. "Let them pass. The temples have the right to send their witnesses. We don't want to offend the Gods."

Laila suspected it was too late for that, considering the Norns had sent her here to eliminate the Demons.

The other looked uncertain but waved them through. "Very well, my apologies, we intended no disrespect."

Laila gave a stiff nod and swept past with the others following. They entered a courtyard where a large crowd gathered around a platform erected in the middle of the yard. Jerrik was bound to the center of it with thick enchanted chains that glowed with red runes. Before him sat a wooden block stained with the blood of past victims. The executioner stood nearby. In his hand was an ax with a large curved blade. She shuddered.

Laila froze as she took in Jerrik's defeated expression. The light in his eyes had dimmed, and he looked tired and broken. Following the thread of their connection, she reached out to him.

Jerrik, I'm here.

His sullen eyes looked up from the executioner's block. *You shouldn't have come. You should have gone back to Midgard, to Ali.*

I told you I won't let them kill you. Be ready.

But Izel—

I'll handle her. We're not alone this time, and I won't let her catch me off-guard.

Overhead, nobles watched from windows and balconies, most of them expressionless, although Laila noticed some of the young women dabbed their eyes with handkerchiefs. Many of the young men looked troubled, although no one spoke out on Jerrik's behalf. On a large terrace, one level above the courtyard, the king sat upon his throne. His face was cold and emotionless as he looked down his nose at his son. Beside him stood Izel, casually leaning against the throne. She watched Jerrik with glee, reminding Laila of a cat with a mouse trapped in its paws. Nearly a dozen guards stood behind them, flanking a set of double doors that led to the throne room.

Laila wondered what Izel had bribed him with to lure him over to her side. Was it power? Land? Immortality? Even from here, Laila could smell her stench. She made sure her aura was masked and hoped it would be enough to prevent Izel from detecting her.

The crowd fell silent as the king stepped forward to address the people. "Subjects, we have gathered here to witness the execution of a traitor to the crown. This man—my own son—has spent years conspiring against me with the rebels who seek to destroy everything we have built." He paused and cast Jerrik a look of utter disgust. "I will not tolerate such insolence—not from our people and not from my own family. All I can hope is that, as my son dies, so too will the rebellion that has protected him."

He waved, and the executioner stepped forward.

Izel smirked from the shadow of the throne. "Do you have any last words, prince?"

Jerrik straightened and looked out at the crowd. "I only ask that the people see my father's acts for the crimes they are. He allows the oppressed poor to starve and die in those mines. Why? To fill his coffers and those of the court!"

Laila caught a muscle twitch in the king's jaw.

Jerrik turned to glare up at Izel. "He stands before this crowd with the head of the Demons at his side. I'm not the traitor. You are, father! You will bring their destruction and damnation!"

The crowd murmured in confusion. Had these people been so oblivious to the presence of Demons amongst them? Or had they simply been too tired and fearful to notice?

King Oddvarr leapt to his feet. "That's enough. Proceed with the execution."

Darien's nerves hummed in anticipation as Donald informed them he had accessed the news station's computers. Now they would wait for Ligeia to make her move. He fidgeted with one of the plastic flex-cuffs in his pocket. It was similar to a zip-tie and wouldn't set off the metal detectors as his handcuffs would. He was ready to get this over with.

The Governor continued his speech in which he threw more accusations at the Supernaturals of Los Angeles. Darien was so damn sick of his anti-Supernatural bullshit. Now that he knew the Governor was just a puppet, it seemed all the more obvious this was just a ploy to generate pandemonium. He played on their fears and provoked the humans and SNPs to turn on each other, oblivious to the real threat.

Finally, he opened the floor to questions.

"Some people believe these new regulations are unconstitutional. How do you respond to that?" a woman in the front asked.

The Governor waved the comment off. "This is no different than setting regulations on firearms. The abilities these creatures have are dangerous, and we have no protection from them. Look at my son—he was mauled to death by a Shape Shifter. He didn't stand a chance! We're not stripping them of their rights; we're ensuring our own."

Another hand shot up a couple of rows away. "But sir, wasn't it the job of the Inter-Realm Security Agency to ensure the peace between humans and Supernaturals? They were established to protect the city, yet you were the one who arrested them."

The Governor seemed to grow irritated with the direction of these questions. "I've said it before, and I'll say it again. That agency was a menace to society. They did more harm than good and failed to keep the humans safe."

The journalist wasn't satisfied. "But statistics show—"

"Your statistics are clearly inaccurate," Stacy snapped.

"But it's a federal agency! You don't have the power—"

"Next question!" called the Governor.

Ligeia stood. "How do we know your statistics are right? For that matter, how do we know that you're not just saying this because you're a puppet for the Demons?"

The Governor faltered, and Darien noticed Lorelei's brow creased into a frown.

"How dare you make such despicable accusations! If you think I'm working with the Demons, then prove it!" The man's composure began to crack.

Ligeia stepped into the aisle and advanced on the pair. "Oh, I intend to, but I'm far more interested in speaking to Lorel."

The secretary stiffened.

"What does she have to do with any of this? You know what? We're done here. Security! Remove her!" he ordered, but no one moved. "What's wrong with you? Do something!"

Lorelei made to sneak out of the room, but she ran straight into a solid wall of air, thanks to Frej. The Demon stumbled back, clutching her nose and swearing.

"Where are you going, Lorelei? Or do you prefer Lorel now? You didn't think your own kind would allow you to run amuck again, did you?" Ligeia moved closer.

"I don't even know you!" Lorelei shrieked, backing away as Ligeia approached.

Ligeia watched her. "You know, I remember the trial. I was there when you were damned. You didn't stand a chance. You knew there was nothing you could do to save yourself. And was it worth it? Did killing all those men really make you feel better about the one who broke your heart? Or was it just a childish tantrum?"

She sneered at the secretary, who trembled with rage as Ligeia tore into the hidden wound. "You know it makes sense. No man or woman in their right mind would go anywhere near you. You're a toxic, self-centered bitch. Not even your mother tried to speak up on your behalf."

"Shut up! You don't know anything about it!" Lorelei snarled, her image flickering. Pale blue lips pulled back from long, needlelike teeth—the true face of Lorelei.

The journalists recoiled and whispered among themselves.

"Shut those cameras off!" Lorelei bellowed.

"Don't!" shouted Darien as he stood. He had removed his contact lenses during Ligeia's confrontation so everyone would know what he was. "Let the people of Los Angeles see you for what you are!"

Two agents stepped up beside the camera crew to ensure the cameras continued to run.

Darien stepped toward Lorelei. "The game's up. We know

you're a Greater Demon, Lorelei. You're outnumbered, so surrender now."

She barked a laugh. "Oh, are you so sure about that?"

The agents and Frej drew their guns and aimed at Darien with eyes that grew cold and emotionless. He gaped at them. How had she done it? Lyn ensured they all had protection spells.

Lyn cursed through Darien's com device. "They must have damaged the runes."

"I can see it. Frej's standing in front of one of the news cameras. Their collars smudged the runes," Donald said.

This was bad. Darien wondered if his own runes had worn off but noticed that all the Vampires seemed unaffected, and Henrik too, for that matter. Was it because their body temperatures were lower and less likely to sweat? The reason didn't matter. He had to find a way to capture Lorelei even if she had the upper hand.

CHAPTER 35

At King Oddvarr's command, a pair of guards stepped onto the platform. They shoved Jerrik to his knees and forced him onto the executioner's block. Laila tensed, her heart pounded in her chest, and the crowd didn't dare to breathe as the executioner raised his ax. Many looked away as the ax began its descent.

Blue light flashed on the platform as Laila appeared in front of Jerrik and used her sword to block the ax. Her robe was gone, and she was clad in armor from the Swordmasters. Her auburn hair rippled around her as blue flames leapt from her blade to engulf the executioner and incinerate him. A murmur of shock rippled through the crowd. Laila turned to the two guards holding Jerrik and flung them back with a blast of air. They toppled backward off the platform.

"Protect the prince!" bellowed the Grandmaster somewhere to her left.

A roar erupted through the crowd as the rebels attacked the sentries surrounding them. Swordmasters leapt onto the platform to form a protective circle and beat back the guards. Laila cleaved through the chains binding Jerrik, her divine sword breaking through the steel and enchantments before she helped Jerrik to his feet. Master Okaenos passed the prince a sword.

"Kill them all! I want that Elf's head!" roared the king.

Guards rushed the platform, and the rebels fighting around it. More civilians joined in to aid the rebels and beat back the guards.

Laila lifted a hand and launched a blinding blue light into the sky—her signal to the others. From caves and crevices along the cavern walls, hulking figures emerged and took to the skies. Two dozen Dragons zeroed in on the courtyard and blasted the guards on the gate with fire and air. They dropped Elven soldiers into the yard in full armor. A few, including the Elven Prince, landed on the platform around Laila. His golden armor shone in the torchlight, and a crown adorned his helmet.

Oddvarr's eyes widened. He turned to Izel. "Do something!"

She gave him a leisurely grin before she spun toward the courtyard and unleashed a blast of shadowy magic. It tore through the crowd and dissolved everyone in its path. The rebels and their allies threw up shields, including Laila, who used hers to cover the entire platform.

"Protect the prince! I'll deal with the Demon," Laila shouted over the chaos.

"Wait!" bellowed Jerrik, but Laila had already vanished.

She appeared on the balcony before Izel and the king. He took one look at her and fled into the palace, a dozen guards on his heels, leaving Izel to face Laila alone. A burst of flame appeared overhead as a Fire Dragon passed, illuminating both of their faces in the flickering light. The shadows it cast over Izel's face gave her an eerie, ghoulish look.

"You know you can't beat me," she said.

"Maybe not, but I can try."

Laila unleashed a barrage of attacks. She cut with her sword and blasted with fire. Her blade bounced off the shadows encircling the Demon, and even her divine fire failed to break through. Laila grunted as she thrust a series of glowing icicles toward the barrier in an attempt to pierce the shield. One of them slipped between the shadows and lodged deep into Izel's shoulder. Another sliced her thigh. The Demon shrieked, and shadows appeared around the wounds to dissolve the ice as blood trickled down her limbs.

The wind swirled around them, carrying with it the smell of decay and grave dust. Laila caught glimpses of skeletal faces in the whirlwind before the Ghosts launched toward her. They piled on top of Laila and tried to smother her with their cold, dead presences—overwhelming her with sheer numbers. As a Goddess of Death, Necromancy was one of Izel's skills.

Laila threw the Ghosts off her with a wave of blue flame, destroying the Ghosts that lingered in its path. She could feel her magic tugging at her, willing her to unleash its full force. Laila allowed the magic to take over her body.

Izel swiped at her with a sword formed by shadows, but Laila easily parried her attack. Gradually, she began to force the Demon back toward the shut doors. The Demon was no longer smiling. Her brow creased in concern. Dodging to the side, Izel reached out to the dead guards standing in the courtyard below the balcony. Their bones crackled and crunched as they rose from the ground. With remarkable speed, they climbed up and over the railing of the balcony.

Laila barked a laugh that was not her own as she conjured a wave of fire. She whipped it around her body, taking out the Zombies as if they were nothing more than cobwebs. As the divine magic consumed them, their bodies were released from Izel's Necromancy. Their spirits rested peacefully once more.

The Demon grit her teeth and lashed out wildly as Laila continued to advance.

"Get out here!" she bellowed.

The doors opened behind her, and a group of Demons leapt to their leader's defense, leaving Laila sorely outnumbered.

Darien held his hands up to the Siren. "You've already been exposed. Killing us isn't going to help you."

Lorelei barked a laugh. "Then I'll take you down with me."

Bang!

Lorelei stumbled back, clutching the wound in her chest. Darien turned to find Sarnai holding the gun she had concealed under her coat.

"Would you shut up already?" Sarnai said as she rolled her eyes.

For a second, those under the Siren's enchantment seemed to snap out of their trance as the Siren's spell waivered. But Lorelei recovered her wits and used the podium to hold herself upright.

"Kill them all!" she snarled.

The room erupted into chaos as the IRSA agents opened fire. Talen's mercenaries tackled the bewitched agents to the ground and attempted to wrestle away the weapons before anyone was hurt.

"Get out!" Darien bellowed at the journalists.

They were already running for the doors, but more security flooding in from the screening checkpoint, blocked the journalists' path. Judging by the indifferent looks on their faces, they were also under Lorelei's influence.

Henrik leapt between the security guards and the journalists, conjuring a thick wall of ice to protect them as bullets thudded into the frozen shield. He started to form more protective barriers when a spell threw him off his feet. He sailed across the room as a blast of air threw him into a wall. Henrik slid to the floor with a groan. Frej grabbed an upturned chair and advanced toward him, intending to bash the ice creature's head in. He was under the Lorelei's spell too.

"Snap out of it!" Henrik rolled out of the way as Frej swung the chair, then he froze the Dragon's feet to the floor with a blast of ice. "You have to fight her!"

Frej ignored him and shot another blast of air at Henrik, who countered with an icy gale.

Darien turned his attention to Lorelei, who was attempting to flee. He surged towards the door where he blocked her path and bared his teeth. "Release them."

She reached into her sleeve and pulled out a knife as she lunged at him. He shoved the blade aside and grabbed her hair before slamming her face-first into the wall. *Crunch.* Blood gushed from her broken nose. It mixed with the blood oozing from the wound on her chest, which was already knitting itself together. He restrained her with a pair of plastic flex-cuffs before she could even cry out. Even so, she didn't release the others.

The Vampires had managed to disarm and restrain a number of the magically controlled agents, and Talen helped Henrik pin Frej to the ground. Fredrik Stacy tried to make a run for it, but Sarnai grabbed him by the front of his shirt.

"Oh no you don't," she purred.

"Jenn, your turn," said Darien into his com device.

Donald nodded as the camera started to stream, and behind him, Jenn could see the split-screen broadcast from his monitor. She paused, feeling like a deer in headlights as she looked at her speech.

"You might recognize me as Agent Holt from the Inter-Realm Security Agency. What you see right now is live from the capitol building. For months now, we have suspected that Demons have attempted to infiltrate our organization and sabotage our investigations. Recently, we were informed that the Governor's secretary was a Demon, escaped from Hell, and with the power to influence others' thoughts and actions."

She glanced at the screen again then thought better of it.

"Look, I'm here because the Demons are pitting us against each other. For months they've been preying on the fears that we humans have—reminding us that Supernaturals are different and terrifying. That they are the creatures of our nightmares and are out for our blood.

"Here's the thing though: Supernaturals and humans aren't any different, not in the ways that count. They are people with morals and feelings and dreams, just like humans. They may not look like us, and they may have different abilities from us, but they are still people!" Jenn could feel herself getting caught up in her own emotions and frustrations. She took a deep breath before continuing.

"My point is that Supernaturals are not the enemy. Humans are not the enemy. *Demons* are the enemy. Just like the terror organizations from before The Event, they are looking to spread their influence here and gain a foothold in our country. What's happened with the Governor and his secretary is a prime example of how far they are willing to go to take over our world."

Her clenched fists were trembling with frustration as she continued. "We need to stand together. We need to face this threat as a united people—as citizens of California and the United States—if we are going to weather this storm. I'm done hiding the severity of the threat the Demons pose. They are here. And they will destroy this country if we don't stop them. I'm not sure what is going to happen moving forward in the next few days, but I will be here, and Special Agent Pavoni will be here, fighting to keep you safe."

Donald ended Jenn's livestream, and she sagged in her seat. She didn't know what to think about that speech, but she needed a drink. But first, Jenn had to get back to the capitol building. Just because they had cornered Lorelei didn't mean Darien had neutralized the threat, and she had a bad feeling this wasn't over yet.

❖

From his phone, Marius watched the spectacle that had become the press conference. He knew Lorelei was a fool for thinking she could handle this on her own. Now she had compromised herself.

The live broadcast showed the Vampire, Darien, frozen as he calculated his next move. The Elf had been a clear threat, but Marius had obviously underestimated the Vampire. The only reason he hadn't placed a Demon in charge of the team was that he assumed the Vampire was incompetent. Yet here he was confronting Lorelei.

The Siren might be able to get out of this on her own, but Marius was done taking chances. He had what remained of IRSA within his grasp. It was time to crush them.

Marius spun around to face the Demons behind him. They were sorting otherworldly drugs from a shipment that arrived this morning.

"Get the cars. We're ending this now. That team has interfered for the last time!" Marius roared.

He stalked out the door, the others scrambling to stash the drugs in safes and follow him. As usual, he was the one left to clean up the mess. All the stress and frustration would be worth it. Once Izel had taken control of Earth, he would have power and status beyond anything he had ever dreamt of. He would have the first claim the worlds they conquered, and when this all ended, no one would ever dare to look down on him again.

CHAPTER 36

Laila was running out of time, and she was beginning to think her magic wasn't strong enough, even wholly unleashed. More Demons emerged from the palace. They vastly outnumbered her, and Laila knew she needed to end this fight somehow. Back when she faced a Demon in the tunnels beneath Los Angeles, she had opened a portal to Hell. Perhaps she could do it again.

Come on, work with me here! I need a portal to Hell, she pleaded with the magic, hoping it would show her how.

You should end this now. You must destroy Izel! echoed the Norn's voice in her head.

I can't, I'm not strong enough, and there are too many Demons.

She swore the Norn grumbled as she replied, *Very well. Send the other Demons back first. Find the link that connects the worlds. Grab the strand and pull. It will create a tear until you release it.*

Laila reached into the ground before the Demons, finding the strands of Yggdrasil's magic that connected the worlds. She found the link to Muspelheim and pulled on the magical thread, tearing open a portal. Dark blue magic crackled and fizzed around a hole that widened in front of her. Rainbow strands of magic formed a tunnel bridging this world to Hell. Laila could feel the corrosive energy of Muspelheim radiating from within the portal.

Laila's voice rumbled with power. "I damn you once more. Return to your prison."

As she spoke, Laila cast a spell pulling the Demons towards the portal. They cried out as they tumbled through one by one—except Izel, who clung to the door handle.

"You won't send me back!" she shrieked.

Izel launched herself through the air, soaring over the portal to tackle Laila to the ground. Her claws reached for Laila's throat, but her gorget blocked them. Tendrils of dark magic snaked from Izel's hands and crept towards Laila's face, smothering her. Summoning her dagger, Laila plunged it blindly towards the Demon's shoulder. It struck flesh, and Izel screamed but kept up her assault. Spots appeared in Laila's vision as she struggled to breathe.

Suddenly, the shadows vanished as Izel was torn off Laila. With a grunt, Jerrik shoved the Demon toward the portal.

"No!" For a moment, Izel teetered on the edge before she fell into the void. Her scream cut off as Laila slammed the portal shut. Izel was back in Hell, where she belonged.

Jerrik offered Laila a hand. She coughed and gasped as she climbed to her feet.

He pulled her into his embrace. "You stubborn, insane woman! I told you not to come!"

Laila relaxed slightly. He was okay. "You can't get rid of me that easily."

Covered in sweat and blood, they both cracked a hint of a smile. Her plan had worked.

The fight still raged around them, but her allies were gaining the upper hand. Guards poured in from around the palace as more Svartalfar fought their way towards the palace from the street, determined to join the fray. But the people of the city were angry and determined. They pushed the guards back.

Prince Haraldur ran across the platform and leapt, using a blast of air to propel himself up to the balcony where Laila stood. A dozen of his soldiers followed. The Swordmasters rushed toward the ramparts to face a stream of approaching guards.

"We need to find my father." Jerrik sprinted toward the doors.

Laila and the others hurried after him, following Jerrik into the throne room beyond, where King Oddvarr stood surrounded by nearly two dozen members of the Red Guard. They were outnumbered, but no one trained their soldiers as Laila's people did. The Elves rushed past and engaged the guards. Spilled blood turned the white marble scarlet as the king's men fell.

"Leave my father to me," growled Jerrik. He advanced toward the skirmish.

Laila and Prince Haraldur fought beside Jerrik as they moved toward the king, keeping the guards at bay as Jerrik faced his father.

"Your reign is over. Surrender," demanded Jerrik. He was calm and composed, but hatred flashed in his eyes.

The king barked a laugh. "I would rather die than surrender myself to a spineless coward who spent years in hiding."

The king was the first to attack. While far better fighter than his guards, Oddvarr was still no match for a Swordmaster. The king lost ground as Jerrik pushed him back toward the throne. Laila struggled to watch as she held back the guards who fought to reach their king.

With a clatter of steel on stone, Jerrik disarmed his father. The king stumbled backward into the throne behind him. His eyes were wide with shock.

Jerrik leveled the point of his sword to his father's throat. "This fight is over."

The king grinned. "You won't kill me."

Jerrik hesitated. Even with all the pain and suffering his father had caused, Laila knew he couldn't take Oddvarr's life.

Oddvarr sneered, and Laila could sense the magic as he prepared the spell. Razor-sharp icicles glittered at his fingertips like claws. With every ounce of divine speed she possessed, Laila lunged, shoving Jerrik out of the way. The ice-claws glanced off her armor and shattered, but Laila didn't see the knife in his offhand—aimed at her eye.

A guttural, unearthly cry tore from Jerrik's throat. Oddvarr's blade slammed into a shield his son conjured. Laila watched the loathing in Jerrik's eyes burn as he drew back his sword. He thrust it forward through his father's chest and deep into the wood of the throne behind him. Oddvarr's eyes widened in shock, followed a moment later by a smug grin spreading across his face.

He choked out a laugh as blood poured from the wound. "I guess you had it in you after all…"

He trailed off. His eyes grew distant, and his heart stopped. King Oddvarr was dead.

Jerrik staggered back, stunned, as the last of the guards fell.

"He's dead. I killed him—my father," Jerrik murmured.

Laila recovered from her shock and pulled him into her embrace.

"I'm sorry," she said against his hair.

"At least… At least he can't hurt anyone anymore. Right?"

She pulled back to look at him. "You didn't have a choice."

Prince Haraldur approached, and Laila stepped away from Jerrik with a bow. Prince Haraldur held up his hand.

"The divine do not bow to mere mortals. I wasn't sure if it was true at first, but your abilities prove it. It was an honor to fight by your side."

Then it hit her. They had succeeded. Jerrik was alive, Izel was gone, and Oddvarr's rein was over. Nidavellir was now safe. Laila's legs nearly buckled with relief. There was still more to do to ensure the palace was safe and secure, but they had won the battle!

Her relief was short-lived.

You must hurry. Your friends are in danger. You must return to Midgard, warned the Norn.

What do you mean? Is it Ali? Laila suddenly realized how much time had passed.

The Vampire faces a Greater Demon, but she will escape if you don't return now, explained the Norn.

Laila froze. What had Darien gotten himself into? She had to get back.

She turned to Jerrik. "I have to go. Darien and the others are in trouble—"

He nodded. "Go."

She hesitated, looking at the carnage around them.

"I'll stay and help Jerrik," insisted Prince Haraldur.

Laila paused long enough to take in Jerrik's face one more time before she vanished.

Erin gripped her sister's hand as Meuric continued to monitor her. She was clinging to life, but barely. Laila better hurry, because they were out of time. Erin didn't know what was taking the others so long, either. Had something gone wrong?

"What's happening in there, Mato?" she asked.

He removed the helmet and shook his head. "I'm not sure. There was an issue with the charms, but I think they're managing."

Erin looked past him to a pair of men lurking down at the alley's entrance. One held a phone to his ear as he peered around the corner. She would've thought him a curious bystander watching the police as they pulled up, but the men seemed far too calm.

Erin climbed into the front seat with Mato and pointed to the helmet. "Can I see that for a second?"

He passed her the helmet, and she pulled it on. The chatter

from the others over the radio met her ears. As she turned towards the men, letters appeared over both of them: Shifters—Wolf. But then they vanished, a red script appearing instead: Demons—Lessor.

"Shit. Guys, we've got company. There are two Lesser Demons in front of us. I don't think they've noticed us—"

One of them turned and stared directly at Erin and Mato. He tapped his companion's shoulder and nodded at the ambulance.

Erin's face paled. "Crap! Never mind. They're headed our way."

"Stay there. I'm coming," said Lyn.

Mato grabbed Erin and shoved her down as one of the Demons opened fire. The windshield shattered, and chunks of glass rained down on top of them.

Erin pushed Mato back and peered over the dash, looking through the shield of the helmet. Both men were armed.

"Stay down!" she called to Mato and Meuric as she ripped off the helmet.

She reached out to the guns and superheated them, just as she had done with the pans when cooking. The men dropped the guns as the bullets exploded in the clip, one striking a Demon in the leg. He howled in pain. Still, the Demons advanced toward the ambulance.

Erin looked back between the seats at her unconscious sister. She wouldn't let them get to Ali. Determined, she reached for the door.

"What are you doing?" hissed Mato.

Erin ignored him and slipped out of the ambulance.

Flames crackled around her fingertips as she faced them. "Back off!"

They smirked, and the uninjured one charged the Dragon. Erin prepared for impact. As he collided with her, she placed a foot on his chest and rocked backward to the ground, throwing him. The surprised Demon sailed over her head and tumbled down the alley.

She rolled to her feet and glanced up at Mato, who gaped at her from the ambulance.

"Seriously? You're just going to sit there?" she howled.

The second Demon lunged for her. Erin ducked under his arms and rammed her knee into his groin. He crumpled to the ground as Erin backed away.

His companion had recovered and reached for the back door of the ambulance.

Erin sent a blast of fire, forcing him back. He narrowed his gaze at her and began to shift into his wolf form. Erin's mind raced. The Werewolf braced to pounce when a mountain of fur plowed into him—Mato. The grizzly bear pinned the wolf under his massive paws and snarled.

Erin turned back to see the other Demon climbing to his feet.

"Stay down!" Flames crackled at her fingertips.

He snarled.

Thwack! He flopped face-forward as Lyn appeared behind him, staff in hand. The Witch tossed Erin a pair of handcuffs, and Erin quickly restrained the Demon's hands behind him. Lyn then approached Mato and the Werewolf. She pulled a sleeping charm out of her pack and carefully slid it over the Werewolf's head. He went limp.

Erin turned to Lyn. "He was on the phone with some-one—"

"Which means there are probably more on their way," finished Lyn.

The Witch hurried to the street with Erin on her heels. They came to a stop when tires screeched in the distance, and they spotted over a dozen cars speeding toward them.

Lyn's eyes grew wide. "Get back to the ambulance and hide. Don't let them see you."

Erin nodded. Two Werewolves were one thing, but a small army of Demons was headed their way, and Erin knew she was no match for them.

CHAPTER 37

Laila didn't bother to mask her glowing aura or appearance as she materialized in the Halls of Portals. She teleported directly into the room that housed the portal to Midgard and startled the guards.

"Intruder!" a guard bellowed, clearly oblivious to the events that just transpired at the palace.

The walls shuddered, and screams echoed down the hallway. A massive Earth Dragon tore through the doors of the chamber and roared. The sound shook the entire room, and the guards dove for cover.

The archers didn't know who to attack first—Laila or the Dragon. Laila conjured a shield and ran for the portal. A guard stood in her path, sword raised. Laila slid under the guard's blade, which narrowly missed her head. As she passed, her sword bit deep into the guard's calf muscles, and he collapsed. Without skipping a beat, she leapt to her feet and dashed through the veil.

In the space between the worlds, Laila sprinted full-tilt with the guards pursuing her through the portal. They had only made it a few steps when she entered Midgard.

An officer with border patrol stood in her path. "Halt! Travelers are not permitted—"

Laila didn't have a chance to hear the rest. She was already teleporting herself out of the building. Her feet hit the sidewalk in front of the Inter-Realm Terminal, and she kept sprinting down toward the street.

She realized she had no idea where to go. Turning to the left, she nearly collided with a security guard on his phone.

He gawked at her as if she was insane. Then again, she was glowing and dressed in armor from the battle.

"I—is that blood?" he stammered.

He clutched his phone to his chest, and Laila could hear the voice of a news reporter from the speakers. "The rouge IRSA agents appear to still be inside the building."

"Where is that?" she demanded.

"The state capitol building."

He cried out in protest as Laila snatched the phone from his hand and peered at the screen. The reporter was standing on the sidewalk across the street from the capitol building. On the road behind her were several police cars with their lights flashing.

Not bothering to return the phone, Laila teleported herself, landing on a restaurant's rooftop across from the capitol building. Crouching down, she peered over the edge toward the street. Several news stations were reporting out front as police officers in riot gear prepared to enter the building.

The reporter on the cellphone continued, "Chaos seems to have erupted in the building with some of the ex-IRSA agents attacking each other. Even though we have the livestream footage of the event unfolding, we are struggling to make sense of it. It appears the governor's secretary may be using some sort of mind control magic to affect them."

"Thor's hammer, what did Darien do now?" Laila muttered, searching for more clues as to what was happening. The Norn had mentioned a Greater Demon, and Erin had told her Darien suspected Colin's ex. He must've gone after her. She considered barging in there.

A familiar voice drew her attention.

"Quickly!" Lyn yelled.

Laila rushed towards the alley to the right of the building. Below, she and spotted Erin and Mato climbing into an ambulance.

What in the worlds was Erin doing here? Was Ali in the ambulance as well? Laila was about to teleport down there when the screech of tires pulled her attention away. Several cars skid to a halt and nearly hit a group of bystanders from the gathering crowd. Dozens of heavily armed humans and Supernaturals emerged from the vehicles. A white-haired figure stepped out of a car. Laila's vision faded to red as she stood there on the edge of the roof. It was Marius.

"Out of our way!" he ordered. The Demons aimed their weapons toward the police.

Boom! Laila landed in the middle of the street between the officers and the Demons. Cries of shock erupted as they stared at her, her divine magic flaring and illuminating the block with rippling blue light.

"You!" Marius hissed and raised his handgun. "I'll put a bullet in your brain myself."

Laila smiled darkly. "I sent Izel back to Hell. Do you really think you can stop me with that?"

She had been waiting for this moment for a long time. For months she searched for any trace of Marius, but to no avail. This time, she would not let him escape.

Laila summoned a massive shield to protect the officers as the Demons opened fire. Bullets hammered against the magical barrier, but it held.

"Laila? Dear Lord, is that you?" shouted Captain Anderson—head of LAPD's Gangs and Narcotics Division. Thank the Gods it was someone she knew.

"Yes. I'm not sure what's going on, though," Laila shouted.

Anderson nodded to the capitol building. "Darien claims

the woman inside is a Demon who controls the governor. We don't know what to do—to listen to Darien or the governor. The city's fallen into chaos."

Laila struggled to keep the shield up as the Demons continued their attack. "Well, I can guarantee these ones are Demons. Mostly Lesser, but one Greater. I can open a portal to hell and send the Demons through, but I'll have to drop the shield to do it."

He nodded, catching on. "Form a wall! Protect the Elf!"

The others rushed to follow his orders by lining up in front of her with their shields. They stood shoulder to shoulder, preparing for the charge that would occur when Laila dropped her magical barrier. Those who weren't in riot gear were trying to get the news crews and bystanders to safety. People screamed and fled the street in search of shelter. The reporters seemed torn between staying and escaping as well. For their sakes, Laila hoped they ran for cover.

Laila took a deep breath and tried to remember how she had opened the portal in Nidavellir. The shield fell, and the Demons surged toward the officers. Blocking out the chaos, Laila focused on the portal and reached into Yggdrasil's magic that connected this spot to Muspelheim. It was difficult here since the magic of Midgard was sparse, but she found the link. Finally, she forced open a portal and widened it to nearly half the size of the street behind the Demons. A couple of them tumbled backward into the abyss.

"Push them back!" ordered the captain. The police tried to gain ground, but sorcerers among the Demons attacked the officers with fire and soaring chunks of asphalt. Laila struggled to hold the massive portal open and shield the officers at the same time.

"Get out of our city!" Lyn appeared at the mouth of an alley. The Witch held a long thin wand of pale blue stone carved with gold runes. The rod glowed, and a gust of wind erupted from the tip. The massive gale swept through the street and scooped up the sorcerers before depositing them into the portal. On the second pass, she grabbed the remaining Lesser Demons and dropped them into the hole just before the wand shattered in Lyn's hand.

"Damn it! This is why I hate single-use spells," the Witch grumbled.

All that remained was Marius.

Laila stepped around the portal to face the Greater Demon. "I'll deal with him."

The scent of Muspelheim clung to his being, clogging her nose with its acrid stench. She resisted the urge to gag as she approached.

Marius continued to shoot, firing rounds into her shield as he retreated into one of the cars. He started the engine and turned the car around back towards the Old City.

Laila shoved her magic into the vehicle and flipped it into the air. Metal groaned, and glass shattered as the car rolled several times. It came to a rest upside down half a block away. Through the smoke and dust, Marius crawled out of the wreck, but Laila was already there. She grabbed him by the back of his dress shirt and dragged him down the street toward the portal as he struggled against her, but her grip was as rigid as steel.

Her voice was emotionless as she spoke, "You know, I've dreamt of this moment for so long. I thought about the things I'd say and the crimes you've committed. After all, I have a feeling that much of this city's suffering has been at your hands." She stopped before the portal and lifted him to face her. "Yet, now that I see you without your guards or those damned enchanted cuffs protecting you from my power, I realize you are nothing. You're weak. Pathetic."

"Just kill me now then!" he hissed, spit flying from his mouth. His eyes were wide with horror, and Laila realized that he genuinely meant it. He would rather die than return to Hell.

Laila chuckled. "No, that would be too kind. I'm tossing you back where you belong. Give my regards to Izel."

There was a flicker of movement as Marius removed some-thing from behind his back. It was a knife etched with famil-iar black runes. It was smaller than the cursed blade that had wounded Ali but equally deadly. He thrust the knife towards an unprotected spot under her arm. Laila threw up a magical shield, just in time. The blade shattered on impact, and the divine magic tore through the deadly curse.

Laila's eyes flicked back to the Demon's face savoring his shock. "Rot in Hell, Marius."

"Please, no!"

Laila snorted in disgust and shoved the Demon. Marius tumbled backward into the portal. His screams echoed through the night as he was swallowed up.

Laila sealed the portal and stared at the empty patch of as-phalt. Marius was gone. She finally found him and sent him back to Hell. Laila wanted to laugh, cry, and dance in victory all at once, but there was still work to do. She had to find Ali.

She took a step toward the ambulance when she found her-self frozen in place.

What are you doing? hissed Senere's voice in her head. *I sent you here to kill the Demons.*

Laila's body refused to move. The Norn was trapping her in place. *I have to get to Ali.*

If you let the Siren go, she'll destroy this entire city. You have to act now!

Laila grit her teeth as a battle raged within her. She was about to retort when visions flashed before her eyes. War, Su-pernaturals slaughtered, and children screaming as a firing squad took their aim. Laila tried to block out the images, but Senere wouldn't allow it. The Norn had full control of her.

Fine, I'll do it. Tears filled Laila's eyes.

She stumbled forward as Senere released her. Laila stole one more look at the ambulance before turning back to the capi-tol building. She would end this quickly and return to Ali. That was her only choice. The Norn had power over her body and magic—she had been the one controlling Laila all along. Deep down, Laila knew that she was powerless to defy Senere. She dashed the tears from her eyes and rushed toward the building.

"Search the vehicles! Make sure no one is hiding!" Captain Anderson shouted to the officers still standing. His right arm hung limp at his side—dislocated in the struggle to hold the Demons back.

Laila hated to leave him in pain, but the paramedics were arriving, and she had to deal with Lorel. She sprinted into the state building. Lyn followed.

"What's happening in there?" she asked the Witch.

"Colin's ex is a Siren. I thought my charms would be enough to protect them, but only the Vampires and Henrik were unaffected. The others are under her control. I think they sweated the charms off."

Inside, humans huddled in the entryway. They flinched and covered their faces.

"It okay, go now. It's safe," Lyn insisted.

They hesitated for a second, then lowered their hands and hurried past them out to the street.

"They're this way." Lyn pointed down a hall.

Laila rushed forward only to realize the Witch wasn't following.

"What's wrong?"

"I can't go with you. Lorelei will control me like the others," Lyn explained.

Laila nodded and continued alone. Through an open doorway, she could see a fight raging inside. Vampires, agents, and her friends battled each other. The scene was chaotic.

"Enough!" roared Laila.

Blue magic rippled through the room, effectively freezing everyone in place as she stepped into the space and scanned those present. Frej was struggling against Talen and Henrik. Talen's Vampires were attempting to disarm IRSA agents and the security guards. Finally, at the front of the room, she found Darien restraining Lorel while Sarnai held Fredrik Stacy. Darien's suspicions had been correct. Laila could sense it. Lorel was a Greater Demon. If only Laila had learned to use her powers sooner, she would have been able to identify it months ago.

Laila examined the others. She couldn't release them from her spell, not yet. If Lorel was controlling them, they would continue to attack each other. She needed to find a way to sever that connection.

Placing her hand on Lorel's head, she searched with her powers until she could feel the magical attachments extending from the woman and wrapping around her victims, like the tentacles of a giant octopus. Laila unsheathed her sword and sliced through the invisible strings. The connections withered and died, instantly releasing her victims from the spell.

"Laila!" Darien gasped.

"I'm going to send Lorel back to Hell," she hastily explained, afraid the Demon would regain control of the others again.

"Wait! Give me just a moment." He looked at the cameras still rolling nearby and then turned to Lorel. "Confess that you were the one controlling Special Agent Colin Grayson."

There was a malicious gleam in her eyes. Blood oozed from her nose and a wound to her chest, but she hardly seemed to notice. It was hard to believe that this was the same stuck-up woman Colin had dated.

Lorel made no move to speak.

Laila's patience had run out. "Look, I've already damned dozens of Demons today—first Izel, then Marius, and all of the Demons working with them. You're all that's left. I'm tired, and I want to go home. If you confess, we'll stick you in a cell instead of tossing you into a portal back to Hell."

"Izel? But how?" stammered Lorel.

Laila gave her an annoyed look, and the Demon jumped to comply.

"Okay, okay. Yeah, I did. I manipulated the Werewolf's poor, conflicted mind and infiltrated your pathetic government. It was ridiculously easy. It was especially easy to manipulate that poor bastard over there." She indicated Frederik Stacy. "He was so deep in his depression that all I had to do was redirect his pain into anger. Is that enough? Please don't send me back there!" beseeched the Siren.

Laila tore open another portal.

Lorel balked. "But you said—"

"The United States Government does not negotiate with Greater Demons." Laila shoved the Siren backward.

"Wait, no!" screamed Lorel. Magic sucked the Demon through the entrance. As soon as she vanished through it, Laila closed the portal. If there were more Demons in the city, they would have to wait. She needed to get to Ali.

"Laila!" Frej rushed over and pulled her into a hug. "By the Gods, what took you so long?"

The others surrounded her with questions, but she waved them off. "There's no time. I have to go."

She raced to the door and prayed she wasn't too late.

CHAPTER 38

Laila raced from the building in a panic as Darien, Frej, and Talen followed her into the street. She could feel Erin's terror echo through her mind and wondered if Senere had blocked the Dragon's prayers from reaching her before.

I'm coming! I'm here! she called to Erin.

As Laila sprinted to the ambulance, she removed the silk pouch and unwrapped it to check the Eirflower. While a little crushed from the fight with Izel, it still glowed with magic. She hoped it would be enough to save Ali.

She skid to a halt and wrenched the ambulance doors open to find Erin and Meuric leaning over Ali.

Laila jumped in and passed Meuric the Eirflower. "You know what to do, right?"

He nodded and got to work with a mortar and pestle to prepare the cure.

Laila knelt beside Ali in the crowded ambulance and used her magic to scan her friend, searching for some way to help her. Ali's pulse was so weak, and she was only holding on by a thread.

Erin trembled beside her, positively terrified. "Can you do anything?"

"I don't know. I don't think so—not any more than the others have." She was panicking.

The others stood outside the doors with Mato, watching helplessly.

"Erin? I can still do it. I can change her," Talen whispered.

Erin looked from him to Laila, and her expression was etched with uncertainty. Meuric finished grinding the flower and poured the juice down Ali's throat.

They waited in silence as nothing happened. Laila continued to scan Ali's body, but the flower didn't appear to have any effect. The seconds ticked by with no improvement.

"It's not working!" Laila's voice cracked with a sob.

This couldn't be happening. Laila remembered both Senere and the Grandmaster's warnings: that not all wounds could be healed. After all that, the Eirflower wasn't the cure.

Erin grabbed Talen's arm. "Do it! Do it now! Save her!"

The Vampire climbed in beside her. He pulled out a knife and made a deep cut across his palm. Talen held his fist over Ali's mouth, allowing the blood to trickle between her lips.

He began to chant an incantation in some ancient language. Laila could feel the thrum of magic around them.

"Come back to us. Arise and join the ranks of the undead," Talen said at last.

No one dared to breathe. Laila reached out to scan Ali one more time, but her pulse had stilled. The magic from Talen's blood was already fading with no effect. The others looked to her, and Laila shook her head. It was too late. They were all too late.

Ali was gone.

Laila held the sobbing Dragon as the girl screamed, and Laila's own burning hot tears streamed down her cheeks. When she asked the Norns if she would be able to save Ali, they hadn't responded. This was why. They knew all along that Ali would die.

A guttural cry escaped her throat. Laila could hardly see through the tears clouding her vision as she placed a hand on Ali's chest. Laila had no idea what she was doing, but she would not give up on Ali. What good was all this power if she couldn't save the people she cared about?

She reached out to Ali's life force as, her spirit left her body to cross over to the river Styx. Laila called to the magic of Yggdrasil to pull Ali's soul back. Laila wrapped her in layers of divine magic to heal, revive, and restore, only to encounter resistance from the curse that still tainted Ali's body, its tendrils of dark magic clinging to the veins. Laila burned them away as she had with the blade Marius pulled on her, finally breaking the curse. There was also the magic of the Eirflower and Vampire blood. They may not be strong enough on their own, but Laila reached out to their powers and intertwined it with her own. She used it to strengthen her spell until the light emanating from their bodies was so blinding that Laila had to shut her eyes.

When the glow finally faded, she heard a gasp. Laila assumed it was Erin. Then she felt Ali's chest expand. She was breathing again. Ali's eyes flickered open, and she looked up.

"Laila? What happened?" Her voice was little more than a whisper.

"It's okay, you're going to be okay," said Laila as more tears rolled down her face.

"Ali!" Erin threw herself on her sister, hugging her tightly. "I thought you were gone! I thought you were dead!"

Ali held her sister. "I think I was. I was standing on the shore of the river Styx when a door opened behind me. I walked back through."

She looked up at Laila, who gasped. Ali's eyes had changed. They were no longer the same shade of violet as before. The outer part of the iris was crimson, fading to purple with a thin band of pale blue at the center that was the same color as Laila's eyes. She had revived Ali with a blend of magic, but how had it affected her body?

Laila exchanged a look with Talen, who seemed to be thinking the same thing.

"We should get her back to the hospital," declared Laila.

"I'll drive." Darien climbed into the front seat.

❖

Laila stood in the corner of the hospital room with Frej as Dr. Elmerson finished his examination. Erin sat in a chair next to her sister's bed, worried Ali's condition might suddenly change. The others waited outside in the hall. Hospital staff tried to send them away to a waiting room, but they had to be cautious until they knew how many Demons remained in the city. Darien insisted that he, Mato, and Lyn stay to keep watch until Talen arranged a new protective detail.

Dr. Elmerson opened his eyes as he finished his magical assessment and turned to Ali. "Well, the good news is that all traces of the curse are gone. It seems Laila effectively eradicated it. However, I've never observed these sorts of physiological changes before."

"What do you mean?" asked Laila.

"Well, when you revived her, the various magics seemed to have fused and created a shift in her magical composition. I can find traces of the Vampire's blood magic interwoven with the Fae magic as well as other things—probably your magic and the Eirflower's. It has mutated her being on a genetic level."

"But will she be alright?" Erin shifted in her seat.

He nodded. "Yes, I'm certain Ali will make a full recovery, but there could be unexpected side effects of this transformation." He turned to Ali, who looked a little dazed. "Before I can discharge you, we'll have to determine if your dietary needs or UV sensitivity have been affected. Even then, I would be careful until you've learned to manage any newly developed abilities."

Ali offered him a weak smile. "Thank you, doctor."

He gave her a sympathetic look. "We'll keep you here for

a few days to monitor you and ensure your recovery is steady. Everything should be fine, though."

He turned to leave, and Frej followed.

"I'll let the others know you're okay, Ali," the Dragon said before he stepped from the room.

When the door clicked shut, Laila took a seat on the edge of Ali's bed. "How do you feel?"

Ali shrugged. "Mostly just tired and hungry. My senses seem different too. I can smell you both. Like, I can smell what kind of creature you are. And my vision seems a little different too, more sensitive."

Erin scooted her chair closer. "Really? Do you think that's because of the Vampire blood? Are you craving blood too?"

Ali wrinkled her nose. "I don't know, but I'm not crazy about the idea of drinking blood. That's kind of gross."

Laila bit her lip. "I'm so sorry. I should have come back sooner with the flower then returned to help Jerrik."

Ali shook her head. "You did the right thing. It's our job to protect people, and I have a feeling that you needed to act there and then. If you returned, there's no telling if you would have been able to return to Nidavellir in time."

Earlier, while they waited for the doctor, Laila had given the sisters and Frej a brief explanation of what had happened in the other worlds. She omitted many details in the process, but she would probably tell Ali the rest later.

Erin grabbed Laila's hand. "At least it all worked out in the end."

Ali nodded. "Exactly. Now, can someone get me a hamburger? I wasn't kidding when I said I'm starving." She made sad puppy-dog eyes at Laila.

"Okay, I'll see what I can do."

She left the two sisters alone in the room and joined the others in the hall. She leaned against the shut door a moment, positively exhausted. She still had her armor on, was in desperate need of a bath, and probably needed food as well, but more than anything, she just wanted a moment to breathe.

"Is everything okay?" Mato asked.

Laila nodded. "Ali's doing okay, just craving a hamburger."

He relaxed. "Yeah, that sounds like Ali. I'll go find some food."

Laila grinned. With her blood-splattered armor, she wasn't exactly dressed to walk into the cafeteria.

"Where are the others?" Laila glanced around as Mato left. All that remained was Frej.

He peered down the hall at a group of nurses watching for anything out of the ordinary. "Talen should be back soon with his mercenaries, and the others went to help deal with things at the capitol building. Lyn is taking one last walk with her girl-friend before the Siren has to wipe our memories. She was the one who helped us with Lorelei."

"What do you mean 'wipe our memories?'" she asked sus-piciously.

"She'll remove all memory of the Sirens from our minds. Unfortunately, what happened with Lorelei is only proof to her that it's not the right time to interact with humanity or even oth-er Supernaturals. The Sirens' powers are simply too strong. I feel bad for Lyn, though." He sighed and shook his head.

Laila struggled to process the news. Lyn had given so much to help them fight the Demons. It just didn't seem right that Lyn would have to sacrifice her relationship for the help Ligeia had given. How much more would they have to give before they were finally able to stop the Demons?

Frej watched her closely. "How are you?"

She shrugged. "I don't know. So much has happened. There is divine magic in Ali's body now, and it usually complicates ev-erything. But I didn't know what else to do."

He hugged her. "Don't be so hard on yourself. I'm sure we'll all figure this out. The important thing is we all survived. Ali won't be alone through the adjustment, either."

They stood there for a movement, and Laila could feel her

nerves begin to ease.

"Do you plan to stay or return to Nidavellir?" asked Frej.

Laila sighed. "I don't think there is much more I can do there. I'm sure the Dragons and Elves will continue to aid Jerrik through this transition. Honestly, Prince Haraldur is better equipped than I am to help him."

He nodded. "Maybe, but does Jerrik want other kingdoms trying to tell him how to run his country?"

"Probably not, but until he can figure out who he can trust, it's his safest bet." She looked up at him. "I spoke with Regina."

"Oh? How did that go?"

"Don't worry. I kept it professional…mostly." Although in Laila's opinion, she let the queen off far too lightly.

Laila knew they were simply prolonging the inevitable discussion about their feelings. She thought back to the ultimatum she had given him. That he seemed to avoid it wasn't encouraging.

"I've decided to return to the Dragon Kingdom," announced Frej, breaking the silence.

"Oh. Right. Of course." She couldn't help but feel a pang of disappointment. That in of itself seemed like an answer, and although she knew it was foolish, a part of her had secretly hoped he would stay.

He took her hand in both of his and looked down into her shimmering eyes. "I know it's too dangerous for Erin here, and I have no doubt the crown will need me in the months to come now that we know the Demons have accessed other worlds. I also realize that our paths pull us in very different directions. I've thought about what you said before you left, and I think I am ready to move past my feelings for Regina—it's possible I already have. I wish I could be with you now, but I have to be realistic."

Laila's lungs refused to work. She had known that this was a possible outcome, but it was different hearing it from his lips, somehow more tragic and final. The fact she was exhausted physically and emotionally didn't help. Tears pricked her eyes as she struggled to keep her composure.

Frej cupped her cheek tenderly. "But even though I know I can't be with you now, I hope that someday when all of this is behind us, we can start over. That you will give me the chance to court you properly and to show you… well, to show you that I love you."

She gazed up with burning eyes at his open face, his tender emotions bared for her. She thought back to the nights she had spent with Jerrik. Frej was the most honorable person she had ever met. How could she stand here and look him in the face when she had slept with another man only nights ago?

"I don't deserve you," she whispered, looking away.

She didn't tell him about Jerrik, but as she looked back up at him, he seemed to realize what had happened. He offered her a look of simple understanding.

"As I said, I think we are both in difficult situations right now. I think—I hope—that the next time around, things will be simpler. But even if they aren't, I still think that this is what I want."

Frej pulled her into his arms, and she rested her head on his shoulder, savoring his musky scent. While she didn't know what would happen with this war and she didn't want to get his hopes up, she couldn't help but feel that maybe this was the sort of man that she needed after all. Jerrik had dared her to live in the now, but Laila knew she wasn't that kind of person. She made planned and deliberate moves.

While she felt her heart break in her chest, she found solace in the knowledge that Frej would still be there for her. That even if now wasn't the time, it didn't mean they weren't somehow right for each other.

She pulled away to tell him that, only to realize he wasn't moving.

"Frej?" she shook his shoulder. He was frozen in place.

She looked past him down the hall and saw a pair of nurses

frozen as well. What the hell was going on?

"You've abused your power," a male voice said behind her.

Laila turned and found a man with coal-black hair and bright white wings. His glowing silver eyes glowered at her. It was Luc—the Angel who worked for the Norns.

"What did you do to them?" demanded Laila. There was something off about this guy. Even if he served the Norns, Laila couldn't help but be on edge.

The Angel's frowned deepened. "They'll be fine. Senere sent me here to ensure you don't step out of line again. That Fae should have died and followed the natural course of things." He gave her a condescending look. "Your emotions are your weakness. I thought Elves were supposed to understand this. There are occurrences in this world that are destined to happen. You cannot shift the natural course of things—there are repercussions."

Laila wasn't listening. Her heart pounded in her chest. She spun around and flew through the door to Ali's room to ensure the others were alright. They were sitting together on the bed and, as with Frej, were frozen in place. As the door clicked shut behind her, she found the Angel had already teleported into the room. He was growing more irritated. Laila knew she should be cautious since this Angel was probably far stronger than her, but the agony of nearly losing Ali was still fresh in her mind. She wouldn't allow Luc to jeopardize Ali's safety.

He folded his arms. "Fate is not yours to decide. You cannot change the course of things simply because the outcome doesn't suit you. It makes you no better than the Demons."

"These are my friends. My family. I won't let you harm them!" Laila snarled, throwing herself between Luc and the sisters frozen on the bed.

Luc's hand lashed out. He dug his fingers into her hair and dragged her toward him. "You serve the Norns. You will learn what actions are acceptable and which are not!"

Laila cried out and clawed at his hand as she glowered at

the Angel.

Crunch! A fist slammed into his face. The Angel released Laila and staggered back as Ali took another step toward him, fists up. Somehow, she had broken through his spell. She looked exhausted, but she also looked ready to kill.

"I've been poisoned, chased out of my home, and brought back from the brink of death in the same week. My tolerance for assholes is gone." Her eyes were a glowing swirl of violet, crimson, and blue.

Luc grunted as blood spurted from his broken nose.

"Do you know who I am?" he hissed at the Fae, his aura shimmering.

"Does it look like I give a shit? No one treats my friends like that!" Ali glared at Luc, who stumbled back.

Laila placed a hand on Ali's shoulder. "Thanks, I've got it from here."

Ali nodded and wavered—this was more excitement than she was ready for. As Ali sank onto the bed, she shot one more dirty look at the Angel.

Laila rounded on Luc. "What the hell is your problem?"

His face turned red. "You're the one who won't see reason. They're just mortals! They'll all die in the end! I was sent by the Norns to educate you, and part of that is knowing when to step back and let nature take its course."

Laila's eyes flared. That was it. Angel or no, she was done with his garbage. She lunged forward and grabbed him by the tunic—

The ground lurched out from under her, and she suddenly stood in the temple ruins beneath the Norn's apartment. Luc was beside her, and Senere was glaring at them.

"Enough! Both of you!" Senere turned to Laila. "You requested instruction. I have tasked Luc with the job. He has served me for millennia and understands the balance of fate. You are to show him respect."

Laila bristled. An ass like Luc didn't deserve her respect.

But instead of strangling the Angel, she forced herself to bow to Senere.

The Norn frowned at Luc next. "And you. You seriously need to work on your interpersonal skills. You've worked alone for far too long. You still represent us, even in the mortal worlds, so don't alienate them."

He bowed then glared at Laila as he straightened.

Senere continued, "Laila, because you refused to kill Izel when you had the chance, you will now have to find a way to get to her. There's also the matter of the Fae you saved. Your actions have major repercussions. Your friends are an emotional attachment that impedes your journey. You'd do well to remove them before fate takes its toll. They'll bring you nothing but pain and suffering."

It felt as though she punched Laila in the stomach. "I won't let that happen."

"You don't have a choice. This is precisely what I was talking about!" huffed Luc, throwing his hands in the air.

Senere massaged the bridge of her nose. "Look, the two of you are going to have to work together to stop the Demons. This means you're going to have to learn to get along. There is no changing what has already happened, so we will merely have to deal with the consequences."

Laila hoped this meant Ali was safe and that Luc would not attempt to kill her to right the balance. Still, though, how far would they be willing to go to ensure Laila's cooperation? Gods were said to have cruel ways of manipulating humans, and she couldn't help but feel this was one such case. It left a bad taste in her mouth. Now that she finally had answers, she wasn't sure she liked them. What if she had only placed her friends in greater danger?

CHAPTER 39

Several days later, Laila stood in the living room of Ali's house, watching a report on the news. The house had been thoroughly cleaned, and most of the damage was repaired. They had to purchase new sofas since the old ones had been partially destroyed, but Ali seemed satisfied with the leather ones she ordered. They replaced the door as well, and the new one was far more sturdy with reinforced locks. Ali was still grumbling about it, saying the door didn't fit the rest of her décor, but Laila and Darien eventually persuaded her it was a necessary precaution.

"Are you sure they're going to show the speech?" Frej asked as he stirred the large pot of pasta sauce.

Just then, the news station cut to a video clip from a press conference. The governor stood at the podium with Jenn at his side. She had received a public apology from the governor earlier in the week, and the trooper who nearly shot her in the back was facing an investigation.

The Governor spoke. "I'm sorry it has taken me so long to address the public personally. I'll be frank with you; I'm still struggling to come to terms with what happened. I never considered myself to be an intolerant person, and I am horrified by the things I have said over the past several months. Lorel—the Greater Demon who influenced my actions—took advantage of my pain and grief and used it to turn me against California's Supernatural communities. This is not an excuse for what I have done, and I'm not sure what I can do to atone for the hurt and unrest I have caused. However, I hope that over time I might work to repair the damage done. I have revoked the curfew placed on Supernaturals and the arrest warrants for all members of the Inter-Realm Security Agency that I had previously issued, and I am working closely with them to assess the threat that the Demons still pose. I will continue to look to them for guidance in the upcoming months to determine how to keep the people of California safe."

Erin leaned against the back of a sofa. "Woah, it's weird to hear him talk like that. It's like he's had a massive personality change. Even his voice sounds different."

Mato stared at the television screen as well. The bread he was slicing was forgotten in his hands. "That's because he's speaking calmly. And he *did* have a personality change. Remember the way Frej and the humans attacked after they accidentally smudged their protective charms?"

Henrik clapped Frej on the back. "No worries, I know it wasn't really you attacking me."

Frej still shifted uneasily. "It's scary how easily she could control a whole room. It's a shame we never figured out what sort of creature she was."

Laila glanced over her shoulder at him. "What are you talking about? Of course we did."

"Do you know something we don't? I thought the whole reason we had a hard time finding her was that we didn't know what she was?" Henrik sounded confused.

Laila looked around at the others, assuming they were joking, but as they continued to stare at her blankly, it dawned on her that Ligeia had wiped their memories. The Siren had stuck around, so Laila had assumed Ligeia had changed her mind. But why did she retain her memories while the others had not?

As if on cue, a knock on the door sounded, and Lyn entered with her girlfriend.

Ali waved them in. "Hey! Are you both getting settled in the apartment?"

Lyn nodded and hugged Ali. "Yeah, it's a little surreal moving back in, but it's nice to be at the beach again. I'm glad to see you up and about!"

"Where would you like this?" Ligeia held up a large bowl of salad.

"I'll take that," offered Laila. Then she lowered her voice and asked. "What's going on? No one here remembers that Lorel was a Siren."

Ligeia looked surprised. "You mean, you do? Well, I guess I shouldn't be too shocked. I suppose my abilities don't work on the divine. I wiped everyone's memory days ago."

"But you're still here! How is it they remember you? I thought you were going to have to leave?"

Ligeia gave her a sly smile. "I found a loophole. I only erased their knowledge of Sirens. Instead, they think I'm human. I convinced the council to let me stay and ensure there is not another threat of a similar nature. I don't like lying to Lyn, but this is the only way I can still be with her."

Laila watched as Lyn chatted with Ali. The Witch looked so happy. "I'm glad you found a way. This is the happiest I've ever seen her."

Darien, Sarnai, and Talen were the next to arrive with several bottles of blood for the party and Ali. The doctor had determined that while Ali could eat ordinary food in moderation, she would also need to supplement her diet with blood. Ali didn't seem to suffer the same sort of bloodlust that caused the Vampires to become ravenous, but she tended to get lethargic. She even fainted one day when she tried to avoid the blood. Since then, Sarnai had been sending over a steady supply. The

Vampire seemed eager to help Ali adjust, even though Darien was technically her sire—or partial sire.

There were other odd effects as well. Ali didn't suffer from the same sensitivity to sunlight as the Vampires, but she would quickly get one nasty sunburn. Sunscreen seemed to help with that for the most part, particularly the enchanted kind Lyn made. Despite Ali's fears, she still retained her Fae abilities to charm and use glamour magic, and they were even stronger than before. With the doctor's precaution in mind, she had been taking it slow, which meant Ali still didn't know the full extent of her abilities. Laila promised she would help sort them out, but they were waiting one more day.

The reason for their little party was that Erin and Frej would be leaving for the Dragon Kingdom in the morning. Many fights between Ali and Erin had broken out over the last few days. Erin didn't want to leave. Not only did she insist Midgard was her home, but she didn't want to abandon Ali after coming so close to losing her.

Laila was sad to see them leave. Erin was like a sister to her, and she loved watching her grow, and her abilities develop. Laila would miss her snarky sense of humor and fiery disposition. She had a feeling it would feel oddly quiet without Erin in the house.

Frej was another matter. Even though they discussed the potential of a future relationship, something about this still felt final. No matter how much she wished it, things would never go back to the way they were, and bit by bit, their circle of friends were being called away.

The last to arrive was Donald. He held a small package wrapped in colorful paper, which he passed to Erin.

"I know they don't have technology in Alfheim, so I wanted to give you a little something to help," he explained.

Erin tore away the paper and pulled out a metallic cube covered in glowing red runes. "What's it do?"

"It's a charging pack for your electronic devices. It's sort of like a solar panel, but it converts magic into electricity. It's strong enough to power your laptop, charge your phone, or whatever you want to do. You won't have Wi-Fi or cell service, but you'll still be able to access your photos and play videogames."

Erin hugged him so tightly it nearly threw the Tech Wiz off balance. "Thank you!"

"Oh! That reminds me, I have something too!" Lyn reached into her bag and removed a little pouch.

Erin opened it and pulled out a sleek black compact with a silver Dragon on it. Erin popped it open, and the mirror within rippled. It was a hand-held scrying glass similar to what Laila's mother used.

"This way, you can stay in touch."

Erin's eyes brimmed with tears and her lower lip wobbled. "I'm going to miss you guys so much!"

Lyn wrapped an arm around the young Dragon. "Aw, it's going to be okay. This just means it's time for you to have your own adventure!"

Darien pulled Laila aside, looking concerned. "Are you expecting anyone else? Jenn?"

Laila frowned. "No. Jenn said she's stuck at the press conference. Why?"

"Someone pulled up. Considering what happened last time…"

Laila nodded. "I'll handle it."

With the others preoccupied, she slipped out the door. In front of the house, a taxi sat with two figures emerging. Jerrik approached in a simple but elegant black suit—the kind the men in Nidavellir wore. His hair was pulled back, and on his brow rested a silver circlet.

"I thought I might find you here." He winked.

"Jerrik? What are you doing here?" she asked.

"I wanted to check on Ali and make sure she was doing okay. I also never got the chance to speak to you after the battle." He paused before her.

Laila recognized his companion, and her eyes lit up. "Master Okaenos!"

He looked around at the cars in fascination. "Hello, Laila! I'm so excited to see Midgard! These self-propelled machines are incredible, and they move so fast! Faster than the ones in Svartalfheim even!"

Laila chuckled and showed them in. "Come in! We've got plenty of food."

Everyone stared at Jerrik as he entered the room.

"Whoa, you look totally different," pointed out Erin.

Jerrik looked down at his clothes with a frown. "Yeah, it doesn't quite feel right. I miss my jeans."

Mato hesitated. "Are we supposed to bow?"

"Don't you dare!" Jerrik pulled him into a hug, and Mato relaxed along with the others.

"Everyone, this is Master Okaenos. He's one of the Swordmasters," announced Laila.

"It's a pleasure to be here!" he said delighted.

Ali led them both towards the kitchen. "Well, don't just stand there! Dig in!"

Together they laughed, ate, and drank. Eventually, Jenn was able to get away from her duties to join them. It was good to have everyone together, but their celebration had a bittersweet edge to it. None of them were willing to say it, but they knew this was the last time they would all be together for quite a while. Laila watched as Master Okaenos chattered excitedly with Frej—eager to discuss the possibility of a Swordmaster taking up residence to teach the Dragons. Mato and Henrik lounged and drank on a sofa with Jerrik—the three of them joking like old times. Ali spoke with the Vampires about the various types of blood they brought. Meanwhile, Lyn and Donald showed Erin a list of basic enchantments for the Dragon to try out while Ligeia listened attentively.

Laila thought over what Darien had informed her regarding Colin. It sounded as though he wasn't truly to blame for leaking information. Between Lorel's confession and the report that came back from the tainted pills Colin had been taking, the chances were high he would be released. Even so, there would be no future for him at the agency, even if they needed the help.

Jerrik wouldn't be returning to the agency either, and tomorrow Frej would leave. Their numbers were dwindling as their paths diverged.

"You look oddly pensive," pointed out Talen as he joined her in the kitchen.

A sad sigh escaped her. "A lot is changing. I want to hold on to this moment."

He nodded. "I know what you mean. At this age, I think I've come to accept that the only thing I can expect is for change to be constant."

Laila watched Ali sip another glass of blood. "Do you think we did the right thing by turning her?"

"I don't think she's upset with you, if that's what you mean. It'll take time for her to adjust, but I think she's okay with that. She wasn't ready to die. I wouldn't have offered to change her otherwise. Sarnai's taken a lot of interest in her. I think she'll continue to offer her support. Something in her changed recently. I noticed it after she spent time with Erin in the safehouse. She seems more human. I think she realized how much she missed her own family. Even her relationship with Darien seems different this time around."

"How so?" she snuck a glance at the pair. Darien seemed to be doing his best to ignore Sarnai, although her eyes constantly drifted to him.

Talen smirked. "Sarnai's used to being in control, but this time Darien has the power. He's stronger now and can resist her if he wants. Sarnai has grown to appreciate it. She's listening to him and respecting his wishes. I'm still not sure that it's healthy, given their history together, but it's also not my place to intervene—not unless I believe it puts his life in danger."

"That's happened before?"

He shrugged. "Yes, but I think she's changed for the better. I think she's learned that if she wants to be a part of his life, then Sarnai will have to prove to him she's a better person than she used to be."

Interesting. Laila knew it was none of her business, but if Sarnai would be spending more time around them, she felt it was prudent to understand the Vampire's background.

Laila noticed Lyn, Ligeia, and Donald saying their goodbyes.

Talen checked his phone. It was well past two in the morning. "It's getting late. We should probably be going too. I'll see you soon, though."

Laila nodded. "Don't be a stranger."

She walked them out into the chilly night and waved from the curb. When she turned back to the house, she found Jerrik leaning against the wall by the door, waiting for her.

"Well, it looks like everything worked out okay," he said as she joined him.

"Not in the way I expected, but yes, I suppose so. How is everything in Nidavellir?"

His shoulders sagged as he looked up at the moon. "Chaotic still. The Elven Prince has stayed to help, but he'll be returning to Alfheim soon. Master Okaenos and Master Bas will be staying to act as advisors, and my mother will be returning. It's reassuring to have their wisdom to pull from. The court is another matter. Many of them are reluctant to accept me as Crowned Prince, and I can't imagine that they will take me any more seriously as King. I won't force them to respect me—I don't want to be like my father—I just hope that I will earn their respect in time."

"The people will stand beside you, though," Laila pointed out.

"Yes, and I hope I can do right by them. I'm already working on establishing a congress of sorts. I want the people to have more say in our political system." He looked more determined than he had before, and Laila was happy to see that he was already taking to his new position.

He glanced down at her lips for a moment before his eyes returned to meet hers. "I know that you feel obligated to stay here in Midgard, but I was hoping we might be able to see each other still."

Her gut wrenched. She had feared this moment. The fact they had grown closer over the past weeks made this more painful. Laila wanted to say yes, and she knew that Jerrik truly made her happy. When he stood by her, he gave her the courage to take on the Demons. But Senere's warning echoed through her mind. If he stayed with her, his life would be at risk. She couldn't allow him to place himself in danger like that—not for her sake and not when his people needed him.

Even if it tore her heart to pieces, she knew what she had to do.

Laila looked away. "Jerrik, we can't. That is no way for you to live. You'll be expected to marry and produce an heir, and I won't be a mistress."

He took her hands in his, his eyes wide and honest. "Then marry me. Be my queen."

Laila removed her hands from his grasp and took a step back. Why did he have to make this so hard for her? She knew this was for his own good, but it didn't lessen the pain.

"Jerrik. We are on different paths now, and my place is here. I can't. I'm sorry."

His face was a mix of shock and confusion. "Laila, don't push me away. We're stronger together. Look what we were able to accomplish with Izel and my father. We can stop the Demons too if we work together! Don't shut me out, please."

She knew he was right. It didn't matter if she had divine powers, she couldn't do this on her own, but she also wouldn't allow him to follow her to his death.

"This is where we part ways." It took all of her strength to force back the tears threatening to spill from her eyes.

The devastation on his face cut her to the core. She wanted

to explain it all to him, but she knew if she did, he would try to follow her down this dangerous path. She couldn't risk it.

The door opened, and out came Mato, Henrik, and Master Okaenos. They were all grinning. Laila didn't know if it was poor timing or a blessing. She wasn't sure she could keep her emotions in check much longer.

Mato paused as he noticed the two of them. "Sorry, we didn't mean to interrupt."

Laila shook her head and forced a smile. "That's okay. We were just wrapping up our conversation."

The Werebear looked eagerly at Jerrik. "Well, Henrik and I thought we'd take you and Okaenos out for a round of drinks!"

Jerrik swallowed hard and plastered on a smile of his own. "Sounds like a great idea."

The group left to wait for their ride by the curb, and Jerrik turned back to Laila. "So, I guess this is goodbye."

She nodded, her throat tight. "You'll be a great king. I'll let you know if I'm ever passing through."

He nodded, and Laila could see the emotions struggling to break through. "I'll always be here for you. I've pledged myself to you, and I still stand by that decision."

Jerrik bowed deeply, then he turned and walked away. Laila bit her lip as she willed the tears in her eyes to vanish. First Frej and now Jerrik. It felt as though her chest was caving in, and her heart was breaking beyond repair. But she had to do this. It was the right thing, and the only way to keep them safe.

After her conversation with the Norn, Laila had given a lot of thought to the matter. She feared that Senere targeted the people she cared about, trying to slowly break the emotional bonds that tethered her here to earth. Laila worried this would only continue to be a problem unless she found a way to distance herself from those closest to her.

She slid down the wall until she sat on the concrete and something nudged her arm. It was Mr. Whiskers.

"Hey buddy," she murmured and scooped up the Bogey. He

purred and rubbed his face against her cheek.

Laila scratched him behind the ears, and the ache in her chest eased ever so slightly. She reminded herself that she was not entirely alone. She still had her friends and coworkers here in Los Angles, and they were some of the most incredible people she had ever met.

She understood why Erin was so reluctant to leave. Despite the chaos and turmoil this city faced daily, there was still so much good. From the Vampires who came to IRSA's aid in their time of need, to Lyn, who helped rid the city of malicious spirits. These were the sort of people who helped build this city back up after the apocalypse and would continue to do so every day. These were her people—the people of Midgard.

She watched as a car came to pick the guys up. As it drove off, Laila was able to regain some semblance of her composure. She cuddled Mr. Whiskers and carried him back into the house to join the others. Even if the moment was bittersweet, it was good to be home.

CHAPTER 40

Laila pulled into the driveway of the Los Angeles International Airport and stopped along the curb of the Inter-Realm Terminal. She helped Frej unload the luggage as Ali pulled on a chic, wide-brimmed hat. Reluctantly, Erin climbed out of the car.

"I know it's not what you want, but I promised mom and dad that I'd keep you safe," Ali said, looking at the terminal mournfully.

Erin shoved her fists into the pockets of her leather jacket. "Mom and dad would want me to stay with you."

"Maybe. I'm honestly not sure what they'd want. But I know Frej will be able to protect you there."

"I'm done being protected! I can fight. I can help you!" reasoned Erin.

Ali pulled her sister into a hug. "I know, but for now, I'd feel better if I knew you were safe, at least until you gain full use of your powers. Hopefully, the Dragons will figure out why you can't shift."

Erin hugged her sister even tighter. "I'm going to miss you

so much."

"Me too. I promise I'll visit when I can."

Erin took a step back and turned to Laila. "You'll visit, too, right?"

Laila hugged her. "Of course, I will. And don't be too hard on Frej. He's still getting used to this guardianship thing. Try not to give him a heart attack by taking up extreme sports or some dangerous hobby. At least not in the first week." She winked.

Erin cracked a smile. "I'll try not to. No promises, though."

Ali hugged Frej next. "Take care of her."

"I swear to you, I will." He turned to Laila as well. "And my home is open to both of you at any time."

Laila nodded and looked up at him. "I'll miss you, but I know this is the way it needs to be."

Frej glanced over at Erin, who was hugging her sister one last time. "I do too."

Laila stepped into his embrace. "You'll do just fine with her. I'm sure Regina will be there to help Erin too."

He frowned and lowered his voice. "That's what I'm afraid of. Regina is, first and foremost, a tactician. I fear she will see Erin's potential and eagerness and use it to her advantage."

"Well, it's a good thing that Regina will listen to you then."

He nodded uncertainly as he stepped away. "Let's hope. Take care, Laila."

Laila and Ali leaned against the hood of the car and watched Erin and Frej walk through the doors and vanish into the crowd. Ali sniffed, and Laila could see a tear rolling down her cheek from under her large sunglasses.

"Aw, come here." Laila pulled Ali into a hug.

Ali broke down sobbing. "I know I have to let her go, but it's tough!"

Laila rubbed soothing circles on her back. "I know. It's okay."

"I just don't think I can keep her safe anymore. Not after the last two weeks."

"Frej will keep her safe," Laila reminded her.

"I know." She paused a moment as a noise escaped her that was somewhere between a sob and a laugh. "He doesn't know what he's getting himself into, does he?"

Laila looked back toward the terminal doors and chuckled. "Probably not, but he'll have help. His friends are good people, and I think Erin's ready to have her own adventures."

Ali pulled off her sunglasses and stared at her reflection in the lenses. "The Morrigan knows I've had enough of those. I don't even know what I am now."

Laila gave her a sympathetic look. "You're Ali, my best friend. Your powers might be a little different now, but you're still the same person you've always been."

Ali looked over at Laila with a half-smile. "I suppose you know better than anyone how that feels, huh?"

"Just like you've been there for me. I'll be there for you. We'll get through this together."

Ali nodded. They were about to get back in the car when a large white feather landed on the hood. It was one of Luc's. Frowning, Laila searched the sky.

Ali picked up the feather, which was the length of her forearm. "Shit! What's *he* doing here?"

Laila slid into the driver's seat. "It's a warning. I guess my training will start soon, and something tells me it won't be as pleasant as Arduinna's."

They still hadn't heard from the Goddess, which was starting to worry Laila. Something was keeping her in Asgard, and Laila had a bad feeling about it. But she had other problems to worry about. She might have dealt with the majority of the Demons here in Los Angeles, but Supernaturals were flocking to the city—fleeing persecution from eerily similar situations across the country. She hadn't stopped the Demons, only slowed their progress. There were bigger fights to come, but she would be ready. Even if it meant having to put up with a jerk like Luc, she would find a way to stop them and save this world.

DID YOU KNOW...

Did you know that leaving a review is one of the most helpful things a reader can do for any author? If you have a moment, please leave a review online.

ACKNOWLEDGMENTS

There is always a magnificent group of people who support me and encourage me as I write each novel. What is different about this book is that I embarked on this journey during the pandemic of COVID-19. I am so used to getting together with friends and bouncing ideas off of them over a cup of coffee, but this was a very different experience. Instead, I hid away in my office, escaping from my frustrations by diving into this story. Laila's series is filled with a variety of worlds and characters that I know so well that it is like returning home. I hope that book provided you with a brief refuge from your troubles.

Now, on to acknowledgments! First, I have to thank my family, who have listened to my ramblings as I worked my way through this novel. They have always been my biggest supporters. I also want to thank Eric, Rene, and Charly for being amazing friends, even if our conversations are only via video calls these days. One day, I hope to see you all in person again.

When it comes to crafting a story, it is also essential to have feedback and a fresh perspective. Sophie and Cathrine, your input is invaluable to me. I also need to thank Zoe Quintin for sharing her wisdom with me and helping me push forward when I was feeling uncertain.

My supporters on Patreon, you are so kind and generous. Your pledges are so helpful, and it's incredible to have your support, particularly my top tier supporter: Kristine.

Finally, thank you to all of my readers. Your support and eagerness to have the next Laila of Midgard book in your hands means more to me than you will ever know. Thank you oof continuing this journey with me!

CHARACTERS

Laila Eyvindr – An Elf hired by the Interrealm Security Agency (IRSA). She is young for an Elf and appears to be in her mid-twenties by human standards but she is really 83 years old. She is a trained warrior and has a good amount of magical training. Laila is determined, hardworking, caring, and passionate.

Colin Grayson – A Werewolf in his mid 30's with brown hair, short beard and grey eyes. He is a descendent of Shifters who have lived amongst humans in hiding for generations. He is the supervisor of the IRSA team, and has been a part of the organization since it's foundation.

Alastrina Fiachra (Ali) – A Fae woman with long curly golden hair and purple eyes. Like Laila, she is an IRSA agent, but she has been around for much longer and has adjusted to life in Midgard. Ali's parents died a few years ago, so she cares for her adopted little sister, Erin. She knows how to have a good time and loves the Los Angeles nightlife.

Darien Pavoni – A male Vampire with black spiky hair, pale skin, and red eyes. Another member of Laila's IRSA team, he is arrogant, and may not always make the most professional decisions, but he genuinely cares about the work he does. In 1724 he died in a duel and was turned into a Vampire.

Erin Fiachra – A young Dragon who is trapped in her human form. She is Ali's adopted sister, and appears to be about fourteen, but she is actually around sixty years old. She's had difficulty contacting other Dragons to discover why she's stopped ageing.

Arduinna – The Celtic Goddess of the Black Forest in Germany. She is down to earth and wise, and is a friend of Ali and Laila's.

Sir Frej Ilmarinen – An Air Dragon and a Knight from the Dragon Kingdom. He has chosen to stay in Los Angeles to train Erin and to help the IRSA agents. He's also Laila's lover.

Orin – The Fae man who owns the Club La Fae. He's cheeky, but a reliable informant.

Lyn – A human witch who lives in Los Angeles. She owns a shop in Venice Beach called Lyn's Charms and Remedies, and helps Laila with the occasional case.

Jerrik Torhild – Svartálfr (plural: Svartalfar) or Dark Elf that was imprisoned in the same cellblock as Laila. He and

Laila had a short-lived romance until he left without a word. He now works with the IRSA team. He is the Prince of the Svartalfar who has been in hiding.

Torsten – A fatherly Dwarf that was also imprisoned in the same cellblock as Laila. He now works for IRSA developing weapons and tools to make the agents' jobs safer.

Donald – A male Witch, or Tech Wiz, as he prefers. A local witch hired to assist Torsten in enchanting equipment for the IRSA team.

Caine Ubel – A Snake Shifter and a Lesser Demon, who was capturing and sending Supernaturals to the Demon-run fight ring and organized the summoning rituals that nearly killed Erin.

Marius – A.K.A. the Master of the Games. He's Fae and was the Greater Demon in charge of the illegal fight ring. He escaped IRSA's raid on the place, and is still at large.

Izel – Unknown. Connected to Marius and the Demons.

Queen Regina Halvard-Hilgard – A Fire Dragon and Queen of the Dragons.

Lord Issac Mavrik – An Earth Dragon and a close friend of Frej's.

Benning – A Giant who was sent, by the Demons, to terrorize Los Angeles. In reality, he wouldn't hurt a fly. He now works as a security guard at IRSA's front desk.

Captain Anderson – A human and captain of the LAPD's Gangs and Narcotics division.

Captain Romero – A human and captain of the LAPD's Homicide division.

Lorel – A Human and Colin's girlfriend.

Fredrik Stacy – A human and avid protester. He believes that strict regulations should be placed on Supernaturals for the safety of humans.

Carlos – A Human who was one of Ali's informants in the Old City until he was assassinated while meeting with Ali and Darien.

Mato – A Bear Shifter who was imprisoned by the Demons in the same cellblock as Laila. He's now dating Ali.

Henrik – A Mörkö (ice creature) who was imprisoned in the same cellblock as Laila. He's Mato's best friend and roommate.

Talen Veryl – A Vampire and Darien's sire. A powerful and influential man who is also kind and compassionate.

Richard – A Vampire who gained his wealth through smuggling and other unsavory business practices.

Jennifer (Jenn) Holdt – A human and special investigator with IRSA. She is practical and level-headed.

Meuric Drisscoll – An Abhartach who works as a medical examiner for IRSA.

Jim Cleary – A human who works as a medical examiner for IRSA.

Adam Johnson – A human and an agent who works for the Inspector General's office. He's been sent to investigate the IRSA team.

Sire Ashford – A rogue Vampire leading a rebellion.

Arnold Koch – A rogue Vampire who is a part of the rebellion.

Dagan – A Vampire on the council, a group of powerful and ancient Vampires that ensure the order and safety of the local Vampires. He is very opinionated and outspoken.

Cedric – A Vampire on the council. He is deliberate in his actions and decisions.

Aalis – A Vampire on the council. Her appearance is rather opulent and gaudy, and she tends to take charge.

Sarnai (**Сарнай**) – A Vampire on the Council and one of Darien's ex-lovers. A cool and ruthless woman.

King Oddvarr - King of the Svartalfar and Jerrik's father.

Queen Birgitta - King of the Svartalfar and Jerrik's mother.

Hallr - A Svartálfr and Jerrik's old friend from the Svartalfar court. He is now a rebel.

Katla - A Svartálfr and one of the rebels.

Folki - A Svartálfr and the leader of the rebels.

Rune - A Svartálfr and one of the rebels.

Ligeia - A Siren and Lyn's girlfriend. She observes the human
    world and reports back to a council.

Master Okaenos - One of the Merfolk and a Swordmaster
    pledged to Poseidon.

Master Bas - One of the Fae and a Swordmaster pledged to
    The Morrigan.

Grandmaster Zorion - The head of the Swordmasters' order.

Wyrd - The oldest surviving Norn. Her specialty is the past.

Verdani - A Norn. Her specialty is the present.

Senere - The youngest of the Norns. Her specialty is the
    future.

Luc - An Angel who serves the Norns.

Prince Haraldur - Prince of the Elves.

WORLDS

Asgard – World of the Gods.

Vanaheim – World of the Ancient Gods.

Alfheim (pronounced "ALF-hame;") – World of the Elves, Fae, Dragons and nature related beings. Large cites of note include:
>Ingegard – Elven City
>Tír na nÓg – City of the Fae
>Schonengard – City of the Dragons

Earth (or Midgard) – The world of the humans. For Millennia it was off limits to the other worlds as humans and other creatures of this world were not gifted in magic or strength. Over time, the humans have become a force to reckon with as they created amazing technologies that rival the magic that others possess. The people of Alfheim were the ones who proposed the truce that would keep the human world safe from the other worlds. There are creatures like human Vampires, human Shifters, and a hand full of other creatures who have managed to stay under the radar during the era before The Event.

Svartalfheim (pronounced "SVART-alf-hame;") – The world of Dark Elves or Svartalfar, Dwarves, and creatures of the earth. They are known for their mines and craftsmanship.

> Nidavellir – The City of the Svartalfar
> Deurgard – The Dwarven City

Jotunheim – The world of brutish creatures like Trolls and Giants. They are constantly at war with the races of Alfheim or other worlds.

Muspelheim – The world of the Dammed. The inter-realm prison where the worst criminals are banished. There is a political organization that has risen to power within this world known as the Demons. They have begun to gain connections in the other worlds, particularly Earth, and have begun to plot their escape and rise to power.

CAN'T WAIT FOR MORE?

Want monthly access to advance announcements, exclusive content and more? Check out Kathryn Blanche's Patreon page for more information!

patreon.com/kathrynblanche

ABOUT THE AUTHOR

Kathryn Blanche writes novels in her favorite local cafes when not indulging her love for travel. Aside from exploring the world, this California native may be found designing for the theatre, reading, fencing, or teaching. *Infiltrated by Demons* is the third novel in her Laila of Midgard series.

FOLLOW KATHRYN BLANCHE FOR UPDATES ON NEW RELEASES, EVENTS, AND MORE!

Website: www.kathrynblanche.com
Email: contact@kathrynblanche.com
Facebook: @LailaofMidgardSeries
Instagram: @kathryn_blanche
Twitter: @_kathrynblanche

CHAPTER 39
(aka the second to last chapter)

Several days later, Laila stood in the living room of Ali's house, watching a report on the news. The house had been thoroughly cleaned, and most of the damage was repaired. They had to purchase new sofas since the old ones had been partially destroyed, but Ali seemed satisfied with the leather ones she ordered. They replaced the door as well, and the new one was far more sturdy with reinforced locks. Ali was still grumbling about it, saying the door didn't fit the rest of her décor, but Laila and Darien eventually persuaded her it was a necessary precaution.

"Are you sure they're going to show the speech?" Frej asked as he stirred the large pot of pasta sauce.

Just then, the news station cut to a video clip from a press conference. The governor stood at the podium with Jenn at his side. She had received a public apology from the governor earlier in the week, and the trooper who nearly shot her in the back was facing an investigation.

The Governor spoke. "I'm sorry it has taken me so long to address the public personally. I'll be frank with you; I'm still struggling to come to terms with what happened. I never considered myself to be an intolerant person, and I am horrified by the things I have said over the past several months. Lorel—the Greater Demon who influenced my actions—took advantage of my pain and grief and used it to turn me against California's Supernatural communities. This is not an excuse for what I have done, and I'm not sure what I can do to atone for the hurt and unrest I have caused. However, I hope that over time I might work to repair the damage done. I have revoked the curfew placed on Supernaturals and the arrest warrants for all members of the Inter-Realm Security Agency that I had previously issued, and I am working closely with them to assess the threat that the Demons still pose. I will continue to look to them for guidance in the upcoming months to determine how to keep the people of California safe."

Erin leaned against the back of a sofa. "Woah, it's weird to hear him talk like that. It's like he's had a massive personality change. Even his voice sounds different."

Mato stared at the television screen as well. The bread he was slicing was forgotten in his hands. "That's because he's speaking calmly. And he *did* have a personality change. Remember the way Frej and the humans attacked after they accidentally smudged their protective charms?"

Henrik clapped Frej on the back. "No worries, I know it wasn't really you attacking me."

Frej still shifted uneasily. "It's scary how easily she could control a whole room. It's a shame we never figured out what sort of creature she was."

Laila glanced over her shoulder at him. "What are you talking about? Of course we did."

"Do you know something we don't? I thought the whole reason we had a hard time finding her was that we didn't know what she was?" Henrik sounded confused.

Laila looked around at the others, assuming they were joking, but as they continued to stare at her blankly, it dawned on her that Ligeia had wiped their memories. The Siren had stuck

I've been searching for a place to introduce Ligeia for awhile now. I wanted to include her earlier, but I needed to wait until it was time to reveal Lorel's identity.

around, so Laila had assumed Ligeia had changed her mind. But why did she retain her memories while the others had not?

As if on cue, a knock on the door sounded, and Lyn entered with her girlfriend.

Ali waved them in. "Hey! Are you both getting settled in the apartment?"

Lyn nodded and hugged Ali. "Yeah, it's a little surreal moving back in, but it's nice to be at the beach again. I'm glad to see you up and about!" I can't wait to write more about Lyn + Ligeia

"Where would you like this?" Ligeia held up a large bowl of salad.

"I'll take that," offered Laila. Then she lowered her voice and asked. "What's going on? No one here remembers that Lorel was a Siren."

Perks of divine magic!.

Ligeia looked surprised. "You mean, you do? Well, I guess I shouldn't be too shocked. I suppose my abilities don't work on the divine. I wiped everyone's memory days ago."

"But you're still here! How is it they remember you? I thought you were going to have to leave?"

Ligeia gave her a sly smile. "I found a loophole. I only erased their knowledge of Sirens. Instead, they think I'm human. I convinced the council to let me stay and ensure there is not another threat of a similar nature. I don't like lying to Lyn, but this is the only way I can still be with her."

Laila watched as Lyn chatted with Ali. The Witch looked so happy. "I'm glad you found a way. This is the happiest I've ever seen her."

Darien, Sarnai, and Talen were the next to arrive with several bottles of blood for the party and Ali. The doctor had determined that while Ali could eat ordinary food in moderation, she would also need to supplement her diet with blood. Ali didn't seem to suffer the same sort of bloodlust that caused the Vampires to become ravenous, but she tended to get lethargic. She even fainted one day when she tried to avoid the blood. Since then, Sarnai had been sending over a steady supply. The

When I started writing this book, I didn't know if Ali would survive or not. When I wrote the scene in the ambulance, I sobbed so hard. I I didn't want to kill her off. Luckily, I didn't have to.

Ali is now part Fae, part Vampire, but also something different + new thanks to the divine magic.

Vampire seemed eager to help Ali adjust, even though Darien was technically her sire—or partial sire.

There were other odd effects as well. Ali didn't suffer from the same sensitivity to sunlight as the Vampires, but she would quickly get one nasty sunburn. Sunscreen seemed to help with that for the most part, particularly the enchanted kind Lyn made. Despite Ali's fears, she still retained her Fae abilities to charm and use glamour magic, and they were even stronger than before. With the doctor's precaution in mind, she had been taking it slow, which meant Ali still didn't know the full extent of her abilities. Laila promised she would help sort them out, but they were waiting one more day.

Fun Fact: Talen has a Fae ancestor

The reason for their little party was that Erin and Frej would be leaving for the Dragon Kingdom in the morning. Many fights between Ali and Erin had broken out over the last few days. Erin didn't want to leave. Not only did she insist Midgard was her home, but she didn't want to abandon Ali after coming so close to losing her.

I've known this was going to happen for a while now. It's sad to see her leave, but now Erin can have her own adventures.

Laila was sad to see them leave. Erin was like a sister to her, and she loved watching her grow, and her abilities develop. Laila would miss her snarky sense of humor and fiery disposition. She had a feeling it would feel oddly quiet without Erin in the house.

Frej was another matter. Even though they discussed the potential of a future relationship, something about this still felt final. No matter how much she wished it, things would never go back to the way they were, and bit by bit, their circle of friends were being called away.

The last to arrive was Donald. He held a small package wrapped in colorful paper, which he passed to Erin.

"I know they don't have technology in Alfheim, so I wanted to give you a little something to help," he explained.

Erin tore away the paper and pulled out a metallic cube covered in glowing red runes. "What's it do?"

"It's a charging pack for your electronic devices. It's sort of

I couldn't send Erin back to Alfheim without some way to use her electronic devices. :)

like a solar panel, but it converts magic into electricity. It's strong enough to power your laptop, charge your phone, or whatever you want to do. You won't have Wi-Fi or cell service, but you'll still be able to access your photos and play videogames."

Erin hugged him so tightly it nearly threw the Tech Wiz off balance. "Thank you!"

"Oh! That reminds me, I have something too!" Lyn reached into her bag and removed a little pouch.

Erin opened it and pulled out a sleek black compact with a silver Dragon on it. Erin popped it open, and the mirror within rippled. It was a hand-held scrying glass similar to what Laila's mother used.

"This way, you can stay in touch."

Erin's eyes brimmed with tears and her lower lip wobbled. "I'm going to miss you guys so much!"

Lyn wrapped an arm around the young Dragon. "Aw, it's going to be okay. This just means it's time for you to have your own adventure!"

Darien pulled Laila aside, looking concerned. "Are you expecting anyone else? Jenn?"

Laila frowned. "No. Jenn said she's stuck at the press conference. Why?"

"Someone pulled up. Considering what happened last time…"

Laila nodded. "I'll handle it."

With the others preoccupied, she slipped out the door. In front of the house, a taxi sat with two figures emerging. Jerrik approached in a simple but elegant black suit—the kind the men in Nidavellir wore. His hair was pulled back, and on his brow rested a silver circlet.

"I thought I might find you here." He winked.

"Jerrik? What are you doing here?" she asked.

"I wanted to check on Ali and make sure she was doing okay. I also never got the chance to speak to you after the battle." He paused before her.

Laila recognized his companion, and her eyes lit up. "Master Okaenos!"

He looked around at the cars in fascination. "Hello, Laila! I'm so excited to see Midgard! These self-propelled machines are incredible, and they move so fast! Faster than the ones in Svartalfheim even!"

Laila chuckled and showed them in. "Come in! We've got plenty of food."

Everyone stared at Jerrik as he entered the room.

"Whoa, you look totally different," pointed out Erin.

Jerrik looked down at his clothes with a frown. "Yeah, it doesn't quite feel right. I miss my jeans."

Mato hesitated. "Are we supposed to bow?"

"Don't you dare!" Jerrik pulled him into a hug, and Mato relaxed along with the others.

"Everyone, this is Master Okaenos. He's one of the Swordmasters," announced Laila.

"It's a pleasure to be here!" he said delighted.

Ali led them both towards the kitchen. "Well, don't just stand there! Dig in!"

Together they laughed, ate, and drank. Eventually, Jenn was able to get away from her duties to join them. It was good to have everyone together, but their celebration had a bittersweet edge to it. None of them were willing to say it, but they knew this was the last time they would all be together for quite a while. Laila watched as Master Okaenos chattered excitedly with Frej—eager to discuss the possibility of a Swordmaster taking up residence to teach the Dragons. Mato and Henrik lounged and drank on a sofa with Jerrik—the three of them joking like old times. Ali spoke with the Vampires about the various types of blood they brought. Meanwhile, Lyn and Donald showed Erin a list of basic enchantments for the Dragon to try out while Ligeia listened attentively.

Laila thought over what Darien had informed her regarding Colin. It sounded as though he wasn't truly to blame for

❖ 323 ❖

leaking information. Between Lorel's confession and the report that came back from the tainted pills Colin had been taking, the chances were high he would be released. Even so, there would be no future for him at the agency, even if they needed the help.

Jerrik wouldn't be returning to the agency either, and tomorrow Frej would leave. Their numbers were dwindling as their paths diverged.

"You look oddly pensive," pointed out Talen as he joined her in the kitchen.

A sad sigh escaped her. "A lot is changing. I want to hold on to this moment."

He nodded. "I know what you mean. At this age, I think I've come to accept that the only thing I can expect is for change to be constant."

Laila watched Ali sip another glass of blood. "Do you think we did the right thing by turning her?"

"I don't think she's upset with you, if that's what you mean. It'll take time for her to adjust, but I think she's okay with that. She wasn't ready to die. I wouldn't have offered to change her otherwise. Sarnai's taken a lot of interest in her. I think she'll continue to offer her support. Something in her changed recently. I noticed it after she spent time with Erin in the safehouse. She seems more human. I think she realized how much she missed her own family. Even her relationship with Darien seems different this time around."

"How so?" she snuck a glance at the pair. Darien seemed to be doing his best to ignore Sarnai, although her eyes constantly drifted to him.

Talen smirked. "Sarnai's used to being in control, but this time Darien has the power. He's stronger now and can resist her if he wants. Sarnai has grown to appreciate it. She's listening to him and respecting his wishes. I'm still not sure that it's healthy, given their history together, but it's also not my place to intervene—not unless I believe it puts his life in danger."

"That's happened before?"

She's got alot of work to do!

He shrugged. "Yes, but I think she's changed for the better. I think she's learned that if she wants to be a part of his life, then Sarnai will have to prove to him she's a better person than she used to be."

Interesting. Laila knew it was none of her business, but if Sarnai would be spending more time around them, she felt it was prudent to understand the Vampire's background.

Laila noticed Lyn, Ligeia, and Donald saying their goodbyes.

Talen checked his phone. It was well past two in the morning. "It's getting late. We should probably be going too. I'll see you soon, though."

Laila nodded. "Don't be a stranger."

She walked them out into the chilly night and waved from the curb. When she turned back to the house, she found Jerrik leaning against the wall by the door, waiting for her.

"Well, it looks like everything worked out okay," he said as she joined him. I rewrote this scene so many times.

"Not in the way I expected, but yes, I suppose so. How is everything in Nidavellir?"

His shoulders sagged as he looked up at the moon. "Chaotic still. The Elven Prince has stayed to help, but he'll be returning to Alfheim soon. Master Okaenos and Master Bas will be staying to act as advisors, and my mother will be returning. It's reassuring to have their wisdom to pull from. The court is another matter. Many of them are reluctant to accept me as Crowned Prince, and I can't imagine that they will take me any more seriously as King. I won't force them to respect me—I don't want to be like my father—I just hope that I will earn their respect in time."

"The people will stand beside you, though," Laila pointed out. Jerrik has definately been inspired by life

"Yes, and I hope I can do right by them. I'm already working on establishing a congress of sorts. I want the people to have in the more say in our political system." He looked more determined USA than he had before, and Laila was happy to see that he was al-

It was so hard for me to keep his true identity secret. I almost had Laila's mother figure it out in book three.

❖ 325 ❖

ready taking to his new position.

He glanced down at her lips for a moment before his eyes returned to meet hers. "I know that you feel obligated to stay here in Midgard, but I was hoping we might be able to see each other still."

Her gut wrenched. She had feared this moment. The fact they had grown closer over the past weeks made this more painful. Laila wanted to say yes, and she knew that Jerrik truly made her happy. When he stood by her, he gave her the courage to take on the Demons. But Senere's warning echoed through her mind. If he stayed with her, his life would be at risk. She couldn't allow him to place himself in danger like that—not for her sake and not when his people needed him.

Even if it tore her heart to pieces, she knew what she had to do.

Laila looked away. "Jerrik, we can't. That is no way for you to live. You'll be expected to marry and produce an heir, and I won't be a mistress."

He took her hands in his, his eyes wide and honest. "Then marry me. Be my queen."

Laila removed her hands from his grasp and took a step back. Why did he have to make this so hard for her? She knew this was for his own good, but it didn't lessen the pain.

"Jerrik. We are on different paths now, and my place is here. I can't. I'm sorry."

His face was a mix of shock and confusion. "Laila, don't push me away. We're stronger together. Look what we were able to accomplish with Izel and my father. We can stop the Demons too if we work together! Don't shut me out, please."

She knew he was right. It didn't matter if she had divine powers, she couldn't do this on her own, but she also wouldn't allow him to follow her to his death.

"This is where we part ways." It took all of her strength to force back the tears threatening to spill from her eyes.

The devastation on his face cut her to the core. She wanted

At least Henrik + Mato are here for Jerrik after this scene.

to explain it all to him, but she knew if she did, he would try to follow her down this dangerous path. She couldn't risk it.

The door opened, and out came Mato, Henrik, and Master Okaenos. They were all grinning. Laila didn't know if it was poor timing or a blessing. She wasn't sure she could keep her emotions in check much longer.

Mato paused as he noticed the two of them. "Sorry, we didn't mean to interrupt."

Laila shook her head and forced a smile. "That's okay. We were just wrapping up our conversation."

The Werebear looked eagerly at Jerrik. "Well, Henrik and I thought we'd take you and Okaenos out for a round of drinks!"

Jerrik swallowed hard and plastered on a smile of his own. "Sounds like a great idea."

The group left to wait for their ride by the curb, and Jerrik turned back to Laila. "So, I guess this is goodbye."

She nodded, her throat tight. "You'll be a great king. I'll let you know if I'm ever passing through."

He nodded, and Laila could see the emotions struggling to break through. "I'll always be here for you. I've pledged myself to you, and I still stand by that decision."

Jerrik bowed deeply, then he turned and walked away. Laila bit her lip as she willed the tears in her eyes to vanish. First Frej and now Jerrik. It felt as though her chest was caving in, and her heart was breaking beyond repair. But she had to do this. It was the right thing, and the only way to keep them safe.

After her conversation with the Norn, Laila had given a lot of thought to the matter. She feared that Senere targeted the people she cared about, trying to slowly break the emotional bonds that tethered her here to earth. Laila worried this would only continue to be a problem unless she found a way to distance herself from those closest to her.

She slid down the wall until she sat on the concrete and something nudged her arm. It was Mr. Whiskers.

"Hey buddy," she murmured and scooped up the Bogey. He

Mr. Whiskers can always sense when Laila is upset...

remember all of the warnings about the Gods?

purred and rubbed his face against her cheek.

Laila scratched him behind the ears, and the ache in her chest eased ever so slightly. She reminded herself that she was not entirely alone. She still had her friends and coworkers here in Los Angles, and they were some of the most incredible people she had ever met.

She understood why Erin was so reluctant to leave. Despite the chaos and turmoil this city faced daily, there was still so much good. From the Vampires who came to IRSA's aid in their time of need, to Lyn, who helped rid the city of malicious spirits. These were the sort of people who helped build this city back up after the apocalypse and would continue to do so every day. These were her people—the people of Midgard.

She watched as a car came to pick the guys up. As it drove off, Laila was able to regain some semblance of her composure. She cuddled Mr. Whiskers and carried him back into the house to join the others. Even if the moment was bittersweet, it was good to be home.